MW01101537

CARROLL & GRAF

Wet Dreams

WET
DREAMS

ANONYMOUS

CARROLL & GRAF PUBLISHERS, INC.
NEW YORK

First Carroll & Graf edition of *Wayward Venus* 1991
Book One was originally published under the title *Of Loin and Cloth*
and Book Two was originally published as *True Love Stories of a
Wayward Teenager*
First Carroll & Graf edition of *The Merry Ménage* 1992

Carroll & Graf Publishers, Inc.
19 West 21st St., Suite 601
New York, NY 10010-6805

ISBN: 0-7867-0500-0

Manufactured in the United States of America

Contents

Wayward Venus   3

The Merry Ménage   233

WET DREAMS

WAYWARD VENUS

WAYWARD VENUS

Contents

Book One   5
Book Two   113

BOOK ONE

BOOK ONE

CHAPTER I

Preliminaries

All that is known of the Count and Countess
of X is that they separated by mutual agreement after two years of married life, thus
breaking by consent, an ill advised union. The
Count, they say, lived a retired life at the other
end of Spain in his ancestral castle. The Countess, after staying for some months in her native Andalusia, pitched her tent in Paris, where
she lived in a small hotel in the Avenue de Messina under a borrowed name.

Whether people knew the lady's social status
or not, they only addressed her by the title
printed on her cards, namely the Countess of
Cythera.

Singular rumors were current in the neighborhood; people never saw any man enter the hotel; all in the household were females; they even say that the coachman, despite the imposing whiskers that adorned his visage, was really a woman in disguise. The three pretty soubrettes who attended to the external business of the household, talked quite freely about everything, except what went on inside the house, having, no doubt, very good reasons for holding their tongues. They were very pretty, prepossessing, each a different style of beauty (one blonde, one brunette, and one with chestnut red hair), and were paid court by the tradesmen, who gave them many presents.

The Countess showed herself at the opera, first night exhibitions, always accompanied by her ladies, some of whom might have been taken for maids of honor to a queen. Sometimes, but not often, she exchanged a bow or a smile as she passed some face she knew. She seemed to wish to cut off the few friends her husband had made in Paris in the first months of their marriage (which had been passed in the capital). The retired and mysterious life that the Countess led under such a significant pseudonym provoked much gossiping, which wearied her. Tired of prowling round the hotel in quest of hypothetical reports, I also at last gave up my investigations.

In the month of August I went to Trouville for some idle leisure. On the day of my arrival, everyone was talking about an intrepid bather, who by her disregard of danger had made the boldest tremble. They pointed out a fair-haired maid who was waiting on the beach for her mistress's frolics to end. I easily recognized one of the handmaids of the Countess of Cythera, who I had met in the Bois. A movement took place—the curious crowd drew near the sea to follow the action. I arrived soon enough to see coming up out of the water a splendid creature that I soon recognized; her bathing-dress was of cream-colored flannel and clung to her skin, admirably indicating the projecting curves of a superb and statuesque woman, drawing murmurs of admiration from the delighted crowd. The soubrette had thrown a peignoir around her, drawn tightly in. It showed a splendid bottom, like a celestial globe, whose two plump curves moved with the undulating hips, rising and falling under the wet and clinging dress. The beauty disappeared and, when she reappeared in her usual dress, an admiring gaze followed her till she was lost to view.

I got back to my hotel, full of an intense will to try once more to penetrate the cloud of mystery that enveloped the Countess of Cythera. This seemed to be easier at Trouville than Paris. Here all the world was acquainted with itself, and it would be the very devil if I couldn't lift a corner of the veil.

The next day before bathing time I was on the beach, having made up my mind to follow the daring swimmer everywhere. I swam quite well enough to know that where she could go I could follow. As soon as I saw the lady advancing, followed by the fair-haired maid, I entered the bathing cabin I had taken; when I came out of it I had the satisfaction of seeing the Countess in her bathing costume, ready to dive into the sea. Not to appear intrusive, I waited till she was some distance out before plunging in myself. I swam after her, gaining on her, and could soon have caught her but I had not quite made up my mind as to how I should board the pretty craft, as I did not want to force myself on her. We had already got well out to sea during my hesitation, when I saw her suddenly stop and turn around with difficulty, trying to float.

"I have a cramp," she said, suddenly perceiving me.

In two powerful strokes I was beside her, and passing my hand under her loins, I held her up.

"Thanks," she said, "it has passed off; I can get to shore alone."

She turned over and began to swim to shore, but the pain had made her left leg stiff, and she was obliged to accept my right hand which allowed us to swim in company, keeping time together.

In a few minutes the cramp was on again. I had to take her on my back. She stretched herself all along my loins, her bosom supported on my shoulders, her arms clasping my neck. Thus free to move, I began to swim vigorously, deliciously enjoying the sweet contact.

From the shore, they had been trying to make out what was going on, and when I laid down my lovely burden on the sands, everyone inquired about the accident. The soubrette, frightened and trembling, her eyes bathed in tears, cast herself on the neck of her dear mistress, unaware of the surprise that the familiarity of these embraces caused, then led her to the cabin. The Countess had thanked me without a word, but with a sweet smile.

Will this smile, I asked myself that evening, authorize me to call and ask how she is? After some hesitation I inclined to the affirmative, and an hour after dinner, about half-past eight, I rang at the Villa des Delices! It was the fair-haired blonde who answered the bell for me. For a moment she was thunderstruck, but she thanked me warmly for having rescued her mistress. After having taken my card, she said she would announce me.

She introduced me into a well-lighted drawing room, where she left me for a moment. Almost immediately the Countess entered. She was quite a vision. I forgot to salute her, struck dumb by the ravishing apparition which advanced towards me with a graceful undulating movement, holding out a snowy hand which I pressed with emotion. Clothed in a simple tea gown, which closely followed the swelling curves of her figure, her unknotted hair, black as night and fine as silver, falling below her waist, she introduced herself without embarrassment.

"I was expecting you," she said, "but not this evening, as you see; will you excuse me for receiving you in such attire? I was too fatigued by the emotions of the day to think of dressing. I didn't wish to let my preserver (for you did save me), think that I could go

11

away without thanking him—for in point of fact, I leave Trouville tomorrow morning."

She certainly could not have presented herself in any attire more charming to me, and I poured from my lips the admiration which shone in my eyes.

After a few minutes' conversation I took leave, just pressing my lips on the tips of her fingers which she extended to me, as she gave me an invitation to visit her on the Avenue de Messina.

I had only taken a few steps through the English garden which surrounded the villa, when I stopped to cast a last glance on the pretty prison that guarded the mysterious beauty, then, step by step, I returned to the threshold. The door was still open. I crossed the hall and found myself without knowing how, in the salon where they had received me, but which was plunged in darkness. My first impulse was to retrace my steps and fly, but the sound of a woman's voice, which came from some place at the side nailed me there. At the same instant a door opened and one of the soubrettes with a silver lamp in her hand, crossed the salon without seeing me. I stepped towards the door which she had left open, and I found myself in a little passage. On the left was a door whose handle I turned. It led into a cabinet. I re-closed the door, and looking around me, saw I was in a large closet which was lit by a glass panel across which was a muslin curtain, which gave into an adjoining room where I heard voices. Soon the soubrette came back, shutting the doors behind her. I saw then that I was a prisoner. The worst that could happen would be that they would discover me, that they wouldn't take me for a burglar, and that I should escape with a scolding.

CHAPTER II

A Quartette of Cytherans

Puzzled by the noise that came from the neighboring room, I stepped carefully towards the glass door, and gently drew aside the curtain. A bright jet of light, which came from a luster lit by many gas jets, nearly blinded me at first, then my eyes fell on the graceful group, chatting in the room. Reversing their roles, the Countess, still in her tea gown, was undressing the fair-haired maid, who willingly submitted to it. The lady unbuttoned the bodice, and drew it off, unlacing the corsets. She pressed up, and out sprang two rounded bosoms of ivory whiteness, tipped with two little rosy nipples which she took for a moment between her lips.

14

She then made her sit down, slipped off her red silk stockings, and held for a moment in her hands the two little white feet. She covered them with kisses, then let them fall again.

"Stand up, Nina," she said. The soubrette raised herself and the lady drew off her drawers and her chemise, which fell in a ring round her feet, making a sort of white pedestal beneath her. The pretty girl stood stark naked, showing her lovely white skin, tinged with blonde at the lower part of her belly by a curled and golden fleece which covered the rounded slope of the hill of Venus.

The Countess gave two slaps on her naked bottom which was just within reach.

"Now for you, Lisette," she said.

The soubrette with the dark red hair took the place of the blonde Nina, and the Countess paid her the same attentions, undressing her with the same profusion of tender caresses. Lissette had a skin of pink and white, that lovely white that so often accompanies red hair; on her mound was a lovely moss of dark red curly hair. She too received two little slaps.

"Lola," cried the Countess.

The rich brunette responded to the call, and gave herself into the hands of her mistress, who stripped her with the same pretty gestures. The velvet skin of Lola indicated her creole and Spanish origin; a forest of jet black curls high and thick, grew at the bottom of her rounded and dimpled belly.

"Clic, clac! Come to me!" cried the Countess.

The three lovely naked girls cast themselves

on the lady who opened her arms; the tea gown fell from her. She had no stays. Her bosoms were rounded and firm, white as the bosom of a virgin of France, and lay in a nest of laces bordering the top of the chemise like the vermilion tips of two roses of Paradise. The loving girls in turn kissed and sucked them with every token of passionate tenderness. The chemise followed the peignoir. The soubrettes at first concealed from me the body that they had stripped, but soon falling on their knees, as if in worship, they revealed to my sight those marble limbs.

I restrained with difficulty a cry of admiration that this apparition of loveliness nearly drew from me. The buttocks, always firm, stood out stiff with excitement like ivory spheres. Her skin, shining satin of a ravishing whiteness, showed her Andalusian origin, which had given her at the center of her attraction a splendid black fleece, forming a rich and bushy triangle which magnificently adorned the grotto of love, a pussy eclipsing the best furred Angora that ever walked. The thighs were round and white, the legs perfectly modeled and terminated by a chef-d'oeuvre of little feet, such as exist nowhere but in Spain.

As though to allow me to admire her beauty in detail, the Countess turned round; the three bending before that superb backside kissed it in adoration. This celestial sphere, dimpled and swelling, was half concealed by the luxuriant hair which fell from her lovely head to the middle of her bottom, half covering it.

But what I did see was of enchanting beauty, and I couldn't take my eyes off her.

After having received the homage they gave to her posterior charms, the Countess made a sign. The three nymphs stretched themselves out on the thick soft carpet which covered the parquet floor. Lying on their sides to form a triangle, each one slipped her head between the thighs of the next girl. They placed their first kisses between the hemispheres, on the little brown jewel which is concealed in that place. And when they had gazed on it, tickled it, played with it as a sort of introduction to love's game, they slipped round to the neighboring aperture, impatient no doubt for its turn. One could hear, as it were, a smacking of lips against other lips, which pressed each other sweetly and fragrantly.

During this, the Countess, on her knees, went from one to the other bending over to follow the different phases of the sport, encouraging the sweet actresses by soft kisses, and by clinging slaps on their pretty bottoms that quivered under her strokes.

She flitted from one tender backside to another. Then, when she guessed that the psychological moment was approaching, she extended herself on the group, cutting the triangle by a straight line, her face on Nina's bottom, her arms stretched out to the two other spheres, tickling the firm flesh with a searching finger, gently nibbling with her teeth the fleshy globes of Nina, lavishing on all three of these her tender stimulants which hastened the approach of pleasure, increasing its intensity, not ceasing till the lascivious girls were writhing in voluptuous enjoyment.

Soon the trio came to their senses. The Countess, then upright, facing the glass door, awaited her turn.

Nina went to a corner of the room and touched a spring; a trapeze that I had not noticed, was let down over the Countess, stopping just over her head. I asked myself what on earth was the use of this gymnastic apparatus here. I soon saw what it was for. Two of the soubrettes knelt down, Lola in front, Lisette behind. Nina, standing up, glued her lips to those of the Countess, and while the others mounted up along the legs and thighs by a sort of chain of kisses, Nina devoured her eyes, her nose, her mouth—in fact, all of her face. Then she bent toward her breasts, and sucked her nipples. Descending lower, she met Lola by the navel, while Lisette was traveling along the curves of her back, over the snowy hills of her bottom, finally reaching the nape of her neck. Each then regained her place by interrupted kisses. Nina stopped at her palpitating bosoms, Lola at love's shaded grotto where she commenced her sweet tongue play, while Lisette stayed at the black jewel. Lola, on her knees, spread her loins, and exposed her brown fat backside and the cleft between in a most seductive manner.

Had I been of the party I should willingly have had a word with them.

The Countess, stretching up her arms, hooked herself on the trapeze bar, sustaining herself on the tips of her toes which scarcely touched the ground. Her bosoms were hard with the tension, jutting forth, her two rosy nipples standing out like two little pricks which Nina sucked in turn, pressing the globes in her hands. Leaving them, she printed a garland of kisses nearby, and they grew pink under her hot and lustful caresses.

The Countess raised herself, obliging her willing slaves to follow her as she rose and descended. Her eyes shone with a strange light, her long silky black eyelashes lowered, veiling their sloe-black light, rose again, moved rapidly. The satin of her belly quivered. Nina caressed her bosoms, pressing them in her hands, rolling the nipples under her fingers, while the lips of the Countess opened, letting forth the rosy tip of her tongue. Then they met and pressed close; the eyes of the Countess rolled upwards, showing the pearly white, her belly rose and fell like the sea, her hips undulated, and for two minutes one saw her writhing in the ecstatic paroxysm of spending as Lola glued her lips to the moist and fragrant quim. Then suddenly relaxing her hold of the bar, she fell panting to the velvet carpets.

Soon the trapeze game recommenced. Lola changed her role. It now was Nina who took her place before her pussy, and the Countess before her bosoms. The dimpled butt of Nina was exposed, no less beautiful than that of Lola if less fat, making me regret in her case too that I could be nothing but an invisible witness to their tender ministrations.

These preliminaries ended, the little harlots

19

worked away with a will, and the Countess
fetched blood from Lisette's lips with her love
bites, as the cries made the soubrette twist in
her arms. It was then the turn of Lola, the
creole brunette. Each changed her place, Lisette at the front door, the Countess at the
back, Nina at the bosom. I noticed that Lisette had also a superb rear, pink and white,
but I had scant time to contemplate it for Lola
was in such a hurry that scarcely had her darlings entered on the "great game" when she
died away, spending with screams of pleasure.

Lastly Nina took her turn under the trapeze.
The Countess knelt before the golden-haired
pussy she was going to suck, while the two
soubrettes took their turns as before. The
Countess made a fine show. Her magnificent
bottom when she bent to kiss the little rosy
feet, displayed itself, jutting out on her heels,
larger, rounder, more dazzling than her companions. The fleece of her cunny was incom-
parably finer in color and thickness, as the
dark curls ran up and fringed her lovely brown
bottom hole. This lovely backside was unrivaled, and when she raised herself a little to
get at the gate of Venus, the lovely sphere
curved and swelled with the arch of her loins.
I had to make the greatest effort not to suc-
cumb to the vehement desire which I had for
this perfect bottom. I could scarcely follow
the various phases of the game of love this
time, and when Nina sank down, lasciviously
spending, even then I could not detach my eyes
from the splendid backside that held me wonder struck, fascinated!

The Countess, her eyes blazing with lust, sought fresh caresses. Lola, the strongest of the band, lay on her back. The Countess lay on her, pressing her cunt to her face, and her nose to Lola's mons veneris. Lisette lay on the Countess's back, her thighs round her neck, her lips and tongue in the soft cleft of her arse. Nina knelt behind the group, behind the Countess, and took her little pink feet in her hands, pressing one to each bosom, tickling and kissing them.

Lola and the Countess gamahuched each other madly, their tongues shooting in between the full lips of their quims, their lips wet with the spunk that flowed. Lisette nibbled the bottom before her, separated the hemispheres, and thrust her agile tongue down the furrow and round the little brown orifice there concealed, which she thrust at with delight, while with her soft thighs she squeezed the neck of the Countess, rubbing her clitoris against the nape of her neck.

Nina was frigging herself at the sight, with one rosy finger thrust deep into her cunny.

Suppressed sighs coming from below announced that the gamahuchers were coming quickly as if they had but been waiting for this moment. Lisette, who was moving convulsively, rubbing her quim against her mistress's neck, and Nina, who frigged herself faster and faster with her finger, both came to the same height of lascivious fury, joined in the magic moment by a murmur of suppressed sighs and wet, clinging kisses.

Each having put on a tea gown, the soubrettes, after having taken fond adieu of their mistress, retired to the side chamber, ready to reappear at the first sound of the bell, if their mistress had need of their services.

CHAPTER III

I Take Part in the Fete

The lights put out, a tiny night light alone
illuminated the room with its dim rays. The
Countess, having put on a nightgown, had
slipped into bed. I didn't exactly know what
to do. If I did not make any attempt on her,
how on earth could I get away decently in the
morning? And if I did try what I could do,
how should I be received by the lovely tribade,
who didn't seem to me to care about what I
had to offer her. Everything was barred and
bolted. I was prisoner, pure and simple. I
couldn't get out by any stroke. Twenty times
I put my hand on the handle of the door. At
last, after an hour of irresolution, I turned it
gently, and the door opened without noise. Lis-

tening intently, I could scarcely hear the calm breathing of the sleeper. I had put off my clothes and shoes, and I advanced on tiptoe to the edge of the bed. The Countess slept, her sweet lips parted, her two arms under her head. The wide sleeves of the nightgown had slipped down, showing the sweet ebony curls of her armpits. How I longed to kiss them!

Having made up my mind for the venture, whatever might turn up, I lifted the sheets and stretched myself out stealthily, without the fair sleeper stirring. Little by little my hand slipped into the hollow of her chemise, and closed upon a round and satin smooth breast whose contour filled it.

She sighed, murmuring the name of a woman. Whatever comes of it, I said to myself, let us push on. I stretched forward. I placed my lips on the half-opened lips of the dreamer, which unconsciously gave me back a long kiss. This kiss put a light to the powder. I clasped my lovely one to me, I strained her to me, and I kissed her with all my power.

My rude attack woke her up, and feeling that it was a man who had assailed her, she cried out: "What assurance, Charles. I did not ring for you, sir! You know that I have changed my mind. As you see, I am all alone, and it is certainly not on me that I wish the experiment tried. Well, why don't you go? Do you want to make me ring?"

"Madame," said I, "it is not Charles, it is—"

I had not time to finish. Sitting up, the Countess recognized me by the glimmer of the night-light. The expression of vexation which had altered her features, had given place to a mocking smile which still was a kind one.

"What do you want of me?" said she. "Indeed, how came you here in my bed."

I told her how I had been led to conceal myself in the dress closet, attracted by her beauty, kept there by my love, and how I had surprised her secret by becoming the happy witness to her tribadic amours. I expected to see her troubled. There was no sign of it.

She answered me in a calm and peaceful voice, that since I had discovered her secret, I might count upon her and on her favors.

"Yes, but this Charles for whom you took me?"

She told me with a frown, in the calmest manner, that she intended to make her coachman take part in the frolics, and that he should take them by the back way, while she managed them by the natural route, the more so that she was sure of the discretion of this man for certain reasons of her own.

Then, sharply—"But you—you are a man of the world, and one can rely on your discretion as to the experiment in question. I shall thus pay my debt to you in offering you what I love best in the world, my love maids, who are equally devoted to me. I am going to ring for Nina, who is on duty, and who will be charmed to pay my debt to the man who saved me, in the way you well know; and I will aid you. But for me, I swore always to consecrate myself to my own sex, after a conclusive experiment that

25

I made of yours, and I am not prepared to alter my decision."

I protested my love for her aloud, a love which I could not lavish on her dear playmates. She would listen to nothing, and so I made up my mind to accept what was offered to me.

She pressed one of the buttons at the head of the bed, and then getting out, she put on her slippers and advanced towards the door, which opened, letting in a blonde soubrette wearing a dressing gown. After a short pause, the two darlings advanced. Nina, throwing off her peignoir without a moment's hesitation, jumped on the bed, followed by her mistress. Without saying a word she lifted up my shirt, took my priapus in her hand, and seeing it raise up, superb and menacing, she showed it to her mistress with a sort of timid yet submissive air. The Countess indicated with her finger first the front aperture, then the back, and seemed to ask me which I would choose. One after the other, thought I, but first the hardest to take. Making the pretty girl turn over, I took her two hemispheres, one in each hand, showing the side I preferred. The Countess seeing me giving up to her the share she loved, thanked me with a smile. Then making Nina stoop down, she made me see, with my lips almost touching the spot, that the pet was virgin on this side—and on the other too.

It was a sweet sacrifice to consummate, but I knew I shouldn't have an easy task in this narrow portal. Kneeling before that lovely bottom I tried, after having wetted both the borders of the sanctuary and the head of my weapon, to pierce the orifice, but I lunged in vain. I remained at the threshold.

The Countess was watching my progress, laughing at the futility of my efforts. I felt that the soubrette, despite her submissive air, lent herself less to the matter than one would have supposed. After a quarter of an hour of vain attempts, I really began to fear I must give in, when the Countess, gradually seized with a desire to assist in the play, disappeared for a moment into the adjoining chamber. Then she came back, followed by her two other maids, as naked as they were born. They no doubt had received careful instructions, for Lola, embracing the backside of the patient, held her immovable while Lisette roughly stretched the clinging ring with the tips of her fingers, enlarging the opening before the head of my prick. The knob slipped in suddenly and the pretty one burst forth into little moans. I pushed on, my standing weapon sliding little by little into the tight scabbard, and thanks to the help given me, was soon sheathed to the limit, facilitating the come-and-go of my prick.

During this the Countess slipped under the girl so satisfactorily impaled, and gamahuched her, madly helping me to follow her to paradise. Lisette let go the edges of the ring, which closed on my weapon like a vise. But I continued my vigorous strokes and soon the victorious member, tightly squeezed by the elastic arsehole, shot its burning jets into the glowing furnace.

The damsel screamed with pleasure as she arrived at the peak of delight under the touches

of the lips and tongue of her dear mistress on
her sensitive clitoris and on the thick lips of
her cunt.

The two soubrettes had disappeared, Lola
casting a lascivious glance on my priapus. The
Countess went with Nina into her cabinet de
toilette, where Nina began to lick her mistress's grotto of love with an agile rosy tongue.
The Countess, without interrupting the action,
told me that now that she doubted me no longer, she could allow me to assist at their Sapphic
sports, being quite sure that, for the moment, I
was not dangerous. Those words seemed to
demand an explication, and I got it later. It
seemed that the Countess's husband, the only
man she had tried, was finished for eight days
after the single skirmish.

"At any rate," she said, showing me how
Nina was engaged, "I dare say you understand
this art. If you like to take my little darling's
place (who is just a shade tired by your performance), I can let you try that."

I hastened to accept this seductive offer, and
when the maid ran off to her room, I took her
place before that superb quim. The fleece which
I had no more than just seen through the glass
door, was remarkable for its triangular shape,
its thickness, its color, and its silky curls. After having admired it and caressed it with my
fingers, I buried my face in it. When I parted
the bush which marked the entrance to the
sanctuary, I could see that her slit was still
very tight, and that the ravages left by her husband had scarcely left a trace. The hymen was
hardly broken through, so that I had almost a

maidenhead before my eyes. Such a windfall as that might have made the most worn out prick rise to the occasion, and mine certainly had no need of such a sight to recover its bony stiffness. The clitoris, which stood out like a miniature prick, perfectly developed, showed that the Countess was most sensitive to every lustful and lascivious delight, as every pretty woman should be.

I began the sport that so pleased the charming tribade and soon showed her with two or three passes of a skillful tongue, that I had nothing to learn from the most skillful Cytheran, but could hold my own in Sapphic play with any lover of her own sex. Having shown a pleasant surprise at this, she remained silent, for I recommenced my sweet task. When she was just going to come the second time, her rosy cunt dilated, opening under my fiery caresses. I threw myself on her body, and before she could recover from her surprise, in three vigorous and rapid strokes, I lodged my prick well into her glowing vagina, where it slipped easily enough along the passage slippery with her recent spending. Then suddenly, the conquered one strove by some bounds and twistings, to dislodge me. I held her tightly, and we were both so mad with pleasure that her resistance soon ceased. When I half-drowned her with the boiling jets of spunk, she moved her bottom from side to side and convulsively spending, swooned away in my arms, biting my lips with her kisses and drowning my balls with her spunk, which shot forth in a hot flood.

At first her immobility frightened me. Her

eyes shut with their dark lashes resting on her pale cheeks, her mouth half opened, she remained senseless. I sucked her, rolled her, tickled her, and then went to her lips, throwing myself on her body. The soft warmth, that so sweet pleasure, the hurt that her burning communicated to my still imprisoned prick soon renewed its vigor, and I commenced a new assault. At the very first push I felt my beauty palpitating under my body, uniting her movements to mine, clasping me in her arms, biting my lips, darting her tongue into my mouth, and frantically spending again before I'm half way there. Then gathering herself together to follow me along the route to pleasure, she quivered and seconded me so well that at the end of the skirmish she mingled her pearly dew with the essence that I shot into the center of her being.

A quarter of an hour afterwards, astonished at seeing Philip Augustus again stiff enough to brilliantly carry on a new struggle, she asked me if the old chap was always thus. I explained to her the phenomenon of erection, while she caressed me with the touch of her soft hands. She then told me why up to now, her idea had been that the aforesaid jewel had need of a long rest after each assault. When I told her she must not accuse it alone, she wanted to begin at once. That shall be my vengeance, said she, and she proved four times before daybreak that vengeance, the joy of gods, is also sometimes the joy of goddesses too. She had not a reproachful word, made no allusion to my roughness. Her aversion for men was based upon a physiological error which I had instantly cor-

rected, hence it was possible that my homeo-
pathic treatment had cured this aversion without at the same time, depriving her of her dominant passion. When we parted, we agreed to
meet at the Avenue de Messina, the Countess
being about to return to Paris the same day.

CHAPTER IV

At the Hotel in the Avenue de Messina

The Countess' Bedchamber

The Countess took the first night train. I took the next, obeying her wish to travel alone. The evening of the next day at eight o'clock as agreed, I presented myself at the Countess' hotel, Avenue de Messina. I was expected, for the door opened at the first sound of the bell, and Lisette, with a roguish smile, showed me the way. We went up by a large staircase to the first floor, and after having gone through several rooms the maid stopped, knocked, and without her moving, the door opened by a spring.

We stood in the Countess' bedchamber,

which was brilliantly lit. The walls were covered with Gobelin tapestries, separated at intervals by tall mirrors of beveled glass which reached up to the wainscot. We walked on a carpet of rich velvet pile, which did not make a sound. No one was in the room, the soubrette having disappeared without my having perceived it. I had leisure in which to look around me. A magnificent bed, very low, encrusted with gold and amber, occupied the center. In one corner stood a low, broad, well-cushioned sofa; armchairs of all sorts stood round, high and low, with movable backs and sides, plump with cushions. Ottomans, low divans and sofas, all were there; from the ceiling hung gymnastic appliances which, after my previous experience, I was not surprised to see there. Curtains concealed certain objects in the corners of the room, and at one end stood a grand piano.

The Countess, who had entered unobserved, surprised me in the midst of my inspection. I saw her reflected in a mirror, advancing with a smile on her lips. I turned sharply round and cast myself on her neck.

"Holy Mary! How brusque you are, my dear," she cried. "Don't you think we ought to have an understanding with each other a little before we recommence our sports? I regret nothing that has passed between us, but I think I should forewarn you of my wishes, so that you should not be taken aback by any caprice of mine, and, my dear man, I am very capricious. You must have perceived by now that my tastes are not the tastes of everyone, not tastes very common to sex. Until now, after an experience that made sex the reverse of attractive, I only desired my own sex. You have destroyed that prejudice. You have convinced me of its falseness, and you therefore shall have cured me of my pet sin, and although I shall be for you alone, as far as men go, you must always let me, as a tribade, follow my love for women without showing any resentment. Without these conditions, my dear Hercules, I shall once more become with you as with others, the icy Countess of Cythera."

A long kiss was my only reply.

"Why, you kiss me as sweetly as my doves, dear. You have perhaps just a shade of advantage even, for if you are equal with your tongue, you have, moreover, somewhere lower down a dear little fellow that makes you their superior. Now for more serious matters. The sight of certain exercises always makes me frightfully excited and randy. You were able to convince yourself of it yesterday when you split up poor little Nina, for you really nearly did split her up, poor little cat. This evening I am going to give you a seance which will do your business. I think it will gratify your wishes, of which I shall remain the single spectator."

I consented to all she wished, and she disappeared for a minute.

Soon the lovely quartette entered the room two by two. All were in walking dress, stays tightly laced, gloves on, piquant little shoes, ready for the Bois. Lola led the Countess, Lisette, and Nina. Each served as waiting maid, for the other undressed her, leaving nothing but her drawers and chemise, silk stockings, and little pointed shoes. Then the turn of the undressers came, who were soon undressed themselves with the same care they had given. As soon as they were all in the same boat, Lola drew a curtain aside and revealed a ladder against the wall, held at top and bottom by two bars of steel, which held it upright and parallel to the wall.

Each girl drew her chemise out from her drawers, and rolled it round her waist. Then Lola caught hold of the upper rungs of the ladder, and went up several steps without moving her hands, in such a manner that her plump bottom, jutting out through the slit of her drawers, showed itself beautifully. The snowy hemispheres, dimpled and forced themselves more and more through the gap, widening as it burst the stitches. She went gradually up, making several halts that showed us each a more enchanting view, and when she came down, her drawers were all split up, letting us see the whole of her arse, the pleasant movement of her hips, and between her thighs, the red, half-open lips of her Venus grotto in a bed of ebony hair. Then, at the bottom of the ladder, her hands and feet on the same rung, she showed all that rounded backside, swaying from side to side with play of the hips and swinging of her spheres.

What a treat, I thought, for Philip Augustus, when he finds his purple head in those charming latitudes. Then it is Lisette who climbs the lady letting her pretty pink and white moon peep through the hole of her drawers, through which her own pretty slit appeared, its coral lips bordered with curls of dark red hair. Nina, in her turn, presented in the same way her fat white arse and her cunt, like a scarlet slash in white satin. The Countess, waiting her turn, gave her two resounding smacks, which caused those rounded cheeks to be suffused with a blush. Then came the turn of the Countess, whose bosoms swelled above her chemise, splitting the fine lace with their pink nipples that stood out unaided. Behind her splendid bottom stretched the wet of her drawers which outlined her form. She spun onto the ladder, her two white satin globes, admirably modeled and dimpled, forming a backside to dream of. She mounted yet higher, showing when she was up, between the two half lips of her thick fleshy cunt, an impudent clitoris the size of one's thumb, surrounded by a forest of black hair. Why wasn't I master of the choice? No other bum would I have worshipped at, but its turn would come.

The ladder game was over. Lola and Lisette were soon stripped, keeping only their silk stockings on. I undressed in a twinkling. Lisette lay on the sofa on her back. Lola, who held my superb weapon in her hand and was gazing at its size, quitted it with regret, but without showing any fear for the fate of her own tight little hole. At a signal from the Countess she climbed on the bed, took Lisette's head between her knees and placed her quim on her lips. When she had received the kiss, she raised her lovely brown bottom, separating the cheeks, and presented her specially small keyhole to my great key.

Before attempting the perforation I passed my moist lips round the passage, wetting the borders, while the Countess did as much for the gland of my weapon, which she took in her mouth. Then I turned the ninepin straight on to the mark. Lola feeling that the dart was going astray, put it back into the right path, herself stretching the ring, helping me to put the awkward creature in first. His nose, then his head, then all the rest slipped in with a sound of meeting flesh; she stifled a sigh, but was soon silent, and let down her pussy on the wet lips of Lisette, keeping still and lending herself to the game of love. I worked away at my case, while Lisette, with her tongue deep in Lola's cunt, pursued her own lust.

I soon felt the canal constrict, sucking up my prick, which shot forth its pearly spunk, while the lascivious Spaniard twisted about in the joys of spending her very life out on the wet and shiny lips of Lisette. The Countess lost none of these details. Lola raised herself with pain, but her sparkling eyes spoke the pleasure she felt, and when the Countess, who accompanied her to the adjoining cabinet, came back, she wanted her turn at once. Lola naturally had instructed her in the sensation, and she wished to personally experience it.

She got stark naked, as did Nina, and when they were all naked, they let down the trapese bar from the ceiling. We were opposite a pier glass which reflected the group. Nina, kneeling before the Countess's well-haired quim, licked between the lips. Eagerly, Lisette caressed the bosoms. Lola, on the right, let her cunt settle down with a hovering motion like a dove, on the sensual lips, while I sought for the straight and narrow way. I had the entire scene before me in the mirror. In order to enter these ecstasies, I wet the little corrugated hole for a long time with my tongue, shooting it inside, and then slipped up my middle finger and frigged her bottom hole gently. Lola came and helped by sucking the knob of my prick, licking up and down my shaft with her hot and humid tongue, tickling my balls tight up against my bottom. I made my beauty bend over; Lisette supported her in front, and helped by Lola, who enlarged the hole with the tips of her fingers, I slipped in the head of my priapus without much trouble, little by little the stiffly-standing cock going gently so as not to tear the flesh. "To the very end! To the bottom!" cried the Countess. Clasping her waist with my arms, I pushed on vigorously without drawing back my weapon.

My love, who received all without a murmur, held the trapeze bar for support, bent her body a little so that each could regain her place, and we began in earnest. I worked well, giving time by my "come and go." I saw in the pier glass the pretty picture—the naked charms of the four beauties—in the pleasantest manner. Nina, her head curled in the thick, black bush of the Countess' cunt, seemed crowned with a jet diadem on her golden head, and showed her great fat bottom spread out, the furrows well marked, parting the celestial globe into two hemispheres.

Lisette, bending forward, showed her profile with its pink and white tits, her plump thighs, while her lips went from one breast to another, leaving marks of little red rings. Lola, straight in front, only shows one side of her arse, brown and downy, her lips planted on those of her well-loved mistress, ready to spend herself from the excitement of this loving kiss.

But the Countess squeezes my weapon in her tight crevice, suddenly stopping its progress, crushed in the constricting folds and ridges of her arsehole, unable to stir. Little by little it relaxed. I could then continue my sweet massage, and the willing victim cried in a choking voice, "More! More!" I went on more easily as she separated the soft cheeks of her bottom, keeping time anew, seconded by her ardent assistants who seemed mad with love and lust. Soon the passage was gripping me anew, and I saw that she was really nearing the end. With my body arched I wildly worked my hips, and conducted myself like a madman. I shot into her a burning shower of bliss, which shot forth in thick threads, prolonging my ecstasy at the same time that the Countess, dropping the bar, gave vent to cries of amorous rage. Lola drank in this voluptuousness, while with two wet fingers she frigged her clitoris and her thick-lipped quim, joining us in the ecstatic moment.

39

After the necessary ablutions the Countess said farewell to all her soubrettes except Lisette who was on duty, and prepared all for bed before saying good night.

CHAPTER V

The Countess' Bath

"Now I'm Mercedes again," said the Countess to me as soon as we were left alone again. "Do as you will with me, my dear Hercules. I leave you in command till tomorrow morning, when I shall once more take the direction of my own heart. I may have visits in which it would not do to have witnesses of your sex, but since these visitors will be ladies, you needn't get jealous, and if you are very discreet, there is just opposite in the bathroom a little Judas hole, well placed for allowing you to await incognito."

Saying these words, she turned down the bed, inviting me to enter, and as we had not much night toilet to make, we soon slipped be-

tween the sheets. I then had all to myself (her
pet tribade not counting), this superb Countess, the wonder of Andalusia. She was mine,
my property, her adorable body was at my
service, to do with as I would. I could have
any fancy, and she would gratify it.

After having amused her in the lazy fashion, letting her lie quiet whil I did all the work,
I wished to try a new method which took my
fancy, and in which the idleness should be on
my side: namely, for the woman to do all the
work, the man not stirring an arm or foot, but
rather lying on his back and carrying upon his
body a sweet burden.

I had to instruct my pretty dear in the
modus operandi, as she had never tried it with
her fool of a husband. When I had her installed in position, I saw one thing was wanting, i.e., a mirror on the top of the bed. I told
her so. The very next day it was in place. God
knows, we had the first use of it. My fair one,
after having thus acted the man declared she
enjoyed the position so much, that she always
wanted to do it thus, which however did not
prevent us going to sleep in the back position
after a mad frolic.

In the morning, after this "Royal George,"
I was getting ready to quit my dear mistress,
when she, holding me back, asked me if I
wouldn't help her to her bath. She jumped out
of bed, put on her slippers, and drew me towards the adjoining room. A great silver bath,
fitted with every convenience of modern comfort, showers, sprays of hot water and cold,
served every day to bathe that lovely body,

which two of her maids then dried with soft and lavender scented towels.

Yes, I did want to assist her with her bath, and to partake of it too if she'd let me. Of course she would—why shouldn't she?

We went back into the bed. At the first sound of the bell the soubrettes ran in, and after having wished me good morning as usual, they went to prepare the bath. One could hear amidst their pleasant laughter the surging of the great water taps that poured in the floods of hot and cold water. Naked, like a modern Adam and Eve, we crossed the room and together plunged beneath the wave of tepid water, scented with rose and eau-de-cologne, while the soubrettes moved about preparing hot towels for our coming out. A sweet heat penetrated our bodies, but my prick remained still soft, though sweetly warmed. Mercedes, who was cuddling up to me, took it in her hand, rubbing it up and down underwater, and squeezing in her other hand the balls that hung at its root. My gentleman suddenly stood stiff and straight, while under my finger slipped into her crack. I felt the little coral button of her clitoris enlarging. We tried to fuck, but in spite of our united efforts I couldn't slip him into the mossy cave. Leaving this game, we amused ourselves by going over the whole of our bodies, our hands wandering over the plains, stopping on the mounts, our fingers searching every hollow, me with my cock as stiff as a capuchine, and her eyes sparkling with lust and made with longing. We rang then, impatient to appease our hunger for love.

Our soubrettes ran in stark naked, their feet in slippers, cast themselves on us, and gave us robes of hot flannel with which then enwrapped our bodies, smoothing and drying us in them with the flat of their hands.

I helped Nina, who sponged the Countess on her quim as Lisette dried her behind, while Lola paid me the same attentions unaided. Above all, I gave my attentions to the rounded form before me, pressing her bosom with one hand, feeling her loins with the other, wandering between her thighs, slipping my fingers up and down the dark furrow that separates the snowy globes of her bottom. Then the Countess shed her robe, giving up all her naked body to the soubrettes who dried her with the damask towels. I wished also to be useful. Lola ran after me to dry me as well. When her hand ran over my loins, my thighs and my bottom, I felt it through all my body. Master Philip Augustus stood up stiffly, and Lola gave it a playful frig, pulling the skin up and down and squeezing the two balls in her left hand, pretending she was drying it. The spunk suddenly flew out in a pearly shower right in her face, streaking her pretty cheeks with boiling tears.

All four burst out laughing at this—Lola with rather the air of one who regrets the waste of such good stuff. The Countess ran to her and kissed the pearls away. Then she stretched herself on the massage table, lying on her back. She offered all her charms spread out. I assisted in the operation of the massage and contemplated with delight this lovely flesh which palpitated, blushing rosy red as our hands rubbed her. One rubbed her thighs, firm as marble, as she lay with them wide apart. Another rubbed the breasts, another the arms, and when the satin skin was all pink, the darling turned on her belly, presenting her smooth and lovely loins, and her well-curved backside. I kept to no one place. I leaned over the table, and while they rubbed her legs and arms, I took her bottom, which reddened under my vigorous friction. I pressed the flesh, I rubbed the satin, passed my hand down the furrow, and bending towards her magnificent arse, I left a thousand hot kisses there, which thrilled from my lips down to my prick, communicating to it a new energy and a splendid erection. The massage ended, and I wished that it had lasted longer.

It was my turn to pass under their hands. I lay myself on my back. My cock, erect and stiffer than ever, beat the air, while that quartette (for the Countess helped) vigorously rubbed me, bringing the blood to the skin. Then I turned over, and I presented my back. Mercedes, not wishing that my standing member should be crushed flat, offered herself as a mattress. I saw what she wanted by the inviting glance that she cast on my triumphant priapus. As soon as she was extended on her back, her thighs wide apart and her legs drawn slightly up so as to show her beautiful quim amid its nest of hair, she took me between her thighs and directed me toward the opening. I made them get me a cushion to raise her bottom well up, and when she presented me with her grotto of love I slipped in the engine, which was engulfed to the hilt. While I proceeded, the maids helped us on. Lola briskly rubbed my bottom, pressing it with her hands, squeezing, tickling and pinching it, bending over to nibble the skin with little bites.

She ran her fingers up and down the hairy furrow, pushing one finger into my arsehole, squeezing my balls. And when she felt the moment approaching, grasping both sides of my bottom in her hands, she helped their motion, ever and anon forcing the finger deeper in my bottom hole, and bending well over to lick my hairy balls with her tongue. Under me the Countess writhed like a madwoman, murmuring obscene words, while her cunt sucked at my prick as a kid sucks the udder of a goat.

We dressed. The Countess led me up to a partition and touched a spring, unmasking a Judas hole which allowed me to see into next room—the bedroom.

"I warned you to accept all my caprices," said she, "and you'll not be slow in being put to the proof. I expect this evening a young lady, rich and titled, who will come with her face masked, not wishing to be recognized. She is a pretty little plump blonde who I love very dearly, and I only see in secrecy. She wants to come and partake of amorous delights without bieng compromised. It suffices for me to love her—for you to be sure that she deserves to be loved. You can convince yourself of it by what you will see. Perhaps she may even unmask. If we are alone for a minute she may not feel your indiscreet glances. She is my passion—for the moment. I have some instruments which will replace a man's cock—godemiches, or dildos. I haven't yet tried them myself. They are so perfectly executed that when they are in position, you might easily mistake them for a man's organ. They have the form, size, shape, and color of a man's prick. They fasten on a woman with straps, and by squeezing the ball at the root with the thighs, they shoot warm milk into the quim at the moment of spending. It is probable that my friend Agnes—that's the name I've given her (and which of course she merits)—will want to try one after her preliminary toyings. I will lay her down ready, and then, if you wish, you can take Lola's place, who will be acting the man. We will fasten the dildo to her in the little pet's presence, and she'll be sure to believe that it is only a sham prick she's taken in. The soubrette, who will be masked, will disappear, and you will take her place, and fuck Agnes as we did together yesterday, in such a position that she can't see you."

I thanked my amiable enchantress and took leave, promising to be punctually at the rendez-vous.

CHAPTER VI

Entrance on the Scene of a Pretty Innocent

Who Is Not Such a Fool as She Pretends

At nine o'clock I was at the meeting place. The lady was to arrive at ten. The Countess held a dildo in her hand. One would have said it was a man's prick at full stand, the knob, the shape, the back, the varied skin of natural color down to the balls covered with curly hair— all was as natural as in life. A strap of three fingers breadth allowed it to be buckled around the loins, and to be carried as a man does his prick in a state of erection. The instrument was hollow, so as to contain boiling milk, pleasantly warm, which by squeezing the elastic ball between the thighs of the operator would squirt forth at the critical moment into the womb of the recipient, just as a man's spunk would do.

I dressed anyhow, a velvet mask covering part of my face so that my moustache should not betray my sex. When I heard the tinkle of the bell, I slipped out and hid myself in the bathroom.

The bedroom door opened, admitting a lady in a dark dress, masked, introduced by Nina.

As soon as the soubrette retired, the new-comer pulled off her mask, and threw herself into the arms of the Countess, and embraced her with a long clinging kiss. When she turned round, I admired her charming virginal face with two soft blue eyes, modestly cast down, everything breathing candor and innocence. A broad forehead, pure and serene as an angel's was crowned with golden curls; one would have taken her for a virgin of Raphael's come down from its frame.

The two beauties formed a delightful contrast. The Countess, with her sensual lips, rosy and moist, the long kiss just imprinted on them, leaving them half open with desire, seemed ready to devour that blonde Madonna she gazed on. The flame that shot from those black eyes told of the fire that consumed her. If I hadn't had my share of the frolics of the lascivious lady, I really might have been jealous. The ardent Andalusian, already on her knees, slipped her head under her petticoats and disappeared there, giving herself up for several minutes to the little game at which she was so adept. I was just opposite Miss Chastity-and-Virtue, but the expression of her features showed what was going on out of sight, for her eyes were glowing with amorous desires, her little pretty nose with its rosy nostrils expanding as though to breathe faster, the motion of her lips vainly kissing the air and showing a row of sparkling pearls, all told the heavenly pleasure that was enrapturing her. Soon her eyelids began to close and unclose quicker, a blush of hot lust spread over her face, her bosoms swelled, lifting up her corsets, and her hands pressed down on the head under her clothes. I saw a tremor come over all her body, especially in her knees, that seemed as if they could not bear her up. And then I saw the face of the Countess emerge, red, moist and glowing from under the petticoats. As soon as she was up she pressed her wet lips on the mouth of her dear friend, who calmly resumed her air of perfect innocence.

The Countess, stepping towards the electric bells, pressed one, telling her golden-haired Agnes to put on her mask if she wished to remain unknown.

The soubrettes soon came. Lola masked, the other two not—all naked, except with stockings and slippers.

The unknown, whose eyes blazed behind her mask, stared at the charming trio as though nervous. To reassure her, the Countess wished to set the example, and at a sign from her eyes, the soubrettes proceeded to undress their mistress in the usual manner, sucking her bosoms, slapping her bottom, and kissing her cunt. Then having put on her slippers, they conducted her under the trapeze; after the preliminary caresses, the promenade of kisses on the white body stopping at the various hollows such as the bushy quim, the furrow of her bottom, and the armpit with its dark curls, the game commenced. Our blonde Madonna shivered with desire in her armchair, greedily following all the details of the frolic. Lola gamahuched her cunt, Lisette licked the arsehole in its dark furrow, while Nina licked the armpits. Seeing lips idle, our unoccupied beauty darted forward, but before she reached her, Nina, who was nearest her lips, kissed them, darting in her tongue, squeezing the great plump bosoms in her caressing hands. The unknown had to remain a simple onlooker, but she didn't waste her time. Putting her hand to her own swimming cunt, she frigged herself madly with one rosy finger, while leaning over Lola. She admired the skill of the tongue which tickled the clitoris. Behind, she gazed on Lisette, frigging with her finger the tight little bottom hole with its ring of tiny curls. Then rising, she saw the two pairs of rosy lips kissing like amorous doves, lips on lips, eyes on eyes. Bending down again, she was just in time to see the lower part of that snowy belly heaving up and down in the spasms of pleasure, while the lips of the cunt were expanding an abundant dew which dappled with creamy pearls the ebony ringlets of hair.

While the three finished with the Countess, the virginal one seemed to await her turn. Six willing hands soon left her without a stitch on while the Countess held her lips pressed on those that showed so sweetly under her mask, and the undressers covered her with kisses. When the toilette was ended, the initiate rose, and went under the trapeze. On the lovely dimpled body blossomed lilies and roses, roses and lilies. She had a firm bosom with breasts well apart, the nipples far from each other. At the bottom of the belly was a black fleece of curls that clashed with her golden locks. As soon as she was under the trapeze, the Cytheran lovers took their several roles; Nina in the pussy, Lola at the dark neighbor, Lisette was at the breasts, sisters yet apart, the Countess near her satin back, waiting for the moment to glue her lips to that little mouth. Scarcely had the overture of kisses commenced, when she quivered all over her whole body, tenderly agitated by the burning contact of such glowing lips, running over her charms, covering them with ineffable caresses which set on fire all they touched. Soon each one was at her post, but scarcely had they opened fire, when the lascivious blonde cried out, in spite of the lips that closed her mouth. When she spent, leaving go of the bar, and heaving great sighs came to herself again, each took on her sweet task. The darling again hung on the bar, and commenced anew to palpitate under the hot kisses by which she was devoured. She swung, rose and fell, giving an oscillation to the whole group which followed their every movement, till suddenly leaving go of the bar, she slipped down, panting, among the quartette. While she was recovering her senses on the soft cushions to which they had carried her, the three maids, who by this time were frightfully randy and ready to fuck and spend at every port, installed themselves on the carpet.

Nina stretched herself on her back. Lola, with her face turned towards her feet, knelt over her head and presented her luscious cunt to Nina's face, which her bottom half hid from view. Then raising Lisette in her strong arms, she turned her head downwards. Lisette supported herself partly on her hands, her mouth on Nina's quim, while Lola kept her legs wide apart in the air, so that she could plunge her tongue and lips between her thighs into her spending cunt. Each made haste to bring on the crisis, overwhelming with reciprocal kisses the sweets she had at her lips.

This scene woke up our fair unknown, and brought her to her senses. Allured by this exciting spectacle, she leapt from the couch, and from a near point admired the talents of each girl. Lisette clapped her feet together in ecstasy, as Lola, embracing her round bottom, pressed her slit up to her lids, keeping them tight there at the same time that she rubbed her own fat backside on Nina's face. She nearly crushed the cheeks of her bottom, rubbing herself lasciviously, the better to feel that fucking tongue along her crack. Lisette, with a face very red from the tiring posture, redoubled her gamahuching of Nina's crimson slash, doubly pressed to finish.

Suddenly the trio quivered and shook with an agony of spending, and fell down like a pack of cards, their cunts throbbing and flowing— Lola especially, who spent almost as if she were passing water.

Our sweet and tender innocent, who always had her mask, threw herself on the group, rubbing herself on these naked and throbbing bodies like a lustful little cat. Lola, suddenly jumping up, seized her, picked her up, swung her upside down with her leg in the air, plunged her lips between her thighs, and licked her hairy quim and the button of her clitoris.

The subject of this attack, head down, her mouth on Lola's grotto, bit all round her lips while she tickled her bottom with her hands clasped round it. Lola carried her light burden around the room, never leaving the sucking and frigging of the quim, fondly licking it and walking backwards and forwards. The legs flew in the air and clasped the neck. Her feet crossed, and when Lola stopped, the slash was still on her lips opposite my peephole, the cheeks of her innocent bottom opened and shut, covered with dimples. They grew rigid with lust, and remained apart as the little darling shook forth her spunk, which trickled down her hair toward her navel. Lola set her lifeless burden down on the couch, and took the dildo full of warm milk. When the tender Agnes reopened her eyes, they showed her the instrument which was going to work her pleasure. Lola tied on the sham prick and advanced with it erect from her belly like a man.

The Countess turned her friend round in such a way, by making her kneel on the bed, that she was ready for a fuck en levrette. Her cunt appeared between the jutting cheeks like a crimson slash in white satin.

Lola then glided out of the room on tiptoe,

pushed me in, slipping her mask on my face, and took my place before the peephole while I noiselessly took hers before that lovely bottom so enticingly ready.

When I arrived, the weapon in my hand, the soubrettes exchanged a smile. The Countess tenderly caressed the secret charms of her friend to dispose her to receive my penetration of her cave of love. I viewed the scene. The superb backside with its dimpled spheres of clear white, arrested my enchanted gaze. To pay it due homage I ought not to carry my regards further, but duty called me lower, and my eyes followed. I saw two vermilion lids pouting with desire, inviting Philip Augustus to do his duty. I hesitated no longer.

The Countess, directing the dart to the target, stimulated its ardor by the sweet touch of her soft white hand. As soon as it had given the preliminary kiss, it entered the grove, where it disappeared entirely, clear up to the burning womb.

Grasping in my hands the sweet globes in front, I go on gently, coming up close to her, warmer at each push, while the complacent Countess gently toyed with my hanging balls. My belly slapped against her arse. Mercedes, with a finger on the clitoris, helped me in my endeavors. The patient manifested by stifled sighs, the pleasure that was coming over her. I mingled my transports with hers, almost unsheathing myself by my involuntary movement. I remained motionless an instant, wishing for a new assault. But fearing that the instrument going down should betray me, I slipped out with regret from the sweet prison. Vain precaution. That was not at all the idea of my sweet partner. The little duck caught hold of my balls between her legs, and squeezed them as if they were made of cast iron. Pain drew a cry from me. Mademoiselle turned round. My mask had come undone during the process—she perceived I was a man.

Thunderstruck for an instant, she at last cried out, "Well, all the better. It's not made of India rubber. Moreover, you don't know, and you never will know whose face is hidden under this mask, my friend," she added, turning to the impossible Countess. "You never told me that among your soubrettes you had one with a horn. I don't mind if you do frighten me a little with your man; you know I love your tongue better than anything else."

The Countess with her eternal smile, always watchful, told her she could trust me implicitly, that she could take off her mask, which was quite useless since I had been a witness to all their frolics since the outset. And as for the soubrettes, they were of proven fidelity, so devoutly discreet that they would submit to torture rather than split.

Our pet having discovered a predilection for Mercedes' tongue, the latter proposed a double action.

"You have there," she said, tapping her bottom, "a little recess, which although very tight will easily take in our friend's eager prick, while in front, dear, to suit your taste, I can give you the 'velvet tip.' You can't conceive, my pet, the pleasure which will penetrate your

56

frame. After a shade of pain inseparable from a first attempt, you will taste heavenly joys, sharp there, soft here."

Agnes consented to anything to make her happy. Lola lay on Lisette, upside down, each offering her cunt to the other for a reciprocal gamahuche.

Agnes, coming between Lola's legs, knelt on the broad backside she presented to view, one knee on each cheek of her bottom, which spread like a luxurious cushion under her weight. The Countess, astride of Lola, leaned forward so as to get her lips on Agnes's quim. Nina, upright at the side of the group, leaned towards our fair innocent (?) and kissed her on the mouth. While she pressed her bosoms in her hands, I attempted the opening of the closed entrance, but its tight ring victoriously repulsed my attack.

The Countess, abandoning her post for a moment, came and helped me vigorously. Thanks to our combined efforts, I forced the gate, not without a little pain for the patient, who raised a little cry when I had passed with the knob. The little clinging sphincter ring gave way to pleasure for her, and Mercedes went back to her place.

My girl, now quite impaled, as I saw in the glass, made a little face, but the ravishing tableau and the sweetness of the double pleasure soon brought back a smile of heavenly delight to her rosy lips. Each lunge of the backside that I gave made my member enter still further.

Her knees sank into Lola's bottom, pressing the cheeks apart. Mercedes, who had one hand between them, thrust a finger up into her brown arsehole with its tiny curls of black hair and frigged it skillfully, while with the other hand she kept Anges's quim open, showing the little button which she lovingly caressed with the velvet tip of her tongue, tenderly exciting the mossy cavern before her.

Under the influence of the neighboring opening, the ring which imprisoned my instrument almost strangled it, but still he kept up the come and go—though with difficulty—till he shot in his wave of burning lava into the soft interior folds of her bottom. At the same time, she spent profusely on the tongue of Mercedes. When we separated, Nina's thighs were streaming with spendings, and on the loving lips of Lola, where the Countess had rubbed her hairy quim, there still remained the frothy dew. Both Lola and Lisette, from their ardent sucking, had quite a glistening moustache.

When Agnes de H. quitted us, she begged the favor of bringing on the next day, her intimate friend, Blanche de R.

"Blanche de R.," said the Countess, looking as if she knew the name. "Why certainly, she will be very welcome."

We went to bed with all the lights lit. I guessed the reason when I saw the glass plaque forming the canopy of the bed. Mercedes wanted to see the effect produced first. I gave her this satisfaction by mounting on the top. She was much delighted in watching the pleasing contortions. Then lending herself to my caprices, she was soon on the top, setting herself over me. She put my swollen prick into her belly, where it soon slipped in up to the hilt. Then gluing her lips to mine and moving her hips, I watched the soft cheeks of her arse rising tight together, then descend open, keeping their pleasant oscillations. At my suggestion, she rubbed herself sideways on my thighs, her bottom performing the "pan and cinder" movement, making little dimples with the effort to move horizontally. Her buttocks swelled as they rose, and spread as they came down, enlarging, straddling as the clinging lips of her juicy cunt sucked my prick in. Then once more she began with the rigid horizontal motion, mixing and intertwining our bushes of curls, her flesh and mine damp with sweat. Suddenly my cock shot forth its spunk, drawn in by the elastic lips of her lustful womb, while obscene and lascivious words fell from her lips.

Four times did we repeat the amorous struggle, and then went to sleep, clasped in each other's arms, till bathing time which brought back renewed desire for fresh fucks and friggings.

This time, however, I underwent a massage at the hands of the soubrettes, and when that was over, we had one more bout on the mattress. During it, Lola acquitted herself as a skillful maid and tribade, at one time smacking her heaving bottom with open palm, at another licking along her arse with a hot and moist tongue, stopping to titillate the little brown hole. She pushed in the tip of her tongue like a dart, and quivered with convulsive bounds.

Philip Augustus felt the throb in his hot prison, and he soon found mutual delights.

It was settled that in the evening I should install myself at my observatory, till a favorable moment for my entrance on the scene.

CHAPTER VII

Between Two Fires

At ten o'clock the two friends made their appearance in the bedchamber. I was at my post, to be sure, with my eye glued to the people. Agnes de P. introduced her friend, Madame Blanche de R. to the Countess; both bowed courteously. Then, to the intense astonishment of Agnes, the Countess cast herself on Blanche's neck, clasping her with her arms, calling her queen, while Blanche returned the caresses with interest, saying, "my sweetest treasure," and treating her as an old friend.

It was nevertheless the first time they had found themselves together. They had often stared at each other as they passed in the Bois, but that was all, and they simply showed the magic sympathy that they both felt when they were brought *"en la pont."*

These effusions having come to an end, Mercedes took Agnes to her bosom, and gave her a long clinging kiss. She wanted a kiss such as this to smooth away the little frown from her brow brought there by just a touch of jealousy. But as soon as she was thus welcomed, her lips soon put on their virginal smile.

"Poor Blanche," she said, "did not know the heavenly joys one tastes in these chambers, and that they would be a snug little party, for the dear girl would be ashamed to face too many indiscreet glances. With us three, my dear, you can well amuse yourself."

"You forget," said the Countess, "that my soubrettes are my friends, and that their discretion, like their devotion, is unlimited. I will commence the seance between ourselves, but we must continue it with my indispensable assistants."

While the Countess was getting ready the necessary aids, I had a good look at the new recruit. Just as brunette as Agnes was blonde, Madame de R. was of middle height. On a pretty figure was a well developed bosom which swelled over a corset of enchanting outlines. From the spring of her hips rounded forth a full-shaped backside. Her face was marble-white, and cut by two little scarlet lips like a split cherry. Her eyebrows were thick and black; her eyelashes, long and silky, shadowed her great soft black eyes, which sparkled even in repose.

The Countess had placed two chairs near one another. She took the fair dame by the hand and made her get up with one foot on each chair, her legs rather wide apart, her back to the partition. She lifted up her petticoats in front and made her hold them up, and stopped a moment before the object that fixed her attention. Then turning up the petticoats behind, she first showed two black silk stockings, a pair of knickerbockers bordered with exquisite lace, and higher up, the tail of a chemise, which stuck out of the slit of her drawers, still concealing what was beneath. Mercedes pushed this in, and opened the slit wider, making the dear creature bend over and hold her clothes well up on her back.

Then advancing, she said, "How d'ye do?" to the beauties before her eyes by placing her lips on them in a sweet kiss. When she left this spot for the land of Venus, I was able to admire the white and dimpled bottom framed in the slit of her drawers.

The Countess, upright between the two chairs but with her neck bent down, glued her mouth to the hairy cunt before her, her right arm embracing the left cheek of her arse, her fingers tickling up and down the furrow between, while the other hand helped keep the clitoris under her tongue.

Agnes, upright behind the Countess, stood on tiptoe, and stretched her arms over Mercedes' head, so as to take the flushed face of Blanche between her hands, which she drew close to her own. The latter bent forward and thrust in an amorous tongue. As she bent forward over the two, the darling burst the stitches of her drawers, and through the widened gap slipped out the whole of her white and quivering bottom with its dark and hairy furrow. By the dimples that came in it and the little creases that appeared and vanished continually, you could tell the lascivious emotions of its fair owner. The hands of the Countess wandered ever between those twin hemispheres, and her fingers traversed the furrow between, stopping a little each time at the back entrance to recommence again.

Soon the snowy cheeks contracted violently, squeezing themselves together, then spreading wide apart with tremulous motion, only to shut tight again. The hand stopped low down, the finger pressed the lovely little crinkled hole of the arse, and pierced it with the tip. Then at a convulsive motion of the bottom, in the ecstasy of spending, she slipped three parts in where they tenderly frigged in and out. I could guess the finale by the enchanted sighs that came from her lips, and the shuddering tremors of pleasure that shook her frame.

When this was over the Countess pressed a button, and immediately the soubrettes made their appearance, being naked save for silk stockings and pretty high buttoned boots with gilt heels—at which sight Madame de R. seemed much astonished. At a signal from their mistress each took one and began to undress her. Nina, upon whom Blanche devolved, prolonged their preliminaries so much, that she hadn't finished as soon as the other. She had scarcely bared one little rosy foot on which she pressed kisses when Lola and Lisette finished stripping the fair dame.

They conducted her to the middle of the room, turning her towards the partition and showed me her pretty dimpled body, every curve of it.

Two rounded breasts on a bosom of alabaster covered the breadth of her, separated in the middle, front and straight. The bottom of her belly, as polished as a gate, was covered with a black fleece, thick, curled, and bushy, shading the little mound and reaching down to the slit itself, so well placed that one could see the pink lips.

But the soubrettes, impatient to astonish their pretty recruit after having covered her with kisses from head to foot, began to try on their great game.

Lola lay on her back, and took the little pet in her arms. She stretched on her so that her cunt was on her lips, while the lady's face rested on her thighs. Nina, in her turn, lay along Blanche's back with her mouth on her bottom. Lisette, kneeling behind, lightly tickled the soles of her feet. The Countess and her fair friend straddled across this ground, facing each other, lasciviously rubbing and frigging their quims on the soubrette's naked flesh, one of them having between her thighs the great fat arse, and the other the middle of the loins. The weight of these two friends rested on the three bodies beneath them, but having their feet on the ground took off some of their weight. Pressing down, they brought all their charms close together, but Lola, who bore it all, was strong as a man, and the burden seemed light from my observatory. I noticed that she didn't stop her movements, and I well guessed that her gamahuching was being reciprocated. Nina pressed between the thighs of the Countess, her lips pushed into the furrow of Blanche's bottom. She rubbed her own cunt on the loins. Lisette kissed and tickled her feet with her left hand. The right had disappeared, but I could see by the movement of her arm that she was lustfully frigging her own cunt. A lascivious smile played on her features and confirmed my guess.

As for me, in my solitude, I was nearly wild. Holding my balls in one hand, I had already frigged myself once, and the warm spunk was flowing over my testicles and my hand in thick drops. I was already stiff again with desire. I was in such a state that soon I was unable to stay still. I made up my mind to assist Lisette to convert her solo of pleasure into a duet. I rushed from my concealment towards the group. Lisette saw me coming with my prick erect, and guessing what I wanted, left her employment for a minute. She lifted up her arse, and opened the lips of her treasure, and took me in easily, her frigging having lubricated her cunt, and my prick having its shaft slippery with the spunk still there.

She then went on amusing Blanche, while I dove into her glowing furnace, and watched the sweet game before me.

I was afraid I had come too late, but I was

so rowdy when I took part in the dance, that the spunk shot out and deluged her already swimming cunt. It mingled with her own; it ran down her thighs at the very moment that the other swam into the sea of voluptuousness.

When the entanglement was unloosed, we had to draw Blanche away from Lola, who held her crushed against her bosom, wishing to continue the sweet folly. We carried her, quite played out, to the sofa. Lola, her face crimson, her eyes shining, her lips humid and her thighs wet with spendings, reeled to her feet, drunk with lust.

The Countess didn't show the least surprise at seeing me there, and when I told her I had not been able to stand the torment any more, only smiled. Then pointing to the little pet lying bottom upwards on the couch, she asked me if I had sufficient "go" in me to take her western virginity, her husband having only opened up the eastern maidenhead. The idea alone of forcing this pretty fortress gave a lift to Philip Augustus, who stood at attention once more.

When the pretty brunette showed signs of life, they prepared her for the process. They showed her a great dildo, destined for her front, and a very little one for the back aperture. They filled the two dildos with hot milk, so soothing to the organs thus pierced.

Concealed behind the curtains, I was not to show myself till a propitious moment. The two friends overwhelmed the darling with the warmest caresses. Lola bound on the larger instrument by a strap that encircled her waist, and two smaller ones round the thick part of each thigh, so that the dildo stood straight out like a man's prick, the belt covered with hair between her thighs. Nina in a like manner adjusted the smaller one.

Lola lay on her back on the bed with Blanche upon her, in the attitude known as the "Royal George" and helped by her friend, she took in the prick, made slippery with scented soap— (my fair readers must remember that no grease must ever be used with India-rubber dildos, as it ruins them) and lowering herself little by little, engulfed the whole in her belly. I then came forward and knelt behind her soft, white arse, and after the soubrettes had made it slippery with wet, tonguing kisses and Nina had sucked the knob of my prick in her mouth, I commenced the insertion. The Countess stretched the opening of the little brown crinkled hole with the tips of her fingers, but it was so tight that the tip of my cock couldn't at first get in. However, as I was sure that the hole was tight enough, I pushed forwards vigorously; the pretty sufferer called out and looking round, perceived the substitution of the natural organ for the artificial.

She struggled against it, and said she couldn't take in such a size, but Lola held her tight in her muscular arms. The soubrettes held her loins steady, and the two friends, with the tips of their fingers, held apart the cheeks of her bottom. My prick, assured of success, pushed forward as I guided it. The tip of the crimson knob entered and then passed in up to the ridge. Then it all entered and disappeared in the tight sheath. The sphincter ring finally yielded. Sighs of pain first came from her lips, and in spite of the resistance of the clinging edges of the orifice, I could work up and down in the tight, warm shelter at my ease. At each motion of my prick which pushed her arse forward, the dildo beneath drove still further into her cunt, coming half out when I drew back, re-entering when I shoved forward, following all my movements. The four witnesses followed the manner religiously, and held the dear patient immovable, which was useless, as now she had no wish to resist. Each instant she took more pleasure in the process, delighted at the new game of love. In fact, both of them tremulously moved under my thrusts, responding to my pushes by convulsive quivers, screaming with pleasure, and muttering obscene and lustful words and phrases. Then my member, crushed in the clinging grasp of her arsehole, shot forth its warm and soothing flood almost to her very heart, and at the same moment the India-rubber prick below shot the warm milk into her spending quim, thanks to Lisette, who squeezed the elastic ball with her fingers. Lola had forgotten to close her thighs on it, as she herself was spending from her frigging with her own middle finger.

As soon as my prick had softened, I withdrew it with a plop from its tight quarters, and going into the bathroom I made myself comfortable once more.

When I came back Blanche was still in the

dressing room with Lola, who was looking after her. While waiting their return, we prepared an amusement in which everyone could participate. When Lola came back, followed by Madame de R., I laid down on the carpet, the back of my neck on a cushion, and my prick in the air. Agnes, the blonde, straddled over the center of my body, and turning her back to my face put my prick between her thighs. She took all its length into her thick-lipped cunt, and thus sitting, waited for the signal to commence.

Next Blanche sat over my face, her back to Agnes, astride my neck, and thus presented her quim to my kiss.

Lisette and Nina got on the backs of Lola and the Countess respectively, their quims resting on the small of the back of their fair supporters just where the arse juts out, their legs crossed in front on the navel, their arms round their necks so that the hands rested in front on their breasts. The Countess with her load then stood astride and upright with one foot on one side of my face and the other on the other, so that her thick, bushy cunt was on a level with Blanche's lips. Thus looking up as I lay, I had a view of the crimson slash of her quim, the tip of her clitoris and the furrow of her bottom. Lola, facing her, stood in a like manner over my legs, and readied her tongue.

The Countess and Lola bent over the two bodies between, to kiss each other amorously like doves. Lisette and Nina kissed also over the heads of their bearers, billing and cooing with pretty murmurs of pleasure. Lisette and Nina rubbed their open cunts on the backs of their bearers, interchanging wet kisses like turtle doves.

Agnes, transfixed by my prick, wriggled her bottom with great agility, and at the same time gamahuched Lola, who covered her face with her black, bushy cunt pressed against it.

Lola, set going by these caresses, amorously sucked the tongue of the Countess. The Countess, excited by the rubbing and spending of the lustful quim of Nina, palpitated and quivered under Blanche's burning lips.

I worked away to complete the pleasure of Blanche, with the agile and skillful tongue of a trained gamahucher, with ardors increased tenfold by the enchanting tableaux I had before my eyes. From time to time I turned my head slightly without stopping my occupation, and saw in the mirrors round, faithful reproductions of the joyous play.

I saw there the outline of the heaving bosoms, of the plump and rounded arses, of the satiny skins, the rosy tinted naked bodies of randy women. I saw an entanglement of limbs and interlacing of lovely forms, showing all their hidden beauties in the tremors of enjoyment, in the agonies of spending, in every bizarre and unusual attitude. The fair riders' bottoms made a slapping noise as their thighs came against Lola and the Countess, giving them a vibrating motion at each fall. Soon ceasing this, they lasciviously rubbed against these curved backs in a voluptuous oscillation.

The jutting forth of Blanche's bosoms prevented my seeing all the beauties about me. Still, through the valley formed by her two great breasts I saw the end of a rosy slit, in which moved a rapid tongue, frigging the clitoris button with skillful agility.

Absorbed now in my sweet task, I felt the pleasures of the clitoris against my tongue, and then suddenly, as if all our organs were bound together by a magnetic fluid, we all—the riders, the gamahuched ones, the impaler and the impaled—spent together as if by electric shock.

The two friends dressed once more, in which we all helped lavish on them the most tender caresses. For my part I took about five minutes, putting on a pretty stocking and garter.

When the darlings were dressed and absolutely ready to go, the four who were still naked and mad with randiness, threw themselves on their knees, and two to each, slipped under the petticoats of the departing ones, pushing aside their laces and taking opposite sides, gamahuching and at the same time frigging themselves madly with their fingers.

Determined to have my part also, and loving a frig as much as a fuck, I put my standing cock into Agnes's hands, telling her to frig it with her soft hand, while I hurried Blanche's hands on my rough and hairy balls.

Then slipping both my hands under their petticoats, I took hold of their bottoms, squeezing them in my fingers, while Agnes skillfully frigged my prick, bringing the skin down and uncovering its head at each of her strokes which succeeded one another more rapidly every moment. Blanche, with equal skill and effect molded and tickled my balls, every now and then slipping her hand behind them little and tickling the root of my prick, forcing her finger into my arsehole.

This gave me the most ecstatic thrill, and when I felt the end approaching for us all, I leaned over and kissed Agnes so fiercely as almost to make her lips bleed, which however she didn't seem to feel. She frigged me still with lustful swiftness, my prick's stiffness in her grasp. Suddenly, I shot out a flood of white spunk which covered her pretty hand. She did not stop her motion till she had extracted the last drops of sweetness from its rosy head. This came as they moved backwards and forwards, spent on the lips their gamahuchers.

This time it was really all over, and the two friends took their leave, frigged, dildoed, and gamahuched to their hearts' content.

I stayed with the Countess, whose languishing eyes promised me some new and fresh sports. Lola only, who was on duty for the night, remained with us. The Countess whispered an order in her ear; the maid slipped on a peignoir, went away for a minute, and came back again with a porcelain pan, which she placed on a tripod over the spirit lamp. Then drawing off her peignoir again, she took a dildo, and when the milk was hot she drew it up into the instrument by squeezing the ball. She fastened it around her loins as before, then standing upright, she was ready for the Countess. Lola bent her knees to allow Mercedes to split herself more easily and so guided the dildo into the ready cunt. The Countess presented her dimpled bum to me. Although the path had been traversed before, and she assisted to smooth away any difficulties, it was only after considerable management that I forced the gate. When I was completely in, and the glowing sheath contracted on my pains, the two women commenced, and each in our way we started the game. We went on in regular cadence, in and out at the same time. Lola shoved her dildo and I my prick, the sham-prick swelling the canal it fucked and narrowing the passage I was in, so that the natural and the artificial were only separated by a thin partition adding to the sweet friction on my pego. After a "come-and-go" of a few minutes, Lola, warned by Mercedes, squeezed the ball between her thighs at the very moment I spent, and we inundated the two canals at the same instant. The maddening lust made Mercedes writhe between the two boiling jets with which her own thick spendings mingled.

Before going off to bed and sending Lola away, her mistress—never selfish—wished her pretty maid to have a turn.

She, in point of fact, was dying for want of it; she hadn't had time to come as we had been too quick for her. I wanted to do it for her, but Philip Augustus was really not in a very brilliant condition. Seeing this as an obstacle to the realization of their desires, they thought of a way to succeed. Kneeling before the poor used-up thing, one took the whole knob in her mouth, passing her tongue round and round it, while the other tickled the hanging balls with a hot and lascivious tongue. What could not happen with such enticement? He got stiffer every moment, and at last stood triumphantly once more.

As soon as he raised his glowing head, the Countess glowing at his unlooked for condition let herself go, seized the dildo, filled it once more with hot milk, and tied it on her; she helped the soubrette to force it up her belly, licking her cunt, and injecting her saliva to make it go easily.

When it was in, and the real curls of Lola were mingled with the false ones on the root of the dildo, Lola presented her bottom and its tight and crinkled hole, surrounded by little curls of hair, which I first sucked and forced my tongue in, and so prepared it.

It still took trouble, and that in spite of the help she gave me and the fact that it was the second time she had tried that entrance. The performance took a little longer this times, and when I gave Mercedes the signal to let go of the juices, I was just beginning to come, and she, by frigging herself readily with two fingers, was able to join us in the ecstatic flow of spunk. I held them up for a minute, but then followed as their knees gave way, and finally I lay motionless on them.

Lola left us, but the insatiable Countess offered me her still spending cunt to lick, to kiss and to suck, while she amused herself with extracting with her pretty red lips the last pearly drops of my spunk. Then, clasped in each other's arms, we slept at last.

CHAPTER VIII

A Russian Princess Who Needs Stimulants

The next day Madame de R. came to tell us of a Russian Princess, Madame Sophie de K., a great friend of hers, from whom she had almost exacted a promise to be presented to the Countess of Lesbos. She hadn't dared to complete this arrangement without leave of the mistress of the house, since the princess was a strange mixture of coldness and flame; sometimes all fire like an African, sometimes cold as a Siberian.

The Countess of Lesbos, always hospitable, willingly gave her consent on the recommendation of Madame de R. she would have accepted anyone with her eyes shut.

At ten o'clock I was at my observatory,

when three ladies came in. The Russian Princess, a ravishing blonde, with pale golden hair and eyes of Myosotis, a full and rounded figure, walked between Blanche de R. and Agnes de P.

The Countess, after a preliminary ceremonious bow, embraced her two friends at once, but hesitated before the newcomer, then making up her mind to take her by storm, she leapt on her neck, kissed her on the eyes, her nose, her mouth, which received these kisses on an icy lip. Excited by her, she accentuated her kisses, trying to force her lips so as to take her tongue, but the princess remained insensible, her teeth clenched. The Countess ran to the electric bell and rang for the soubrettes who ran in stark naked.

Sophie gave them only an indifferent glance. However, she let them take off her clothes, receiving the most intimate caresses of her attendants with complete, apparent indifference, though their kisses were on her most secret charms. The princess was, no doubt, in one of her wintry moods, for she received the most ardent caresses without emotion.

When she was quite naked, except for her stockings and pretty bottines, the trio commenced the great game, trying on all the pretty frolics, seeking the naughtinesses of theirs which was unrivaled, still without result.

From my observatory I gazed on this splendid, naked woman, so hard to warm. She was a perfect model, with her round and dimpled arms, her alabaster bosom, a bust of perfect curves, a bush of golden hair on the white skin of her belly, two plump thighs and perfect legs, with tiny feet.

The soubrettes tried in vain to animate this marble statue, but it remained cold in spite of their warmth.

Upon this obstinate coldness the Countess quitted the room, and ran in to pour forth her woes to me.

"I know what she wants," said I, "and if you'll let me, I know how to give it to her. Russian women often want stimulating—my remedy is a sovereign one; you must let me give her a liberal dose of it."

"Get along then," said Mercedes, "and try your remedy."

I was just in the mood for the struggle; without hesitating, I went into the other room. The princess turned round without showing the slightest surprise at seeing a naked man walk in with a cockstand of grand dimensions. I pushed Lisette aside, who was resting with her cheek on that lovely dimpled bum. Without giving her any warning, I cruelly spanked this broad bottom, on which the slaps resounded loudly. She made no movement to avoid this smacking.

The Countess, who at first seemed as if she would oppose this brutality of mine, seeing that Sophie did not stir more than once, let me go on. Soon the cheeks of her arse had quite lost their paleness and began to blush and move lasciviously, feeling the warmth that penetrated them.

Nina, who was molding her breasts in her hands, felt them heave. The lips that she had on her own returned her kisses, and Lola, in the slit, was gamahuching. She could hardly keep under her tongue the stiffened clitoris which stood out, so the lips of her cunt became covered with a fresh dew, while Sophie manifested by the convulsive movements of her bottom, the pleasure that she felt.

As soon as she had come she turned over. Her eyes of Myosotis blazed with voluptuousness, her icy manner had changed to a smile of blissfulness and thanking me for my services.

While she squeezed me to her, my shaft, which was as hard and stiff as a bar, beat against her thighs and the bottom of her plump belly. She took it in her hand, and directed it towards its native goal, trying to force it in. Kneeling down, I helped her, and when it was right up her, I got up, lifting her as well, with her arms round my neck and her legs crossed over my bum. Then turning her head, she asked for a birch rod. Lola, at a sign from her mistress, brought a nice birch, tied up with blue ribbons, and presented it to Mercedes, who giving way to the lust of the princess, gave her some light cuts on the bottom.

"Harder! Harder!" cried the victim. The Countess, bothered by her dress, and not having the nerve to slash the velvety satin of such an arse, passed the instrument to Lola.

To lose nothing of the sight, I moved with my precious burden in front of a mirror, which reflected the expansive bottom, well placed to be flagellated.

Lola lifted the birch, which whistled as it fell on the cheeks, gently, without much pain for the patient.

The crimsoning arse demeaned itself after a pleasant fashion, rising and falling in time. Her vagina followed these movements of her backside, showing half the shaft of my prick, the clinging lips of her cunt round it, both shining with spendings when the bum rose and fell. She greedily sucked it in, till our hairs mingled, alternately drawing it in and rejecting it with a gentle sucking, slapping noise.

Lola began to like her amusement. Her cheeks blushed with pleasure, her eyes sparkled with lust, her lips quivered, murmuring obscene words, her nostrils dilated. She redoubled her strokes on the bottom, blushing under the birch. Then she commenced to frig herself furiously with her unoccupied hand.

At last my girl stopped for an instant, her belly pressed to mine. My prick plunged into her quim and remained motionless. In the mirror I could see her bum moving convulsively under the birch, opening and shutting, initiated by her vagina which closed and opened on my member, squeezing and relaxing, following the play of the arse.

All this, reflected in the mirror, added to my pleasure. Try it, fair reader!

Soon the bottom moved more swiftly, and the lips of her vagina palpitated and swelled. The cheeks of her arse remained still, then squeezed together, contracting on each other. Her luscious cunt sucked on my prick, drawing in drop by drop the warm liquor. While the birch operator sank down panting, the finger of one hand forced deep into her cunt, the other madly frigged the clitoris. Her spunk shot out like a man's, covering her thick thighs, her slit, and the black brush that overshadowed it with dew like scattered pearls.

I carried my fair rider to the bed, where, slipping from her, I let her have a minute's breathing space. I turned her over, and kissed the furrow of her bottom, its curls damp with spunk and sweat. She was not much damaged, and soon regained her breath and color.

During the time that she was in the dressing room with Lola, I explained to the others that certain temperaments have need of stimulants—above all in cold countries like Russia, where flagellation is quite fashionable. Then our beauties got ready for exercise, in order to be able to proceed freely to the amusements which were to follow. When all was ready, and Lola and the princess had joined in again, the soubrettes lay on their backs side by side, with their curly fleeces in a row. Mercedes, Agnes, and Blanche extended themselves on them the reverse way, bottoms upwards, in the proper position for a mutual gamahuche. The three backsides being well in line, Sophie then threw herself across these three bottoms at full length. Her belly was in the air, and the back of her neck rested on Blanche's bum, which was in the middle. Her legs were thrown right and left over the Countess's back legs, leaving her splendid buttocks exposed between them, on which I was to kneel. I extended myself on Sophie's body, and she helped me to adjust myself by lifting her bottom, which fell back on Agnes' as soon as I was in her. The come-and-go began, putting into motion all these pretty bums, swinging to and fro with us. Softly lying on her swelling and firm bust, my belly pressed to the satin of hers and our bushy curls entangled and mingled together. I fucked on and on. I kept my burning lips on hers. I was cradled, as it were, on her firm and rounded form, which I crushed with my weight. The gamahuchers beneath us redoubled their caresses, forcing me to accelerate the movement, and follow them to the goal of Venus. With a few vigorous shoves, to which Sophie responded by upward heaves on her part, I finished the work and my charming girl, joining her sighs to mine, mingled in the center of our two bodies. Her warm and sticky fluid shot forth around my delighted pego at the very moment that the six fair ones, who formed our living mattress, covered each other's lips with a mutual spend. For a moment Sophie remained motionless, with her arms stretched behind her neck, showing the curls under her armpits damp with sweat. I kissed them lasciviously, and breathed in amorously the lustful odor that exhaled from her.

At length we all rose, and restored ourselves with champagne and liqueurs. The Russian princess was now like a burning firebrand; scarcely had we quit the field of battle, when springing on the Countess, she clasped her to her heart and returned with interest the caresses she had so coldly received on her arrival. Mercedes, whose Spanish blood was instantly on fire, clung to Sophie, lip to lip, breasts crushed against breasts, manly rubbing their bushes against each other. They forced the open lips of their cunts together, clitoris against clitoris, curving their loins, moving their great bottoms. Their bosoms flattened against each other, nipple to nipple, their breasts mingled.

Lola and Nina knelt behind these two lustful tribades, tickling the little brown holes of their arses with sharp penetrating tongues. Following their motions, we looked on, a most interested and appreciative audience.

In an instant the two bottoms swelled, squeezed together, swung to and fro, went down. The cheeks shut tight together, opened and closed in one final push as they both spent. Still spending, they separated their lips, looking at each other with lustful eyes, and withdrew from their mutual embrace.

After a few minutes' rest we went in for a little gymnastics. The soubrettes uncovered the ladder which was clamped to the wall and the women put on shoes with felt soles. Then Nina, setting the example, climbed to the top of the ladder, slowly twisting her bottom as she went, showing many pleasant sights. At the top of the ladder she turned round, and holding the top rung, went up backwards a step or two with her feet. She remained with her knees bent, showing her blonde bush between her opened thighs, the pretty pink and gaping lips of her love slit.

Lola went up in her turn with many a twist of her great white hemispheres, and when her nose was close to Nina's mount of Venus, she took hold of the ladder, went up three steps. She remained with her loins bowed out, showing her great arse, and her cunt like a crimson slash. Agnes climbed up and when her head touched Lola's backside, she turned, taking the same attitude as Nina. She slipped her head under Lola's belly, only showing her chin framed in curls of hair, and lower down, her alabaster bosoms, her ivory belly, and her black haired quim. Lisette came in her turn and took up the same position before Nina, and bringing her hands and feet together, she showed her round, fair bottom, pink and white, and lower down, her love's grotto. Blanche then slipped in with her back to the ladder, so that she could stick her tongue into the crack as she sat on the last rung but one of the ladder, her feet on the ground, her thighs at full stretch to receive the tongue of the princess.

The latter, kneeling on the carpet, stretched out her mouth to the downy crack. While bending her loins, she jutted out her buttocks, elevating her arse to take me into her the back way. Her bum was lily white once more, with no signs of the recent birching.

The Countess reserved for herself the part of the gymnast. She helped me first to gain an entrance, and when she had safely lodged the implement, she sprang towards the ladder, and placing her feet on the ends of the rungs, she climbed like a cat to the top of the human pyramid. At the top of the ladder she kissed Nina on the mouth, slipped down to her breasts, nibbled her bosoms, rolled her tongue round the nipples, traversed the satiny skin, tickled the navel to begin again. She moved to Lola, stopped at the hemispheres, gave them a playful bite with her pearly teeth, stayed an instant on Agnes's bosoms, and went down the slope of the belly to her cunt. Then with the agility of an acrobat she leapt on the bum of Lola, and wriggled herself there like one possessed. She rode her like a man, rubbed her open cunt on it, and when her spasmodic contractions excited her, twisted her loins convulsively, sending a quiver of love down the human chain, finishing with me. When I raised my eyes, I saw bosoms palpitating and bottoms heaving in a pleasant oscillation. The crisis arrived! Lola's arse was covered with the profuse spendings of Mercedes, which trickled down in thick drops on to the belly of the one beneath, sprinkling the open cunt. The princess and I got up first, then Blanche stood up, then Lisette and Agnes. The Countess remained glued to Lola's bottom. The latter came down the steps, bearing her precious burden, which she carried to the sofa. Then Nina came down backwards, wriggling her bottom, and showing many pleasant glimpses of her organ of generation.

When the hour came for parting, the princess, whose lust was far from appeased, asked to pass the night between us. The Countess was delighted, and Sophie remained as the two friends left with great regret, their engagements not permitting them to stay longer.

CHAPTER IX

A Well Occupied Night

Sophie and Mercedes, after having given each other a kiss, came and stood upright in the middle of the room, back to back, loin to loin, separated by the hollow of the back for a short distance above the group. Then touching lower down, the two bottoms pressed against each other. The women twisted their arms behind, in a position which threw into relief their plump and rounded bosoms with their nipples up like tiny pricks. Lower down was the Mons Veneris of each, the enticing pink slits shaded with their frizzy coverings. Lola knelt down before the Countess, Nina before the princess. Lisette and I remained simple spectators while the two soubrettes ran their lips over the naked flesh, leaving pink marks as they crossed from the feet to the knee, from the knee to the thigh, then to the slope of the Mount of Venus, which they saluted en passant. Then making the tour of each bosom, they tickled the nipples with a knowing tongue, making them then harder than ever. They pressed higher up, their lips kissed the red lips opposite, then passed once more over the breasts on their downward course, tonguing the smooth plain of their bellies. Kneeling once more before the curls below, they gently separated the fat outer lips already shining with spunk, and began their pious pilgrimage to Temple of Venus.

Lisette hung on the Countess' lips as I did on those of the princess, pressing her round firm breasts which sprung back against the hand that enclosed them, pushing them high, letting them fall, molding them softly with many kisses on their satiny surface. I titillated the nipples with my fingers, making dimples in the smooth surface with my fingertips. I wanted to suck her tongue, but her clenched teeth prevented me. Still, I glued my mouth to hers during the madness of spending, urging on the lascivious game for the two tribades in every way, making them turn and writhe voluptuously.

This randy sight fired me at once. Philip Augustus flew upwards and the insatiable Sophie, seeing him thus randy for the fray, took him in her hand. At the mere touch my gentleman grew enormously thick and threatening.

"Where shall we put him?" asked the Countess.

"Wherever he likes to go," said Sophie, desirous of trying everything.

Another maidenhead! So much the better! Mr. Augustus was quite agreeable.

The Countess told them to go and fetch four dildos without straps. Then they filled them with hot milk which they warmed in the night lamp. Then the soubrettes rolled three armchairs side by side and sat well forward on the edge, being of course naked except stockings and slippers. Their legs were on the arms of the chairs, showing three lovely bums, one snow white, one pink and white, and one brown, all in a row. They also showed bushy cunts to match, one blonde, one with dark red curls, and the last jet black. Between their wide opened thighs, among the curls, could be seen the crimson slash and the pink lips of their quims, the slit terminating just above the other hole with its little fringe of curls at the bottom of the furrow. From the top, the clitoris peeped out in each, eager for pleasure, glistening with randiness.

Each had a dildo in her right hand, ready to penetrate the longing slit. In front of the lovely scene Sophie awaited the attack on her rear. The Countess lubricated the edges with a lustful tongue, and taking the knob of my prick in her lips, prepared him in like manner for the fray. Then, making my beauty bend over, she offered the ample rounded backside for my attack.

Mercedes helped me with eager fingers to

overcome the resistance of the corrugated arse-hole which tantalized me by its tightness.

The attack lasted some moments, but the fair patient lent herself so courageously and pluckily to the operation, and her friend aided me with such skill on each side of the aperture, that I at last got the knob in by force. The column followed and disappeared altogether in her warm bottom hole, without a word of complaint on her part and even with a murmur of pleasure.

Mercedes took the fourth dildo, and installing herself before the soft pussy of the princess, she opened the lips of her cunt with one hand and slipped in the dildo with the other. At this sight the three soubrettes inserted their dildos with one push. Holding a bosom firmly in each hand to keep in place, I commenced the in and out movement in slow time. All hands went together, imitating in the three lovely quims, opposite me, the come-and-go of my priapus in the other place. During this, each with her other finger madly rubbed her clitoris.

My chin resting on Sophie's shoulder, I contemplated with rapture the spectacle of three women writhing in contortions of the wildest lust. The two friends did not lose a detail of it, and the soubrettes, their eyes fixed on us, drank in our motions while frigging themselves with dildos and hands.

These three perfect bottoms of different tints, these three sweet curl-shadowed cunts of different shades, these three imitation pricks so skillfully handled, acting just as real ones would do, separating the clinging lips they entered, these palpitating breasts with their hard nipples projecting with lust, the three mouths open, the tips of their tongues appearing through their pearly teeth, kissing the air—all formed an absolutely enchanting sight. Philip Augustus, lodged like a prince in his sweet new home, remained comfortable and delightfully placed.

But this time there was too much excitement for the actors in the scene, and soon Mr. Augustus, although his motions were very slow, was so amorously squeezed in his sheath that he shot forth his soul almost to Sophie's heart, who showed her delight by cries of amorous rage. At this the three charmers on the chairs came together, pushing the dildos to the hilt in their spending cunts, and squeezing the India rubber balls. Thus they procured for themselves an exact imitation of the liquor of love shooting into their longing gaps, thrown them into convulsive spasms as it went in, making their thighs, and bottoms quiver again with lust. Then they threw themselves back in their chairs, with the spunk running down their streaming thighs, the lips of their quims clinging to the dildos.

The Countess, who had not had her turn—and who wanted one—dismissed the maids, and invited us to follow her to the bed. I got in the middle and on each side my fair companions worked away to restore some vigor to Philip Augustus. He began to look up once more at the sweet contact of their warm little hands.

Mercedes, as soon as he was up, threw herself on him, straddled him, and putting him into her longing belly through her moist hairs, sat on me and he disappeared to the hilt. Then pressing her lips to mine, she began to ride like one possessed.

Sophie contemplated this luscious sight; she didn't long resist the burning desire that tortured her. She knelt and took my face between her thighs in front of the Countess. With her forehead resting on the bed and her cunt hair on my face, she pushed her arse backwards. She dislodged Mercedes' head from its position on my face, and placed her longing slit on my lips, so as to present her fair bum to the kiss of the Countess. I lost nothing by the exchange. Instead of lips of the face, I had lips of the quim, and these last were burning and half opening to receive my eager tongue. With the delicious odor of sweet woman's cunt, I was maddened with desire. I could see no reflection of this in the mirror, but I sacrificed the sense of sight willingly for those of touch and scent.

I allowed myself to be conducted to paradise by my pretty jockey, who rode fast and furiously in love's race, all the time exciting herself lustfully by gamahuching the pretty brown hole in front of her. Keeping the time that she gave me with the rise and fall of her backside, I drove my tongue in and out of the luscious retreat, sucking, nibbling and molding with my lips the randy clitoris—half as long as my finger—that stiffened itself and felt like the prick of a young boy in my mouth.

I frigged it quicker and quicker with my tongue, drawing it into my lips, and soon received over them the sweet shower of her spendings. It flowed profusely over my face while Mercedes, engulfing my member to the root, drew forth the warm jets of spunk from it into the elastic and clinging sheath of her burning vagina.

But these two little devils were insatiable. Philip Augustus being obliged to rest, they began to tease each other with hands and mouths. The princess threw herself all along on the Countess like a man, belly to belly, breasts to breasts, their mouths joined, their bushy mounts pressed together. They opened their cunts with their fingers, so that the interior of the lips and their clitorises should glide against each other. They lustfully rubbed their thighs and bellies, the one who rode pressing against the one who was ridden, naked flesh to flesh.

Lying on one side, I pressed myself against these glowing bodies. I slipped my hand under der Mercedes' backside, which I patted; the other hand played on the hemispheres of Sophie's buttocks and caressed them. Sometimes I spanked them, and pretty hard too. They quivered under the slaps. Then when I felt they were near the end I pushed a finger into each pretty bum hole, frigging the thin partition that separated the two holes. The sphincter rings closed on my fingers in the ecstasy of spending. My position added to their sensations and made it more intense as they shot jets of hot spunk into each other's open cunts, wetting their thighs and greasing down all their matted curls.

They rested for an instant pressed, one on the other. Then the princess, stretching out a hand, found my prick in a fine state, and soon leaving the Countess, she threw herself on me. Mercedes was too burnt to take her share in the fete. Not to leave anyone out, I lay flat on my back with my head on the bolster, body straight, legs squeezed together, and my shaft vertically erect. The Princess sat astride him on the middle of my body with her fair bum to my face. She put my prick up her belly and leaned forwards, her head towards the foot of the bed, flat on my legs, her breasts on my knees, her face towards my feet, her bottom opposite my eyes, large and spread out. I made her try to move, and following my advice, she lifted her arse up, leaving three parts of my cock outside her vagina. Then she brought it down, quite engulfing it—and did this three or four times. When she had the action right, the Countess knelt astride of my face, bottom upwards, the inner part of her thighs on my cheeks, her bush on my lips. Then bending over towards her friend, she supported herself on her hands, her bosoms on my hairy belly, and her mouth on Sophie's bottom-hole, which she gamahuched as she worked my prick. The maneuvers commenced. As I lay I could admire in the mirror over the bed the pleasant tableau that the two satiny backsides above me made. These splendid, fat, spreading arses quivered with lust. One rested on my face, and was of the whitest hue. The other, which worked on my cock, still retained its redness as a souvenir of the rude contact of my hand.

But I moved my finger from the brown jewel to its loving neighbor, giving the hottest kisses on its crimson little button. Impatient in its mossy cave, it was still wet with its last voyage to paradise, and seemed to move under the ardent kisses that I poured on it. I held it shut in my lips, and turned it round and round till the expected moment, which was heralded by the loosing of a few drops of spunk. Then I sucked it and drew it in; the drops became a shower of oily pearls that I greedily swallowed while my ravished member discharged copiously into the burning furnace of Sophie, who soon drew forth all my marrow.

After these three pilgrimages to the shrine of Cythera, always on my prick, they seemed tired but not satisfied. Their wombs were still rigid with lust, the lips gaping for more. But as I was of no further use for the time, they went to sleep.

I awoke in the morning to an agreeable sensation! The princess, who had enclosed my prick in her mouth, was sweetly sucking it. The Countess seeing her thus employed, proposed to organize a pleasant revel.

I leapt from the bed, followed by the two Bacchantes. I went and sat on a chair, my back against the cushion. Philip Augustus, with a fine morning cockstand, stood up erect between my thighs, his rough and hairy balls, covered with fleece, hung down below, hard and firm. The princess straddled over me as I sat, and on tiptoe presented the opening of the grotto to the crimson head of my instrument that she held in her hand. It was as stiff as wood. When the head was in, she slowly settled down on it, and in it went, into her belly.

The Countess put a chair on each side of us, and mounted on one. Sophie leaned back a little, leaving a free space between our breasts so that Mercedes, passing her left leg between our bodies, could place her foot on the other chair. Placing herself thus between our chests, her thick black fleece rested on a level with my nose, and her white bottom sat on the lips of the princess. This latter began to rise anyhow, out of all time. I was obliged to guide her, with my hands flat under her backside. I lifted her up and down in regular cadence, showing her the exact motion at each ascent of her bum. The vagina rose too, leaving my shaft half exposed, then swallowing him anew in her descent. Her tongue went up and down the dark moist furrow of Mercedes' bottom, while, on my side, I overwhelmed with burning kisses the center of attraction which opened out under such lascivious caresses. My fair rider rode faster and faster. Still, I accelerated my caressing in front, and she leapt, bounded, and writhed on my cock so as almost to snap it off. My tongue flew to the clitoris. Mercedes rubbed herself like a randy cat on my face, pushing with her belly and putting her two hands behind my head, almost crushing her clitoris against my teeth. Looking up, I could just see the masses of curls under her armpits, wet with the perspiration caused by her mad frigging. At this very moment the shell burst and I flooded Sophie in and out. Her spendings mingled with mine, and opened to us the gates of heaven.

We rang for the bath, which, as a matter of course we all took together, with many pleasant evolutions. After the bath, we wrapped ourselves in warmed peignoirs and placed ourselves in the hands of the soubrettes who sponged us with coquettish ticklings.

Then our two beauties lay flat on the massage table. Nina and Lisette took charge of Sophie, extended on her back. These two splendid nudities made the most ravishing contrast by the opposition of their various attractions, and we had all sorts of fun on these reversed bodies. When it was my turn, the two friends tickled my bottom and my front, amusing themselves by testing Philip Augustus, who stood up furious at the way they treated him. They tickled me under the balls, slipping a naughty finger into my arsehole. I was wild. I saw they were on fire too. The soubrettes were as randy as they could be, and I foresaw that all would soon have to satisfy a sweet want.

We passed into the bedroom and drew a long chaise out into the middle of the room—a sort of cushioned and stuffed bench, very low, without a back, with a cushion like a small bolster for the head. Lola lay down on it, with her body stretched out, her back on the little bolster, her legs straddled to take me between them. I went between her thighs, and while she arched herself to help me penetrate, I directed my weapon to the temple of love, in which it disappeared after two jerks of my bottom. I was flat on her belly, my breast on her bosoms, my lips on hers, my legs between hers, and in this position I waited for the four tribades to take their respective places on my back. The Countess first put herself astride over my neck, her face to my feet. Secondly, the princess took the same position over my shoulder, with her face to her friend. Then Lisette mounted on my loins with her backside against that of the princess. Lastly, Lisette mounted on my loins with her backside against that of the princess. Nina sat straddled over my bottom, giving a movement to my instrument which sent it into Lola's cunt up to the hilt. Lisette and Nina kissed each other's lips, Mercedes and Sophie the same, and at a given signal, the two couples on me moved backward and forward.

They made me follow their motions, pushing my prick into Lola when they squeezed their thighs together, and letting me go back when they widened them. My whole frame was on fire, from the nape of my neck to my arse. Their hot randy flesh, the oozing of spunk from all their cunts on my body was like a continued burning. It was like a large mouth, whose hot lips covered all my body with one delicious kiss. The regular swing, slow and measured, was ruled by the motion of the naked thighs. The two fair ones in front, at each push of their backsides, crushed my breast against Lola's lovely bosoms, whose firm round globes made for me a lascivious cushion, soft, yet firm. The two lower down, pulling on my loins, pushed my prick to the bottom of her swimming quim, mingling our hair together. Soon all cadence ceased. I continued my come-and-go as well as I could.

Sophie and Mercedes approached each other, glued together, and rubbed up and down on me, where the lips of their glowing quims kissed me. Then Nina, pressing her thighs together, forced me to remain buried to the hilt. The three others moved furiously, and while I penetrated Lola with my favors I felt my body inundated at once, everywhere, from my neck to my bottom, just as if four taps had been turned on. Drop by drop the warm flood exuded, augmented by sweet titillation the thrilling voluptuousness which ravished me.

When I disengaged myself, my flesh glued to the wet skin of Lola, I left some marks. Her face was red, her bosom palpitating; she rose breathless, panting, her eyes swimming with lust, begging more love.

To make up for her rather uncomfortable position, her four sister tribades divided all the different sources of pleasure on her body. Between them she let them love her. The Countess and the princess had a turn with her, the first in front, the second behind. The two soubrettes each sucked a nipple. Seeing her lips free, I leaned over the Countess and kissed her. Our five hot sets of lips reuniting their fire, nearly drove the passionate Spaniard mad from head to foot. Soon a thrill ran through the whole of her body, spasm followed spasm, a

shudder of bliss pervaded her. I gave her sucking kisses, and she bent down as her knees
trembled, obliging me to follow her, still writhing and panting. Spending still, she remained
for a long time plunged in ineffable ecstasy.

CHAPTER X

Varied Sports

For eight entire days our Russian Princess, the busiest at the soirees of the Countess of Cythera, burnt with unassuaged fire. Ever since the first disposition to love, she arranged all our sports, prolonging them even beyond ordinary limits, sending herself into every fantasy, lavishing her tenderness.

One evening, however, she came in a very different frame of mind, which she showed by the chilliness of her greeting. She received with absolute indifference the caresses of the whole band, which exerted themselves to put her in tune. In face of the uselessness of our united efforts, they determined to resort to stronger means. Lola disappeared for a moment, and then came back with a birch, which she gave to me. We stripped the princess of all her clothes. Two soubrettes conducted her towards an armchair, where they made her kneel down, her forehead supported on the back cushions, and kept in position by the two maids, so that she couldn't stir to avoid the flagellation. She showed—full and fat—her white arse, and displayed between her cheeks and thighs, wide apart, the slit with pink lips pressed one against each other.

Swish, swish, the tips of the birch fell, gently at first, marking the bum with rosy lines, which soon vanished. Nothing stirred; her thighs were still and the lips of her quim remained tightly closed.

Swish, swish, again I struck a little harder this time; the cheeks of her bottom got redder, but did not move. Swish, swish, her bottom blushed deeply, but showed no fooling. Soon, however, at a skillful cut, just touching love's grotto, the lips pouted a little. With another swishing stroke, they bareply parted. I recommenced on the backside, which now moved, separated, closed again, communicating their impressions on the center of attraction which began to gape, showing between and lower down the impudent little rosy clitoris, visibly stiffening.

At this result I stopped the flagellation for a short time, but the princess, without stirring, called out: "Go on! Go on!"

To make use of this result, we conducted the princess to a sofa. Lola undressed in a jiffy and lay down on her back. The princess stretched herself on Lola, with her cunt resting on the lips of the soubrette, who began to gamahuche her. I continued the flogging on the fat backside, which displayed its two rounded hemispheres highly crimsoned by the birch. Lola sucked and licked the red lips of this lustful quim, rolling her tongue up and down and round the clitoris. I resumed the piquant exercise, letting the tips of the birch cut well into the tightly stretched skin. Then, indeed, that bottom, now quite ruddy, began to demean itself very pleasantly, bounding on Lola's nose. She clasped the bum in her arms, held it unflinching under a shower of cuts, and pretty sharp ones. It soon trembled and opened—and shut. The princess at this moment plunged her head between the thighs of the maid, and returned her the ardent caresses she herself received, hurrying to get her to the same pitch of delight as herself. Lola, who had no need of stimulants, went ahead rapidly, and, for her part, heightened the pace of her tongue fucking. As I birched away, I saw the lips of her tongue hastening its motions. The crisis approached, and the shuddering tremors which ever precede the orgasm, were soon seen. Sophie squeezed her bottom together, making little dimples all over the surface like the summer rain makes on the surface of a lake. Then she violently contracted as I threw away the birch and slipped my finger up her arsehole, which I frigged. She let the free tide of pleasure flow, which Lola greedily swallowed. When the prisoner quitted the field of battle, Lola remained, her eyes turned up, her thighs widely straddled and swimming with the spunk that covered them.

The princess, as soon as she was upright again, showed a most smiling face. Her eyes sparkled with pleasure; then precipitating herself on me, she began to rummage with a lascivious hand into my breeches and drew out my prick in a most triumphant state. Turning her back to me, she showed me the route she wished me to take. I felt her bottom; it was burning. Mr. Augustus will be warm there, thought I. Soon all is ready for everything. The soubrettes each seized a dildo full of warm milk. They gave one to Sophie to frig herself in front, while I should slip in the back way. Lola, Nina, and Lisette lay on their backs, their sham pricks erect, the balls between their thighs. The Countess, Blanche, and Agnes straddled each over a mouth—the Countess on Lola, Blanche on Nina, and Agnes on Lisette. They lowered themselves on to these India rubber cocks, which penetrated their longing cunts to the hilt with a gliding motion.

The princess, all this time bending forward, held me, with the tips of her willing fingers, to stretch her little bum hole. I soon slipped in, not without some trouble. My member seemed to be in a furnace; her arse actually burnt my belly. She forced the dildo into her cunt, and fucked herself with it like an unattached prick, frigging herself in and out. The group showed us a ravishing sight. I admired the three splendid bums, white and lustrous, that rose and fell in cadence on the dildos that transfixed them. This mingling of clinging quims, this interlacing of limbs over which ran tremors of lust, the avant-courier of spending, was a sufficiently attractive vision for our longing eyes. But they soon fell out of time, and all these regular movements became erratic, as each took her own course and time. One bounded on the belly under her making a slapping noise; another writhed upon the dildo, engulfed to the hair with a voluptuous undulation. Another by a succession of short and quick jerks, swallowed up the fictitious prick and then let it slip out. The princess, with the wild fixed stare of intense readiness, kept her eyes fixed on this delicious sight, one hand frigging herself with the dildo, and the middle finger of the other on her clitoris. I worked hard with my prick in the tight sheath of her arse, and soon the edges of her hole closed hard on me, squeezing the prisoner within. He shot his spunk into her bowels, giving her the most exquisite pleasure, so that leaning back and turning her head, she kissed and bit me till my lips bled, her body twisting in my arms. The other pairs, at the same moment, heaved delighted sighs. The princess, now disengaged, contemplated for a moment these pretty groups, watching their little quiverings of satisfied pleasure. Suddenly Sophie sprang to the prostrate group, her hand raised, and distributed from one to the other a perfect salvo of well applied slaps which reddened the flesh and made them rise from their position.

The soubrettes, who had unstrapped their dildos, were still half mad with lust, although they had spent to a certain extent, as one could see by the spunk that trickled down their thighs. They continued interlacing and clasping each other, rubbing themselves together like amorous cats.

The princess threw herself on Lola. She drew her away and dragged her to the sofa. She got underneath her and pulled her quim down on her face. The two began a quiet and reciprocal gamahuche.

Blanche took Nina into a corner, where they began to frig facing each other, each putting two fingers through the curls into their respective slits. Agnes and Lisette kissed each other on the bosoms and the curls of their armpits, and were soon occupied in frigging themselves with their fingers.

The Countess, seeing my prick rather soft, took the prick in her hand, drawing down the skin below the knob, and frigging me. This not being quite enough, she took it in her mouth. This soon restored its presence. She gazed at me with love and approached with open arms. Then, quite upright, she tried to put it in the right route. Bending my knees, I helped to introduce it, and after a few short struggles my lord took possession of his place. Raising her up by main force, still impaled with her legs clasped round my waist, I carried her round to the grounds, with my prick embedded in her cunt, and our hairs commingled. We excited ourselves with the sights of the various modes of enjoyment, and terminated near Lola and the princess. Lola's opulent hemispheres made an inviting and springy couch on which I rested the splendid bum of the Countess, and on that soft cushion proceeded with my luscious game. Comfortably settled down on her warm and living seat, Mercedes clasped me in her arms, crossed her legs on my loins, and straining me to her bosom with her rosy heels. I answered every thrust with an upward heave which communicated a motion to the two underneath us, pressed by the weight of her body. I was sweetly cradled on her body, my hairy chest crushing flat the full bosoms of her beautiful breast. I continued on, till I finished in the sweetest transports, kissing her on the mouth and under her arms. The same crisis came on the two below, and the other couples joined in with soft sighs and murmurs.

As soon as their disorder was a little smoothed over, the Countess asked, "Who can waltz?"

The princess offered herself, and the two dancers put on their black silk stockings and pretty slippers. Nina, who I had not given credit for so much talent, sat down at the piano, and after a prelude of brilliant arpeggios, began the introduction to the *Blue Danube,* while our two beauties, taking each other by the waist, walked into the center of the room. We installed ourselves and prepared to be mute admirers of the delicious spectacle they presented. Our two darlings swam circling round the room, letting us see their bosoms, which rose and fell with each step. The introduction over, our pretty ladies clasped themselves closer, bosom to bosom, belly to belly, their thighs interlacing, their hairs crushed together, ready to begin in earnest. The waltz went on. The couples started, turned a moment, then whirled round the room swiftly and passionately, reserving, marking the time, touring on one spot, coming, going, offering to our charmed gaze the richest treasures, one after the other. They looked fondly into each other's eyes, their mouths ever kissing each other, breast pressed to breast, two Cytherean tribades, mad with love and lust. An arm white, round, and dimpled, pressed with love the bust it encircled; in the tight embrace of these lovely bodies you could catch glimpses of a bosom here and there, with a vermilion tip jutting out like a ripe strawberry. The bodies of shining white satin sloped towards the plump buttocks, which looked like a lovely full moon cloven into four hemispheres, curved and rounded, admirable pendans to the breasts above. One felt as if one could bite those firm, white, dimpled masses of flesh, as if one would wish to crush them in one's fingers, to slap them, to nibble them, to redden them with the touch. They turned and waltzed under the bright light of the lustres overhead.

Their snowy orbs seemed sometimes to open like a flash of light, and again to close. And all the time the waltzer swept on in a rapid whirl, scarcely brushing the carpet with their little forms swinging and balancing in the cadence of the dance. But the waltz and waltzers soon lost breath; they moved slower and slower with the last dying notes of the waltz, then parted with regret, separating their caressing lips.

When they parted at last, they stood with their bosoms heaving, their perfumed breath coming and going, their breasts with the little nipples all scarlet from the tight pressure with which they had pressed each other.

Lola and Blanche sprang to the Countess, kneeling—the first before, the second behind. Agnes and Lisette went to the princess, Agnes to her pussy, and Lisette with her finger busy behind. The four began anew the old sweet game, the two darlings upright and pressing their lips to each other over the heads of their gamahuchers.

While this went on, Nina at the piano still played Mendelssohn's *Fileuse*. I thought she well deserved to be rewarded for her self-denial. Making her push back her music stool a little, I knelt down before her, between the stool and the piano. I made her sit well forward so as to offer her cunt to my lips and searching tongue. While her fingers ran over the keys, my tongue played a prelude on her little instrument, which vibrated to the touch of my tongue. The fair player never ceased till the end. As the music grew slower and died away, so did I, with lips pressed into her curls, keeping time. Last of all, her fingers rested on a chord, and as she had her little foot on the pedal, the sound lasted the whole time of her pleasure and only died away as her head fell back in the ecstasy of overpowering bliss.

WAYWARD VENUS

BOOK TWO

CHAPTER I

Jenny has made quite a rite of pressing me to her, all the time encircling my waist, often kissing my face and hugging me to her firm and well-developed breasts. Her caresses would immediately excite my genitals though the amorous attention lavished on them by Mrs. Barnett would have been sufficient to satiate even a grown-up's desires. Now, I was even denied those lascivious delights, for the sparse and meager pleasures I was taking with my sister Lilian were nothing comparatively with the amorous deeds I had performed during a whole month with an expert addict of the art of fucking.

Since the day where I noticed the elation Miss Jenny felt in ascribing to her looks and to her sighs my obvious absent-mindness—though it had been entirely due to Mrs. Barnett's departure,—she had increased her affectionate caresses and she ought surely feel my stiff prick fluttering against her thigh, when she hugged me to her bosom: I often noticed how her eyes shone then and that she was blushing when she kissed me and I did no more than brush her cheeks with my fingers. Sometimes she would push me roughly away from her, telling me to go back to my seat. Many times did she leave the room in a dreadful state of agitation. So I understood that a violent struggle was taking place between her reason and her passions. Remembering the wise advices my beloved and ravishing mistress, Mrs. Barnett, had given me, I made up my mind to play the innocent lad and to let her nurture her passions to fulfill the purpose of my wild expectations.

I don't know if I could have waited so long had I not had the relief I found in my dear little sister Lilian's crack; every time we were able to meet by stealth, I would notice with rapture that she was growing more and more attractive and talented in the give-and-take-love-game. We could hardly prevent my other sister, Dorothy, to see what was taking place between us. At last, Lilian made up her mind to initiate Dorothy to the sucking pleasures; then, she explained to the youngest girl that I was playing with her when we were shut in together and promised her that I would initiate her to the same pleasures if she promised to keep it a secret. She added that it was necessary that one of them keep watch lest Miss Jenny should come and discover us. Lilian began to suck Dorothy who enjoyed it inordinately, for, though eighteen months younger than Lilian, she showed at once that her passions were more developped than her sister's.

At the beginning, I only sucked her, letting her play with my prick, without telling her that it might be driven into her lovely little slit which was already beginning to be covered by a smooth bush on her prominent and firmly rounded mount of Venus. When I had sucked her to my content, Lilian, whom I had already fucked, came back and Dorothy went outside (for we used to meet in a small summer-pavilion at the end of the garden), and kept watch while I was quenching in the delicious cunt of Lilian the fire kindled by my sucking Dorothy.

However sparse and paltry those pleasures may have been, compared with Mrs. Barnett's fucking abilities, anyway they enabled me to wait dispassionately for the anticipated issue of Miss Jenny's love for her pupil. Obviously she was struggling against her inclination for me, but her passion was increasing. I noticed it in the nervous pressing of her hands, when she would draw me to her burning lips then push me back, her body fluttering all over and her face turning at once very pale. I fancied that in those occurrences, she was a slave to her lubric dispositions, and that her sudden squeezings were really the love-crisis approach, and that while she was trembling and pushing me back, she was having an orgasm.

Obviously it could not go on very much longer. At last, the happy, so wished-for day came. Mummy had to go to the town and intended to take my sisters with her, in order to buy them sundry pieces of clothes. She asked Miss Jenny to share the ride, but the latter refused, alleging a painful headache; truly, the violent struggle which opposed her passions to her prudence had somehow injured her health; now she was pale and seemed so upset that my mother was very anxious about her health. So she told her not to overwork herself with my lessons that day, to make me study only for one hour and then to take a walk in the garden and to get as much rest as possible.

As she was leaving us, she recommended me to be gentle and obedient, for Miss Jenny was not feeling well. Mummy departed with my sisters. Miss Jenny, deathly pale and shivering all over, asked me to go to the study-room and to learn the lesson she had given me the day before, and said she would join me soon. I went there, but I was not in a mood to learn any lesson that day. I was absent-minded and somewhat frightened by the obvious agitation and visible illness of Miss Jenny; I was then too inexperienced to understand the nature of the struggle that was taking place in her innermost self: it was a phase of the character of women which I did not understand yet.

*   *   *

However I had a vague notion that all that would come to an end with the fulfillment of my libidinous wishes; I followed only the directions that my charming lover had given me and I waited quietly for the issue of the crisis I had so eagerly hoped for. Miss Jenny came downstairs at last and joined me; her eyes were red and swollen as if she had been crying; mine filled with tears when I saw her. I went and stood by her side. Then I told her shyly:

—Oh, my dear governess, I am so sad to see you are sick. Oh, don't work today and I promise you I'll work twice more to-morrow.

For a minute I was quite frightened by the pain her sunken features revealed. Then, she smiled languidly and, catching me in her arms, she squeezed me against her breasts, smothering my face with kisses; her eyes shone strangely.

—Oh, my dear, beloved boy! I love you above all words. Kiss me, oh, kiss me, my darling, and relieve me for I love you too much.

Then again, she altered her attitude; anxious lest she had said too much, she averted her head and tears spurted out of her eyes, but her arms did not loosen their hold on me. I was deeply stirred by her extreme agitation. I thought that she was really sick and suffered very much; so I threw my arms around her neck, kissing her tenderly, crying my heart out, trying to relieve her, I told her, in my inexperience, while I sobbed:

—Oh, my dear, dear Miss Jenny! You must be better, I love you so tenderly that my heart

119

bleeds to see you so unhappy. Oh, please, smile to me. Try not to cry. Why are you so unhappy? Oh, how glad should I be if I knew how to make you happy!

And, increasing the rhythm of my caresses, I saw her turn her pale face towards me. Her eyes still shone with an extraordinary fire, and a feverish redness pervaded on her cheeks.

—Oh, my dear angel, dear love "you" are the one who makes me unhappy!

I fell back with surprise.

—Why, I make you unhappy! Oh! Miss Jenny, it cannot be so. I am worshipping the very earth you walk on and I love. . . (*sob*) I love . . . (*sob*) I love you more than anybody in the world.

She took my head between her hands, stuck her lips to mine and gave me a long, long and loving kiss; then squeezing me against her breast:

—Oh! tell me that again, my love, my beloved boy; it's love that I feel for you, and you are breaking my heart, but I cannot stand it any longer. Will my George love his Jenny always as he loves her now?

—Oh! How could it be otherwise! I cherished you from the first moment of your arrival and I have never had any other thought. What may I do to prove it? I have never even whispered a syllable of my love, not only to yourself, but to anyone.

Her eyes, shining excitedly, were seeking to probe my thoughts in the deepness of mine. I was beginning too to feel my amorous excitation

120

roused by her burning kisses and her fiery caresses. She was holding me tight against her body and was surely feeling the hard piece that was fluttering against her.

—I believe you, my George, and I want to entrust you my life, my honour! I cannot resist any more. But, oh! George, you must for ever, for it's an awful danger to love you as much as I do.

She drew me again to her lips, and I wound my hands around her neck in a tight grasp. Her hands were running all over my body and stopped on my thrilled prick. With shivering hands she unbuttoned, she rather tore my trousers, and with her sweet fingers she gripped my naked tool.

—Oh, I shall die, dear miss Jenny, what can I do to make you happy?

My visible ignorance could only delight her. She reclined back on the rocking chair on which she was sitting, picking up with her hand her petticoats while she fell back, seemingly not doing it on purpose.

I fell down on my knees and, lifting her petticoats some more, I gazed at her beautiful cunt covered by a thick bush of black and curled hair. She hid her burning face in her hands, while, pushing my head ahead, I began to lick her magnificent cunt without forgetting to tip the erectness of the clitoris. At first, she tried to push me back.

—No! No! No! I should not! I should not!

But I suppose that my behaviour could only

set her passions aflame more effectively, for her cunt was all wet with burning juice, and I was then convinced that she had come wildly while she kissed me.

She told me abruptly:

—Come, then, my dear child, I want to be all yours.

Getting up, I fell down on top of her, lying prone over her willing body, and crushing my throbbing prick against her cunt. I was still very careful not to betray myself and to make her believe that I had not the slightest notion of what was coming after the first daring step.

O! My beloved Miss Jenny! Help me, I don't know what to do!

She slipped her hand between our bellies and she guided my burning tool between the greedy lips of her delicious cunt. I pushed and with the first stroke I drove the head and two inches more of my prick into it. At the second stroke I met with an unexpected obstacle, because I had never thought that Miss Jenny would be a virgin. So I pushed more fiercely.

—Oh! George! My love! Go gently, you are hurting me awfully! Please, George!

Knowing that the best way was to excite her by little strokes without trying to go all the way in at once, because it should hurt her too much, I did likewise and she began to feel the violent desires that such an enormous prick as mine can't fail to excite when it is driven into the velvet-smooth folds of such a tight and juicy slit as she was endowed with. I held on the post and kept the rhythm of my piston-like thrusts, until the convulsive movements of her loins and the rhythmic pressions of the crab-like folds of her cunt told me that she was nearing a crisis and was on the verge of coming. She squeezed me tightly in her arms and at the first spasm of pleasure she heaved her ass clear from the chair. I had been expecting this difficult instant. I withdrew my cock a little and dived it again into the constricted ring of her cunt with an irresistible thrust. I tore open the taut flesh of her virgin hymen and drove my prick up to the balls into her palpitating cunt. The attack had been as hurtful as unexpected. Miss Jenny uttered a scream of pain and fainted.

Availing myself at once of the occasion, I worked my rod in and out with a forcible eagerness, tearing at all obstacles and widening as much as possible the burning gash by seesaw movements directed sideways while she was still numbed by pain. I fainted myself in an ecstasy of satiated lust. I remained engulfed in her delicious crack until some convulsive quiverings and short sobs indicated that my mistress, now quite expertly devirginized, was coming back to her senses. The idea that I had won an unexpected victory made my prick stiffen again, though it was still somehow limp. Then she got quite conscious of her position. I felt an involuntary pression on my peter. She threw her arms around my neck, gave me a passionate kiss and began to cry, with heart-rending sobs that stirred in me a very excitable spot.

It is one of the most curious trends of my temper that the tears of women excite my lascivious passions, and, though I was truly anguished to see her in such a state, I was feeling my prick stiffen and swell to an extraordinary size. I tried to comfort her with sweet names and lovey-dovey words, but she was all the more sobbing.

Suddenly I thought that if I went again to give it to her it might alter her sensations for the best and I began my strenuous movements; she sighed deeply but I was aware by the nervous jerks of her loins that her passions were beginning to be excited.

It was quickly evident. She put her arms around my waist, hugged me against her and ate up my mouth with kisses. Nature helped her movements and soon both of us made a plentiful offering on Venus' altar. She shivered and writhed when she felt the hot liquor flowing in her and she tightened her grasp around me, pressing me again her breast with all her strength.

We remained motionless for at least ten minutes; my lovely mistress fainted with pleasure, giving my ravished prick lascivious pressions which inflamed it at once with new desires. Miss Jenny herself was madly excited and we plunged again in a delirious fucking bout, via the newly discovered love's path, which ended as usual in a spasm of fulfilled passion. While we were coming back to our senses, my lovely mistress kissed me tenderly and said to me:

—Oh! My dear beloved child, you made me suffer tremendously at first, but you succeeded later in giving me heavenly joys. But my dear

George, we must get up, because we might be discovered.

In our earnestness we had not even locked the door and we were running the risk of being caught in a kind of very peculiar teaching. So I got my prick out of her fuming crack, which seemed by its pressions to let it go regretfully, and I noticed then that it was covered with blood.

—Wait, Georgie. Let me wipe it with my handkerchief, else you will stain your shirt and your mother will find us out.

She wiped the friendly peter with loving care, then, folding the handkerchief and putting it in her breast, she added:

—I shall keep this precious relic as a token of the sacrifice I have offered for the love of you, my worshipped child. Ah, George! You cannot yet understand the value of this sacrifice. I love you as I have never loved before and as I shall never love any more. My honour and my happiness are now resting in your hands and they depend wholly on your power of secrecy. Be careful not to take any open liberties with me in your future behaviour, nor to tell anyone what has just been taking place between us.

It will be easily understood that I gave her all possible assurances about my discretion; telling her that I loved her too tenderly and was too grateful for this new happiness to do anything that might give her trouble and that she would never be endangered by any indiscretion on my part. She kissed me warmly and told me to go for a walk in the garden, because she needed some rest after all those blessed happenings and that we would meet again after lunch.

I complied with her request, thinking back on all the exquisite enjoyments she had given me and already eager to see the coming of the afternoon so as to reenact such a ravishing union of our bodies and souls.

Miss Jenny did not go down for lunch, but she took a light meal in her room. Nevertheless, she met me again at two o'clock as usual, in the study-room. She was very pale and very caressing and kissed me tenderly. At once I became very excited and I had a beautiful hard-on.

I became very enterprising, but she repelled me in a sweet manner, and asked me to let her rest now for not only was she feeling annihilated but she was still suffering and it would be better for her to relax. I besought her eagerly to allow me some little favours if not all but she remained unyielding. Seeing that I could not concentrate on my work, and not even be quiet, she said to me:

—Let us go to the garden, I think that the air and a quiet walk will make me feel well.

I thought at once that should I succeed in leading her to the pavilion I should have a better luck and I could enjoy again her delicious caresses. So, while she was going upstairs and fetched her cloak and her hat, I seized the key, and I was ready for any chance.

We walked a little amid the bed of flowers. Miss Jenny let me hold her arm and all the time she was talking to me in the tenderest manner. She walked with some stiffness. We sat down

126

to rest a little, but soon she complained of the hardness of the sun, so I ventured to offer her a walk under the shadowing trees. I chattered as much as I could in order to prevent her to notice how far we had walked. So she was utterly astonished when she saw that we were nearing the summer pavilion.

—Oh! dear George, I am afraid I shall not be able to go back to the house if I don't rest. But we have not the key and we cant enter the pavilion.

—Sometimes it is left in the lock; I'll go and see if it is so to-day.

I sprang ahead, slipped the key into the lock and came back to say to her that it was there; she followed me inside and fell heavily on the sofa which I had already used so often, and reclined on it.

I put a cushion under her head and drew a chair to sit down near her. She did not imagine that I might want to make love to her, so she turned her body toward me, took my hand in hers and we started a most interesting conversation; indeed the matter was how we were going to behave so as not to waken any suspicion about our love-meetings and equally how we should manage to meet each other alone now and then.

—Dear child, she said to me, I can't live any more without the joy of your caresses, but you must remember that, in my actual condition of governess, the discovery of our love would be my ruin.

I trust your silence and your discretion, and,

beloved George, if you are as fond of me, as I am fond of you, I may wholly trust you.

I threw an arm around her neck and told her that I loved her so much and wanted so madly to feel again her delicious caresses that she must not be afraid of any indiscretion from me. She hugged me and kissed me passionately; I began to burn with passion, my hand was running everywhere, her position did not allow her a great resistance, so I reached for her crisp, so richly furnished crack, while she was whispering to me to be quiet and keeping her thighs tightly shut. She did not know that I had a superlative knowledge of this particular place so, inserting my finger in the upper part of her crotch, between the sealed lips, I tipped her clitoris and began to rub it with a seesaw motion with a most proper care to rouse burning desires in the right place.

—George, my Georgie, oh! please, do not do it . . . do not it . . . I . . . cannot . . . bear it.

And so saying she encircled my neck with her arms and drew me to her lips which she stuck to mine. I felt her thighs come slightly apart. At once I availed myself of the occasion and began to frig her by inserting my medium finger in her slit. Her passions were aflame at once.

—Come, dear and beloved child, come in my arm, I cannot resist any longer.

At once I was unbuttoned, my trousers in a heap on the ground, and I was between her legs before she had ended her sentence. The excitement of my frigging had got her already wet, so the head of my prick entered without any difficulty. In my eagerness I pushed and thrust it into her with a strenuous stroke, but she entreated me to go gently, because she was still suffering after our morning bout. Moderating my movements and slipping my stiff too in her, I went through by degrees as far as the utmost limits and did not hurt her. Then I stopped, letting my prick engulfed up to the balls, only making it thrill softly now and then; then seeking for my beloved Jenny's mouth, we intermingled our lips and tongues. Her arms encircling my waist began to press me tighter; the delicious folds of her lascivious and juicy cunt fluttered and pressed my swollen member. I wanted her to become utterly excited, so I waited and she reached her climax and came in a flow of fuming come, a heavenly pleasure to my prick flooded by her juice. Still I remained motionless to let her rest after the enjoyment of her unloading which was surely the first when she had felt a total happiness; for since I was an idle actor nothing could give her any pain in spite of the torn brims of her hymen which I had properly lacerated in deflowering her. The internal pressions were the most exquisite; our lips and tongues were like the doves' cooing and led her quickly to desire me with fury.

Then I began gentle and slow movements, drawing back my prick almost all the way out, then driving it in again slowly as far as my balls. Her previous and so abundant unloading had oiled the brims of her cunt so effectively that she did not feel any more pain, but a boundless enjoyment. At last she could not resist any more; her arms were thrown around my waist and her legs locked over my buttocks; nature inspired her ass with movements of an almost diabolical precision; she was meeting my forward strokes and answering them in the most lascivious way.

—Push, push, darling George, quicker, quicker . . . that's it!

I needed not be spurred. My movements grew quick and furious until, uttering together a scream of happiness, we fainted embraced in a delicious ecstasy of gratified lust.

We remained senseless for several minutes before awakening but all the time our respective genital apparatus were still fluttering, one inside the other, with all the lascivious delight of a satiated passion. Her magnificent legs were stretched along mine. She wound her arm around my neck, kissed me with sensuality and mingled her sweetest words of thanks with praises of my virility, all the time lavishing me with passionate caresses.

I remained in the grove of Paphos, feeling an exquisite sensation which it is impossible to put into words, my pleasure was greater than in the moments where my movements had been the most active. I should have stayed thus but for the excitation in my prick, the sensibility of which was too quickly roused by the lascivious pressions of the delicious cunt I was engulfed in. By degrees it had grown again very stiff and was now quite swollen, fluttering impatiently for some new struggles. I began to move, but Miss Jenny said to me:

—Oh! my George that is enough, my dear child. Not only we must be careful, but we must think of your health and youth; yes, oh! yes, my dear child, oh! please, stop.

Her words were stopped by the strenuous movements my prick was exercizing in her wide open cunt. She could not resist any longer, but squeezing me close in her legs and arms, and eating me up with kisses, she threw herself into the souffle and helped me so well body and soul that we swooned with a scream of delight and remained unconscious in one another's arms.

We stayed so during several minutes before moving. I was still engulfed in her delicious cunt and I should have liked to remain in it longer and feel again the crab-like squeezings of the soft walls of her love-grotto; but miss Jenny asked me so much to stop this time, telling me it was an absolute necessity, if we wanted to meet again, that I had the wiseness to get my prick out of her body. But, getting up, I slipped down to her feet, and before she could prevent it, I struck my lips on her slit and ate up greedily all her delicious creamish spunk and retreated only after I had licked her clitoris so efficiently that she came again in my mouth. At first, she had tried to resist and said:

—George, what are you doing? You must not do that, my dear child, it's awful.

But since I had excited her passions, her hand, instead of driving me away, was holding my head fast against her throbbing slit, her thighs were tightened along my cheeks and she almost fainted at the unloading ecstasy. I voluptuously swallowed all and, getting up at last, I took her in my arms and, pushing her gently so that she lay on her back, I kissed her tenderly.

—Oh! what a lovely creature you are, my beloved Jenny, I love you so much.

—And you, my beloved George, you have done more than justify my imprudence. You have given me so much joy that I should never even have dreamed of it. I am yours, body and soul; you can do as you please with me; I worship the earth you walk on. I am your willing slave.

We went on so, exchanging the sweetest oaths of love and affection, until she saw my prick taking again its ordinary stiffness, and she said:

—Oh! my dearling, hide it away from me, please; it would not be wise to do it again. Let me button it myself into your trousers.

She kneeled down and began to kiss my prick; then, she put it back in my trousers which she could hardly button and we went back to the house.

We talked about the luck we had met with our last fucking session. I had to promise her I should keep quiet the next day; she would try to figure some way for a meeting the day after, though the continual presence of my sisters was a very unfortunate hindrance.

I suggested her the idea to shut herself in with me, like when she had been whipping me and that she might even whip me if she was fond of it.

She laughed at my idea but said that we could make up some story of this kind. I answered then:

—I shall neglect my lessons to give you a plausible justification.

—We shall see, we shall see. Nevertheless, remember that you have got to be very careful.

We came back to the house; she withdrew up to her room till the return of my mother who enquired kindly about her health, she answered that she had been suffering very much from her headache, but that now she felt better and hoped that a good night's rest would make her recover fully. We withdrew early because mummy and my sisters were tired by their tour and shopping in the town. I had recovered my bed in the little dressing-room and I went to sleep thinking of the delicious things that had happened during the day and went to dream that we were reenacting them again, will all the voluptuous excesses that the greatest lewdness might imagine.

CHAPTER II

The next day, miss Jenny's complexion took on some colouring, the fight was out. She was very sweet in her manners and seemed fonder than usual of my sisters who, thinking she was not well, were very attentive, almost trying to forestall her wishes rather than complying with them.

She was almost more reserved than usually with me; but when I came by her to recite my lessons, she pressed me more warmly, keeping a tight grasp around my waist and I saw that she was sorry for not being able to hug me to her breast. Her face reddened and she looked at me with such an affectionate expression that

I would have thrown myself into her arms if her arms if her own reserve had not forbidden it.

Nothing peculiar took place between us that day. At our usual play-time, from four to five o'clock, miss Jenny withdrew up to her room, to rest from the striving she had accomplished all day long to control herself, and left us all alone. There is no need to say that we flew at once to the summer pavilion. There I plunged at first deliciously through Lilian's lovely crack, then I sucked Dorothy, pushing gently a finger a little way up inside her slit, and for a finish I fucked Lilian a second time. I was thus able to bear the otherwise painful deprivation of being denied access to Miss Jenny's love grotto and I seemed more reasonable than I truly was.

The next day she could not yet give me what I so eagerly wanted from her. Thinking that she was wavering, afraid to be discovered, and realizing that she had no good excuse to shut herself in with me, I made up my mind to be unruly the next day. When it was my turn to show her my work, my copybook was blank; I had not done anything. Miss Jenny looked sternly at me, but could not help blushing at the same time.

—What are you thinking about, George? You are so lazy. Go and learn your lessons. If you dont know them, you will be punished.

She caught me by an arm and pressed it gently, telling me to go back to my seat. Of course, at four o'clock I did not know a word of my lesson and I was peculiarly happy about my failure.

—Lilian, Dorothy, you may go in the garden. George will stay to work and learn his lessons or he will be punished for his bad behaviour.

They left, and miss Jenny went to the door and locked it. Then we threw into each other's arms and smothered the partner's body with wild caresses for several seconds. For a long time I had had a powerful erection, so that I immediately slipped my hand under her petticoats. I pushed her down gently on the rocking-chair, and kneeling in front of her, at first I thrust my head between her thighs, and with a quick glance at her cunt, magnificently furnished with hairs, already all wet and juicy, revealing that she was as hot as I, I licked her until she unloaded into my mouth, and I swallowed the delicious liquor with a greedy sensual pleasure. Her juice was peculiarly sweet, and my tongue went inside and fetched as far as it could the delicious nectar in the most secret folds of this delicious slit, really worthy of a god, so as not lose the least drop.

The excitation I aroused in her was almost too strong; she could not bear it longer, so drawing me to her, she said to me:

—Oh! George, my child, my angel, come, oh! come in my arms.

I got up, I threw myself in her arms, and I was at once engulfed up to the balls into her thrilling cunt; she had clasped me in her arms and her legs were locked around my waist. We

136

were both too much excited to be satisfied by the slow movements of less violent desires, so we rushed into the most savage ecstasy of passion and, both too eager to control ourselves, we achieved our first round with a surprising quickness and with the fury of unbridled lust. My dear Jenny was not feeling any more pain and was superlatively ravished by the vigour of my attack and the violence of my amorous energy. We fainted at the same second unloading at ecstasy-time a brook of juice which cooled the burning parts which a moment before had partaken of so furious a fight. My beloved Miss Jenny was holding me tight against her breast and was rolling her magnificent eyes toward the sky as to thank it for the libidinous pleasures she had felt. Our mouths met and we glued our lips in a long, long love-kiss which soon woke up our lewdness. She was as hot as I and we resumed a hearty fucking which ended, like the first one, by the final spasms of delirious orgasms. Then, after a long interlude of passionate caresses and whispered cooing love-words, we attained again the heights of pleasure with a total forgetfulness, extending our exquisite sensations as far as possible by slower or quicker movements with halts in which my superb governess began to develop an art in which she quickly became even superior to the most experienced Mrs. Barnett who had initiated me in a so expert and affectionate way to the love's mysteries.

Miss Jenny had some very peculiar gifts, and above all a caressing, seducing and ravishing sweetness. That was even obvious in her way of manipulating a prick; she did not grasp a rod, but her hand seemed to go over it, only brushing it, but with such an exciting touch that even after a wild fucking party, it could make a peter horny in an instant, only by its light handling and expert fondling. Our third love tournament lasted half an hour; when we were plunged in the coming ecstacy our souls themselves seemed to desert us along with our fucking's distilling. It was long before we were thoroughly awake again. I was still engulfed inside her delicious cunt, but she asked me to relieve her from the weight of my body. We got up, she brushed her petticoats down and helped me to put my trousers on. Then I sat down and pulled her on my knees. Our lips met in a burning kiss of mutually-fulfilled passion. She thanked me for the heavenly joys I had given her and for my idea of an excuse for our meeting. She admitted that she had been as impatient as I, but she ought to be the most careful not to give the least suspicion to anybody in the house.

—You must always remember, my beloved child, that if we were discovered it would ruin me forever. I should venture all to be yours, my lovely child, neither should I be afraid to be discovered if this discovery were not to separate us for ever. My darling George, I cannot even bear this thought. I could not live any more without you.

Then she put her arms around my neck and burst into tears.

I have already told about the action of tears

on my ill-bred peter; since I was comforting my beloved mistress and swearing her eternal love, it went out from its hiding-place and appeared naked in all its glory. I took her soft and beautiful hand and forced her to grip it. She squeezed it tightly and looking at it with a smile in spite of her tears. Then she said:

—My George, what a big thing it is. I wonder how it could come into me and not kill me.

—You'll soon be in a perfect position to verify your empiric science, said I.

And standing up, I threw her down, tucked up her skirts and gave it to her at once, so that she was impaled by the big tool she had been looking at wonderingly not two minutes ago, and still perfectly living. She asked me to go slowly and to make our pleasure last as long as possible. We fucked in one of the most glorious and delicious way, my lovely mistress giving me the most exquisite enjoyment by the ravishing internal pressions of the walls of her so delicious and so lewd cunt.

We remained in rapture long after our coming, then we took back our usual seats because it was the time when my sisters ought to come back from the playground.

Under cover of a laborious drilling in English history, we began to discuss about how and when we would meet again. Miss Jenny dwelt on the point that we ought not to try to meet again intimately before three or four days or else we should run the risk to rouse suspicions which would eventually lead to the horror of the disclosure of our intimacy. Though her reasons were perfectly sane, I could not bear the idea of so long a postponement, and besought her to give me a closer "rendez-vous."

—It is impossible, my darling child, remember that we should be separated for ever if our love happened to be discovered. If we are careful we may go on as long as we want with those delicious meetings.

Suddenly I suggested to her that, since I was sleeping alone in the little room which was far from all the others' bedrooms, when the guest-room by which was my cell was free she might come by stealth during the night, when everybody was asleep, and I might enjoy her rapturous presence in all her naked and unveiled charms. She did not answer, but I saw her eyes shine, and her cheeks got very red as if she was already thinking about all the sensual pleasure of lewd enjoyment that such a plan might involve.

Nevertheless she did not agree at once, but kissing me with passion, she called me her dear and clever little boy and she said that she would think about my idea. We resumed our lessons when my sisters came back.

Four endless days elapsed before Miss Jenny allowed me to fuck her again good and sure. It was only by means of the most obvious insubordination that I succeeded in bringing her and myself to that so wished-for opportunity. We plunged again in an orgy of sensual pleasures, running the whole scale of the thrills of voluptuousness, though we were much hindered by our clothes and the relative security of the place. Asking her again more eagerly than ever for a "ren-dez-vous" in my room, I besought her so much that she promised me to come the next night. I had to be satisfied with her promise though I had hoped she would come the same night, but, as she was more and more a prey to her passions and as she grew more loving and more voluptuous than ever, I was confident that the next night my lovely governess would not deceive me.

With the delicious thinking that I should see her unveiled charms of which I had so often caught sight by stealth. I kept away from my sisters during all the following day. Alleging a violent headache, I went to sleep early, taking the precaution to carry some oil to my room, in order to lubricate the hinges of the door through which my beloved mistress would enter my bedroom. I lay in my bed for long, excruciating moments, and I was beginning to despair when I heard the clock downstairs strike midnight.

All at once I felt that she was near me. She had come into the room with so light a foot that, though I was expecting her, I had not heard her come in nor lock the door. She had wrapped herself in a grey cloak and when, standing near me, she dropped it, she had nothing on but her filmy night-gown. She hurled herself in my arms as I was getting up to grasp her, and we fell down clasped in each other's arms. I was too horny to busy myself with any preliminary; clumsily I forced her to lie on her back and I sank my prick into her, with an eager stroke

141

which left her out of breath and gave her an intense pleasure. I came to a finish too quickly for her because after two or three strokes I could not check my impulses and I came into her ravishing cunt. But as the fire of my too eager desires were not relieved, the convulsive movements of her unsatisfied vagina succeeded quickly in helping my peter to resume its usual stiffness which, since its powers had been revealed to me, had been its normal state.

Miss Jenny, very much excited by my first stroke which had not satisfied her was very hot now; so she clasped her arms behind my neck and wrapped her legs around my waist, we plunged ahead into the big fucking's fury; since my first unloading had reduced the possibility of an immediate new ones, I was able to rhythm my movements with my active partner's ones and we sank in the sensual pleasure of our fulfilled desires, remaining a long time tightly in each other's arms, before we resumed our fucking struggles. Meantime we swore each other eternal love and exchanged burning caresses all over our naked bodies fondling in the other what was fondled in ourselves in a reciprocated frenzy of lust.

At last, Miss Jenny stared at my huge rod which she began to kiss and to caress softly, giving it, for all her attentions, an extraordinarily powerful erection. I was lying on my back and she half-rose to kiss my tremendous tool; so, pulling her gently over me, I said to her it was now her turn to work. She laughed very much of my idea, but straddled me at once and, bringing her delicious cunt exactly over my belly, she seized my prick and, leading it to the entrance of the love grotto, she impaled herself on it and engulfed it in her crack so far that our hairs mixed. Then she worked her haunches up and down, but growing quite excited, she lay at last on my belly and began to move her loins and buttocks with the greatest eagerness. I helped her as much as possible and, when I saw that she was nearing her climax I slipped my hand around her behind and inserted my middle-finger in the little, pink and very narrow hole of her beautiful ass. I worked it up and down, tuning it with her own movements; that seemed to give her more vigour and, with panting breath and stifled sighs, she almost fainted on my breast. I had quickened my thrusts too and I spread a torrent of foaming juice into her burning vagina.

During a long time we remained in the ecstasy of our fulfilled desires. At last she came back to her senses and, kissing me with passion, she stretched on one side and we hugged each other in a loving embrace.

—Oh! my beloved George, what an immense pleasure you have given me. You are the lovingest and the most delicious being in the world. You almost killed me with happiness, but what you done with my ass? How were you able to think about such a thing?

—I don't know, I answered, I had put my hand behind to feel the magnificent globes of your buttocks, and, by squeezing one of them, my finger happened to be in front of a hole, all wetted by our previous unloadings, and by skirting it, my finger slipped inside; and you squeezed it so delightfully that I happened to think how it was similar to the delightful pressions your other charming hole gives my stick when it is inside; so I believed that this orifice would like such a movement as my tool was doing inside your slit. Therefore I did so and it seemed that your excitement was growing greater with that, having regard to the extraordinary convulsive pressions you have given my finger when you came into our final pleasure spasm.

Tell me, my beloved Jenny, has that increased your happiness as much as I have fancied.

—Yes, my dear George, I wonder about it but I must own it was so; it seemed that I was reaching an almost too much exciting peak of pleasure to be able to bear it, and I may only say that it is a happy accident which has increased my enjoyment so much that is impossible, I think to outdo it. Bad scamp, I feel your big tool; it is still quite stiff, but you must check yourself, my darling, it's enough for this night. No, no, no! I do not want to let it go in any more.

Putting her hand down, she removed the head of my prick from the lovely entrance of her cunt, and began to handle and caress it with an obvious admiration for its stiffness, its size and its length. With her expert and soft fondling the fever of my passion could hardly lessen; so, sucking one of her titties while I held her against me with one hand, I slipped the other between our two bodies, and reached her lovely clitoris, already burning from the stiff prick's handling. My ticklings made her at once aflame, and putting my arm under her body, I gently helped her to place herself upon me. She made an objection but she did not show any resistance; on the contrary, she guided my furious and throbbing prick into the voluptuous slit which wanted nothing but to eat it up. This time our movements were much slower and more voluptuous; at times she was almost standing up, raising herself as far as possible and falling back again on her knees. I was shaking her clitoris and so added to the sensual pleasure's ecstasy she was so lewdly feeling. She was soon aware that she had to move faster and more strongly, so dropping herself on my belly, she grasped me and kissed me madly. I put my arm around her waist and held her strongly while her superb buttocks and supple loins gave my up-to-the-hair-sunk tool lascivious movements and ravishing squeezings.

I increased her desire's excitement to the supreme degree by putting my finger in her asshole, and we reached together the end-crisis in a fit of rapture.

We remained so at least thirty minutes, both oblivious of anything else but the fullest enjoyments of our fulfilled passions.

Miss Jenny was the first to remember where we were. She jumped out of the bed, kissed me softly and told me she had to leave at once, that she was afraid she had stayed too long already;

indeed it was about five o'clock. I got up from the bed in order to enfold her lovely body with my arms, to kiss and titillate her exquisite breasts. She freed herself sadly of my loving grasp. I followed her to the door and she left. I went back to my bed to dream about this delicious night of voluptuous fucking.

CHAPTER III

She came back again four times during the six following nights; each time we renewed our mutual enjoyments that seemed always to increase in intensity. Coming to see me for the fifth, time, she said to me:

—Dear George, I come only to kiss you and to tell you that I cannot stay.

—You cant stay, I cried out, and why not, beloved miss Jenny?

—I am not well, but I cant tell you any more.

I jumped out of bed and grasped her in my arms; then putting my hand on her superb and bushy crack, I noticed that it was covered with a cloth. I remembered at once that the same thing had happened with Mrs. Barnett. I noticed too the peculiar smell of her breath, but simulating ignorance, I asked her what had happened to my dear little grotto.

—I cannot tell you anything, my dear child, but that I cant come and see you for five or six nights.

—But why? Did I do something wrong? Cant you let me go only once into this delightful source of heavenly pleasures.

—No, no, it is impossible, my dear George, quite impossible! it will hurt me and you too. Be quiet and so I shall recover the sooner and we will be able to make love again.

—Oh! my darling, how could I bear your absence for five nights, I shall grow wild with desires, see how it throbs and wants to come into its dear partner.

She began to caress my prick with her soft hand. For once, I thought I was going to succeed but she was swifter than I.

—No, George, I am talking in earnest and you must not try to do violence to me or I shall never come back to see you at night.

I noticed that she was resolute, so I threw myself suddenly on the bed.

—Oh! darling George, be reasonable. I shall try to do my best to please you. Lie on your back, like that. I shall kneel down, because I do not want you to touch my little slit. Please, be a nice boy.

Taking my prick with her soft hand, she started to shake it with a perfect mastering of

the operation then, stopping abruptly, she put it
in her mouth, tickling the head with her tongue,
while with one hand she kept on shaking it, circling its base where it touched my belly, and
with the other hand she was manipulating my
hanging balls. She extended the pleasure with
savant handlings and, at last, feeling the
unloading's arrival, she quickened her movements and I sent forth a torrent of juice into
her mouth. She went on and sucked it till she
had swallowed the last drop. It was the first
time she sucked me but it was not the last; she
did it often later on and devised technical
improvements. When she did not have her periods, we sucked each other and she used to do
what I had often done with her, that is to say
she poked her finger in my ass-hole and it
caused her a very great pleasure while she was
sucking me.

Now she had somehow relieved my sensual
lust, so she kissed me tenderly and left me with
my dreams. Of course, during the four following
days, save two short visits "in order to take
patience," as she said, I fucked and shaked my
two sisters who were delighted and enraptured
by my brotherly attentions devoted chiefly to
their girlish slits.

Thus did I spent four months during which
miss Jenny became a perfect pupil for the delicious mysteries of love; but though I had tried
several times to enjoy her nice pink hole situ-
ated under the Venus' temple, I had never quite
succeeded, because my penis was too big and

caused her too much pain, so that I was the most devoted worshipper of the most legitimate altar of Venus. My sisters began to develop extraordinarily, chiefly Lilian. The hairs on her cunt had grown plentiful and curled; her hips were broad, her firm and big behind promised to grow very broad. Dorothy too began to have breasts and a broad and foamy crack.

It was the beginning of spring and the time of the full moon. Lilian was complaining; she was not well and wanted to cry; I tried to console her and thought my attempts would be more successful if I fucked her. And so, taking her to the garden, I led her away to the summer-pavilion and started at once to work on her. She was not eager, without knowing why, but filled with instinctive loathing for. Nevertheless she let me do anything I wanted though with some disgust, and I fucked her but she did not enjoy it as usual. Therefore I drew my prick out as soon as I had come and I discovered the reason why Lilian was not well. My prick was covered with blood; she had her things for the first time. She was very frightened, but I told her I had heard that it was a very natural thing for all the young girls about a certain age; she ought at once to advise mummy who would give her directions about that; I carefully wiped my blood-stained peter and withdrew to my room to wash; when miss Jenny came to my room the same night. I noticed she was in the same condition. She gave me my usual relief with her soft hands and her stroking lips and left me alone during five nights as she was accustomed when she was indisposed in such a way.

Then I happened to have only my dear little sister Dorothy. Till then I had never fucked her and her virginity was intact. She was nearing fourteen years and her cunt was beginning to be full-grown. Her nipples too, by my frigging and suckings erotic excitement, were now prominent. My finger had widened her little pink cunt' opening; so I decided upon putting the finishing touch to her love training and to fuck her thoroughfully. Circumstances were good: Miss Jenny and Lilian, at the usual play-time, withdrew to their rooms in order to rest; Dorothy and I ran to the summer-pavilion where we shut ourselves up. At once I threw her down on the sofa, and made her come in my mouth by sucking her and I kept on sucking her up to make her wild with desires. Then I told her that I was going to initiate her in a new mystery more delightful than all she had tried until now, but that the first initiation was always very painful.

—Oh! What is it? my dear George, everything you did with me is so good that I am sure I shall like it, what is it?

—At first you must know, my dear Dorothy, that your little cunt is especially made to receive a prick inside; but since mine is too big and you are too young and little, I was afraid to give you too much pain and to make it too soon; but now I believe I could get it in by going slowly.

—Oh! dear Georgie, put it inside at once; I

had often felt I should like that; but as you had never tried to get it in I fancied it was a mere foolish idea of me. Have you ever slipped it into Lilian's slit.

—Often, about each time, my dear.

—Does she like it?

—She loves it.

—Then slip it into me at once, Georgie.

I wanted nothing better than that: I told her that in order to enjoy it more fully she ought to be quite naked. All at once she took everything off, while I discarded my trousers, for I had already taken off my jacket and my singlet. I had brought a towel to put on the sofa under her behind in order to avoid telltale stains. Lying on her back, her behind near the edge, her legs wide apart, her feet upon the sofa and drawn toward her buttocks, with her knees leaning outside, she was in the most favourable position for the working I was thinking of. I put a cushion on the ground, I kneeled on it, I brought my prick out and started the whole process by a careful and extensive sucking of her crack, so that at last she came in my mouth, and cried out:

—Oh! push it in me, George, I feel I want it.

She was already quite drenched by her first unloadings and by my sucking of her cunt which I had covered with spittle, and I had oiled the head of my prick by spitting on it too. Then I aimed my penis at the luscious target the bright red lips of her little and so soft cunt offered me, rubbing it up and down between the petal-like lips, before pushing its head inside. Owing to those preliminaries as well as to the widening I had achieved by my previous working with tongue and prick, I made an immediate entering quite easier that it might have been fancied.

Scarcely had I pushed one inch more inside when the excitement of the passion I gave her stimulated so much the natural lewdness of Dorothy's temperament that she started wriggling her behind, letting her knees fall on each side, helping as much as possible the fierce thrusts I did at this moment so that my prick went in halfway and, without the virginity's impediment which it met then, it would have been quite engulfed. At that time she felt a very sharp pain which made her recline more backwards and cry:

—Oh! Georgie! What is going to happen! I dont understand it!

—Don't be afraid, I'll go slowly; be quiet for a while and you'll feel the pain vanish out and instead you'll feel a great pleasure.

We stayed motionless for a while, until I felt her unconscious inside pressions, real forerunners and infallible indicators of awakening desires; so, beginning a slow up and down motion, I soon brought forth such a sensual pleasure's excess into her delightful cunt that her movements became almost furious and nature inspired her to help me with as much efficiency as if she had been from long acquainted with the delightful movements which are alone able to increase the enjoyment of real pleasure.

But Dorothy was a most unusual example of an impetuous and lewd temperament, and was ranking much higher than Lilian in that respect. Though the latter was a very hot number, Dorothy's passions were much more violent and later on she became one of the best fuckers, letting herself plunge in all the most savage pleasures that the most lascivious nature might offer.

But I must not speak of what took place later. Just now I had excited her at the highest degree, she was about to come and as I withdrew my cock a little to give her the final stroke, she heaved her behind in an enjoyment's agony. I perceived it was now or never, and plunging my throbbing prick into her with all my strength, I went through every impediment and pursued my forward course till I was engulfed in it up to the balls.

Poor Dorothy! When she thought she had reached the happiness paradise she felt the most grievous pain. She screamed and fainted: her arms fell down listlessly along her body; her legs would have fallen too, but for my arms holding them. I went on with a series of several successive strokes to explore fully each internal crevice, for I was by then very much excited. I fainted in an excess of pleasure, throwing a torrent of balsamic liquor which appeased and diminished the suffering of her awfully torn slit.

As I saw that Dorothy did not recover, I got up, a bit frightened, and was terrified to see all the blood she had lost after my withdrawal.

Luckily I had not forgotten to put the towel under her for, not only the sofa was safe from any stains but I used it to stanch her swollen and bleeding slit and to wipe the blood which covered her thighs and her buttocks. I did all that before the dear girl showed the least symptom of recovering. At first she sighed, then shivered and at last opened her eyes, asking me with an haggard look:

—What has happened, George?

Then noticing she was lying quite naked, she was at once fully aware of all that had happened.

—Oh! George! Now I know; I felt as if you were killing me; George, oh! I suffered awfully. How could you hurt me so much, just when I was about to feel the greatest pleasure I had ever felt in my life.

—My darling, now all your troubles are over, and you'll never suffer any more, and we shall have together more pleasure than ever, but not at once: it hurts you more than I should have thought, and now we must stop.

I helped her to get up, but she thought she was about to faint and it was hard to help her dressing. She was astonished to see the towel full of blood. I told her to put her handkerchief between her thighs and to push a corner of it into the slit so that her shirt would not be bloodstained. Then I laid her on the sofa, while I ran and fetched some water at the garden fountain. I took a glass and the towel with me. I came back with water which refreshed Dorothy very much. I told her she ought to remain lying very quiet without moving as long as we might stay in the pavilion. Nevertheless, when she tried to walk, she felt very disturbed by a sharp pain. I was awfully afraid that they may catch sight of something wrong when we would arrive to the house, so I suggested Dorothy to simulate a fall as soon as we should see somebody and to say that she could not walk any more because she had knocked her knee in falling down.

This stratagem succeeded wonderfully. Miss Jenny, my mother, Lilian looked at us as we arrived. Dear Dorothy played her part wonderfully, she was seen falling down heavily and she screamed. Everybody ran up, we picked her up carefully and we helped her to the house; she was complaining of a pain in her ankle and her knee. Mummy insisted to put her to bed at once and hot linens were applied on her legs. Dorothy let them do everything they judged fit for her ailment; we soon left her to get some rest, which relieved her from the painful duty of playing the hurt baby.

The next day she complained of a great stiffness, and she was limping, though hot linens had stopped the swelling; anyway we had been able to avoid remarks and suspicions of what had really happened. Three days elapsed before I tried to put it in her again. Obviously I had, for the first time, excited her very much as I had sucked her for a long time. I did likewise and only after did she let me, though fearful and shuddering, bring my burning prick in the tender folds of her cunt. Since I moved very slowly she hardly felt a slight pain, and when I had at last poked the bottom of the warm canal, after I had slowly and lewdly given some strokes, her lascivious temper was roused and just when I was ready to come she had two or three powerful orgasms, and we sank together in an ecstasy of delightful voluptuousness. She was holding me close and did not want to let me take my prick out of her foaming crack.

—No George! It hurts too much to put it back, let it where it is so tenderly poked in.

Anticipating her natural desires, she began exercizing upon my penis the most delightful squeezings which soon led us to the point requiring more active motions. However I refrained her a little and said to her that we ought to moderate our movements in order to increase our pleasure, because so frequent repetitions would do nothing but pump us out without our enjoying the real ecstasies of sensual pleasure. Then I taught her the happiness of slow motions and made her come but I did not come myself. The dear little creature stuck herself close to me with one of the most intimate and highly exciting embraces, as if she wanted our two bodies to achieve a perfect amalgam and she fainted in the sweetest rapture of fulfilled desires, with an expression of heavenly ecstasy on her face which I started eating ravenously with kisses. I could hardly help following her erotic rhythm for her delightful movements when she had orgasms as well as the pressions and squeezings of the walls of her cunt on my prick were so much exciting that it was a real victory if I could resist. However I succeeded and kept quiet and motionless, though powerfully tempted by the delightful suckings of her lovely little cunt's exquisite folds which were squeezing my prick the most expertly. I let her free either to leave me as soon as she felt calling an end to it or to start again the delightful pumping through which we should run again a furious race to end as usual in so ravishing an ecstasy of lascivious delight.

Dorothy went at it again and I helped her eagerly. It was a twofold stroke; my sister swooned with pleasure when the fuming jet of my spunk mixed up with hers. She declared it was an unutterable delightful kind of momentaneous death. She glued her lips on mine, kissing me in the most highly exciting way, telling me how at last I had made her happy by getting all of my prick into her cunt. It was worth suffering more than the first time to get so ravishing a result. At last we straightened our clothes and went out of the pavilion.

We turned to the flower-bed, so as to be seen playing together and not suspected for our long absence, for now there was only the two of us together.

Of course Lilian knew what we were doing and suspected I was wholly initiating Dorothy. She smiled and significantly pressed my hand when we met in the study-room in order to learn our lessons.

During the two following days I experienced pleasure only with Dorothy; at each new fucking she was getting skillfuller and apter to give or receive sensual pleasure.

The third day, miss Jenny muttered to me "see you to-night" and squeezed my hand stealthily. She came and we enjoyed fucking in every conceivable way. I was lucky again and contemplated her in all her naked glory for it was broad daylight when she left me; I had sucked her twice and fucked her crack five times. She allowed me that on account of my long abstinence, but told me that in the future I ought to be soberer for her health if not for mine. Three nights went by before meeting again. I cannot say I was sorry for now I had initiated Dorothy as well as Lilian and, we plunged ourselves in the greatest revels, fucking and sucking at the same time. At first we started by having one girl lie on her back, ready to be fucked while the other, kneeling over her head, was sucked by the fucked one and I was inserting my finger in the ass-hole which was in front of me. But the most voluptuous posture, one that we liked above all was the following: one girl was lying on her back and the other standing over her on all fours. The latter one drew her mouth near the cunt of the one who was lying on her back and offered me her buttocks behind which I was kneeling. The under one was leading my prick to the cunt over her face, and was thus satisfied by seeing the whole process of the thrusting in while with one hand she tickled my balls and with the other she dug a finger into my ass-hole; all that time she was sucked by the one I fucked and who fingered too her ass-hole and the three of us would faint in a ravishing agony of happiness to do it all over again after the two girls had swapped places. Sometimes I tried to insert my prick into Dorothy's tight little ass-hole, but, though the fingering increased her pleasure very much while my virile member was working in her cunt, she could not yet bear the inserting of my broad prick. I had not yet tried with Dorothy, except once when Miss Jenny and Lilian had their periods. Once I happened to be alone with my sister who, suddenly overtaken by the evac-uating need, withdrew in the nick of time behind a bush and bent down. I stayed there and waited, when she called me and asked for paper. I moved forward to give her some; she was half crouching with her skirts tucked up and held around her waist. As I handed her the paper, I gazed at her shit. I was amazed by the extraordinary size of the piece.

I said nothing but I was disturbed by this fact which aroused an idea about which I became very much preoccupied. I had often thought of the pleasure I had felt by fucking Mrs. Barnett's ass, and from that day on I had tried to initiate Miss Jenny and Lilian in this pleasure's delightful road, but, as I have already told, I had not succeeded with them on account of my tool's unusual size. Since they could not bear such an insertion I stood no more chance of succeeding with my less developped sister and I had not tried anything with Dorothy except with my finger. As a matter of fact, it seemed to work better on her than on Lilian or on Miss Jenny. The very sight of the unusual size of her little pink ass-hole, though very narrow, could let such a big lump go out, it could all the same receive my huge screw. I resolved to try the next day an initiation on this side. By remembering that Mrs. Barnett was accustomed to be rightly sucked and fucked before it, so that the prick was very wet, I began to excite Dorothy as much as possible at first; I worked my prick in her and made her come twice; then I sucked her till she begged me to thrust my prick into her cunt. I had managed to dig at once two fingers into her ass-hole and I was masturbating her there while I sucked her in front, and it did not seem to hurt her in any respect; on the contrary, I noticed that my movements excited her still more. I tried to widen her as much as possible or rather to keep her ass-hole as open as possible with my two fingers. Then when she had her greatest excitement, as she urged me to fuck her at once, I said to her:

—My beloved sister, there is another mystery for getting voluptuous feelings; you have not yet tested it, you have not been initiated to it yet and I want to train you for it.

—Oh! what is it? dear George, do as you like, but do it as soon as possible.

—Ho! my darling, it's into the sweet little hole of your ass that I'm going to push my prick; it will hurt you a little at the beginning, but by going slowly and stopping now and then when you'll be suffering too much, I'll succeed in putting it in all and both of us shall enjoy a tremendous pleasure.

—Dear, dear Georgie, do as you like, your beloved prick can only give me pleasure; I am eager for feeling it in me anywhere since I can feel it running through me; I think I must stand on all fours.

So saying, she quickly turned over and offered me the two round and firm globes of her ravishing buttocks. I hurried and pushed my prick up to the balls into her cunt in order to oil it; she was thrilled with lust and she squeezed it so much in her cunt that I could hardly withdraw it; it was so good and so sweet in that cunt that I was seduced and hesitated to unload inside, but I aimed at the other hole and knew that I needed all my stiffness to succeed with this new one, so I took it out of her cunt; I spit a lot upon my prick already very wet with fucking juice, I put a bit of spittle too on her ass-hole by inserting my wet finger in it, and I drew the head of my tremendous rod near the little orifice in front of me. I judged so flagrant the disproportion that, even should I succeed, it would not be without great sufferings for her, but remembering the size of what had gone out of it I began at once. I forced the whole head in and she did not move, but as I pushed it forward, forcing about two inches more in, she cried out:

—Stop a little, George, I feel a strange sensation. I cannot bear it any longer.

I stopped immediately, then, slipping my hand under her, I groped for her clitoris with a hand, holding her buttocks close against me with my other arm which I had put around her waist in order not to lose the position. My active finger quickly inflamed her passions and I was aware that her behind squeezed my prick convulsively. I let her become more excited, then I softly and slightly pushed ahead and I noticed I imperceptibly moved forward. Two thirds of my prick were already enfulfed in, when a too sudden motion from me made her scream and I should have been dismounted if my arm had not held strongly her haunches close against me.

—Oh! darling George, stop; it suffocates me, it gives me such a strange feeling that I am about to faint.

—Now, I'll be quiet, my dear Dorothy, besides all is in and when the pain of my thrusting will be out, in one or two minutes, you'll feel nothing but pleasure.

So I held my prick where it was, but I busied myself with frigging her clitoris and so she quickly came, for I was resolute to attempt the last strain when I should feel the juice of her coming run out, what happened very quickly and with her wriggling and squirming her buttocks she had swallowed my prick up to the balls in her tiny puckered ring; I was not straining any more and instead of suffering, she began to shriek with pleasure, so great was the delight she felt by coming in wild orgasms.

For several minutes she could not speak; she kept on squeezing my prick with the muscles of her anal sphincter. But I had resolved not to come at once and to wait for a second helping in order to initiate my dear Dorothy wholly to the ecstatic lust of this new fucking way. I was very much rewarded for my self control. The first words my dear Dorothy uttered were those of a wild joy for the extraordinary delights she had felt and received from me; never, never had she enjoyed fucking so much and so extensively. She turned her lovely face towards me and I saw her eyes filled with great tears of sensual pleasure.

Again I applied my titillations on her still excited clitoris; it had notably grown; so she was as eager as me for a second round. I could still control myself enough to thrust my prick back and forth so as to give Dorothy such an exquisite pleasure that another time she would be quite ready to offer me her nice ass-hole as often as I should want it; I led her up to the highest degree of excitement and, when she unloaded, in an agony of delight, I spurted out a real stream of fucking juice into her womb and both of us fell down ahead, crushed by the powerfulness of her pleasure, but nonetheless very careful not to let my rod slip out of her ass-hole.

When we recovered, I withdrew my prick slowly from her tight anal canal, and I noticed it was covered with some blood stains. I wiped my screw with my handkerchief and wiped too my dear Dorothy by running it in the deep furrow of the line dividing her buttocks, for fear her clothes should be soiled. Then I helped her to rise up; she encircled my neck with her arms and, kissing me very softly, she thanked me for this new love lesson which had exhausted her with happiness.

164

Thus was completed Dorothy's first drilling in the exploration of that pleasure-path, and I owe it to the truth to say that she was peculiarly well-shaped to give and receive such heavenly pleasures. Later on she turned into a beautiful woman, with one of the prettiest and broadest behinds I have ever met with; and she was always very fond of being fucked from behind.

When she was married, she told me that her husband was a bastard who knew only one way to make love and kept strictly to it. And so she often deceived him and slipped his prick into her ass-hole without his noticing the kind of pleasure he was giving her.

Three months elapsed as quickly as a dream, while we were engrossed in these delightful and lubric occupations of giving and receiving sensual pleasure, but nobody in the house caught any sight of that intimacy and even Miss Jenny did not suspect anything about what was taking between my sisters and me, thanks to the natural teen-agers natural trend for double-dealing place. Miss Jenny and my sisters believed from their personal standpoint, that they gave me as much pleasure as I wanted and therefore they could not think I might go and derive sensual enjoyments from another woman's cunt. But events occurred which turned out the whole dealing for the best but first brought me much sorrow.

CHAPTER IV

There was a neighbour of us, a very nice bachelor about thirty five years old, and a very rich landlord at that, who had formed quite a habit, every Saturday, of waiting for us after mass, in front of the church, and he used to chat a little with Miss Jenny, mummy or us. He was taking us for mere children and never paid any attention to us.

On a particular Monday, mummy received a letter from him, asking her for a short meeting the next day, for he needed her advice about a very important matter. Mummy answered back asking him to come at eleven o'clock, adding she would be glad to receive him.

He came in full dress. My mother had been very restless during the whole morning and had grown more and more nervous as the meeting-time was nearer. I think the old lady believed she was concerned in his coming. But he was concerned in his coming. But he was merely coming in order to ask Miss Jenny to marry him, that is to ask mummy for the governess'hand; he was ready to give her all and everything she would ask for; he told my mother that before presenting himself to Miss Jenny whom he had loved since her first appearance at church, and whose sweet and modest character moved him more day after day, as an open suitor, he had thought he ought first to open his heart to my mother and ask her leave for meeting Miss Jenny and, should they agree together, to allow him to come to the house and to court her. He added yet that he would never be bold enough to declare his own sentiments to Miss Jenny and begged mummy to be good enough and to interfere with it and to Miss Jenny and him for the day after; then he would be able to declare himself and to hear from her very lips what his fate would be and if he could hope for her future surrendering.

My mother, though at first a little disappointed, felt so much concern for Miss Jenny that she agreed heartily to his request and told him she would be his ambassador.

Miss Jenny was genuinely astonished by such an offer and seemed to need some time to think about it.

—It would not be wise, my dear, to reject

him. You are actually depending wholly on strangers, and you must think about the benefits of his proposal. You must not waver very long. Think about it. He will come to-morrow and I hope his amorous eloquence will quickly clear up the matter in his favour.

My poor Jenny burst into tears, saying it was too sudden and she was not ready to take an definitive decision. However she was going to think very earnestly about it so as to be able to give an answer the next day. My mother, noticing she was disturbed by the proposal she had transmitted her, told her in a very friendly way:

—You may give the children a vacation for the afternoon, and I advise you to withdraw to your room where you'll write to your mother who was left a widow; tell her what is happening and ask her for a piece of advice.

So we were left to ourselves for several hours. I knew all that was happening and I felt very sad when I noticed that if Mr. Bank's proposal was accepted I should be for ever deprived of Miss Jenny. This idea made me very gloomy and I did not play very much with my sisters till Dorothy came to me and laughed at my sadness, asking me what it meant.

—Don't you see! if Miss Jenny gets married with Mr. Bank, we shall have another mistress and we cannot hope to have such a good one who disturbs us so little in our pretty "little plays."

—Oh! That's true and we should be awfully troubled if some busybody took a fancy to spy on us and forced us to stop. However we must use our momentary freedom, so come with us, George, and let us enjoy ourselves with a good and square fucking. We have much time to be quietly by ourselves, mummy is not very well and has retired to her room; nobody will come near us and nothing keeps us from making good use of the time, the three of us will be for once stark naked, the way you do like so much, please, come, Georgie.

Her words had already diverted the course of my mind; my prick had answered her words before she had stopped talking; her inquiring eyes had at once noticed it, so, stroking it with her hand, she began to talk to it:

—Oh! my dear little rascal, I see you agree with my proposal, so you see, George, you have got to come, the dear little fellow wants it too.

I followed her and we spent the most voluptuous afternoon in fucking delightfully.

Miss Jenny came to see me at night and rushed in my arms, sobbing and crying; she said to me, pressing me on her breast:

—Oh! my darling George, I love you so tenderly, I need you as much as my own life. I cannot think of departing my only love. You have initiated me to all the enjoyments of reciprocated love. Oh! the idea of parting from you is awful and ruins my heart. Oh! I love you, my beloved boy. Kiss me, and hold me tight on your heart.

I did better; I have already confessed that women's tears had an immediate action on me;

it was only the beginning of one of the most voluptuous nights.

Miss Jenny had no restraint that night, and she gave free rein to all her lewdness as if she was already aware that those nights of abandon and libidinous delights were soon to come to an end.

Indeed, when she left in the morning and I began to recall all the things she had told me during that night, I was convinced that she had made up her mind to accept the profitable offers which she had received. With woman's instinctive intelligence she had understood that she could not decline such a proposition for the sake of a little boy whom incidental events could part from her any time.

And in the same time she was convinced that I was entirely hers for she never suspected my first initiation. And the idea pleased her very much indeed, to say nothing of my huge screw that she was happy to have at her disposal and which had so great an action on her passions. We spent a wild night of enjoyment, without sleeping for a minute, and my afternoon's riots must not be forgotten. But such is natural strength and energy in a strongly-built young man of fifteen that Miss Jenny had to check me rather than give some forced excitements to make my prick stiffen. I made her promise to come back the next night and to let me know about what she had decided regarding Mr. Bank's connubial hopes.

The next day, Mr. Bank was punctual for his visit; mummy received him, with Miss Jenny by her side, and after the usual formal greetings, she got up and asked them to excuse her for she had to look to some very urgent household matters. Later on Miss Jenny told me that as soon as mummy had left the room, Mr. Bank got up from his chair and, coming near her, said to her in his best gentlemanly manners and with the greatest visible sincerity:

—You know, my dear Miss Jenny, the purpose of my visit and I augur, from your kindness in granting me this meeting, that I stand a fair chance of being accepted by you.

Then taking her motionless hand and pressing it to his heart, he added:

—I have been in love with you, Miss Jenny, from the first day I have seen you, I feel my future happiness hangs on your lips, for without your love my life will be broken. To-day I am here in order to offer you my hand and my wealth. If I have not yet reached your heart, I hope that if you allow me to court you, may be I shall manage to win it, at least I shall try and I shall always be your devoted worshipper.

Then noticing she was peculiarly moved, he asked her to sit down (for she had got up when he had come to take her hand), he led her towards the sofa and sat down close to her. As he urged her to give him an answer, she told him:

—You will easily understand, Mr. Bank, that I have been very surprised by your generous offer; I am very grateful for it, but I must beg you to let me wait for some time until I have received an answer from my mother; I am

171

going to write to her about the generous proposal you have made me, a poor governess who can only be grateful for the delicate way you have been kind enough to deal with, in such an important matter.

—Ah! do not speak so, my dear Miss Jenny, and believe me; I have not thrown myself at your feet on a sudden impulse, but with an eager love and true admiration for your great beauty and for your wonderful behaviour since you have entered this family.

The dear girl was smiling through her tears as she was repeating to me those affectionate words with which Mr. Bank overflowed her.

To be short, before his departure she confessed to him that the frequent meetings at church or elsewhere had given birth, in her, too a thing greater than mere sympathy but nevertheless she had never hoped to become his wife and she had very much endeavoured to escape those too sweet feelings because she was unworthy of a rich landlord. Oh! woman, your name is deceiving! So he left the happiest man in the world. Later on he came to see her every day and remained with her from four to five o'clock, and owing to their meetings we often spent half an hour longer at playtime. Often too he dined with us. Miss Jenny's mother welcomed the opportunity and gave her her assent with the greatest joy.

When Mr. Bank heard of the news, he become very urging and wanted to bring closer the day when he ought to become the happiest of men. Miss Jenny still wished to postpone it for six weeks, but he complained so much about it that at last my mother helped him and Miss Jenny to agree, at first for reducing the six weeks to one month, then to a mere fortnight from that day; so everybody became very busy ordering wedding-gowns, picking up the right material and getting the best seamstress from the near-by town.

The wedding was to take place in our house, and my mother insisted to offer the wedding-dinner. Jenny's mother was invited to spend a week with us, at the time of the wedding, and to keep my mother company. My two sisters and Mr. Bank's young sister were to be the bridesmaids and a young man who was courting miss Bank would be the bestman.

Everything had been so set in order that things went very smoothly to everybody's evident satisfaction. When Miss Jenny's mother came to our house, she occupied the room where the lovely Mrs. Barnett had so eagerly initiated me to the whole scale of amourous emotions and libidinous pleasures.

To return to the day when Mr. Bank obtained his first meeting, proclaiming his love and closing it with a wedding-proposal, before he left he asked to see mummy in order to thank her for her kindness and to tell her how he had been delighted to hear that Miss Jenny allowed him to court her and to try to win her heart, and so on . . . Asking for the favour of a pure kiss, he left dazzled with hope.

Of course Miss Jenny was very tired by the

meeting, she was obviously very nervous and my mother bade her to withdraw to her room and to go to bed until she had quite recovered from this disturbing though happy event for she was unable to give us our lessons in such a plight as she was; mummy would teach us herself in the morning and would give us leave for the whole afternoon, in honour of the happy event that had just happened.

So my sisters and I were gratified with a new opportunity and were able to dedicate ourselves freely to our exhaustive and far-reaching love-delight; but notwithstanding the wonderful strength which nature had gratified me with, I was aware that if I wanted to enjoy again my dear Jenny's cunt the next night as I had sworn myself I would, I ought not only to keep from such excesses as had filled part of the previous day, but to sleep a little too, for I had not slept at all the night before; so I contented myself with sucking my sisters and fucked them only once each; then I sucked them again, making them come five times, so as to satisfy them fully without exhausting me, and I closed the whole session by fucking my dear Dorothy's ass, while they busied themselves with sucking each other most affectionately. That seemed to gratify them and they allowed me to go stealthily up to my room to sleep, Lilian promising me to wake me up for the tea.

I fully slept for three hours, and when I came down and drank my tea, I felt well and ready to face whatever might happen during the night. What a lucky idea I had had, for as parting-time was near, Miss Jenny needed more and more sensual pleasure, and we devised all possible postures and means to increase and stimulate our passions. She came to my bedroom every night, even on the last one before her wedding, though during the three nights before that event the room near mine was occupied by her mother; in spite of that we met and gave ourselves up to love delight, muffling our sighs and cutting out too noisy motions.

At the end, in the moments of her greatest excitement, she had tried several times to insert my prick into the puckered rosebud of her lovely little ass-hole.

Once, by a sudden jerk, I managed to push my prick into it at the very moment when she had a drenching orgasm; with one stroke I was able to drive two inches in, not counting the head, and I believe I should have succeeded to put the whole in her that time if, in consequence of too much a great excitement on my part, I had not spurted out a fuming jet of come. It had lubricated the way, and my prick which had already unloaded several times was now too limp and was driven out of her pouting ring by the squeezings she did with the anal muscles of her sphincter. As it were, she was naturally relieving herself of a huge pudding that happened to be meat instead of the usual stinking substance. I think that at that time she should have wished to see me succeed wholly; however I succeeded entirely the night before her wedding: she was on her knees, her head falling down on the pillow, and I stood behind her, kneeling down too (she loved fucking that way, declaring that so I could get more of my prick inside her cunt and it was as if I reached her very heart and filled up all her body; besides titillations made by a deft finger and the inserting of another finger in her ass-hole added a great deal to the pleasure that may be felt in that posture).

I had already fucked her wonderfully well, we had reciprocated sucking each other, so that she was very much excited and wet with her own juice and mine. By inserting two fingers in her behind, I managed to make them work so as to widen her ass-hole as much as possible, while I excited her still more by pushing my prick against her cunt and frigging her clitoris. Just when she was going to unload, I wetted her ass-hole with spittle I had taken out of my mouth with my fingers, and as she was pushing her buttocks against me to get my prick in a little way farther, I withdrew it quickly and by a strong motion drove it half way into the ass-hole. She uttered a scream, amazed by the swiftness of the attack and she would surely have dismounted me if I had not held her firmly by locking my two arms around her hips; I gave her ass-hole another fierce thrust, and I sank up to the balls in her wonderful buttocks that I felt now pressed against my belly. She muttered:

—For God's sake, darling Georgie, stop a little. I cannot bear it! I shall scream aloud if you don't stand quiet and motionless for some time.

As I was very firmly settled, it suited me too to stand motionless for if I had done one or two movements I should have come at once into her anal canal. Now I was wholly engulfed and I wished not only to enjoy myself but chiefly to make my dear Jenny enjoy it. So keeping my prick absolutely motionless, I slipped one hand towards her clitoris and started stroking it; I brought the other hand to her titties, and I played with the nipples, which excited her as much as the tickling of her clitoris as I had noticed several times before. Her passions were soon aroused again, and the unintentional squeezings and pressings of her behind and sphincter showed me she would soon reach the pick of excitement; I was right and it happened almost at once and she came with a wild orgiastic fury not only from her unloading, but chiefly from mine when she felt I was overflowing her inside cavities with a burning hot and plentiful fucking juice.

After that ecstatic coming, we lay panting on our side, but I did not draw my prick out of her buttocks; and after we had kissed, fucked, frigged, tickled, sucked, licked each other, we felt once more ready to resume the delightful fight; we worked a second time into the delightful retreat of Venus Callipyge, second temple of the sensual pleasure. It was our last fuck, for unhappily everybody in the house was now beginning to get up. My ravishing mistress kissed me sweetly and thanked me for the new pleasure I had made her discover. We cried in each other's arms, and I cried again alone when she had left me, for I understood I had lost her forever as a mistress, and what a lovely mistress she had always been for me!!!

On the morning, the bridesmaids, the best-man and the husband came to our house. We all departed for church; my sisters were delighted to be bridesmaids and very proud to wear pretty gowns; but they became enraptured when they saw the beautiful jewels Mr. Bank offered them. They looked at him and truly, in that instant, he was the best man and the nicest human being they had ever known. The wedding dinner went off well according to custom and when the bride, who had gone upstairs and had changed from her white wedding-gown into a sober but "chic" travel-dress, came down, everybody burst into tears. She kissed us tenderly and said good bye in a poor wavering voice. She pressed me gently on her breast and whispered in my ear:

—Be brave, darling George!

—It was too much for me but I succeeded in choking back my tears; the door of the car was shut and they left to spend their honey moon at Bezonla. All the guests remained till the night and after the emotions of the day and the sadness of the parting, added to my overtiring preceding night, I was glad to go to bed. I started crying instead of sleeping, thinking that another one, at this very moment, was enjoying all the wonderful graces which I had till now been the only master of.

* * *

Thus came to a close one of the most delightful amourous experiences of my life, and though I have had since the renewed opportunity to fuck my former mistress now and then, it was only some furtive fucking party, very delightful but which never gratified us fully.

It was the first great event that for some time, altered the course of our life, but I want to lay by the details of my future adventures which I shall relate in their swift succession.

The house was not the same any more after the wedding; the first following day was desolate. Jenny's mother was still home and she left us only two days later.

My mother and hers spent every afternoon in the summer-pavilion so that we could give ourselves up to our love-games. Dorothy was complaining from a violent head-ache; she was about to have her things and indeed they came plentifully in the evening. I had planned with my sisters that I should slip into their room as soon as everybody would be asleep, for now our governess was not there any more and they were quite elated by the prospect of seeing me at night. I arrived, but Lilian was the only one fit to partake of our amorous feast. I made her lie with me in Miss Jenny's bed and during all the time I was running my rod through her I was thinking of my dear governess; even when I fucked her ass I remembered the insertion of my big screw in Jenny's asshole the very night before her wedding and I wondered if her husband would fail to notice that she had lost her cherry or not.

Nevertheless I fancied that he would not notice anything and that his wife would be unfaithful to him as several millions of others had been in such a way. As she had just chosen the very day when she ought to have her periods to be wed, I was supposing that she wished to make her husband believe that her deflowering blood be mixed with her menstrual flow. Later on we shall see how my reckoning was correct and how the first bridal night was spent.

I spent a delightful night in my lovely Lilian's arms and withdrew out of her cunt only when it was time to go back to my room; I could not run the risk to be seen and the household was already stirring significantly.

Jenny's mother left us on that same day; my mother, who did not feel very well, wanted Lilian to sleep with her, so I was forced to spend a very quiet night, but I endured it easily owing to the love excesses I had performed during the whole week.

Another week elapsed without any event worthy of being related, except that Dorothy could join us again in our fucking parties. The doctor had enjoined my mother to go and spend several weeks on the seaside and she had decided we would all go and spend about six weeks over there, after what she would hire a new governess.

CHAPTER V

We left the house and went to a lovely southern village, very remote and cosily perched on high cliffs. It was a very little hamlet with only one street and a few houses scattered here and there, but with a wonderful beach that was bound by very steep and high rocky cliffs. Our lodging was small, a drawing-room and bedroom above a store, topped by two other bedrooms. I slept in a little room that was behind the drawing-room, my mother had taken the room on the front of the house and my sisters the room in the back.

Those two rooms were only parted by a very thin partition, so that we were obliged to choose a place outside where we could gave ourselves up to our lovers' pleasures. Very few visitors came to that so remote little village; in our searches, at one end of the beach we found some favourable places amid the rocks; they soon became our elected grounds where we could throw ourselves into our amorous pleasures and gratify all our lewdness. The place was farther than one league from the village and we commanded a very large area; however as we might have forgotten how quickly time elapses, we agreed that one or the other of my sisters would be posted as a sentry so that she could warn the others should somebody be coming near our retreat. So I took each one in turn, laying her on the ground, and beginning, by a hearty sucking of her cunt which she reciprocated on my throbbing peter, then I fucked each one good and square. We kept at our childish pleasures for three days and we were congratulating ourselves in having found such a safe spot for our enjoyments. During the morning we used to remain with mummy who taught us for two or three hours and made us recite our lessons. But after lunch, mummy had to withdraw to take a nap and we would go out to take a long walk or to do a few more interesting incursions. I have already said how for three days we had played our nice amorous games without being troubled even by the sight of a remote passer-by.

On the fourth day, while Dorothy was keeping watch and Lilian and I had just been coming with foaming orgasms in a voluptuous agony, after we had nicely licked each other's genitals clean, I was telling her:

—Was it not delightful when I pushed it in up to the balls!

—I think it was, without doubt she had her cunt full of it, answered near us an unknown voice.

—It is easy to fancy that we got up at once, overwhelmed by astonishment.

—Oh! don't be uneasy, I do not want to trouble you at all, added the same voice.

It was a very good-looking man, with a quiet and sweet voice, kind and amiable manners, who was standing near us, smiling, his fly unbuttoned and his very stiff prick firmly held in one hand. So great was our surprise that we were not realizing in what a plight we were now finding ourselves. Lilian was lying, her legs set wide apart, her belly stark naked and her cunt open like a little red mouth; as for me, my trousers were on my knees and my big prick was hanging, that is true, but it had hardly shrunk. The stranger added:

—I do not want to trouble you, but on the contrary, I want to help you in your pleasures. By accident I have watched you two days ago: here I am a foreigner like you. I know that you are sisters and brother and I admire you all the more because you dont set any value on family and relationship prejudices; but you must know that, since I have discovered your secret, it is better to make me partake of your pleasures; not only you will thus be sure that I shall not tell anybody, but that will surely increase your voluptuous enjoyments very much and in the same time I'll get a very great satisfaction myself. Why, I am convinced that your oldest sister, who was going to take the place of the young one who is now watching over would be undoubtedly very pleased if, for a trial-run, I should plunge this rod into her. Do not be afraid, my dear, he said, noticing the sudden alarmed movement of Lilian who was only now getting conscious of her indecent posture, I shall do nothing which you did not give your fullest assent to, but I am sure that your brother who fucks you one after the other will be very pleased to see you in my arms unless I am much mistaken about his erotic temperament, which I doubt very much.

I could not help myself to think inwardly how he had rightly found out my most secret thoughts for I was just now reckoning how it would be much better for all of us to let him share our enjoyments rather than making an enemy of him by an unaccountable-for rejection. So at once I owned that, the way things were, the three of us ought to be satisfied with the plans of the stranger and I took quite a secret fancy for the prospect of a four-cornered fucking. So I asked Lilian to allow him to do what he would like.

Woman's natural aversion to seem to be yielding too easily brought a refusal from Lilian, but as she was still lying on her back, I stooped a little over her, opened her thighs and asked him to kneel between her legs and for the rest to manage by himself. Kneeling down, he bent

184

down forward and in a gentlemanly gesture, he started licking all the fucking juice the foaming cream of which covered the lips of her cunt. Then he sucked her and she was himself for fucking her.

As soon as they were quite entangled in that occupation, I whistled and called for Dorothy. Her amazement may be imagined when she saw Lilian in the arms of a stranger; but as this libidinous sight had suscited, as usual, a powerful erection in my sensitive organ, which was rising quite stiff on the verge of bursting, I made her kneel in front of them and slipped my prick from behind into her cunt, so that both of us could enjoy the spectacle of the fucking that was talking place in front of us. It increased our excitement and the four of us ejaculated at the same moment in a voluptuous agony.

Then we sat down in order to further our acquaintance with him, and it was no problem after such an introduction. Our new friend gave us some advices for our future lustful entertainments, while, stroking Dorothy's cunt with one hand and my prick with the other, he kept tickling both of us with a perfect masterfulness. Soon he succeeded in giving me a tremendous hard-on, then made me lie on my back; he began to gaze at it and to meditate upon the extraordinary power of stretching of my prick, saying he had never seen such a big one in a young man of my age, though he had already seen many and many.

When the throbbing tool had got very stiff, he bent his head and started to suck it in the most delightful way. It was more exciting for me than when I was sucked by my sisters, by Miss Jenny or even by Mrs. Barnett. Moreover he drove a finger in my ass-hole and made me come in his mouth; he swallowed all the juice which trickled out of my burning rod, then went at it again and sucked me till the last drop was exhausted. Of course he had grown very much excited in the process, and he said:

—Now it's the younger's turn to be fucked by me.

Dorothy, without wavering, lay down at once on the grass; I led his prick toward her cunt and stroked his ass-hole as he was fucking her. His prick was middle sized, not too long, not too big, but evenly large from beginning to end, the head was not bigger than the rest of it. He advised us to leave it at that for the first time and to go back to the village; by walking, we would arrive where the village is in sight but where we are yet out of ears' reach; there we could sit down and figure up the best way to meet all together again to enjoy the greatest lewdness. We were so young that the utmost caution was advisable:

—I notice that you all like it very much, said he, I'll increase your pleasure as you'll increase mine. You have yet to further your knowledge and I am the one who can teach you all the tricks you don't know yet. There are many various ways of fucking and I know them all. And I am a willing teacher.

We followed him as he wished, we sat down on a rock where our talk was chiefly concerned with our future pleasures; plans were laid, time tables computed, and a rendez-vous was taken for our next fucking-party. We agreed to meet together the next day in the rocks and at the usual time; he would come before us in order to inspect the spot and see if anybody was there who could fall on us by surprise as he had himself. At night he would think about it and see if he could not find a way of meeting us at a place where we could be quite at ease, that is to play together stark naked, and enjoy freely an orgy of the most delightful lewdness.

He showed us where he was living, in a small inn a little out of the village and on the road-side; behind the cow-sheds there was a very tiny house comprising, on the ground-floor, a passage and a drawing-room, and below a bedroom and a dressing-room; the door opened on the hill and there was no communication with the inn except by passing behind the cow-sheds and going around the house to enter the house.

The maid of the inn came every morning and brought his breakfast with tea, eggs and ham and when he had finished she took the tray back, made his room, and so on . . . He dined with the proprietors of the inn, in the dining-room. No window was looking down on his, he was far enough from the village so that nobody could watch him not even the people of the inn; and seen from the beach his lodging was about as sheltered from lookouts as if he had lived in a house secluded of the other ones by a great distance. I have described so scrupulously that dwelling-house because the advantages of its unusual situation led us later on in using it for our fucking sessions.

Our friend's name was De Burnon, Hector de Burnon, and he was a scion of the famous family. He was about thirty years old, very fond of any sport, chiefly fishing. His room was full of fishings implements and he liked the South better because there were several streams where beautiful trouts could be caught, that is if you knew how to fish trout. He wanted to initiate me to the art of fishing; later on I went with him to many fishing parties which often ended by new erotic adventures that I may decide to narrate one day. He was usually living in Paris and our actual acquaintance grew into more intimate relations which I shall narrate in due time.

On the next day we met among the rocks. It was on a Saturday. We found Mr. De Burnon at his post; as we were confident that nobody could fall on us by surprise, we started at once. It was Lilian's turn to assume the first round of watch. Our friend became our leader. He asked me to take my trousers off and Dorothy to pull her dress off and unlace her corset for she was not yet wearing knickers; he made me lie on my back, made Dorothy kneel over my head, instructing her to bend down so that her lovely little cunt was just upon my mouth, her petticoats quite tucked up and her chemise on her shoulders. So I could tickle her clitoris with my tongue and she could lower her buttocks right upon my face so that I could drive my tongue

188

into her cunt and lick her juice when she had unloaded. At the same time, with one hand I could caress her firm and round ass, and I could with the other tickle her ass-hole and so excite her passions in an extraordinary way. I have already said how fond she was of the ass pleasures.

As we were so engaged in, De Burnon started sucking my prick in the most delightful way for he was worthy of the best in the art of sucking a penis. And he outdid all those who had sucked me before and have sucked me ever since. Of course he tried to satisfy me wholly and all the time he tickled my ass-hole with a saliva-coated finger. He made me come in his mouth in the most delightful way as my dear Dorothy inundated mine with her fuming juice.

We remained overwhelmed for some time before recovering gradually. Then, getting up, I wanted to return the compliment by sucking his prick too; but he declined and told me:

—I shall acquaint you with a new enjoyment before we leave, and my strength is not as great as yours, for you are young; now we must content ourselves by watching each other's parts, and mutually stroking our pricks. In a few moments, by pleasant titillations, I shall have both of you fit for a new amorous struggle. Now that's fine. Let me work on you.

He sucked Dorothy as he was stroking my prick and quickly led us up to such an unbridled excitement that we were ready to do anything he might instruct us to do. Again he made me lie on my back, but he put Dorothy over me and he aimed my prick at her narrow little cunt. When it was quite wholly engulfed, what was achieved before she was fully lying on top of me, he asked us to start giving it to each other. For a short time, his face came near my balls and he watched my prick coming and going out, as he drove a finger in Dorothy's ass-hole and another in mine. Then he got up and said:

—Stop a little, dear children, but without taking it out. I am going to give your sister a double-enjoyment's lesson.

Then spitting on his prick and lubricating the little pink orifice of her puckered ass-hole with a lot of spittle, he started driving his prick into it, yet wholly unaware that it was one of her favorite fucking enjoyments and that many were the times when I had given it to her hindways to our mutual delight. He took very much care not to hurt her, going in as slowly as possible, instructing her to push her buttocks backwards and to do as if she wanted to relieve nature, explaining that it would make the insertion easier for him and that she would suffer less. It is easy to understand how happy was Dorothy; she did everything he requested her to do and he succeeded nicely in putting all of his prick inside her, insomuch that his belly was touching Dorothy's buttocks.

Wonderful, my dear, you have undergone it beautifully; I see that you will be a good pupil; now you are going to feel the delightful raptures that can be given by the simultaneous working of two pricks in two adjoining cavities. Now, George, it's your turn to work, as for your sister she has only to keep on the exquisite squeezings she makes now on our two penises before and behind.

So we began the first lesson about double fucking. Dear Dorothy was almost wild with the exquisite sensations that those two pricks suscited in her excited senses. I too was feeling De Burnon's prick rubbing against mine through the tin partition, so thin that since our two peters were pushing on it on each side, it was stretched to such a point that it could be said there was none. Such an excitement led to a quick end. In pleasure excess, Dorothy screamed so loudly that Lilian got frightened and ran towards us to know what had happened.

Her surprise was great when she saw how things stood, but we were too much engrossed in the little enjoyments of lust and lewdness to have little care for any interruption. Dear Dorothy recovered only after a while and she bursted into tears, saying that till then she had not known what pleasure was, she had gone as far as paradise, she wished no other death than to die in such a delirious pleasure.

Thereupon she threw herself into De Burnon's arms and, kissing him with the greatest eagerness, she said:

—Oh! dear man, how I love you for the teaching you gave us of this new way of reaching pleasure peaks; you can always possess me where and when you feel like it, I'll love you as much as I love my very dear brother George.

Then she turned towards me and tenderly kissed me too. She put her dress on and went to keep watch in order to liberate Lilian whose turn it was to be initiated to double fucking.

She dreaded the experience somehow, but, as she had witnessed the voluptuous pangs of pleasure of Dorothy, she would have liked to try if De Burnon's prick had not been that big. As a preliminary drilling, he made Lilian kneel over my head and while he was sucking my prick, he had a full view of the wonderful buttocks of Lilian which promised him a great enjoyment in a very short while; he even asked me to yield her ass to his little finger, so that he was stroking the sister's ass and sucking the brother's prick at the same time, and it was an arrangement that filled him with exquisite pleasure. Lilian was very excited and came plentifully in my mouth, while I did so in the mouth of our friend who let no drop get lost.

When we had taken enough rest, his lascivious caresses and his compliments had quickly excited us again enough to make him see that we were ready to do what he liked. Following a previous pattern, I lay down on my back and Lilian stood on all fours over me, impaling herself on my prick which De Burnon himself led in her wide open cunt. When my big peter was wholly engulfed in her hot and fluttering cunt, she began her "nutcracker" squeezings, a speciality she mastered perfectly; then drawing her to me I held her tight in my arms and glued my lips to hers in a long and voluptuous kiss. Her buttocks were so wonderfully displayed in front of our dear fucking teacher that, enraptured by these charms much more fullgrown than my younger sister's ones, he paid them his first compliments by kissing them lovingly and making his tongue go far inside the little pink orifice, tickling her as swiftly as possible. Then wetting his prick he tried to insert it in her ass hole, but at first he could not succeed and Lilian told him that she did not think he might achieve his tentative.

—With patience and perseverance, my dear girl, he said, I should put it in a rat; we are going to try another way; it is that monstruous prick in your cunt which bars me from the path of the secret temple's delightful pleasures. Will you withdraw for a while, George?

I got my peter out of her cunt; then he dived at once up to the balls into the gaping cunt where he applied frenzied thrusts to excite her and to make her forget her dread, for, as he told us later, the chief difficulty came from the unintentional resistance of Lilian who was tightening her ass-hole instead of opening it. When he thought she was enough excited and she could suppose that he was going to fuck her cunt good and square and only to fuck it, he withdrew abruptly the two fingers he had plunged in her behind, put his prick inside instead, and before Lilian could understand what was happening to her, he had already entered more than halfway her tight anal tunnel.

She uttered a smothered scream, but with her hips tightly held by our friend and her waist tightly grasped by me (for I had guessed what might happened) she could not escape nor reject him, which had been her first impulse. Then he said:

—I'm going to keep quiet, and in a while the pain you feel now will be all over.

He stopped for two or three minutes during which I kept stroking her clitoris now fully erect with the head of my rod. Then when I noticed her movements that her passions were excited again, I slipped it rather easily in the gaping cunt. Mr. De Burnon availed himself of the opportunity to consolidate his advantages in his attack-point up to the highest degree. Lilian sighed again and said she was suffocating. Nevertheless with some more patience and thanks to the slowness of our movements, we led progressively her to an extraordinary excitement and the three of us came madly in a frenzy of unutterable bliss. She remained shivering and exhausted between us for more than a quarter of an hour.

I was already up and about to begin again, but De Burnon reversed to an erect position and withdrew his limp prick from the narrow nook where it had felt so exquisite enjoyments; he told us we ought to be satisfied with that for today, chiefly because he had made up a plan in his mind for the next day and we would need all our strength.

So when we happened to be in sight of the village, but not near enough to be heard, so as not to attract any suspicion by going too far, De Burnon informed us that in the afternoon, we would go to his little house instead of meeting amid the rocks and there we might be stark naked and celebrate a great licentious revel of delightful fucking and masturbation as well. We approved heartily of his idea and after chatting some more we parted. He had given us an appointment for the next day on the beach, but in the opposite direction, with the purpose of meeting near his house, from the side where we could not be seen arriving.

The next day after lunch we left at our usual time to take our daily walk; but after we had gone beyond the village limits and let most of people come in church to hear divine service, we turned towards De Burnon's door. He had seen us coming and opened the door himself before we had knocked. He led us at once to his upstairs bedroom and we did not lose a minute to be stark naked; after a preliminary admiration of our two lassies whose voluptuous shapes were really moulded, we lay down on the bed. Dorothy and I sucked each other, each one of course inserting a finger in the other's ass-hole. Lilian and De Burnon followed our example, for naturally he liked her better because she had a more full-grown ass. After all of us had delightfully unloaded, after many kisses and mutual caresses, we made the girls take all the possible postures, until we were ready to do something better than merely sucking each other. De Burnon as usual was our appointed leader. He ordered Lilian to lie down on her back, Dorothy stretched herself on top of her in the opposite direction, so that she could suck her cunt and insert her finger in her ass-hole while Lilian could with one hand stroke her clitoris and with the other play with my balls. De Burnon led my prick in Dorothy's nice little cunt; when we were all rightly in position and after he had tickled my ass-hole with two fingers, he said:

—Now, I am going to initiate George to the delights to be at the same time operator and operated.

So saying, he wetted his screw and my ass-hole with his spittle and very slowly proceeded to insert his prick in it.

I have already described his prick; its head was not very big, so that its first part was easily inserted, but when the remnant too was forcibly pushed in I felt a strange and funny sensation as if I was quartered, so I had to ask him to stop for a while. He was too much experienced about it not to understand my feelings, and knew very well that this pain would soon vanish if he was keeping motionless. So he stopped till I had told him he could resume his efforts; he withdrew, and again wetting his prick's remnant with spittle, gently but firmly and slowly he inserted it in me up to the end, as far as allowed him his belly and my buttocks which were touching each other. Keeping motionless for a while he waited until he felt, by my prick's flutterings which were echoed by the squeezings of my ass-hole, that I had reached the due excitement degree, and he began slow back and forth motions of which, along with the nice flutterings of Dorothy's cunt, excited by the titillations exercised on her clitoris by Lilian's finger and my big prick,—set my passions on fire, and at once we began some movements as quick as savage. I could not have fancied anything which could give me such a delightful enjoyment as the one produced on my erotic nerves by that double working. I was sighing, I was shivering in a violent agony of pleasure, and when I reached the great and voluptuous final crisis time, I shouted literally like a fool, for which we laughed very much together later on, when our senses were less excited. We came all together at the same time and fell down all in an inert heap on poor Lilian. We were astonished to see that she could bear all of us but she had been so excited by this sight that she had not suffered from our weight. Then we got up and after we had refreshed a bit, we strengthened our forces with wine and cakes which De Burnon had thought of supplying us with. He did not allow us to fuck again for a while, we began to play around in the room, which much diverted us and nothing was heard but slaps ringing on our buttocks and our wild laughs, till our two pricks, rising hard and stiff, pointed out that we were ready for new fights.

This time Dorothy lay down on her back and Lilian sucked her; De Burnon fucked her ass and I tried to do the same but without success for I was too big for her ass-hole which was really very little for a man.

He would have much appreciated it had I succeeded, but in spite of all striving for, I could not surmount physical hindrances. Therefore, inverting our positions, Lilian lay over me with my prick in her cunt, thus offering her anus to

De Burnon who engulfed his prick in it without great difficulty.

Dorothy was standing up, her two legs wide apart, one on each side of my body and Lilian's, and was offering her cunt to the mouth of De Burnon who was sucking her with a mad frenzy while he was driving his finger into her behind. Erotic fury raged with an unbridled frenzy for a long enough time till our movements getting quicker and quicker we all fell in a thorough exhaustion of satisfied lust after we had plentifully drenched our partners with foaming spunk.

We remained lying still embraced in one another's arms. By recovering we refreshed again with some wine and cakes and as our passions could not be as quickly excited as our partners' ones, we started sucking them and did not allow them the least touch on our pricks. We began again our frolics around the room; then Lilian placed herself under and Dorothy over her; she requested especially that I fuck her cunt this time, because she said it had not to be quite forgotten. As previously, De Burnon took my behind, and pleasure was so great that he went in with very much ease, so we made our erotic pleasure last as long as possible, till at last we died in agony of voluptuous and heavenly raptures.

We ordered again a general fucking before we left. Dorothy's cunt was fucked again by her devoted brother and her ass by De Burnon. She declared she liked this arrangement better than any other one for my prick filled up her cunt so exactly that it made her tighten her ass-hole in the place where De Burnon's prick, though smaller than mine, worked just as mine when I fucked her ass and Lilian plunged her fingers into her cunt.

We went through this new fucking round with more delight and lust than before. Dorothy was quite hysteric, so violent was her pleasure and we fell down exhausted over poor Lilian, and we remained a long time motionless, crushed in one another's embrace. So was closed, for that day, our most voluptuous revel. We washed and dressed. We parted after exchanging kisses, with promises to reenact as often as possible those delightful plays and indeed we often carried them out again going now and then to the rocks in order to get a change and not to draw attention to us by coming too often to his nice and hospitable little house.

Our six weeks elapsed so quickly that we could hardly realize how we had spent our time. One morning mummy informed us that we should leave the day after the morrow. Our disappointment was great, but we could do nothing. We met on that day amid the rocks and we were all sad and tearful any time we happened to think of our imminent parting from our dear friend, of whom the three of us had become so very fond of. We were not up to our usual level that day, but we made up our mind to perform on the next day, at his little house, an extraordinary orgy, as a farewell meeting. The three of us arrived at the appointed time and we put forth all the art which we were able of to increase our enjoyments. De Burnon and I had ejaculated at least six or seven times each; but the lassies, more easily excitable, had at least nine or ten juicy orgasms till, at last, exhausted and utterly crushed with the violence of our orgiastic fury, we dressed and parted, hoping sincerely that we should meet again later. My sisters wept as we parted from our dear friend to whom we owed so many delightful and licentious revels. We exchanged addresses and he promised to go and make a fishing party in our neighbourhood where he hoped he could find a way to meet us and reenact our voluptuous lovematches from which we had already derived so many lustful delights; at the end, we tore ourselves away from his caresses. We shall see later how as I happened to come to Paris, it was in that town, in his own lodging, that we were able to revive those lovely and voluptuous plays and to practise the dear Venus' art at his best.

CHAPTER VI

We came back home, and mummy inserted a new advertisement in the paper for a governess, mentioning expressly that she ought at least to be thirty and very experienced in teaching. There were many answers; but a young girl wanted to see mummy and her children in order to know if she would accept the post; she was sending along very elogious certificates.

Mummy was surprised by the style of the letter and by the request to see her pupils before reaching a final agreement. Therefore she wrote to Miss Imogen to come and spend three days with us and if her visit proved successful on both sides, she was sure that things could be managed to their mutual satisfaction.

Consequently Miss Imogen arrived at the appointed day and hour. In our opinion, she was already almost an old maid, looking rather over thirty than less, a large girl, a little big but not too fat, with wide shoulders, well-shaped hips, well-parted but not too prominent breasts. Her hair was coal-black and so were her shining eyes but with a serious expression, enforced yet by black and thick eyebrows that joined over the bridge of her nose. Moreover she had a very visible moustache of light but very black fuzz, and on the back of her head little curled hair covered her nape and vanished in her dress the collar of which was very old-fashionedly high and stiff.

She always wore very long sleeves and she never showed her arms naked; later on I discovered the reason; her arms were covered with thick and black hairs; so she was ashamed to show them though they were wonderfully well-shaped; her mouth was great and sensual but was revealing a great firmness of temper too. You could not say she was really attractive, but there was in her whole body something that made you say she truly was a beautiful woman. As for us, at the beginning, we noticed nothing but her firm temper and at once we were frightened when we realized she was going to become our governess, for we felt that not only we were going to have somebody who would direct us but we foresaw that she would be stern and would hardly let us have a good time. Youth is often a better physiognomist than most people usually think. We shall see later if our opinion was right or wrong: it suffices to know that three days after her arrival she looked perfectly satisfied with the offered post and mummy was pleased with her too. We did not know at once, but we heard later that she had set as a "sine qua non" condition that she could use the rod freely when she would think it necessary.

She made Mummy understand that our last governess had not been severe enough with us, that it was necessary to exercise a sterner discipline with which she had got excellent results from her own experience. Mummy who had thought us very unsteady during those two last months wholly agreed with her and allowed her to do anything she might think necessary, in the field of disciplinary measures, as well with her daughters as with her son.

All was thus settled and Miss Imogen asked for a week to bring her preparations to an end before she came and lived definitively at home.

During that week we were quite free, for mummy thought when Miss Imogen would be there we should be kept more severely and she let us do what we chose to do. Of course we availed ourselves of the opportunity and attempted by all means to forget the deprival of our dear and priceless friend De Burnon. Not only did we use the summer-pavilion in the daytime, but each night I went stealthily to my sisters' bedroom where we attempted to reenact the voluptuous and lewd games that we had lately enjoyed so much on the seashore.

Of course the week flew much too quickly, and, at the appointed day, mummy went to the town in order to meet Miss Imogen who was arriving by coach. My two sisters went with her for they always needed one thing or another and since what with Miss Imogen and her luggage the carriage would have been filled up, they left me at home alone, and it was a happy circumstance as we are going to see.

I was a little worried to stay alone; but how true is the proverb: "Man proposes and God disposes". If my sisters had been there I should have lost an unexpected and very delightful happiness. I had gone to the summer-pavilion in a kind of despair for I had lost the opportunity of fucking my sisters again before the arrival of our feared governess.

I was looking absent-mindedly out of the window when I thought I saw a lady, waving her hand, who was coming along the path which led to the pavilion where I was hidden. At once I recognized Mrs. Bank. Running to the gate, opening the door, welcoming her, were the matter of a mere instant. I begged her to get out from her carriage and to come to the house by the circular walk around the park; her coachman would bring the carriage in the stable where he would wait orders. She immediately agreed with my proposal. I did not tell her a word about the absence of every member of the household until we had arrived together to the pavilion. We came in and I closed the door. Without saying a word. I took her by the waist, and pushing her on the sofa I quickly unbuttoned my trousers, tucked up her petticoats and pushed my hard and stiff prick against her belly before she could realize what my intentions really were.

—My dear George. she cried out, what are you doing? We are going to be discovered and I shall be dishonoured.

—Oh! no, my dear Mrs. Bank, my eternally beloved, everybody is in town and we have nothing to fear.

She was loving me too much for displaying very long a false resistance; on the contrary, she helped me with all her usual science and we soon came wildly and streams of fuming spunk were the proof of the voluptuous enjoyments of our satisfied desires. I did not want to lose my position, but kissing her with passion, I pushed my tongue in her mouth in order to keep her from rebuking me.

The pleasure of encountering her after so long a parting which had lasted for more than two months, excited my passions at the highest degree, and I had no time to relax, I began a second fucking session though with a greater moderation and being very careful to make her share all the heavenly pleasures I was feeling myself. She enjoyed it uncommonly and, no more afraid of surprise, as I had informed her that my whole family was out, she gave herself up to the eagerness of her loving inclinations. She enjoyed immensely that delightful fucking and unloaded at the very time I did, uttering wild screams of gratified passion. Then I got my prick out of her cunt; she kissed me tenderly and said to me that I was always as wild and as rascally clever as before, but she was loving me so much that she could not refuse me anything which I might want; she made me sit down close to her for a good talk about old time.

—No, said I, on the contrary let us speak about you. I have not seen you since your wedding-day and I wish to know everything that happened on that day and later. I was afraid that your husband would have noticed our caresses and would not have found you such as he had thought.

—You are a funny boy, my dear George, and manlier than many other men even ten years older than you. Who would think that such ideas could roll in so young a head. Well, my dear beloved, I was very anxious too about that, and I had settled for my wedding to take place on the day where I thought I should have my periods, but I was deceived about it; nothing happened and I had to get out of as well as I could. I closed my thighs tightly, I covered with my hand this part of my body and I managed to make my sex as inaccessible as I could. I pressed hard on his toll with my fingers when he tried to force his way through, and all at once I screamed as if I was suffering very much, and while he pushed violently forward I let him enter fully with one stroke.

An experienced husband is often relying on his own imagination. He was sure that he was the first to possess me, but, oh! my beloved George, I noticed I was already pregnant, and you, dear lover, you are the father of the child whom I'm bearing in my womb.

—What! I! I! the father of a child? Oh! dear Mrs. Bank, oh! say it again.

—It is only the truth, my dear George, and I must say that it is only by thinking that I had been the first to possess you as you had been the first to possess me that I have found enough courage to bring my husband a child who is not his own.

—My child! my child!

I shouted and I danced and I jumped with joy in thinking that I could be the father of a child. It must be said that it made me feel manlier and I was very proud of it. I rushed towards poor Mrs. Bank, took her in my arms, kissed her with fury, and pushing her down on the sofa, I said:

—I must see how this little angel behaves in his jail.

I tucked up her petticoats, uncovering her magnificent belly of which the already noticeable roundness proved she had swallowed my sperm very efficiently through that part, though I remembered the eagerness of her mouth in that respect. Her cunt was more prominent too. I bent down to kiss her nice slit that I licked a bit, then I sucked her till she screamed to me to fuck her with my big prick and we achieved one of the most delightful strokes. The thought of baptizing my baby with my own semen stimulated my lubricity.

—George, my love, get up; remember you may hurt the dear little being by too great an excess, please, get up.

At once I got up but I squeezed her very tenderly upon my heart. She complained of feeling a little exhausted and we turned to the house in order to refresh her with some wine. Thinking of my fatherhood, I walked as proudly as a peacock, for I was no more a child. I did not know if I stood on my feet or on my head and I behaved foolishly. Dear Mrs. Bank had to bring me to reason so that I could behave decently in front of the servants. She rested about half an hour and was going to order her carriage to come and take her to the gate, when I begged her to send it waiting for her in the path below the summer-pavilion, for so I should have the pleasure of staying longer with her. She smiled and slapped my cheek lightly, as if she wanted to say: "I understand you, my little rascal" but she did what I was asking her, and we crossed the garden up to the pavilion where we arrived before the horse was harnessed. I did not lose any time, but embracing Mrs. Bank I wanted to make her on the sofa.

—No, no my dear Georgie, my dress would be too much rumpled and we should not have time to get up, were we discovered. I am going to kneel on a cushion and you will place yourself behind me; I shall lead your screw myself and you know I like that position better for thus you go in much farther and I enjoy it much more than in any other way.

She knelt and pulled her skirts over her

shoulders, showing her magnificent buttocks which, since she was pregnant, had still grown much fatter and rounder. At first I kissed them greedily, then I pushed my prick against them. Mrs. Bank slipped her hand between her legs, seized it and led it into her juicy and greedy cunt where it was at once engulfed up to the hairs.

—Slowly, darling George, she cried, remember there is our baby and you must not be too violent.

Those words somehow quieted my furious attack I had put a hand on each hip and while I was slowly working my way in her cunt, I pulled her beautiful buttocks toward me. I was standing very straight in order to enjoy the voluptuous sight the movements of her behind offered me.

—Put your hand over me, my dear George, and tickle my clitoris.

I did as she wished for a minute, then I whispered to her:

—It's truly very voluptuous to see you move your behind, so frig your clitoris yourself and let me enjoy that delightful sight.

—Then, very well, darling.

And I felt her stroking herself with fury; this allowed me to push at first one, then two fingers, into her ass-hole. When I was aware she happened to be very much excited, I suddenly drew my prick out and substituted it for my fingers. She was so excited that she could not offer any resistance, besides my movement had been quick and I pushed my rod in as far as

I could go, but not too fiercely. She resisted somewhat and called me a nasty pig, but I was holding her too strongly by the hips to allow her to shake me out, had she wanted it, which I doubted. I asked her to let me go on that way, for I had never forgotten the delights she had made me feel the day before her wedding. She did not answer but I felt she was stroking herself with a greater fury; and by the nervous flutterings of her anal sphincter, I was soon convinced that nothing could please her more than my remaining where I was and working in it; it was indeed delightful. We should have come with enjoyment-screams, but we were restrained by caution, for, at that time, the carriage must have been already waiting for her on the road which was only a few yards away from the pavilion.

My lovely mistress looked like she did not wish to let me go out of her ass; she was squeezing my prick very tightly, pressing it now and then with convulsive motions and exciting it so much that soon she felt it stiffen again in her ass.

She rose to stand and so drove me out by this movement. Then she turned and wound her arms around my neck; and she kissed me tenderly for I had given her so delightful love tokens.

—But I must leave, my darling George, and I hope that we shall again find out again some good opportunities to feel so exquisite enjoyments. Give my best regards to your mother and to your sisters and tell them I shall come soon and call on everybody.

I saw her get into her carriage and looked after her as far as the road turned. I came back to the pavilion and kissed the spot where her adorable body had lain. My soul was full of love for her and I was proud of having been man enough to make her pregnant. I walked to and fro in the room, and if anybody had seen me he could have thought I was becoming crazy.

Mummy, my sisters and our new governess came back at tea-time. I related them Mrs. Bank's visit, how sorry she was for missing them and her promise that she would soon come back to see them. Mummy said to me she hoped I had been very attentive to her. I answered that I had done all my possible, and I had offered her some wine and cakes for she did not feel well, and I thought the ride had tired her.

It may be supposed that, after the impression our new governess had made over us, we were for some time very studious. As a matter of fact, her way of teaching was very much higher than our previous governesses'. She was endowed with the gift of making us interested by what she was teaching us, and during two months we were so careful and made so marked progress that she could not keep herself from paying high compliments to us one day when mummy was in our study.

—It was a right shrewdness, for, by youth's natural unconcern, we thought we were so learned that we became less careful. So she gave us a light rein for some time without saying anything, very likely on account of our previous good behaviour. But one day Dorothy showed some stubbornness about a somewhat rough reproof miss Imogen had addressed her.

—Well! Since you think you make have your own ways, dont you? We are going to see about that.

She taught us as usual till four o'clock, then she made Dorothy stay with her, dismissing me with Lilian. She locked the door on Dorothy and went out, likely in order to fetch and rod. Soon she came back, and she shut herself in with Dorothy whose poor behind she whipped strongly. She dismissed her when it was over, and Dorothy joined us and cried plentifully from the sufferings she was feeling.

We laid her on the sofa and turned her petticoats up over her head in order to cool her behind which was burning, as she said, as if it was covered with red hot coals. I kissed these dear wholly reddened buttocks, covered with wales that made them looked like a piece of raw beef, although no blood had come. We fanned her with our pocket handkerchiefs and it gave her a delightful relief.

After a few minutes, she began squirming her behind, looking very excited and cried out:

—Darling George, stuff your prick in my cunt, will you, for I'm beginning to want to be fucked tremendously.

I did not ask for any more encouragement to start working on her because the very sight of her naked ass had made my prick stiffened as hard as iron.

She stood on all fours, offering me her cunt's entrance and telling me it was there she wanted at once to feel my prick. I drove it into her with one stroke up to the balls, for she was as wet as if she had already unloaded, which was about sure. After I had thrust my prick in and out of her cunt a few times, she ejaculated again, uttering screams of joy and squeezing my prick to such a point that she almost hurt me. She hardly stopped a moment and cried out:

—Push, dear Georgie, put it in all the way. It does not matter if it hurts, I am burning with desires.

She wriggled her behind most effectively and in the most delightful and lewd way, and when she felt my prick swell up and stiffen as well as the usual liquid effect of love-crisis, she received my flood of semen and she spurted out so much spunk that she sluiced my balls and hairs. She was holding me tightly enfolded and she would not let me withdraw at all before I had unloaded four times and she at least seven times. Then she got up and her nerves had quite nicely relaxed from the repeated doses of hot fucking juice that I had injected in her womb. She proclaimed that never, since she had begun to fuck, had she felt such desires and a more ravishing enjoyment in gratifying them, and that she would willingly suffer a dozen spankings in order to feel again such a ravishment.

—I am sure, she said, that it is the effect of

the beating with the rod, for I had never, till then, felt such a feeling.

All the while, Lilian had stayed as a mere onlooker and had been happy to see the erotic fury of her sister and how I had been of use to relieve her. It must be said that we had fucked together quite nicely while poor Dorothy got spanked, and after that I had wonderfully sucked her until Dorothy had arrived and I had turned my attention to her poor suffering buttocks.

Miss Imogen had withdrawn to her room, and when she joined us again after the end of our usual play-time, she was still very red in the face and looked somehow haggard. As it may be supposed, the three of us were as guarded as possible and quiet and submissive. There was a thing which pleased greatly Miss Imogen. When it was Dorothy's turn to recite her lesson, she impulsively surrounded the neck of Miss Imogen with her arms and whispered her letting her tears run on her cheeks:

—Please, dear Miss Imogen, forgive me and let me kiss you for I like you very tenderly.

There was in the eyes of Miss Imogen a flash of pleasure. She grasped Dorothy's waist with her arms and kissed her fully on the lips. The kiss was obviously an amourous one, and it lasted so long that I thought it would never end. We noticed that Miss Imogen had reddened very much. In the end, she dismissed Dorothy, saying to her that she was a kind and dear little girl whom she could not help herself to love very much.

—Go and sit down, you are too disturbed now to recite your lesson. Send me Lilian.

So she came back to her seat, but I could not keep myself from noticing in her countenance an expression of erotic desires. When later on we were alone together, she told me that when the governess had kissed her, she had felt Miss Imogen's tongue go in her mouth and tickle her in the most delightful and exciting way, and she believed that if they had been alone, they would had embraced in a quite different way and would have left nature have her ways. This made me think that Miss Imogen had given the rod.

During all the next week, Dorothy thought only of the uncommon excitement that the spanking had given her and the utmost enjoyment she had felt by gratifying her lascivious desires.

We could not be by ourselves every day, for very often Miss Imogen was going along with us and joining in our young children's plays. Dorothy was keeping on thinking of the great pleasure that the rod had got her when the spanking was over, and she inflamed so much Lilian's mind, that the latter was in her turn eager to be spanked, and hoping for it to be as cruel as possible. Under such conditions, it was easy to bring the punishment upon oneself; she had only not to do her work, not to learn her lessons, and she was sure to would get what she was asking for. Indeed that was the very pattern she followed, and it led to what she hoped so wildly for. When she had got her spanking, she ran to the pavilion and, without any preliminary, entreated me to fuck her at once, and then everything happened exactly as when Dorothy had when been whipped; however Lilian did not throw herself into Miss Imogen's arms, the way Dorothy had.

Like the previous time, Miss Imogen had withdrawn to her room after she had given chastisement, and later on she went downstairs again with a face quite red and shining eyes. And so I was convinced that she had excited herself very much by the whipping process and I began to believe that, with such passions, if I could excite her in any way, I should get what I wished.

When those libertine thoughts had entered my mind, the lust of possessing her made me see her with every spell of beauty and I became very eager and anxious to possess her. The more I looked at her and wondered at the magnificent proportions of her fully-developed shapes, the more I was impelled to fuck her, and my lust grew fiercer and fiercer.

About that time, Miss Imogen, who had become mummy's great favourite, get the privilege to use the guest-room for her bed-room, and she would give it up if any guest happened to come. Of course this last circumstance made me want more eagerly to get into her good graces, seeing that then it would be easier for us to spend a night together.

I resolved to watch her as she would go to

bed and to try to have a look at her naked forms. Consequently I took off the crumb-bow I had put to dissimulate the hole I had bored in the door of my own room in order to see Mr. Barnett give it to his wife, which was my beloved first and unforgettable mistress. I remained awake until she went up to bed. I watched her undressing, but I could only see her naked breasts above her chemise. As I have already said, they were not big, but well-parted. I saw that her neck-bones were not appearing, which is a great beauty in a woman. She had obviously quite undressed to use the bidet, but the length of the crack did not allow me to see the corner of the room where she had used it. The next day I bored a larger hole, and I was rewarded on the following night the most delightful beholdings.

It may be supposed that I did not let myself be caught by sleep, and I was at my post as soon as I heard her entering her room. I knelt at once, my eye riveted on the hole, and I saw her slip her day-shirt off, without any wavering. Then she prepared her beautiful hair for the night, brushing them as far as her arm could stretch; after she had brushed extensively and combed very carefully, she rolled them in a big pack behind her head, then she washed her hands and pulled the bidet that she filled with water. She was standing in front of the dressing-table, with two candles on each side, so that I could look as much as I wanted at her belly uncommonly covered with hairs as black as coal where curls were shining as if they had been smooted. Now I am old, but I have never seen a woman with as much hairs as Miss Imogen. Her crack was fully covered with thick moss and they went down along her thighs at least several inches, and passing between her thighs, went on and were lost in the hole of her ass where they ended into two magnificent tufts as thick and even thicker than those other women had on their Venus' mount.

She had equally a wonderful mane of little curls-row that were running up all along her belly and stretching as far as between her two breasts, to say nothing of the hair that covered her arms, her legs and her thighs as well. I had never seen a so delightfully hairy woman, and she was quite such as her hairyness might wholly imply, that is to say passionate and lewd at the highest degree, when she trusted her partner enough to surrender herself to her passions. Of course, I am now describing things, I got to know in my future experiences, for at that time I was only dazzled by the uncommon luxuriance and extent of that adornment. I mean of the superb mane of hair which covered her head so beautifully that I have never seen such an uncommon headdress in any other woman. I was bewildered with astonishment and admiration. She washed her hairy cunt and all the surrounding parts, wiped herself long with the utmost care slipped into her nightgown, blew the light out and of course went to bed. I went to lay in me too but I tossed up and turned over in my bed; at last I fell asleep but I spent a restless night, dreaming of that wonderful cunt covered with. hairs and fancying myself inserting my big friendly peter in it. My excitement was so great that I had the first wet dream I had ever had. It is useful to say that I was dreaming at that time about fucking that marvellous cunt and coming in it in a flood of burning semen.

On the morning, after such a night, I was not only very absent-minded, but I was truly so weary that I could not do my work.

Of course Miss Imogen noticed it, and knowing not the reason, she ascribed it to laziness and to a daring from me against her authority. She spoke to me very severely and earnestly and said me that if I did not behave well the next day, she ought to punish me very rigorously.

—I hope that your behaviour will be different to-morrow, otherwise you will compel me to do what I should not want to do.

It rained very much during the afternoon, and we ought to play in the house. While going to bed I resolved to look again at Miss Imogen, but the need of rest seized me and I fell deep asleep as soon as I was in bed, only waking up in the middle of the night. I got up, looked through the hole, but all was black and really I could not see anything; I was hearing Miss Imogen breathing heavily. I thought I could easily slip to my sisters' bedroom, for they were alone since Miss Imogen had settled in the guest-room where now she was deeply sleeping. Therefore, opening the door softly I slipped in the passage, and reached the bedroom of my sisters; I awoke them gently, and jumped between them both, for their great gladness and contentment.

We began at once by a sucking-party, I caught hold of the cunt of Lilian who was sucking Dorothy who had put her cunt over her mouth and at the same time had her behind tickled by Lilian's finger, while I had just before me the magnificent sight of all those workings. As soon as Lilian had unloaded, I made Dorothy lie on her back, her head turned towards the foot of the bed, Lilian knelt above her in the opposite direction, thus offering fully her lovely behind which was growing every day more luscious. I sank into her cunt, pushing my middle-finger in her tight little pink ass-hole, and Dorothy was doing as much for me and was rubbing with her thumb the clitoris of Lilian, who, fucked herself and masturbated all the while, busied herself with sucking Dorothy, all the while shoving two fingers in her ass-hole. For Dorothy had pointed out that with only one finger it was as if she was feeling nothing.

As long as possible we kept those delightful proceedings going on, until our excitement prevented us to go on much longer in the tempestuous fight of the lustful fury of our sensations, and we unloaded all together with such a lewd and ravishing bliss that we remained exhausted for some time. Then we had a delightful fawning, each of my sisters having one my prick and the other after my balls.

When we were ready to begin again, my sisters went back to her previous posture, but Lilian under and Dorothy over her, and I fucked the latter. Lilian was sucked by Dorothy who all the time was tickling her ass-hole, while she was busied with Dorothy's clitoris and my own ass-hole. Dorothy was much more excited and lewder than any of us, so she quickly and plentifully unloaded on my ravished prick which hugely enjoyed the hot bath provided by the sticky liquid with which it was inundated. I made some back and forth movements so as to wet it fully everywhere, and drawing my two fingers out of her ravishing behind which I wetted with spittle, I pulled my prick out of her cunt, and, at her great contentment, I lodged it in her greedy and so exquisitely delightful asshole, now keeping motionless, in order not to unload before Dorothy was about to do the same. I was feeling with pleasure her body's delightful flutterings, which at the end became so exciting that I put a hand under her belly, moved the finger of Lilian and stroked her clitoris myself, while Lilian pushed two fingers in her cunt. We quickly arrived at the unloading and we fell down exhausted in the raptured trances of our gratified lewdness. As day-light was beginning to peep, I tore myself away from their tender and lovely caresses, returned to my room safe and slept soundly till very late in the morning.

My orgy with my sisters had so much satisfied my amourous passions that I was beginning to be almost afraid of the sternness which Miss Imogen would make use of if should fall into her hands. Therefore I was very careful on that day and she was satisfied with me; as the weather was very fine, she went and took a walk in the garden while we were innocently entertaining ourselves. On that night I kept awake and could again enjoy the delightful sight of the so uncommonly hairy cunt of Miss Imogen; all the lower part of her body was as black as a chimney-sweep's one. That sight awakened all my erotic fury. I felt I ought to possess her and I was decided to run the risk of the most severe punishment from the rod. I do not know how, but I got so far that I fancied that nature had only grown such an abundance of hair in the very spots where it had implanted too the hotest and more amorous passions. I resolved to get to a definitive solution as early as to-morrow, and wanting to keep all my strength for that, I went at once to bed and did not try to go for a love call on my sister's.

The next day, Miss Imogen could get noting out of me and she advised me very severely that if my behaviour was not better on the afternoon, she would punish me with a right spanking. As I had made up my mind, I did not change my lazyness and I was more disobedient than ever; Miss Imogen was very angry. At four o'clock she ordered me to stay and dismissed my sisters. Then she locked the door, brought out of her desk a formidable rod and made me come near her; I came, truly a little frightened, for she looked very furious and resolute. I went near her.

222

—Now, George, she said, your behaviour, during these last two or three days, has been such that cant accept it; your mother has given me full powers to punish you very severely when you would deserve it; you are old enough and I hoped that never would you compel me to get so angry as being obliged to punish you so, but I am sorry to see you have betrayed my hopes. Now I am going to punish you, and you are going to submit to it willingly, else I shall punish you again more severely. Unbutton your trousers and let them down.

I saw I had to submit, but at that time I was so afraid of her that my prick was not rising up at all.

While I was undoing my trousers, I noticed that Miss Imogen had carefully tucked up her under petticoats and had sat with the obvious purpose of whipping me by putting me across her knees. When both of us were ready, she told me to bring a little footstool near her and ordered me to kneel upon it; wanting to make me bend down on my knees, she passed an arm round my body in order to hold me lying on her knees, then uncovering my behind and seizing the rod which was near her, she raised her arm and gave me so violent a cut with it, that not only did I shudder back but I uttered a loud pain-shriek. Cuts followed one another, bringing about me at first a great suffering which made me utter again some pain shrieks; then as the hurtful cuts succeeded each other, it seemed that my sufferings were ceasing, and at the end, I was hardly feeling them. At that time I felt titillations and a great excitement which led my prick to his wholly strength. Then I started pushing it against the thighs of Miss Imogen and wriggling my body in such a way that I was about to fall from her knees. In order to avoid that, she passed her left hand round my body, led her hand under my belly and apparently by accident, against my prick which she grasped; I felt she was running her fingers over it from top to base likely to measure its size and length, going on showering cuts like hell on my behind, one after another. As she was holding my prick squeezed in her hand I was pretending to want to avoid the cuts, but as a matter of fact I made my prick coming and going in her hand with the greatest energy! which led quickly to the delightful crisis, and I spurted in her hand a plentiful flow of spunk and screamed with voluptly; I almost fainted right on her thighs instead of slipping to the ground, I was pretending to be fully sense less! She believed it and began to stroke my prick and even to masturbate it a bit, squeezing me against her body, and I felt a shiver running along her body. I am sure she was at the highest degree of happiness and she had just unloaded. I let her better for a while, then I was pretending to recover myself, but with very dim thoughts; I cried out:

—Oh! what has happened? I was in Paradise!

Then getting up and seeming only now to recognize Miss Imogen, I threw my arms round her neck, saying:

—Dear Miss Imogen, whip me again if I

must feel such ecstasies as I have never felt up to that day.

Her face flared up and her eyes shone with the fire of the most voluptuous passion. My prick had lost nothing of its stiffness after unloading, and moved forward stiffer than ever.

—Why, George, up to now I thought were a child, but, on the contrary, you are quite a man, with such a big thing.

Her hand had seized it again with a very obvious contentment.

—Oh! I cried out, keep on holding it, that pleases me so much.

—Has anybody held it in such a way?

—No, I had never felt such a thing before.

—But, don't you know what is the use of it?

—Oh yes! it's used to piss.

She laughed and asked me if it was often in that state of stiffness.

—Every morning when I wake up it is in that state, and that hurts me till I have pissed.

—And has not anybody ever taught you what other use it might be of?

—No, what may be the other use of it?

—Oh! dear and innocent child, if I could trust you, I would teach you a secret that this dear thing would be happy to know. But may I trust you?

—Oh! assuredly, dear Miss Imogen, I know what you want now: to renew the delightful sensations that you made me feel close on some minutes ago. Oh! do, do, do it again, it was really too good for me and I shall never tell anybody, as long as you will do it for me.

225

—Well! George, I do trust you; do you know that women are not like you?

—Yes, when I slept in mummy's bedroom, I often noticed she pissed through a big hole and she had no little tail to get a leak with.

—My dear and innocent George, that big hole is made to be filled up by this dear thing which is fluttering hot in my hand, and if you swear never to tell anyone, I shall teach you how it must be done.

Of course my protestations about the secret were very earnest.

—Then please, my dear child, look at what I have between my thighs.

She lay down on the lounge, tucked up her petticoats and offered my delighted eyes the wonderful forest covering her crotch. Opening her thighs, I saw her little pink lips which made a lovely contrast with the black hairs that grew with an uncommon plentiness all about the great lips and ran at least five or six inches down each inner thigh. But at that time I was chiefly amazed and all my attention engrossed by the sight of a long red clitoris that was coming out of the upper part of her cunt; it was as long and as big as the middle finger of a man. Seeing that, I was on the point of betraying myself, but luckily I could keep on my innocent and seemingly unknowing air by saying:

—You have a little tail to piss with too?

She burst out laughing and answered:

—It is not like yours. Give me yours and I'll kiss it.

She stroked it for one or two minutes and

could not help bringing it to her mouth and sucking it.

—Oh! what a pleasure! I'm going to die!

—Not yet, dear child: kneel there and I'm going to teach you the secret of real pleasure.

But before she could do anything, I sank my head between her thighs and said:

—This little friend too must taste the same pleasure you had just given me.

In a moment's notice the whole delightful piece was in my mouth and I was sucking it with fury. Her haunches' wrigglings and her loins' up and down motions showed me how far I was exciting her; indeed, I led to the crisis during which she was holding my head tightly squeezed against her cunt, pressing it between her magnificent thighs, overflowing my mouth and breast with a true torrent of juice. One minute later, she seized me by the arms and brought me top of her, lying on her belly; then slipping her hand between us, she caught hold of my prick that she led into her burning and steaming cunt. She put her hands on my buttocks and drove me in up to the hairs, beginning a backward and forward movement that she told me I ought reciprocate in order to meet her thrusts, which in a very short time led to a delightful unloading from me. The thought she was giving me my first fucking lesson and that she was the first to possess me seemed to excite her at the utmost degree, and she unloaded so plentifully (as I myself did), that she overflew my thighs everywhere with it. During her enjoyment-trance she was so strongly squeezing my prick in her cunt, that she hurt me. I had never known anybody who could so vigorously squeeze a prick into an amiable cunt; she often brought tears into my eyes in such a way, so powerful were her compressions, I think I can really say that she was squeezing you as with a vise.

She was lying, her eyes closed, her breast palpitating with volupty; her quivering cunt was keeping me tightly enclosed in a delightful jail and squeezing now and then my prick which quickly recovered all her strength and stiffness.

She was as hot as fire and she answered at once when she felt my screw getting back its hardness.

She gave way to her lewdness again with more passion, if possible than at the first time. My huge tool seemed to excite lascivious pleasure so much that it looked like it would be impossible to gratify her. Her hands were squeezing my buttocks convulsively and it seemed she wished to get my whole body into her hot cunt. The fucking was led with such a strength that the crisis happened swiftly; it was delightful for both of us, but it made Miss Imogen almost crazy. The motions of her body and the sighs of her throat were those of an hysteric woman, and she squeezed my prick so strongly that I thought for a while she had broken it in two pieces. More than ten minutes elapsed till she recovered from her swoon. Then she took my head between her hands, kissed me warmly and announced I was the dearest being in the world; she had never known anyone who had satisfied her so much in every respect, I had made her feel sensations too strong to be put into words, and so on.

Again my prick was as stiff as ever. Miss Imogen said:

—My dear George, we must be very careful, for it's about time your sisters are coming back.

But nothing could stop me, the exquisite pleasure given by the inside pressures of her cunt was overwhelming. My movements soon led the things right on my side. Miss Imogen's temper was very much too hot to leave her long senseless, and we had one of the most delightful fuckings, and it lasted much longer than the others for the three previous unloadings had already quieted the fierceness of her desires a little bit. We gave way with more ease to the ecstasies of a voluptuous mutual unloading which just now fulfilled our lewdness.

Miss Imogen kept my prick still engulfed in her burning gash for a while, then, raising herself a bit, she said to me:

—George, we must stop now.

She pushed me away from her and I had to go out of her cunt; but her dear cunt was as worried as me and was keeping my prick so tightly squeezed that I had to strain violently to draw it out, and in the end it went out with the very sound of a cork being forcibly pulled out of a bottle. Before I got up and before she could prevent me from it I dashed between her thighs, and sticking my lips on her over flowed cunt, I started licking all the gluey fucking-juice that was oozing out of her filled-to-the-brim crack. She withdrew uneasily, but when I was standing up, she enfolded in her arms and kissed me eagerly, licking her own fucking-juice with which my lips were still voluptuously smeared.

After she had buttoned me and got to her feet, she made me sit near her. She wiped my mouth with her pocket handkerchief and set my neck-tie, my collar and my hair in order. Then we kissed very tenderly and she thanked me for the immeasurable enjoyment I had given her; she paid compliments to me about the huge size of my prick, saying to me that it had given her more pleasure that any other she had tried till then. It was the second time she was speaking about her previous experiences. I did not notice of it at that moment, for I was playing the part of the boy too ignorant or too innocent to think there was some evil in that, but I was resolved to make her, in a moment of passion, tell about her previous experiences.

Before the coming of my sisters, she said me:

—I'm going to try to make up a story so that we can met again to-morrow. However, you must look as if you had been very severely punished, and I shall say that you rebelled against my rightful authority to chastise and consequently, in order to punish you more, I did not allow you to leave the study-room.

Many were the times, later on, when I was gratified with the lustful access and proper use of her magnificent cunt.

And, when we happened to be separated fate spared me and allowed me to meet again all my former loves: Mrs. Barnett, Jenny, the actual Mrs. Bank, De Burnon who sodomised me more than once. Needless to say that all those stories would require again a whole book to be related. The time for it may come one day.

THE END

THE MERRY MÉNAGE

THE MERRY MÉNAGE

Contents

Book One   239
Book Two   389

INTRODUCTION

It is hardly surprising when one looks into Victorian morality, that appearances were to be held high in importance, and behaviour, only secondary, if misbehaviour were discreetly indulged in. Such is the code of morality in "THE MERRY MENAGE," a manuscript that clearly mirrors the social and sexual behaviour of ladies and gentlemen of fashion.

Two widows and a virginal companion cheerfully invite the stud services of the guardian and mentor, and all is acceptable, including a menáge a quatre, provided there is no scandal.

The characters in this novel are based on actual persons in actual situations. The family, itself, was highly respected and at no time did a breath of scandal so much as tarnish one initial of the good name of these 'good' people.

Documents, if reliable, would have it that the widow Helen, eventually marries Jack and the rich, young widowed daughter, Maud lives in the same household, thereby implementing now a menage á trois. There is no further reference to the young Alice, who served as a companion earlier. It is hoped that she was suitably rewarded, and what is more, respectably placed 'n appreciation ot her services rendered.

The novelette "Old Fashioned Discipline," included as an addendum, was originally in the hands ot collectors and has just recently become available for publication.

Editor

BOOK I

CHAPTER ONE

One morning, when I came down to breakfast, I found the following letter of my plate:

The Nunnery, Wednesday.

Dear Jack,

What are you doing with yourself? I have come here for a few days, but find the place most terribly dull, only Mother and Alice being here. Can't you come down for a long week end and amuse three lonely females. I am writing at Mother's suggestion. Do come!

Yours ever.

The invitation was very welcome. I *was* at a loose end, that week, and London in July is not the pleasantest of places. The Nunnery was a charming house to visit, so promptly I wired grateful acceptance, adding that I would arrive that same afternoon by tea time.

Now allow me to introduce my reader to my Dramatis Personae and to the scene.

"Mother" was my old friend, Mrs. Helen Bell; we were children together, and I was present at her wedding and godfather to her only child, Maud, my correspondent. Helen was scarcely seventeen when she married. Maud was born the following year, and was now twenty-two; Mrs. Bell was therefore not yet forty, and was frequently taken for Maud's elder sister. She now was in her prime, a splendidly shaped woman, rather tall, slightly inclining towards embonpoint but very graceful in her movements, and very attractive. Her husband had died three years ago, and had left her a pretty place and ample means; and her re-marriage had been confidently predicted but so far she had shewn no desire to re-enter into the wedded state.

She lived quietly and was the Lady Bountiful of the neighbourhood. She was wonderfully free of prejudices and particularly tolerant of the frailties of her own sex.

Maud, her daughter, was also a widow, her husband having died just a year ago, leaving her well provided for so long as she did not marry again, and lived "a chaste and proper life," to quote from his will. I was her Trustee as well as her godfather, and it devolved on me to see that the conditions of the will were conformed to. But she was of a particularly ardent temperament—as also was her mother—and her involuntary cry of dismay when she heard her husband's will read warned me that there would be trouble unless I took care.

She was a beautiful girl, having inherited her mother's good looks together with her father's height,—in fact she was unusually tall. She possessed a most voluptuous figure and loved to display it. Unlike her mother (who was a brunette) Maud was a charming blonde with a mass of golden hair and blue eyes, which fairly captivated me when after some years absence from England I returned home just in time for her wedding and I found myself horribly envious of the good fellow whom she married and who thus obtained the fullest rights over her charms! On his death my duties as her Trustee constantly brought us into close relations, and it was impossible for me not to note how her enforced celibacy was distressing her, while she could not but be aware of my passion for her. One day when I was nearly mad with desire after her and she had been unusually confidential, I ventured to suggest that so long as the Trustee was satisfied in his capacity as such, he in his capacity as godfather and dear friend might afford her the relief she so ardently craved. She delightedly con-

ferred on me the further appointment of lover, and
as opportunities presented themselves she received
in my arms the solace that her ardent feminine
temperament required from time to time, the
happy gratification of which tended to heighten
and ripen her attractions as well as to maintain her
in perfect health.

"Alice" was Mrs. Bell's companion, practically
her adopted daughter. Her mother was a school-
mate and dear friend of Mrs. Bell; and on her
death the latter took charge of Alice (who was
totally unprovided for) and had her educated properly. When Maud married, Mrs. Bell brought
Alice home as her companion. She was a charming
little maiden of that almost indescribable English
type that necessitates the use of adjectives such as
"sweet," "cuddlesome," "dainty," "scrumptious,"
etc., a universal favorite and one of the accepted
belles of the neighbourhood; and although she had
only just turned eighteen she had received more
than one good offer of marriage, all of which she
had refused. Mrs. Bell used to say half in fun and
half in earnest that Alice was in love with me and
that no one else would ever get her. I cannot say
that I reciprocated the affection, but I will confess
that I began to think Alice was a flower the pluck-
ing of which would be a treat for a god.

She absolutely worshipped Mrs. Bell, and whatever her own private opinions and ideas might be
she was ready to conform to the slightest wish Mrs.

Bell might express—a characteristic that will be found to greatly affect the events that I am about to relate.

Mrs. Bell's residence, *"The Nunnery,"* was a comfortable old-fashioned house that stood in its own grounds some four miles from a country town. There were really two buildings, the house itself, and the wing that contained the domestic offices and the servants' rooms. The house had a ground floor and first floor; a sort of one storeyed passage gave the servants access—so that at night the family and visitors were quite separated from the domestics, a feature that also will be found to affect my narrative. Mrs. Bell's bedroom occupied the whole of one end, and looked out over the grounds, and communicated with Alice's bedroom and the room generally allotted to visitors by curtained doors.

As I journeyed down I wondered whether Maud's invitation meant anything of special significance. I knew that she had told her mother of our relations, and that Mrs. bell in her broadminded way did not object (in view of the terms of the will and knowing her daughter's erotic temperament) so long as no scandal arose. But to allow Maud and me to have each other under her own roof seemed to me too improbable to be expected.

Maud met me at the station. She was driving herself in a waggonette without a groom. My light baggage was soon put inside—I took my place beside her and we started off for "*The Nunnery*".

When clear of the town the road began a long and somewhat steep ascent. Maud made the horse walk, then turning to me said: "Now Jack, I want to talk to you seriously."

"Good Heaven!, what have I done now!" I exclaimed.

Maud laughed. "It is not what you have done but what you are required to do that I want to talk about!" she replied; "now Jack, be a good boy and promise you'll do as we all want—all of us mind!"

"Of course I will if I can!", I rejoined gallantly —"what is it?—anything very serious or very difficult?"

Maud shook with laughter. "Jack, you're too funny! Yes!, it is very serious and it may be difficult! I'm going to call a spade a spade as it will be the easiest and quickest way! Jack, we all—all, mind you, including Alice—want you to ... have us! There!"

"What!", I exclaimed, staring at her in absolute surprise.

"It's quite true, Jack dear!" Maud replied, colouring faintly, "that's what we want you to do! Now listen!"

"I've been wanting you badly, my lover!—oh so badly—till I told mother that either you must come to me or I must go to you! She didn't like your having me under her own roof! I didn't want

246

to go up to Town! A sudden idea struck me! As you know, Jack, Mother is still a young woman,—I get my hot temperament from her, and I know how she hates her lonely bed! And she loves you, Jack! So I slipped my arm round her, and whispered coaxingly: Look here, Mummy, let us get Jack down and . . . share him! She blushed like a schoolgirl! "Mummy," I again whispered—" you know you want . . . something . . . very badly, just as badly as I do!— (she quivered responsively)— won't you let me get it for you?—(again she blushed deeply). — "Come, Mummy darling, share Jack with me!" And I kissed her and kept whispering—it's sweet of you! if Jack is willing it shall be as you wish!" "There, Sir, what do you say?"

"I'm lost in astonishment!" I stammered—and so I was! "Maud," I added presently, "you're not playing a trick on me, are you?"

"I'm telling you God's truth, Jack!" she replied speaking now quite seriously and looking me straight in the eyes. "You won't say "No" to Mother, will you Jack?".

"Of course not, dear!" I replied as I placed my hand on hers—I place myself absolutely at your disposal and hers in all honour and loyalty, and will not spare myself in your service!"

Maud looked lovingly at me and I saw her eyes were dewy. Presently she said softly "Thank you for what you have said, my own true lover. I am proud and happy to think that you will at my request do to Mother what you have so often done so sweetly to me!" Then after a pause she added in a lighter vein "And you'll find your virtue being its own reward, Jack!—for Mother is a lovely woman, Sir!"

I laughed. "But what about little Alice!", I asked.

"Oh! we managed to square her without much difficulty!", Maud replied, smiling at the recollection." You know Jack, that Alice will do anything if Mother wishes her to do it. We got her quietly the same afternoon, and told her that we both were getting very anxious about her because we could see that her stifled natural desires were beginning to affect her health and looks! She was awfully staggered! Then Mother drew her on her lap and took her in her arms, kissed her tenderly and said lovingly: "My darling, my second daughter, the one man in the world we believe your love is coming down here for a few days, your Jack! (Alice blushed deeply)—if you will consent to let him put you right, Maud and I will keep you company and let him have us also, so that we can be together in my room where we can look after you! Will you consent, darling?" Poor Alice didn't know what to say—she was dreadfully taken aback! "Say yes, darling?" whispered Mother lovingly. Slowly came the answer "If you wish it, Auntie, Yes!" Between us we hugged and kissed and soothed her, and now

248

she's all right about it though very timid! Jack, you're going to be a lucky man!"

"Going to be!" I exclaimed, looking tenderly at her as my hand slid on to her leg and amorously pressed the region of Love—"am I not so already, seeing that I have the run of this treasure!"—and again my hand rested over the organ of her sex! "And as if that was not enough luck for any man, you are going to put me in possession of the finest woman and the prettiest girl in this part of the County! Maud darling, how can I ever thank you sufficiently?"

Maud laughed wickedly. "Just keep a little bit in hand for me, darling," she replied,— "we are going to work you very hard, but don't forget my brokerage!"

I laughed. "If there should be only one drop left in me and you want it, darling, you shall have it! Now tell me, how do you propose to work this job? —have you made out a list of hours and appointments for me as they do for stallions, or am I to sit on the landing till some door opens and I am beckoned in?"

Maud laughed amusedly. "You must arrange all that with Mother after tea," she said— "she wants a talk with you and I have arranged to take Alice off, so as to leave you together. *Entre nous*, Jack, I think her idea is that we shall always meet in her bedroom as soon as the house is quiet, attired only in our "nighties", and there and then decide on the evening's programme." As she spoke we drove through the gates. "There she is! . . . see, she has got Alice by the hand so as to make her meet you and get it over! . . . how Alice is blushing!"

"We're delighted to see you, Jack dear!" said Mrs. Bell as we alighted. "We were so glad to get your wire saying you would come!" And she kissed me affectionately, somewhat to Maud's surprise, for this was an unusual proceeding.

"You don't know how glad I was to get out of town, Helen!", I replied as I returned her salute. "How are you, Alice?—why, you're not looking quite yourself!" I added as I took her little hands in mind and drew her towards me— "I really must look after you!", I continued, as for the first time I kissed her virgin cheeks, now covered with blushes at what she evidently thought was a reference to the trouble alleged by Mrs. Bell and Maud. They regarded her affectionately, but I could see they had difficulty to smother a smile at my audacity and its effect on Alice.

"Show Jack his room, Maud", said Mrs. Bell as she passed her arm lovingly round the still blushing Alice— "tea will be ready in five minutes, and I expect you will want it!"

"Jack! how could you!" exclaimed Maud, choking with laughter when we reached the security of my room— "poor Alice! how a certain part of her must have tingled!"

"I couldn't help it!" I replied, as I joined in her

silent mirth "it was a sudden inspiration, and I think a happy one!"

"Very!", she rejoined—then pressed herself amorously against me looking tenderly into my eyes. I divined her desire and whispered softly "Finger or tongue, darling?"

"Finger!" she murmured—" no time for the other just now, but I must have something quickly!" Promptly I dropped into an easy chair and took her on my knees—as my hand stole up under her clothes and travelled along her delicious legs she threw her arms round my neck, pressed her lips on mind, and parted her thighs to assist my hand which just then was searching for the slit in her drawers—which it soon found; then my eager fingers rested on the already moist lips of Maud's cunt, now throbbing and pouting with sexual excitement! Hugging me tightly to her, Maud now began to wriggle on my knees in the most divine way as she felt my finger penetrate her cunt in delicious agitation and then craftily attack her excited clitoris! "Oh! Jack! ... oh! ... d-a-r-l-i-n-g!!," she gasped brokenly in blissful ecstasy!—then straining me to her she ejaculated "I'm coming!! ... I'm coming !!! ... oh! finish me!!" Promptly my finger played on her clitoris!—I felt an indescribable quiver pass through her—and then she inundated my happy finger with a profuse emission as her head dropped on my shoulder in her ecstatic rapture!

I allowed her to rest undisturbed by any movement on my part till she recovered from her half-swoon. As she came to herself, Maud drew a long breath, slowly raised her head—then looking lovingly at me with still humid eyes she passionately kissed me, murmuring. "Oh! darling! that was good!", and slowly rose from off my knees. Suddenly she stooped and whispered in my ear "Shall I do anything to you, Jack?" at the same time placing her hand gently on the fly of my trousers. I shivered with delight at her touch and nearly yielded to temptation, but retained sufficient self-control to deny myself the sweet pleasure she was offering to me. "No, dearie!" I said, "I'd like it awfully, but I must reserve myself to tonight and you three!" "Oh you good boy" she whispered —then after kissing me again she said in her usual voice "now I'll leave you and will join you presently at tea; I can now get on well till tonight! Oh Jack!, I do hope you'll have me first?" then disappeared.

I found Mrs. Bell and Alice already at the tea table. Alice again blushed on seeing me, and I fancied that Mrs. Bell looked somewhat enquiringly at me. "Where's Maud?" she asked. "I expected to find her here", I replied— "she went on to her room after showing me to mine; here she comes!" And then we chatted gaily. I gave them the latest news from London and they detailed the County gossip to me, for I knew many of the families. And so tea passed, and when we rose I was glad to note that Alice's shyness and restraint had disappeared.

True to her undertaking, Maud drew Alice's arm through hers and led her off into the garden, while I chatted with Mrs. Bell and followed her into her own particular boudoir. As I closed the door she came towards me with open arms and love in her beautiful eyes, drew me to her and kissed me sweetly, whispering "Jack!! it is good of you to come to the help of us poor women—but what can you think of us to ask it!"

I returned her kiss lovingly, then passed my arm round her waist and led her to a settee for two, into which we settled ourselves in delightfully close contact. "There is only one thing I can think, Mrs. Bell", I replied softly as I looked into her eyes— "you, Maud, and Alice are simply angels." She laughed and blushed prettily, then whispered "you called me Helen when you arrived—I want to continue to be Helen to you now that we are going to be so ... so ... intimate!" I drew her to me and tenderly kissed her, and for a moment she rested silent in my embrace.

Presently she freed herself. "I want to talk with you, Jack—you and I have to arrange matters! Maud has told me that you will ... play! now have you anything to suggest?"

"I'd rather leave myself in your hands, Helen darling", I said, noting delightedly her pleasure at my form of address. "I'm sure that you and Maud have discussed matters and that you have some scheme cut and dry. And there is sweet little Alice, who is differently placed to you two—I'm sure you can arrange for her initiation better than I possibly can! But tell me, Helen, is Alice really willing to ... surrender her maiden treasure to me?—it seems incredible!"

"She really is willing, Jack", Mrs. Bell replied; "you have her heart and her love, Jack, and she is quite willing to let you have her body, her maidenhead! And Jack, may I say that I also love you, dear, and willingly give myself to you!" And drawing me to her she kissed me passionately.

I was very touched. "I haven't words to˵say what I feel, Helen darling", I whispered in her ear, — "but may I have a chance tonight to show you how I appreciate your wonderful kindness and love!"

She blushed prettily. "This is what I want to talk about and to arrange with you, Jack dear", she replied softly. "May I tell you our ideas?"

"Please do!" I answered, and drew her against me so that she could whisper—for I recognized she could whisper what she could not say in the usual way. And to indicate my recognition of the sweet intimacy into which she had now admitted me, my disengaged hand stole towards her corsage and lovingly wandered over her voluptuous bust!

Mrs. Bell began. "You know, Jack, that all the servants sleep in the domestic wing, leaving us

254

along in the house. They cannot see the lights in my room and they know that I sometimes read for hours after I retire—because I am alone!" she added with a blush and smile "By half-past ten the house is quite quiet. My idea is that instead of your visiting us in our own rooms in turn and perhaps attracting attention by the lights, we all should meet in my bedroom, clad only in our "nighties", and that you should work your sweet will on us in the presence of each other. There will then be no jealousies—things will more or less be done on the spur of the moment—and the feeling that each one is assisting the others and contributing by her presence to the piquancy of the proceedings will add zest to our pleasures. How does it strike you?—I see a smile on your lips!"

"I think your idea a most charming one", I replied, looking fondly at her and amorously playing with the swell of her bosom— "may I confess that I know from personal experience how much the pleasure of ... having a woman ... is enhanced by the presence of another girl. But our case is so exceptional that I could not refrain from a smile as its peculiarities struck me!"

"In what way?" she asked, somewhat anxiously I thought.

"You will let me use plain words and not beat about the bush?" I enquired.

"Certainly, Jack", she replied with a conscious smile and blush.

"Well, Helen, you and Maud are mother and daughter—not many daughters are ... fucked ... in the sight of their mothers, and fewer mothers still allow their daughters to watch them being fucked! Are you sure you and Maud won't mind? I shall insist on your being stark naked!"

"Quite sure!" Helen replied stoutly—but she coloured violently. I kissed her tenderly.

"It will be awfully delicious!" I said delightedly, and I felt a responsive quiver run through her.

I continued. "Now we come to Alice. To speak plainly, she has to be ravished by me, eh Helen?"

"That's really what it is, Jack!" she replied slowly, blushing deeply.

"Will she agree to be violated in public, so-to-speak,—will she not prefer the privacy of her own room and to lose her maindenhead alone with me?"

"I don't think so, Jack" Helen replied, looking soberly at me; "she is very young and very timid and nervous, and really both Maud and I thought that she she seemed relieved when we told her that we would be present to look after her while she was being ravished!"

"Then, Helen, I think your idea is really splendid and am ready to fall in with it. I would like to make just one suggestion—some one of us should be appointed each evening to direct the proceedings and to say what is to be cone, and the others are to give implicit obedience. Deal the cards round every evening when we meet in your room, and whoever gets the Ace of Spades is to be the Queen or King of that evening."

"Oh Jack! what a lovely idea!" she exclaimed delightedly— "we can have a regular revel or games at every meeting then!"

I kissed her. "I have seen the game played, Helen, and I'm sure you all will love it!" One question more—do we meet this evening?"

She blushed "We thought we might do so, Jack, if you were willing and not too tired after your long journey!"

"The prospect of seeing you in all your naked beauty, Helen, and of making you die of esctacy in my arms would be enough to banish all fatigue did it exist, which it does not. So we will meet!" She kissed me rapturously.

"Is Alice to be ... sacrificed ... this evening, or do you propose that she should be saved for tomorrow, and be educated a little by the help of object lessons furnished by you and Maud. What do you think, Helen?"

"We thought we would leave that to you, Jack," she replied—" "we considered that you ought to have the right to choose."

I drew her closely to me. "Then we'll keep Alice for tomorrow night, darling, and I'll devote myself to you and Maud tonight. But we will make Alice show herself to us naked tonight—and as our loving pranks are sure to excite her virgin self, I must claim the privilege of affording her the relief she will crave. Now Helen dear, just one point more; will you mind if I have Maud first, and then you?"

"Of course not, Jack," Helen replied with a smile— "I think you ought to, especially if she wishes it."

"I'm sure she will, for she is so terribly mad with desire!" I said, "the sight of you in my arms, quivering with ecstacy, will probably drive her wild! Besides this, Helen, it will be better for Alice to have you with her when she sees ... fucking ... for the first time!" (Helen kissed me rapturously). "I'll do Maud as soon as I can arrange it—then we'll play for a bit with Alice and utilise her naked charms to excite us—and then, my darling, you and I will have a long sweet fuck!" (Helen kissed me rapturously). "I'll then dissolve the meeting— but I'll slip back to you, and we'll have a sweet time by ourselves! Now, one final kiss, and we'll join the others. Get Maud away and tell her what we have arranged, —I'll entertain Alice; perhaps you'll also tell her that she is to be reserved as tomorrow night's *bonne bouche*, —she then will be more at her ease tonight, and we'll use her to excite us. Now Helen darling!" and after a long passionate kiss, lips on lips, we strolled into the garden. As arranged, Helen soon disappeared with Maud, leaving me with Alice, who at first was very shy and timid—but when she found that I did not touch on the topic of her sacrifice she soon regained her

258

usual easy and charming demeànour. In due course came dinner, then cards and music—and so bedtime was comfortably and happily reached.

CHAPTER TWO

Carefully and ceremoniously we wished each other good night while the servants were removing the cakes and glasses and closing for house. When I was undressed and ready for the fray I glanced at the clock and to my disgust found it was only ten minutes past the hour and that I had twenty horrid minutes to wait. It could not be helped. I got into a comfortable chair and recalled the dinner table with the three ladies in their dainty evening attire—how my eyes dwelt on what they were kind enough to display in the way of bosom—how my prick throbbed at the thought that very soon I should see those bosoms unveiled and bare! Then my thoughts wandered to the surroudning bedrooms and their occupants—I could imagine Maud dragging off her garments in her excitement and surveying herself naked in the mirror preparatory to slipping on her only robe—I could picture Mrs. Bell's agitation as she carefully prepared herself for the fucking for which she so longed—and I could almost see Alice as she nervously undressed herself to appear before me clad in her "nightie" only! At dinner she chattered away so freely and delightfully and seemed so much at her ease save for a certain suppressed excitement that I felt certain she had been told that her ordeal had been postponed to the following night and that she therefore was to play the part chiefly of spectator and Maid of Honour.

At last the clock in the hall chimed the half-hour; promptly I rose, turned out my lights and noiselessly slipped into the landing; a thin line of light indicated Mrs. Bell's room and that the door was ajar. Into it I went.

Mrs. Bell and Alice were there, sitting together, their "nighties" on, the most dainty and provoking garments I ever saw! As I approached them they both rose. Helen opened her arms to me and clasping me to her she said "Welcome here Jack!" and kissed me; then pushing me towards the blushing Alice she said "Now Alice!"—whereupon the sweet girl threw her arms round me and held up her face to be kissed. I took her in my arms and pressing her closely to me I showered hot kisses on her lips till she gasped for breath, when I released her, and she took refuge alongside of Mrs. Bell again.

Just then Maud appeared, wearing the most ravishing "nightie" I had ever seen—for it was semi-transparent! She kissed us all in turn, then looked inquiringly at her mother.

"Jack dear, we want you to direct the proceedings tonight instead of someone being chosen by the fall of a card—then we shall learn the game better and how to play it!" said Mrs. Bell, looking at me and slightly colouring;—"we'll all promise to do whatever you wish and in the way you wish. Will you be so kind?"

"Why, of course, Helen!" I answered, concealing my joy—for was not I now master of the situation!

"And if you don't mind, Jack, will you be content with Maud and me only tonight, and let Alice see for herself how the game is played; then tomorrow we will put her at your disposal!, added Mrs. Bell, passing her arm round Alice's waist protectingly as the blushing girl nestled closely against her.

"Why, certainly, Helen dear!" I replied with a smile to Alice; but I suppose that Alice is willing to take her part in everything else that we may play at?"

Mrs. Bell turned to Alice. "What do you say, dear?" she asked lovingly.

Alice hesitated for a moment, then colouring

deeply replied in a low voice "Yes, Auntie, if you wish it!"

"There's your answer Jack!", said Mrs. Bell with a smile. "Now my Lord, your handmaidens await your commands!"

"Alice, dear, come and sit on my knees!" I said. Hesitatingly Alice left her Aunt's sheltering arm and gently placed herself on my knees, sitting so that she faced Maud and her mother. I slipped my left arm round her to hold her in position and lovingly kissed her. It was a delicious sensation to feel her soft weight on my thighs and to note the little tremors that pulsated through her, for she now was fairly quivering with excitement.

"Helen, will you now show yourself to us?" I said—" Maud, dear please strip your Mother stark naked, and then come here to look at her with us!"

"Oh! Jack!, no, no," protested Helen, flushing furiously. But Maud delightedly seized her. "Stand up, Mummy!" she cried as she set to work to unbutton Mrs. Bell's "nightie". Slowly and reluctantly Helen complied; quickly Maud pulled the "nightie" off her and threw it on the bed—and Mrs. Bell stood naked in front of us, one arm and hand in front of her breasts while with the other hand she covered her cunt!

I felt Alice thrill! I glanced at her—she was rosy red, but her eyes were rivetted on her Aunt's naked figure. Maud remained by her Mother as if expecting further orders—I could see that she was quivering with suppressed excitement.

"Maud, pull your Mother's hands away and clasp them together at the back of her head—and then come here!" I commanded.

"No Jack!, no!" pleaded Helen, who evidently was reluctant to expose her cunt to our gaze. But Maud slipped behind her, gripped her wrists in her strong young arms and pulling them backwards she placed them in the desired position, and quickly joined Alice and me, standing behind my chair her eyes glittering with something very like lust!

In silence we three gazed at Helen—the broken breathing of the two girls betraying their suppressed excitement! Helen naked was certainly a thrilling spectacle—her flushd face, her glorious figure, her wonderful breasts heaving in her agitation, her splendidly round thighs and legs, her grandly swelling hips and haunches, and the bewitching forest of close curling silky hair that clustered over and concealed her cunt!

"Jack! isn't she glorious!" whispered Maud in glowing admiration. I nodded. "Make Mother turn slowly round, Jack, so that we can see her from all points and in profile!" whispered Maud again breathlessly. A quick flush told me that Helen had heard her daughter's suggestion. "Please, Helen!" I said gently,— "very slowly, please!" Reluctantly Helen complied, affording us the most charming succession of views of her magnificent naked self.

When she was in full profile I made her stand still
—the sight of her in this position was simply wonderful, the sweep and spring of her back and bottom, the curve of her belly, her proud upstanding
breasts with their saucy nipples, and the glorious
bush of hairs—it simply fascinated us and I could
feel my prick beginning to stiffen and began to
wonder if Alice noticed it! After gazing our fill I
made Helen continue her revolving—but stopped
her again to revel in the view of her splendid
buttocks and haunches and her plump thighs. Then
starting her again I allowed her to complete the
round, and again she faced us, now visibly trembling with apprehension and shame!

"Go and kiss her, girls!" I whispered. Up sprang
Alice—simultaneously she and Maud seized Mrs.
Bell and smothered her with their ardent kisses. It
was a sweet sight to watch—but time was valuable
and so I joined the group and rescuing Helen from
the excited girls I installed her on my knees, naked
as she was, showering burning kisses on her quivering lips, while my hands sought her glorious breasts
and squeezed them.

"Now Maud, its your turn!" I said; "strip dear
and how us your naked beauties. Help her to take
off her 'nightie', Alice!"

In a trice Maud stood naked before her Mother
and me, a lovely vision of voluptuous slenderness.
To me the sight was familiar, but to her mother
and to Alice it was a revelation which struck them

dumb with admiration. Helen's broken breathing told me how much the sight of her daughter's naked loveliness was affecting her, while Alice simply thrilled with undisguised pleasure, her eyes dwelling almost wonderingly on the glorious wealth of golden fluffy hair that grew on Maud's Mount of Venus and sheltered her cunt. We made Maud turn herself slowly round, just as her Mother did, revelling in the spectacle of her bewitching slenderness; and when she again faced us, her cheeks suffused with blushes, I stealthily watched Helen's eyes as they wandered over her daughter's voluptuously naked body and her delicious breasts and her golden haired cunt!

"Haven't you seen her like this before?" I whispered in her ear. Helen blushed. "No!" she replied softly— "Maud was quite a little thing when I last undressed her—now, well Jack, I'm beginning to wish I was a man, for her sake!"—and she laughed wickedly, while Alice who was standing just behind us, leaning on the back of our chair, broke into a ripple of amused girlish mirthful laughter.

"Then you can appreciate what my sensations are, dear!" said as I amorously played with her breasts— "I can guess them, Jack, by the mutinous movements of something I am sitting on!" Helen replied as she moved herself provokingly on my knees, smiling significantly at me.

It was only too true! The sight of her glorious

nakedness, so quickly followed by the display of Maud's voluptuous charms, the inflammatory influence of our close contact and arising from my handling of her breasts (her cunt I did not dare to touch at the moment) all set me on fire! My prick was like a rod of iron! It was full time to have Maud!

I glanced over my shoulder at Alice. She was still intently gazing at Maud, and evidently very excited by her naked beauty. Her eyes were gleaming, her lips partly open, while her bosom throbbed and heaved. She evidently was dominated by intense curiosity which for the time being overpowered her maidenly instincts and training, and some subtle instinct (probably sexual) told her that a crisis was approaching.

"Helen!" I whispered loudly enough for Maud and Alice to hear, "I must have Maud!—do you mind?" Maud blushed prettily, but Alice became crimson as she glanced quickly at me.

"Do, Jack!" Helen replied, kissing me ardently —then she rose so as to set me free. "Come, Alice," she added, reseating herself and pointing to her lap, on which Alice instantly installed herself, quivering with suppressed eagerness. Helen kissed her affectionately and whispered something in her ear that I could not catch but which made Alice colour still more furiously.

In an instant I was naked, my prick standing stiff and rampant in magnificent erection! Maud's eyes glistened joyfully at the sight, but Alice shrank back, startled, in Helen's arms, exclaiming "Oh! oh! Auntie!" her eyes widely dilating with surprise and alarm! "Come here, Jack," said Helen quietly, as she passed her hands caressingly and re-assuringly over Alice. I slipped an arm round Maud, and the pair of us went up together to Helen's chair an stood in front of and close to her and the still startled Alice. "Now look again, dear!" said Helen softly as she pointed to my prick. Timidly Alice did so, flushing a rosy red, her astonished eyes travelling from the threatening rubicond head along the shaft to its root in my forest of hairs, under which my dangling balls were clearly visible, the sight of which evidently filled her with wonder and amazement. With silent curiosity we watched Alice as she gazed on the masculine organ which was so shortly to be lodged in her virgin cunt, and we wondered as to what thoughts were then flashing through her mind at the sight of the instrument of her approaching violation.

Presently Alice drew a deep breath and hid her face against Helen's shoulder, a tremulous wriggle passing through her as she did so! Our eyes met Helen's in an amused smile—Had Alice's sexual excitement at the sight of my prick proved too much for her?—had she spent? But the very idea that Alice's maiden cunt was quivering in ecstacy set Maud and me on fire. "Come, darling!" I exclaimed—and quickly I led her to Helen's bed, which was covered with a plum-coloured counter-pane well calculated to set off our nudity—and on it Maud hastily extended herself on her back!

"Quick, Alice! wait a moment, Jack!" cried Helen, as she hurriedly rose, and slipping an arm round the flushed trembling and wildly excited girl she brought Alice to the bedside. Maud's legs were now widely parted to accommodate me, and her golden haired cunt was in full view, its pouting coral lips being clearly visible through the cluster of fluffy golden curls. "Look, dear!", whispered Helen to Alice, indicating Maud's cunt with her finger—"isn't it lovely!" Alice's eyes gleamed as they glanced from Maud's cunt to my impatient prick, intently watching our every movement. "Go on, Jack!" said Helen softly. Quickly I placed myself in position between Maud's legs, and let myself down on to her breasts; and as her arms closed lovingly round me, I brought my prick to bear against the lips of her throbbing excited cunt and gently forced it in! "Look, Alice, look!" whispered Helen excitedly, Alice's eyes dilating with astonishment as she saw how easily Maud's cunt engulfed my prick! Soon it was buried in Maud till our hairs intermingled! "Oh! Jack! . . . darling!" Maud murmured ecstatically with half closed eyes, as after showering burning kisses on her sweet lips I began to fuck her! Instantly she threw her legs across my loins and strained me against her breasts with her strong young arms. "Watch them, darling!" whis-

pered Helen eagerly her voice betraying her own
agitation at the sight. But the injunction was un-
necessary. Alice's eyes were rivetted on our quivering, wriggling, heaving naked bodies, and not a
single movement passed unnoticed! Soon mutual
ecstasy began to steal over us!—wilder and fiercer
became my down-thrustings, madder and more
frenzied became Maud's wriggles and plunges
under me. Then the blissful climax was reached—
an indescribable convulsion swept through both of
us—"Ah! ... ah! ... A-H-H-!!" ejaculated Maud
brokenly as she felt herself inundated with the
boiling torrent that I frantically shot from me as I
spent rapturously into her! For a moment or two
we lay rigid, locked in the closest and sweetest of
embraces—then we collapsed into temporary forgetfulness of everything but the heavenly bliss we
had tasted in each others arms, the echoes of which
were still thrilling through us! Alice had witnessed
a fuck!

When I had recovered myself and remembered
my surroundings I looked cautiously round for Hel-
en and Alice. I found they had returned to the
chair. Helen, still naked, was seated in it, and Alice,
still in her "nightie" was on her lap, but she had
coiled herself up and had twisted herself round so
as to be lying face to face with Helen, tightly
clasped bosom against bosom in her arms. Her
attitude had somehow pulled her "nightie" tightly
across her bottom, and revealed so delicious an

outline that I involuntarily quivered with pleasure! This quiver aroused Maud, who dreamily opened her eyes; as they met mine a smile of heavenly satisfaction irradiated her countenance—her lips met mine and we exchanged long passionate kisses expressive of our gratitude for the divine raptures we had communicated to each other.

"Look at your Mother and Alice!" I whispered softly. Maud looked and broke into a merry laugh, which made Helen and Alice start up almost guiltily; and as we slowly slipped out of each other's embrace and rose from Helen's bed, they came to meet us, blushing consciously. Maud rushed into her Mother's arms murmuring "Oh Mummy darling!" while Helen responded "Oh Maud dear! oh you happy girl!" as they kissed each other passionately. I held out my arms silently to Alice, who timidly slipped into my embrace and let me kiss her lips. "Darling!' did we please you?" I whispered with a twinkle in my eye. She blushed crimson, averted her eyes, but remained silent; whereupon I added "never mind, dear, you'll tell me better tomorrow night!" whereupon she quivered nervously. Then to my utter surprise she raised herself on tiptoe, turned her blushing face to me and whispered very softly in a voice full of emotion "Kiss me again, Jack, and promise to be kind to me tomorrow when my time comes! "My darling!" I exclaimed, strangely moved,—and again clasping her to me I kissed her passionately over and over again!

Helen's voice interrupted us. "Jack, you can get to your room through that door, its open tonight; Alice dear, come with us!" The three women disappeared into Helen's bathroom, and acting on her hint I slipped into my room and indulged in a most welcome ablution and purification of my organs; then feeling greatly refreshed by the operation I, still naked, returned to Helen's room just as she, also naked, came in alone from her bathroom.

Having the room to ourselves we rushed into each others arms and kissed each other tenderly; the "feel" of her flesh against mine was simply exquisite, and I thrilled to think that before long she would be locked in my arms in the closest of embraces!

"Jack! it was just wonderful!" she murmured; "Maud says it was the best ... fuck ... she ever had!" "And what did Alice think of it, Helen?" I asked eagerly. She laughed. "Alice is absolutely staggered, Jack! In her wildest and wickedest moments she never imagined anything like what she has now seen; the sight of you and Maud in each others arms excited her terribly—and when the wonderful finale was reached, I took her away and made her sit on my lap in the fashion you saw, for I am sure that otherwise she would have used her hands to get relief for her feelings! I was very bad myself!" she added with a conscious blush. "Did you spend, Helen?", I asked mischievously. "No, no, Jack!" she responded smilingly, "but I was hard put to control myself!" "Do you think Alice spent?" I asked somewhat anxiously. "No, Jack, I know she didn't, but she admitted to Maud in the bathroom just now that she very nearly did!" "Where is she now?" I enquired. "In my bathroom with Maud," Helen replied. I thought it as well to leave the two girls together and I expect Alice is plying Maud with questions! I think you will have the sweetest of pupils tomorrow night, Jack dear!", she added with a smile— "I am looking forward to it with very pleasurable expectations."

"When the girls join us, Helen, we'll make Alice show us herself naked," I said; "We'll play with her and tease her and excite her again and then I'll satisfy her desires and cravings in a way she will think is just heavenly. By that time I shall be ready to fuck you, my darling" (she kissed me rapturously) "a good, long and slow fuck?" (another passionate kiss). "After that we'll dissolve the meeting—but I'll slip back to you through that door, it won't be midnight, so we can have a long sweet time together by ourselves in your bed and in each others arms" (more passionate kisses) "here they come!"

As we disengaged ourselves from our sweet embrace Maud and Alice with arms interlaced emerged from Helen's bathroom, Maud looking radiant, while Alice's face simply beamed with happiness; for she had now witnessed an act of fucking, and her maiden dread had been chased away by the sight of our rapturous transports. Also she had the pleasurable knowledge that she would presently be watching Helen in my arms; and so when Maud sank into an easy chair Alice settled herself down comfortably on Maud's lap and smiled brightly at us.

But her happy complacency was about to be rudely disturbed! I had drawn Helen again on to my knees and was playing with her glorious breasts while she exchanged a laughing badinage with Maud which greatly amused Alice. Presently my right hand slipped down over Helen's stomach, and after gently tickling her naval it descended towards her cunt, which up to now I had not yet touched. Hastily she stopped me. "No, Jack, you mustn't!" she exclaimed somewhat shamefacedly, "you mustn't touch me there!—I'm too excited!—I should go off." Maud and Alice shook with silent laughter, then Maud said mischievously "Hurry up, Jack, or you'll lose the train," which provoked further laughter in which Helen and I joined. "I've got at least twenty minutes yet, Maud," I replied, "I'm not built on the revolver principle and keep on firing—I've got to load my gun again and must not hurry the process or I will not be able to do your Mother justice!"

"Twenty minutes!" exclaimed Maud dolefully, —"what shall we do all that time?"

"Let me see," I replied. "I am Director tonight! I think that we cannot fill up the time better than by putting Alice through some of her paces; come, Alice dear, slip out of your nightie and show us yourself naked, to begin with!"

The happy smile fled from Alice's face and a look of dismay succeeded it as she cried "Oh no, Jack!, please no!" "An excellent idea Jack," cried Maud delightedly—"come Alice, let me undress you!"— and she commenced to unbutton Alice's "nightie." "No, no, don't Maud!" cried Alice, resisting stoutly, but Helen rushed to Maud's assistance. Between them they got the "nightie" off Alice, then each seized a wrist and gently forced her to stand in front of me stark naked!

Delightedly did my eyes rove over Alice's shrinking naked body. Helen held her firmly by one wrist, Maud by the other; her arms were thus forced away from her sides and so allowed her lovely outlines the fullest display,—and as her hands were captive she could not hide her most private parts from my eager gaze. Her skin was like milk! She had the loveliest little breasts I ever saw, so sweetly full and ripe, and so deliciously saucy! The little pink nipples pointing outwards; while the exquisitely subtle curves of her figure as it swept inwards to her waist and then swelled outwards over her hips and on to her legs were dreams

276

of beauty! Her thighs were gloriously plump and round, and melted into the daintiest of calves with slender ankles and tiny arched feet! Her beautifully rounded belly was surmounted with a large and deep navel and sloped gently down to its junction with her thighs, her Hill of Venus being unusually large and prominent and fleshy, and covered with a delicious tangle of closely curling silky hair, through which the delicate pink lips of her cunt were visible! She was just the daintiest, sweetest, prettiest little maiden one could imagine,—and her delicious young freshness crowned everything!

I sat still, simply enraptured! Before me stood a wonderful trio—Helen and Maud, tall, splendidly voluptuous, stark naked, holding between them Alice in her dainty nakedness, her face suffused with deep blushes which surged down to her dear little breasts, as half-laughingly and half-nervously she begged to be let loose.

"Bring her here to me," I said at last, separating my legs widely an act that seemed really to alarm Alice and compelled Helen and Maud to use gentle force; and soon the naked struggling girl stood between my thighs held firmly there by Helen and Maud, now deeply interested in the proceedings. "Don't touch me, Jack! please don't!" begged Alice, now quite frightened and trembling violently with flushed face and cast down eyes! I placed my hands just behind her hips, noting delightedly how she squirmed when I touched her, while the sight

277

of her palpitating bosom and heaving breasts began to re-animate my prick!

"Alice dear," I said softly, "You're behaving very naughtily, and you are breaking your promise to do everything I might wish if you were let off from doing one special thing tonight! Do you think we would hurt you, dear? On the contrary, we're going to give you the sweetest time you've ever had, and prepare you for tomorrow! Now darling, take courage! Come and kiss me, and smile again!"

I pressed her coaxingly towards me as I spoke; for a brief moment Alice stood irresolute—then she raised her eyes looked lovingly at me, smiled trustfully, and, yielding to the gentle pressure of my hands, she allowed herself to be drawn forward till she was resting against me. Then she held up her lips to me to be kissed. "My darling!" I whispered passionately, clasping her in my arms, and pressing her warm soft body against mine. I kissed her over and over again!

"Now you can let go of her hands, Helen, for Alice has become a good girl again!" I said with a smile, as I arranged Alice on my knees, retaining her in that position with my left arm and keeping my right in readiness to feel her naked person—the sweet warmth and pressure of her bottom on my prick beginning to infuse fresh life to my somewhat limp organ. Helen, meanwhile, had settled herself again in her chair and faced me; she took Maud on her lap and then began to play with Maud's lovely breasts and generally to feel her, all the time looking significantly at me.

I took the hint and said to Alice, "Look at those two, dear, it's a pretty game, isn't it!" Alice coloured vividly, then laughed uneasily, but watched Helen and Maud attentively.

Helen then exclaimed "Don't you know this game, Jack?—its only 'Follow my Leader'! I'm leader!—whatever I do to Maud you are to do to Alice!"

"Oh! Auntie!" exclaimed Alice, considerably startled at the idea. She turned and looked at me inquiringly.

I smiled encouragingly and asked "Shall we play, dear?"

Her colour rose, she hesitated, then whispered "Yes, if you wish it, Jack!"—then laughed gaily as if amused by her audacity!

Helen commenced by kissing Maud on her lips; I did the same to Alice. Helen next placed her hand just below Maud's breasts and felt her all over her stomach, roving backwards and forwards at her sweet will, sometimes going perilously near Maud's cunt. I followed suit, revelling in the feel of Alice's firm, soft and springy flesh and sweet skin, smiling mischievously at her as she winced when my hand neared her cunt. Helen then devoted her attention to Maud's hips, haunches, buttocks and thighs, her hand dwelling lovingly on the plumper and fleshier parts, which she gently squeezed and caressed,

279

visiting them again and again. Delightedly, I did the same to Alice, who now began to show signs of agitation. When I followed Helen's lead and forced my hand between Alice's plump thighs, so closely prssed together, and began to luxuriate in her rich, juicy, smooth flesh (my hand travelling dangerously near to her cunt) she ejaculated confusedly, "Oh Jack! ... Oh Jack! ..."—then laughed nervously at her own discomfiture!

Helen here refreshed herself by kissing Maud, a proceeding I was not slow to follow with Alice and which she appreciated.

"Shall we go on, Jack?" then asked Helen.

"Shall we, Alice?" I queried with a smile.

"I'm quite willing, Jack," she replied with a blush, then added laughingly "only Auntie is getting very daring!"

"I'll pay you out, my beauty!" retorted Helen as she joined in the laugh: "Now Maud!"—and she began to tickle Maud's navel, making her wriggle prettily with the titillation.

I applied my finger to Alice's navel. "Oh! Jack dear!" she exclaimed with heightening colour and increasing agitation as she began squirming and writhing and twisting herself about, joining nevertheless in Helen's triumphant laughter.

"Now we'll try something else!" said Helen mischievously—and to Alice's dismay she gently attacked Maud's breasts, keeping her eyes on Alice! Delightedly, I followed suit, and before Alice could interpose her free hand my eager hand had flown up to her bosom and had captured her left breast! Jack!" cried Alice, flushing furiously as she seized my hand and endeavoured to drag it away from its tempting prey, nevertheless laughing (though somewhat uneasily) at her complete discomfiture—but she found me too strong for her.

When I whispered gently, "You must submit dear—this is part of your preparation for tomorrow," she loyally, though reluctantly, accepted the position and surrendered her sweet twin globes to my tender mercies, her agitated breathing and restless movements indicating her perturbation and emotion at my hand's invasion of her maiden breasts!

Helen and Maud had suspended their game—that is to say, Maud was still on her Mother's lap with her mother's arm round her, and Helen's right hand was still playing with her daughter's beautiful breasts, but they evidently found it much more interesting and exciting to watch Alice's first experience with kind but inquisitive male fingers! The shock of feeling a man's hand on her maiden breasts had to a certain extent died away, and Alice was now lying resting on me, her right arm clasping me round my neck, her left hanging by her side, the hand tightly gripping the chair rail—the distant expression in her eyes as they idly fell on objects without seeming to see them, indicating her intense absorption in the sensations of the moment as she felt her virgin breasts stroked, caressed, and squeezed by my eager though gentle hands! For me it was a delicious occupation! Alice's little bubbies were so firm, and yet so springy and fleshy and, above all, so virginal, that my fingers absolutely revelled in their feel; and for some considerable time I could not bring myself to relinquish them!

At last, with a strong effort, I tore my hand away, and sliding it down to her navel, I brought Alice back to a consciousness of her surroundings and whereabouts by gently tickling that sensitive part of her! As her eyes resumed their duties they met those of Helen and Maud, beaming sympathy and signalling encouragement, and she smiled gratefully at them as she roused herself, murmuring, "Oh Jack dear, don't!" At this juncture Helen caught my eye, then slowly ran her hand from Maud's breasts over her stomach and down to her cunt, where her fingers began gently to pull and play with the lovely tangle of fluffy golden hair that clustered there! Alice became scarlet! It had never ocurred to her that her cunt was to be felt, and when my hand followed Helen's lead and slipped downwards over her belly she clutched my wrist wildly, threw one thigh closely over the other so as to defend the approach, and exclaimed agitatedly, "No, no darling!—no, Jack dear!—you mustn't touch me there!"—then kissed me frenziedly as if to dissuade me!

I let my hand remain in her grip and said quietly

and soothingly, "You must play the game, dear!—besides that, what did I tell you just now?" She looked questioningly and imploringly at me with eyes full of dismay! I drew her to me and kissed her lovingly, whispering "Cannot you trust yourself to me, darling?"

For reply she nestled her soft cheek against mine, and then murmured, "Jack, must you do it?"

"Yes, Alice dear!" I replied softly—"and tomorrow you will thank me for insisting!" For a moment she hesitated,—then without a word she released my wrist and slowly and reluctantly unlocked her thighs!

"May I, darling?" I asked gently.

"Yes, dear!" she replied softly and tremulously, then pressed her cheek still more closely against mine till our lips nearly rested on each other—she tightened her clasp round my neck as if to nerve her for the ordeal, while her eyes sought Helen's and rested appealing on her as if asking for her sympathy and guidance!

I decided that this time I would invade Alice's maiden cunt by the valley formed by her closely pressed thighs, at the head of which I should find her Hill of Venus, its unusual size and prominence being intensified by her sitting position—which made the tangle of curly silky hairs stand out like a bush. Accordingly I did so. To Alice's surprise, I dropped my hand lightly on her thighs, about half way down them, then it travelled upwards between their soft smooth surface till it arrived at her shrubbery, when (following Helen's lead) I played amorously with her hairs, now pulling them gently, now twining them round my fingers, now softly brushing them—a proceeding that seemed to excite Alice judging from the way in which she agitated her bottom on my knees! After a little of this toying I proceeded with forefinger and thumb to explore the region covered by her hairs, pressing and squeezing its delicious soft springy flesh, but carefully avoiding the tender sensitive opening— till Alice's involuntary wrigglings and squirmings and the increasing agitation of her bosom told me that she had arrived at the condition of erotic sexual excitement that I desired. Then I gently applied my forefinger to the lips of Alice's tender maiden cunt!

"Oh! Jack!" she cried, drawing herself back hurriedly, as if to escape from my finger, which, however, not only retained, but improved its position, and now began to move along the delicate slit— creating the most exquisite tickling sensations, which Alice evidently enjoyed! She clutched me tighter than ever round my neck, she quivered voluptously, she brought her lips to bear upon mine and began to kiss me ardently—and where my finger inserted itself into the virgin recesses of her cunt and commenced to agitate itself seductively, Alice fairly lost control of herself and surrendered herself unrestrainedly to the gratification of her sexual desires and her newly born erotic lust!

I glanced triumphantly at Helen—but to my astonishment, she was busily engaged with Maud! Her hand was buried well between Maud's thighs, and her finger was evidently hard at work in her daughter's cunt, for Maud was wriggling and quivering and jerking herself about in extreme lascivious frenzy—and it was clear that the ecstatic crisis was at hand. The piquant spectacle of Helen frigging Maud—of a mother frigging her daughter was too much for me!—I redoubled my ministrations to Alice and set to work deliberately to make her spend! She and Maud were by now far too excitedly absorbed in their own voluptuous sensations to pay any attention to each other. "Jack! Oh! Darling!" gasped Alice almost incoherently as, wriggling violently, she jerked herself madly forward as if to encourage my finger to more furious exertion in her cunt.

"Oh! Mummy! oh Mummy dear! . . . keep on! . . . keep on!" ejaculated Maud wildly in her lascivious frenzy!

Seeing that Alice was now on the verge of erotic collapse I attached her virgin clitoris and furiously tickled it! "Ha! . . . ha! . . . ha!! . . . " she gasped—then, with an indescribable spasmodic paroxysm, she spent voluptuously, bedewing my finger with her creamy virgin essence.

Almost simultaneously Maud went off with a

half-strangled cry of "Ah! ... Mummy darling!!" clinging frantically to Helen as the spasms of her sexual rapture vibrated through her and quenched the fires of her lust!

Maud was the first to come to herself which she did very soon. She kissed her Mother gratefully, and they both came across to me to welcome Alice back "from the angels," she being still unconscious! I cautiously drew my finger out of her cunt, and with the air of the victor I exhibited it to them; wet, glistening and sticky with Alice's maiden spend, the display provoking them to silent laughter! Just then Alice moved herself uneasily, then drew a long breath and dreamily opened her eyes. As they met Helen's, the recollection of her whereabouts and of what she had been doing flashed on her! She blushed violently, sprang to her feet, and buried her face in her hands, murmuring shamedly, "Oh Auntie!, Auntie!"

Helen took her affectionately in her arms and said, "There is nothing to be ashamed of, darling— we've not come to scold but to congratulate you on your debut!"

Overjoyed, Alice kissed her gratefully, embraced Maud, then threw herself into my arms (I had then risen) murmuring "Oh darling! Darling!" But my prick had been so irritated and inflamed by the movements of her soft warm bottom on it that it stood rampant and stiff and stark!

"Oh, look at poor Jack!" cried Maud as she

pointed to it—"And poor Mother too, who has not yet had anything. Wait half a minute for us Jack. Come, Alice!" and the two girls rushed off into Helen's bathroom. Hurriedly Helen and I performed our ablutions, mad for each other, then I placed her on her bed, put a hard cushion under her bottom, separated her thighs, and sat by her, impatiently waiting for the girls' re-appearance— the while feasting my eyes on Helen's beautiful cunt now so gloriously displayed, while Helen gently stroked my raging prick!

Very soon the girls hurried in, beaming with pleasurable excitement and anticipation. "Now Jack! into Mother!" cried Maud.

I needed no encouragement! In a trice I was on the bed and between Helen's legs, and was just about to plunge my prick into her cunt when Alice innocently intervened! "Please Jack, may I feel it?" she asked.

In spite of ourselves we all laughed! "Yes, dear!" I replied, "You may feel me, and you may put me into Helen!" The touch of her soft maiden hand nearly made my tool burst with pleasure. "Now, Alice dear!" I cried as I let myself down on to Helen. Holding my prick in her dainty fingers, Alice cleverly guided its head into Helen's throbbing and expectant cunt and delightedly watched it as it disappeared inch by inch, Helen all the time whinnying with the rapture of again feeling a male organ lodged in her! But we both were too ardent

287

and excited to take our pleasure slowly, as we had intended! As soon as Helen found me well up her cunt and felt my arms close firmly round her till her breasts flattened against me, she began to agitate herself under me wildly, wriggling and writhing, jerking herself about, moving her legs restlessly—sometimes stretching them, at other times twisting them round me! To prolong her blissful transports, I lay on her as motionless and as rigid as I possibly could, leaving her to really fuck herself, in the hope that her furious movements would provoke her into spending quickly— and so it happened, for soon she strained me passionately to her and jogging herself upwards violently she spent rapturously, ejaclating brokenly "Oh my darling! ... my dar ... ling ... ," with such voluptuous quivers and tremors that she nearly sent me spending also! I was, however, able to resist the sweet temptation, and when her spasms of pleasure ceased to thrill through her, I began to fuck her delightedly slowly; but another cyclone of sexual passion and just swept through Helen, and again she began to riot under me in furious plungings and curvettings, her head rolling from side to side in the vehemence of her desires! I could not any longer control myself, I let myself go and rammed fiercely into her! Helen responded by jerking herself madly upwards as if to meet my down thrusts! Then ensued a veritable cyclone of heaves from her and fierce ramming thrusts from me in the wildest fury—then the ecstatic crisis overtook me, and frantically I spent into Helen, she receiving my boiling tribute with the most voluptuous and rapturous transports of bliss as she herself yielded to nature and spent madly in thrills of delight!

For some little while we lay lost to the world, tightly casped in each other's arms—then slowly we came to; our lips met in tender kisses, and then I slowly drew my prick out of Helen's cunt and rcse. Maud and Alice at once fell on her and kissed her passionately—then Maud whispered something in her Mother's ear and promptly Helen rose and, with a loving glance at me, she disappeared with the two girls. I slipped into my room and quickly performed a most necessary and welcome ablution; then I put on my night attire as a hint to Maud and Alice that the seance was closed.

Before long they all returned and following my lead they put on their "nighties" ... then Helen said "Now my dears, it is time for bed. Good night, Jack dear! Oh how good you have been to all of us!" and tenderly she kissed me.

"Good night, Jack! And thank you so much!" said Maud archly as she kissed me.

Alice said nothing, but when our lips met in a passionate kiss she breathed, "Oh my darling!" Then we retired to our separate rooms.

CHAPTER THREE

In about fifteen minutes Helen noiselessly opened my door and said softly, "Jack!" and promptly I went into her room, still naked. She was still in her nightie; I begged her to take it off, and again she stood before me in all her glorious nudity! I pointed to her bed, and soon we lay on it side by side, my left arm 'round her, whil emy right hand, after playing a little with her lovely breasts, wandered down to her cunt.

Presently I took hold of her and gently conducted it to my prick, which still lay limp and inert. With a loving smile she began to play with it, sometimes stroking it, sometimes caressing it, feeling my balls and pulling my hairs, evidently delighted in her occupation. Needless to say, it was not long before my organ began to show signs of returning life, and soon it was in fair erection again.

"Why Jack! You're ready again!" she whispered admiringly as she continued to play and fondle it

"Yes, darling!, thanks to you!" I murmured with a kiss of gratitude—"and you?" Helen blushed prettily, then wriggled lasciviously as my finger slipped into the warm and moist interior of her cunt—no answer was necessary as her eyes proclaimed my readiness.

My prick now was in full erection! I whispered to Helen "put it into you, darling!" She looked uncomprehendingly at me! I whispered again "straddle across me, dear, . . . that's right, now take hold of my prick and put it into your cunt yourself . . . now sink down on it, and let yourself take it all in . . . slowly darling, that's the way . . . now lie on me!"

In surprise and wondering astonishment Helen obeyed, hesitatingly at first—but when she began to impale herself on my rampant prick, she comprehended the sweet manvever and lent herself almost too energetically to it; but soon she had my prick stiffly lodged up her cunt, then she lowered herself gently on to me murmuring "Oh Jack! How delicious! How heavenly!" as with a few voluptuous wriggles she settled herself luxuriously on me, her eyes sparkling with delight as my arms closed round her and imprisoned her! As for me I was in the seventh heaven of bliss as I lay under Helen, clasping her luscious and palpitating naked body in my arms with my prick engulfed in her moist, warm, and throbbing cunt! Her full large breasts lay sweetly on my chest, our eyes looked straight into each other's, her ripe lips rested on mine and our breaths mingled as we exchanged long passionate and burning kisses in our mutual rapture! And so we lay silent for a while, absorbed in the exquisite sensations of the moment!

"Am I to do anything, Jack?" Helen presently whispered.

"Not just now, darling," I replied softly—"Just keep as you are and rest yourself on me, lie limply, dear, and let me enjoy your delicious weight on me! We'll have a sweet talk, all the time tasting each other—then when we can no longer wait you'll have to ... fuck me!—and yourself on me!—you'll have to do all the work this time!"

"Oh Jack!" Helen murmured delightedly, her eyes sparkling again with pleasurable anticipation —and involuntarily she began to agitate herself voluptuously on me. Quickly I passed my hands along her back to her bottom, and gripping her gloriously plump fleshy buttocks, I checked her movements whispering "Steady, Helen darling! Lie still, dear—or you'll set us both off!—let us prolong this delicious agony, and when we let ourselves go our pleasure will be all the greater".

"Oh Jack! I couldn't help it!" Helen murmured faintly, then she suddenly caught her breath, her eyes half-closed and an indescribable tremor quivered through her. She had provoked herself into spending! I patted her bottom tenderly. Then she raised her humid eyes to mine, and kissed me rapturously as she whispered "Oh Jack, that was lovely! Now I will lie quiet and be a good girl!" And again she voluptuously settled herself on me.

I transferred my hands from her bottom to her breasts and fondly caressed Helen's delicious bubbies as they rested sweetly on me, and again we lay silent for a while.

Presently she whispered in my ear "Jack, are you going to ... to ravish Alice this evening?"

"I think so, darling!" I replied, "Provided, of course, that she is willing to let me have her! Has she said anything to you?"

"No," Helen answered, "But I'm sure she wishes you to ... fuck her, dear! The sight of first Maud and then me in your arms excited her terribly—you should have heard her questions when we were in the bathroom,—I think she would have liked to have been ravished there and then!"

"Then she shall be deflowered this evening!" I said—"The very idea of holding her tight in my arms while I force my prick into her maiden cunt is enough to ... make me spend now!" Helen kissed me passionately, and began to jog herself gently on me!

"Steady, darling!" I whispered warningly as I

soothed her. "Alice has a largish cunt, has she not?"

"Yes," Helen replied with an arch smile, "Alice has quite a large cunt—as large as mine!" she added with a conscious blush and an involuntary wriggle. "You'll hurt her very little, I fancy, Jack, and it will be sweet to see her in your arms, especially when she feels herself inundated for the first time with warm love juice!" and her eyes glistened as she amorously kissed me. Then she whispered in sudden agitation "Jack! I must . . . ! —may I, darling?"

I nodded with a loving smile and folded my arms again 'round Helen so as to hold her firmly against me. Again she whispered, this time flushing deeply, "Darling, promise to lie quite still, and let me do . . . everything!" and again I nodded smilingly.

Voluptuously, Helen arranged herself on me, kissed me tenderly, laid her cheek against mine and, gripping me tightly, she began to jog herself up and down on my prick, agitating herself on me in the most delicious way and making me fairly thrill with delight! At first she moved herself slowly and rythmically—but before long the increasing flutters of her bosom clasped so tightly against me, and her broken breathing indicated her rapidly growing lust; soon she was wriggling furiously on me, her bottom heaving and tossing wildly as she worked herself up and down on my stiff and rampant prick with riotously rapid movements. Soon the blissful crisis overtook her—a convulsive quiver thrilled thrrough her, and with a half-strangled inarticulate cry Helen spent rapturously and collapsed, her whole body pulsating as the spasm of pleasure shot through her!

True to my promise, I lay absolutely rigid and motionless—but I had to exercise all my powers of self-control to prevent myself from joining her in spending!—and as she lay quiet on me, I gradually regained complete hold over myself again. Then I whispered in her ear "Go on again, darling!" Helen instantly roused herself from her semi-swoon, and soon she was again raging wildly on me, wriggling furiously and ramming herself down on my prick in the wildest erotic excitement! Then, for the second time, she spent blissfully, quivering voluptuously in my arms in the throes of her ecstasy! Again I allowed her to lie quiet till she could collect herself—and then I whispered, "Now, darling, we'll finish together!" As if stimulated by the knowledge that her excited cunt was now about to receive the blissful injection Helen clasped me more tightly than ever to her, kissed me passionately and set to work to fuck me (I really cannot describe her movements more truly!). It did not take her long to break down my defense—and I was a willing victim! With long furious strokes of her wildly agitated bottom she worked herself up and down on my now raging prick—then, when my involuntary and uncontrollable quivers told her that she had overcome my stubborn resistance, she agitated herself madly on me in a hurricane of wild heavings and wrigglings and squirmings, in which I joined with frenzied up-thrusting—till, no longer able to refrain, I shot a torrent of boiling love juice into Helen just as she, for the third time, yielded to nature and spent in exquisite transports of rapture! Oh God!, how I spent into her—and how ecstatically Helen received the deluge of hot semen that I poured frantically into her! Then we both collapsed and lay motionless, clinging rapturously to each other!

How long we thus lay I do not know! I came to first. Helen was lying on me limp and nerveless, her head resting on my shoulder—she had fainted under the violence of her spending and the intensity of her spasm of pleasure! Gently and caressingly I passed my hands over her naked self, squeezing her breasts and endeavouring to bring her to herself, all the while whispering fond words of love in her ear! Presently Helen moved uneasily, then drew a long breath, or rather a deep sigh, of utter satisfaction and slowly raised her head half-consciously with a glazed look. As her humid eyes opened they met mine and flashed instant recognition. A wonderful smile indicative of the intense satisfaction and happiness radiated her face— "Jack! My darling!" she murmured rapturously, as she pressed her lips to mine and showered kisses on me till we both gasped for breath! Then slowly and reluctantly she drew herself off my now limp and dejected prick, rose, and tottered to her bathroom. Promptly I slipped into my room and indulged in a welcome and necessary ablution, then returned to Helen's room just as she herself re-appeared. She ran straight into my welcoming arms. I led her to a chair and installed her on my knees, and in soft murmurs and with loving kisses we testified to each other the pleasure we had mutually tasted!

"Now my darling, good night!" I said finally and drew Helen tenderly to me!

"Goddd night, my darling, darling Jack!" she murmured as our lips sought each other—"Oh! how happy you have made me!" and passionately she kissed me, then rose and led me to my door, as she had to lock it after me.

"Sleep well, my darling!" she added archly—"Do not forget that tomorrow night you have to violate Alice!" I laughed, gave her a final kiss and thus we parted!

And so ended our first evening at *The Nunnery*!

CHAPTER FOUR

We all met at breakfast next morning, the ladies looking radiant; Helen and Maud's faces wore a look of happy satisfaction, while Alice was a veritable blush-rose! After the usual bright meal, Helen disappeared into her boudoir to write letters, and Maud adjourned to her bedroom for mysteries in millinery connected with a visit she was about to pay. Alice confessed to having no plans; to me she seemed nervous and pre-occupied, her thoughts no doubt reverting constantly to her ordeal of the evening. Since I arrived and had been told of the wonderful and almost incredible thing she was willing to do, I was most anxious to get her by herself for a little so that I might let her understand how I appreciated it—but no opportunity had been vouchsafed; and so I decided to monopolize her all the morning, for I felt morally certain that she then would be all the happier when she was made over to me that evening in Helen's room,—and to that end I suggested that I should take her on the river till lunch time. Delightedly she accepted the proposition, and soon we were in the boat and off, she in the stern seats with the tiller ropes, and I on the rowing thwart, in easy chatting distance of her.

She had on a walking dress—and what between the lowness of her seat and the shortness of her dress, more of her shapely legs and slender ankles cased in dainty stockings were visible to my delighted eyes than she quite approved of; and she strove by sundry tugs and re-adjustments to lessen the exhibition—but without success. I watched her in amused silence—and when she resigned herself to the inevitable and resumed her usual pose on the stern cushions with slightly heightened colour, conscious that my eyes were admiringly dwelling on her pretty extremities, I frankly laughed out and said chaffingly, "Well, you are a funny girl, Alice—why are you so unkind this morning in the matter of showing yourself to me, when you were so sweet and kind last night, and are going to be so again to-night!"

Alice coloured deeply, then laughed in pretty confusion and said, "Places and surroundings have to be considered, Jack my dear,—I am quite sure that you would not like me here now just as I was last night!"

"Wouldn't I!" I rejoined ardently,—"When we get to that little sheltered backwater on the left, I'll row in, so as to give you an opportunity of changing your attire!"

"You're very considerate—and I'm much obliged to you, Jack," she replied, laughing merrily and apparently quite at her ease with me—" but I'm afraid you must deny yourself the ... may I say, pleasure!" she added archly.

"Well, I suppose lovely woman must have her way! At all events, we'll go in all the same," I replied with mock resignation—"Steer in, dear, and take us right to the end in the thick of the trees,"—and soon we found ourselves in a delicious nook and in absolute privacy. I tied the boat to a convenient root so that we could not drift, then I squeezed myself into the stern seats by Alice's side (she sweetly making room for me) and slipped my left arm round her waist.

"This is very romantic!" I remarked softly as I drew her to me—"Will not the poetry of the spot tempt you to become a wood nymph?"

Alice laughed gaily and shook her head. "I never went in for theatricals, Jack," she rejoined.

"I'm not asking you to do so now, dear," I replied—"Theatrics mean dressing up, my suggestion implied the very contrary!"

She laughed merrily, then nestling close to me

she whispered gently, blushing divinely "In less than twelve hours you'll see what you wish, Jack won't that do, dear?"

I clasped her tightly to me and made her shift herself onto my lap, then I kissed her passionately. "My darling!" I whispered, "I was only teasing you! ... And are you really going to be so sweet and kind to me to-night as to give me your ... maiden self!"

Alice smiled tenderly and gently nodded her hear, her eyes looking lovingly into mine. I kissed her sweetly and gratefully and for a moment or two our emotions enforced silence.

Presently I whispered "Tell me, darling, do you really wish this? Are you really willing to ... lose your virginity, your maidenhead?"

A vivid blush suffused her cheeks—for a few moments she was silent and I could feel how she was trembling; then she murmured with deep emotion "Had anyone else ... been suggested, I would have said indignantly No! ... No! ... No! ... — but to you, Jack, I say Yes! ... Yes! ... Yes! ..."

I was too moved to speak! ... I could only kiss her sweet lips over and over again,—and she could read in my eyes my emotion! Helen's chaffing remark that no one but myself would ever win Alice flashed through my brain—and an overwhelming desire to reward in the one and only right way Alice's love and trust as evidenced by the wonderful sacrifice of her virginity that she was willing to make, surged through me!

I held her to me more closely than ever, and looking straight into her loving eyes I said softly "Darling, you rebuke me! You are willing to surrender to a girl's most precious treasure, and to give it to me freely and without regard to your future happiness! Will you let me do what I can to ensure that happiness to you? Alice, my darling, will you become my wife?"

She gazed at me in absolute wonder, her eyes widely open in startled surprise; it was clear that she could not believe her ears! I smiled tenderly at her and whispered, "Would you like to hear it again? Alice darling, will you become my dear little wife?"

The look of startled surprise vanished,—in its place came a simply wonderful smile,—she caught her breath,—her eyes filled with happy tears which, however, could not put out the lovelight that was in them,—her lips parted, and she murmured brokenly "Oh! Jack! ... Jack!" as she clung lovingly to me!

I bent down and kissed her tenderly on her quivering lips, and said gently, "That means Yes! ... Oh! My darling! ... my darling!" And for a while we remained silent, our eyes looking into each other's and brimming over with love!

Presently Alice whispered with a curious smile,

303

half anxious and half roguish, "Jack! what about to-night, darling?"

I laughed, she also after a moment's hesitation. "We had better let the arrangement stand good, darling," I replied, "We must think of Helen and Maud, for were it not for them we should not now be ... sweethearts!" (she kissed me delightedly) "We must not disappoint them. I don't think we will tell them anything until after ... after." Alice blushed vividly and kissed me sweetly, "After you have tasted Love's raptured in my arms! You're happier now about it, eh darling?"

"I'm yours now entirely and absolutely, Jack," Alice murmured gently, her eyes full of love—"I'm your happy sweetheart now!—I'll gladly be your mistress to-night, and your little wife as soon as ever you like! So do just what you like with me and to me!" and she smiled lovingly and trustfully.

I kissed her gratefully, and a sweet idea came into my brain; with a mischievous smile I said "I'm going to take you at your word, darling!"— and slipped my right hand under her clothes, arresting its movement upwards when it got to her dainty knees. "Oh Jack!" she exclaimed as she started up hurriedly and strove to defend herself, at the same time laughing merrily at her discomfiture and the way I had turned her words against herself. I looked smilingly at her but kept my hand where it was on her knees. "What do you wish to do, darling?" she whispered in pretty confusion. "I want to call on a maiden that has just become engaged, and to offer her my congratulations," I replied with mock gravity—"I know she is at home and so with your leave I'll go on." Alice laughed merrily and gently reparted her thighs as my hand passed along them, as if to facilitate its approach to her cunt, all the while looking at me with eyes full of love. Delightedly, my hand travelled over her luscious thighs clad in dainty drawers, till it reached the tender junction,—then slipping through the opening it arrived at its destination. "Oh darling!" breathed Alice, squirming deliciously as she felt my fingers on her maiden cunt,—and as I pulled and played with her silky hairs and stroked and caressed her exquisitely springy and juicy flesh, she threw her arms 'round my neck and pressing her lips on mine she kissed me passionately, agitating herself charmingly all the time. Soon my finger gently made its way between the lips of her cunt and into the warm throbbing moist interior, where it inquisitively explored its sweet recesses, dwelling significantly on the weblike hymeneal membrane that I was that same evening to break through, and then as she was now beginning to wriggle in earnest I challenged her excited clitoris and set to work to frig Alice! "Oh Jack! . . . darling!" she panted rapturously as she jogged herself to meet my finger, gently at first and then more and more wildly and rapidly till in a storm of uncontrollable jerks and

305

squirmings and wriggles the ecstatic crisis overtook her and she inundated my happy finger with her virginal love-juice!

Alice had kept her lips pressed on mine throughout, deliciously punctuating with ardent kisses her transports while being felt and frigged! When the last spasms of pleasure had died away she gave me one long clinging burning kiss and looking gratefully at me with her still humid eyes she murmured rapturously, "Oh Jack! it was just heavenly!" "Nicer than last night, dear?" I asked quizzingly. "Oh! yes, yes!" she replied in tones of the deepest conviction that set me off in a laugh in which she soon joined. "Last night I was too timid and nervous, and so awfully surprised by everything I saw, and so excited also, that I could not let myself go as I did just now!" she added colouring prettily. "Then you'll let yourself go to-night, darling!" I whispered significantly. She blushed like a peony, looked tenderly at me, and with a loving smile she nodded her head assuringly!

"Now it is time for us to start home,—one final kiss, darling! I said feelingly. "We're going to be very happy, love, for we are wise enough to recognise that a bedroom has joys as well as a drawing room! Now, my sweet . . .!" and lovingly we kissed each other. Then we resumed our proper places in the boat and soon were out in the river again, this time homeward bound, talking sweet nothings in supreme happiness.

Presently, Alice, with a little hesitation, said somewhat seriously, "Please promise me one thing, Jack!—When we are married please keep on being kind and good to Auntie Helen and to Maud!—I shall be so very miserable if I should be the cause of their being left without the sexual satisfaction they so ardently desire and need! You will promise this, Jack darling?"

I was very touched by her devotion. "I promise willingly, dear," I replied earnestly—then with a mischievous smile I added, "We'll have our bedrooms arranged like those in the Nunnery, darling. We will always put up Auntie Helen and Maud in the rooms that communicate with ours, so that they can slip in quietly—and we'll have regular orgies when they come up, eh, darling!"

Alice beamed on me, then laughed merrily, exclaiming, "Oh Jack! It will be fun!"

As we neared the house, Helen came down to meet us. "I've been wondering what became of you two!" she exclaimed,— "Now come along, lunch is ready—we must feed you up, Alice darling, and you also, Jack," she added laughingly, and, slipping her arm round Alice, she led her towards the house. I fastened the boat and tidied up generally, and then followed them.

CHAPTER FIVE

After lunch the ladies retired, frankly admitting that they were going to "rest" so as to better fit them for the excitements of the evening. I announced my intention of walking to the neighbouring little town to try and do some shopping; but they all so vigorously protested against my taking an eight mile walk and knocking myself up that at Helen's pressing request I consented to be driven in. The object of my visit was to try to obtain two pairs of strong leather wristlets, softly padded and fitted with a brass "D" so that they could be strapped together or each arm secured singly. I was fortunate enough to find the very thing at the saddler's; he stitched the "D"s on while I waited, and I bore them off in triumph. My readers will come across them presently.

I was back to The Nunnery by tea time, after which Maud took Alice off for a short walk, while Helen and I strolled in the gardens. She was delightfully full of the pleasures she had tasted in my arms on the previous night,—"Jack! I'm another woman today!" she exclaimed rapturously, adding with a merry smile "I didn't know I wanted it so badly!" She went on to tell me that she had kept Alice with her all that afternoon as she feared that the girl's natural apprehension of the ordeal of being ravished might make her nervous and perhaps hysterical when the moment arrived, were she allowed to think about it too much previously— but, she said, "While Alice does seem a little to dread the ... operation itself, she really seems to be almost looking forward to surrendering her maidenhead to you! I'm sure she loves you, Jack!"

"Dear little thing!" I replied with feeling—"The thought of having to ravish her this evening excites me terribly!"

Half-past ten again was a very long time in coming, but at last the clock chimed the half hour, and promptly I entered Helen's room, where I found Maud and Alice, the latter really looking nervous and agitated, although she greeted me with a sweet smile. We kissed each other all round, and then Helen placed Alice in my arms with a significant smile that made the blushing girl grow still more rosy as I fondly kissed her again, and then passed my arm round her waist so as to keep her with me.

"Now let us begin!" I said briskly. "Helen, may we move that long dress box of yours with the padded top into the middle of the room?" Quickly she and Maud effected the change, then looked enquiringly at me. "Thanks, dears!" I said—"Now Helen, lie down on your back, naked, with your legs widely apart, and let me have a good study of your cunt!"

"Oh Jack!" she exclaimed, colouring vividly as she looked pleadingly at me—but I only laughed at her and pointed to the box; whereupon Helen reluctantly took off her nightie and placed herself on her back in the position desired. Quickly I knelt between her knees with Maud and Alice on either side of me, their eyes gleaming with excitement, and together we delightedly inspected Helen's superb cunt—gazing admiring on the thickly clustering growth of hairs of Venus' Hill and the delicate salmon-pink of its lips, poor Helen all the while blushing like a schoolgirl! Then with gentle fingers I drew the lips apart and disclosed Helen's clitoris (evidently much excited), the quivering folds of pink tender flesh, and the delicious passage in which I had already been twice voluptuously lodged!

At last I removed my hands, and leaning forward I ardently kissed Helen on her cunt, she squirming

311

prettily,—and rose. "Don't move yet dear," I said, —"Now Maud, strip yourself naked and lie on your Mother face upwards—let your legs hand down outside hers, so that we can compare both cunts!"

"Oh Jack!" both Mother and daughter cried aghast as they looked ashamedly at each other; but I was obdurate. Alice was now rosy red, but her eyes glittered with eager anticipation, and she smiled delightedly at me as our eyes met; she undoubtedly was enjoying herself!

Reluctantly Maud complied. When she had stripped herself naked I made her straddle across Helen, then gently lowered her backwards till she lay flat on her Mother, who passed her arms round her daughter and maintained her in the desired position! Their cunts now were displayed one just above the other, a charming spectacle!

"Now Alice dear, strip yourself naked also!" I said gently to her. Much surprised and somewhat disconcerted, Alice slowly complied, and shamefacedly stood naked before me; after a delightful but hasty glance at her lovely timid shrinking naked figure I made her kneel between Helen's parted legs and sit on her heels, then I myself knelt behind her, passed my arms round her and gently seized her breasts—my chin resting on her right shoulder, so that we could together feast our eyes on the piquant sight, the cunts of mother and daughter!

In admiring silence we gazed our fill, Alice's trembles testifying to her suppressed excitement: "Aren't they sweet!" I whispered. Alice nodded eagerly, too excited to speak, her eyes shining with something akin to lust! After a little further silent contemplation I whispered again "Open Maud's cunt, dear, so that we can see what the inside is like!" Joyously Alice complied, and with her pretty little fingers she pulled widely apart the delicate lips of Maud's cunt and revealed the lovely interior, salmon-tinted and juicy, surmounted by a projecting and angry-looking clitoris, which seemed to attract Alice's eyes.

"Now open Auntie Helen's dear;" I whispered. Quickly Alice lowered her hands, and placing the tips of her fingers on either side of Helen's well-defined and pouting slit she held Helen's cunt open for my inspection! "Do you see any family likeness, dear?" I asked with a smile.

Alice laughed silently—"Of course!" she said softly, "They're exactly like each other, only Auntie's is so much bigger and ... and ... looser!" she added with a mischievous smile which made me fondle and squeeze her dear little breasts more actively than before! Then of her own accord Alice began to stroke and play with the glorious pair of cunts in front of her, devoting a hand to each—while Helen and Maud wriggled and squirmed deliciously, uttering involuntarily little cries of pleasure as Alice's gentle fingers wandered caressingly over their sensitive and ticklish cunts—her eyes dancing with delight!

"I think they have had enough, dear!" I said presently and Alice and I rose and assisted Helen and Maud to their feet.

"Now Jack, Alice must let us examine her virgin cunt before you alter it forever!" cried Maud excitedly.

"Oh no, Maud! Oh no, Jack, please!" Alice pleaded, blushing vividly.

"I'd also like to study it, dear?" I said, "and this will be our last chance. So lie down, darling!"

Shamefacedly and with burning blushes Alice showly complied; delightedly Helen and Maud forced her legs widely apart and, kneeling together between them, they proceeded to examine Alice's maiden treasure, while behind them I also knelt, my head between theirs, my arms round them both, my hands each occupied with a breast of each. After minutely inspecting Alice's full and prominent *Mons Veneris* and gently playing with the hair that grew so prettily on it, they tenderly pulled the delicate close-fitting lips apart and excitedly gazed at the virgin interior, the web-like membrane that defended the stronghold of Alice's virginity receiving their closest and most interested attention. "There's your job, Jack!" exclaimed Maud wickedly, as she pointed to it—on hearing which, poor Alice shivered involuntarily but most prettily.

314

At last they rose. "Darling! it's very sweet!" murmured Helen in Alice's ear as she fondly kissed her and began to help her to rise. Meanwhile, I had attracted Maud's attention, and protruding the tip of my tongue between my lips I made her understand my intentions. She nodded delightedly and quickly got behind Alice and caught hold of her breasts and so prevented her from getting up, while I said gently, "Lie still, dear, we want you a little longer!" and knelt down on her right motioning to Helen to place herself similarly on Alice's left.

"Oh! Jack! what are you going to do to me?" Alice cried, half alarmed by these mysterious preparations. "Something very sweet, darling!" cried Maud,—"Don't be frightened, just lie still!" In an undertone, I directed Helen to hold Alice's left leg firmly while I imprisoned her right leg between my right arm and my side,—then bending down, I placed my lips on Alice's tender cunt and lovingly kissed it!!

In spite of Maud's re-assuring words, Alice had been watching my every movement intently; she saw my head bend forward and down—then she felt my lips touch her cunt and imprint on it a kiss that sent a quiver through her. Startled by the sensations now aroused she cried, "Oh Jack! don't," and tried to close her legs and rise—but we were too strong for her and forced her to remain as she was. Again I kissed her sweet cunt,—again she quivered violently and struggled to get free, crying

"Don't Jack! Please don't!" Her face was now like a peony and she was thrilling every limb—my kisses on her maiden cunt had evidently set her on fire and her lustful desires had passed beyond her control. Just then I imprinted a burning kiss on her clitoris itself, pressing my lips down on her soft springing flesh as I did so.

"Ah!" Alice ejaculated sharply, agitating herself divinely as her lust began to dominate her. Then I lightly ran the tip of my tongue along her tender slit, and began to lick the lips of her cunt!

"Oh! ... oh! ..." Alice gasped in a strange half-strangled voice, closing her eyes in ecstasy,—no longer resisting but yielding to her now imperious erotic desires! Helen to whom this sweet pastime was an absolutely new revelation, was a study— with eager gleaming eyes, dilated nostrils, and slightly parted lips watched Alice with the keenest interest, Alice now being in the throes of the wildest erotic frenzy, wriggling, quivering deliciously, thrilling with rapture as my loving tongue tickled and licked her now inflamed cunt! I ceased for a moment to feast my eyes on her and to exchange significant smiles with Maud and Helen—then I whispered to the latter "Help me to hold Alice's cunt open so that I can get my tongue inside!" at the same time placing my left hand alongside of Alice's slit. Quickly comprehending my wishes Helen placed her fingers opposite to mine, and together we pulled Alice's cunt widely open,—then after an admiring glance at its pinky juicy luscious interior now evidently throbbing in intense sexual excitement I inserted my tongue deeply into it and began to agitate it subtly with uncontrollable desire! Wildly she tossed and jerked herself upwards as if to meet the thrusts of my tongue, her head rolling from side to side in her blissful transports and her breasts dancing with the palpitations of her heaving bosom, while she ejaculated brokenly incoherent exclamations in the fury of her erotic rage! I saw it was time to bring on the ecstatic crisis, and so my tongue attacked her throbbing and excited clitoris, sucking and tickling it passionately! "Ha! ... ha! ... ha! ...", she cried chokingly in a paroxysm of rapture, then she spent frantically in exquisite bliss and delicious spasmodic quivering as my still devoted tongue absorbed the sweet maiden love-juice of her hot discharge as it revelled in its delicious environment between the lips of her cunt!

When I found that the spasms of pleasure were ceasing to thrill through Alice, I withdrew my tongue and lips from her cunt and rose. As I did so, Helen gave a gasp of astonishment and pointed to my mouth with an expression of horror, for my moustache was plentifully bedewed with Alice's spendings. I chuckled contentedly at her and disappeared into my room where I quickly put myself in order again and then rejoined her. Alice had just come to herself,—Helen and Maud were kneeling on each side of her and kissing her fondly as they stroked her breasts as if to stimulate her. I heard Maud say softly "Didn't I tell you, dear, that you were going to taste something very delicious?—Oh! you are a lucky girl!"

Just then Alice caught sight of me—she sprang up, threw herself into my erms, flung hers round my neck and kissed me passionately over and over again, murmuring, "Oh darling! . . . Darling!" till she had to cease for want of breath. Then Maud took her off for a necessary toilet, leaving me with Helen.

By now I was in a furious state of erection—it was absolutely necessary to me to get some relief from somebody. I seized Helen and whispered fiercely "Will Alice be ready to be ravished when she comes back or must she be allowed to wait a bit?"

"Better let her wait a little, dear," she answered looking sympathisingly at me—and I could see that she also was very erotically excited and was longing for relief!

"Then either you or Maud will have to take me on, dear!" I replied, "I must have one of you,—feel," and I conducted her hand to my raging prick!

"Oh, Poor thing!" she exclaimed, adding with a smile, "Either Maud or I will e delighted to have it inserted into us, dear. Who shall it be?"

"You, darling, if I dare choose!" I answered,

"but we had better get Alice to deal the cards and settle that way. Here she comes!" and as I spoke, Alice and Maud appeared, Alice absolutely radiant with delight.

I tore off my night kit and pointed to my prick in tremendous erection. "Alice darling, please deal the cards to Helen and Maud and settle who is to have the honour—whoever gets the Ace of Spades must be the one to relieve me!"

Excitedly, Alice shuffled and cut the cards, then dealt them face upwards to Maud and Helen; after a few rounds the Ace of Spades fell before Helen. A look of delight flashed over her face as she looked delightedly at me.

"Come, darling!" I said. She wanted no pressing, but quickly slipped on the bed and placed herself in position. In a moment I was on her—in another I had buried my prick in her expectant cunt. Then, clasping her tightly against me, I rammed fiercely into her—she ably seconded my furious movements, and soon we both spent ecstatically, she quivering rapturously as she felt herself inundated by my boiling discharge! A rapid but most delicious fuck!

"Quick Jack! Let me up!" Helen whispered. Hastily, but reluctantly, I rose off her and set her free, laughing as she rushed off to her bathroom followed by Maud.

"May I come with you, Jack?" whispered Alice timidly. "Yes, of course, dear, come along!" I re-

319

plied, looking fondly at her, then slipping my arm round her waist, I led into my room and put the door to. "Oh Jack! do let me do you, dear!" she asked excitedly, her eyes beaming merrily,—and without waiting for a reply she set to work, and in the sweetest and most delicious fashion she sponged and bathed my prick, the touch of her gentle little hands thrilling through me and reviving me wonderfully.

When she had finished I took her little hands in mine and thanked her with a kiss—then said softly, "Now dear, in about quarter of an hour I propose to take you and ... violate you sweetly! May I do so?"

Alice looked straight in the eyes lovingly and trustfully, then replied gently "Yes, darling!" then held up her lips to be kissed. "You are quite sure, sweetheart?" I asked searchingly, but with a tender smile. "Quite sure, Jack!" she replied, blushing prettily as she again met my eyes squarely and bravely, "Take me, and ... fuck me, darling!" she whispered and hid her face on my shoulder in bashful confusion. I clasped her closely against me and sought her lips with mine, and kissed her passionately over and over again till she gasped for breath.

"Now let us go back," I said, and we returned together to Helen's room which we found empty. "Oh! I'm so glad we're first back," Alice exclaimed delightedly—"They won't know that I've been

320

with you!—Jack. Don't tell them, dear!" she added merrily, smiling her thanks as I gave the required promise. Just then Helen and Maud appeared. Helen ran up to me, threw herself into my
arms and kissed me, saying laughingly, "Jack dear,
it was just heavenly!"

"Darling, of course it was," ·I replied, "For
you fuck like an angel!"—at which interchange of
compliments Alice and Maud laughed heartily, Hel-
en soon joining them.

"Come to me, Alice dear," said Helen as she
seated herself in her favorite chair, "You and I are
entitled to a rest!"—and quickly Alice settled herself in Helen's lap and, greatly daring, gently
played with her Auntie's breasts.

"I suppose that means· that you and I are not
entitled at present to rest, eh dear?" I said to
Maud meaningly,—"Come and discuss the situation!" and seating myself I drew her on my knees
and gently toyed with her cunt.

"Well Jack," she said presently, "What are we
to do?"

"I'm afraid your choice is limited to finger or
tongue, dear," I replied with a significant smile.

"And a very sweet option too!" Maud answered
cheerily,—"Jack, I'd like to be sucked, a long slow
suck!" And she looked at me invitingly. We rose,
and I arranged her on Helen's box, face upwards,
with her legs nicely apart, Helen and Alice kneeling
one on each side of her the better to watch the

proceedings, Alice being particularly keen to witness what she herself had just tasted so deliciously.

After a little sweet toying with Maud's cunt, I stooped down and kissed it ardently, my lips travelling right along the coral slit and making Maud quiver voluptuously—while Helen and Alice intuitively commenced to play with her breasts. Then I ran my tongue slowly along the lovely opening, touching it very lightly, and evidently giving Maud exquisite pleasure—for she began to wriggle delightfully, half jogging herself up as if to meet my tongue, whereupon I stiffened it and forced the tip well into her orifice, then stabbed and darted and thrust downwards strongly, first slowly and then more rapidly as I noticed her agitation increase. Again I ran my tongue along her slit, this time with more of a licking action, reverting to the orifice every now and then—till I had worked her up to a frenzy of unsatisfied longing lust without touching her clitoris. Maud's movements now became tumultuous, even lascivious, and wanton in their wrigglings and writhings, their twistings and contortions; she was evidently on the point of spending and longing to spend, but yet delaying the culmination of her pleasure in order to prolong the blissful agony of the struggle against herself! Being desirous of humouring her desires I continued my alternate lickings and thrustings, avoiding touching her clitoris—but soon it was patent to me that Maud was losing her power of self-control.

Promptly I attacked her clitoris, sometimes simply licking and tickling it, sometimes taking it gently between my lips and sucking it! Maud now seemed to go mad! Alice told me afterwards that she was an extraordinary sight in her erotic fury! She plunged, curvetted, wriggled, and tossed herself about so wildly that I had the greatest difficulty in keeping my mouth planted on her cunt! Suddenly her body stiffened, her breasts became tense, an indescribable spasm convulsed her —and with a delirously strangled, "Ah ... h!" she spent rapturously, her whole body thrilling voluptuously as the spasms of pleasure quivered through her, while she distilled her love juice so plentifully that my tongue lips and moustache all were spattered with her feminine essence of love!

Again Helen's shocked eyes met mine as I raised my head from her daughter's cunt, and again I chuckled contentedly at her as I went off to my room, leaving Maud in her charge till she came to! I was more than jubilant—I had now done my duty to both Helen and Maud, and now I was about to enjoy the exquisite pleasure of depriving Alice of her virginity!

I hurried back as quickly as I could. Maud had recovered and had got up, and was on her way to the bathroom when I appeared. She stopped, threw her arms round me fondly and kissed me passionately over and over again,—then said roguishly, "Jack, your tongue is really almost as good as you

323

... prick!" then vanished, followed by Alice and our merry laughter.

"Now I suppose you will take Alice, Jack!" said Helen eagerly. I nodded. "Then I'll get everything ready for her!" she rejoined, with a meaning smile as she produced the towels she had provided to protect her bed quilt from the tell-tale stains that Alice's defloration was sure to cause. She glanced at my prick. "You are hardly ready yet, Jack!— We'll have to work you up, Sir!" she added smilingly. "Let me make a start," and seating me at her side she commenced to play with my limp and flaccid penis. The touch of her hand was heavenly, and soon I began to feel my forces revive.

Maud and Alice now re-appeared, and when the latter caught sight of the bed so obviously prepared for her and saw Helen getting me ready, her courage seemed suddenly to leave her; she nervously exclaimed, "Oh! I can't! ... I can't do it!" and tried to run away into her room! But Maud caught her and held her gently but firmly, and said with an encouraging smile "Nonsense dear! Here Mother, will you take Alice and give me Jack, and I'll have him ready in two twos in a way that you do not know! Come along, Jack!" I guessed her intention and laughed, then made way for Alice—who was quickly folded in Helen's arms and soon soothed and caressed till she had recovered from her sudden timidity. I think, however, that the sight of Maud and me had more to do with her reviving interest.

324

Maud had made me lie on my back on Helen's dress box—with a gentle thumb and forefinger she had raised my limp prick and with the other hand she had gently captured my balls—and she was just beginning to sweetly lick the latter and tickle the former with her kind tongue, to the unbounded astonishment of both Helen and Alice, the latter evidently forgetting her nervousness in the excitement caused by Maud's proceedings! "See, mother," exclaimed Maud presently, "Jack is coming along finely!—I'll have him ready for you, Alice, in a minute!" and with eyes dancing with delight, she resumed her delicious ministrations and soon my prick was standing stiff and rampant and ready to ravish Alice!

"Come dear!" said Helen to Alice as soon as she saw I was ready; then she and Maud let the still reluctant and nervous girl to the bed, and having made her lie down, they drew her legs apart and generally arranged her to receive me. Then each kissed her tenderly, whispering something that I did not catch, but which brought the blushes again to Alice's cheeks. "Now, Jack!" said Helen invitingly, "She's ready for you!" and she pointed to Alice's maiden cunt lying so deliciously and temptingly open to attack.

I hurried to the bed, stooped over Alice, and whispered, "Give me your last maiden kiss, darling! and fairly sucked the life out of her mouth, then quickly I slipped on to the bed, got between

Alice's legs, and lowering myself gently on to her I brought the head of my prick to bear on her little cunt—then shoving firmly, but gently, I succeeded in getting it into her a little way, then my progress was blocked!

Tightening my clasp of her, I shoved harder and harder, but without breaking through her maiden defences, and evidently hurting her, for she cried "Oh Jack!", as if in pain, at the same time wriggling uncomfortably and apprehensively! Collecting myself, I lunged strongly downwards—something seemed to give way, and my prick seemed to glide into a sheath of delicious warmth and exquisite softness, while a smothered shriek from Alice proclaimed to Helen and Maud that she had lost her maidenhead! Taking every care not to hurt her needlessly, I drove my prick deeper and deeper up her virgin sheath till I was fully buried in her, our hairs intermingling, then my mouth sought hers, and passionately I kissed her quivering lips, receiving from her her first kiss as a woman!

Oh! my sensations of triumph! I was possessing Alice, I had captured her maidenhead, and she was now lying quivering and trembling, closely locked in my arms with my prick buried in her—and now I was about to give her the sweetest of lessons! Delightedly I set to work to fuck her in earnest, going slowly and gently at first for I was afraid of hurting her—but when I noted that her nervousness and pain were turning deliciously to wondering rapture and heavenly ecstasy as I agitated myself on her, holding her tightly clasped against me, I began to move more and more freely. Soon Alice herself began to respond—I could feel her bosom commencing to heave and palpitate, her breathing became broken and agitated, and then she commenced to move herself under me in the most deliciously provocative manner, which fairly set me going. Quicker and quicker I rammed into her—wilder and more tumultuous became our movements! Then came the climax, and deliriously I spent into Alice, deluging her virgin interior with my boiling tribute which she received with wondering rapture and indescribable bliss while she simultaneously surrendered herself to the dictates of her newly-born lust and spent in the most exquisite transports of delight!

We lay locked tightly in each other's arms, motionless save for the involuntary quivers occasioned by lingering spasms of pleasure. Gladly would I have continued to remain so, but Helen begged me to get off Alice so as to set her free to be carried off to the bathroom and looked after! And after imprinting a passionate kiss on her unconscious lips I reluctantly rose and hurried off to my room.

When I returned I found Maud waiting for me. In reply to my eager enquiries she told me with an assuring smile that Alice was "quite all right and very happy now that the ordeal had been passed"

327

—that I had hurt her very little indeed, but not unnaturally her cunt was sore and should be left for the present untouched till tomorrow evening when I would find Alice only too ready to be fucked again.

While we were talking, Helen and Alice returned. I took Alice in my arms and after some tender kisses I told Helen and Maud of our arrangements for the future and (at Alice's request) of her wish that we all should continue to live as we then were doing and enjoy each other all round. Their surprise and delight I will not attempt to describe. Suffice it to say that after mutual congratulations and compliments, Helen insisted on the seance being closed, so that we all might get the benefit of a long night's rest so as to enjoy the following evening thoroughly—for, as she said with an arch smile, "We women will all be equal and ready for anything and everything whenever wanted!" And then after tender good-nights all round we retired to our respective rooms.

CHAPTER SIX

At breakfast next morning I was delighted to see all three ladies appear as radiant as ever, Alice especially. She was looking more charming and attractive than I had ever seen her; her nervo-erotic excitement had been sweetly allayed, she had now no ordeal to dread, and she had the proud satisfaction of feeling that she now stood level with Maud and Helen in matters sexual, and could do whatever they did—and this combination of happy circumstances made her eyes sparkle and imparted to her a pretty vivacity that was simply bewitching and made me look forward to enjoying her in the coming evening. There was no doubt that all three had been badly in need of sexual satisfaction and were revelling in the pleasures they had tasted naked in my arms and I doubt whether a happier trio could have been found in the country.

But the morning post brought a danger in the form of a letter to Maud from the friends she was looking forward to visit. It begged her to come to them at once—not later at all events than the following day—so that she might join in sundry frivolities that had been hastily organized.

"I must go!" she wailed half-mournfully—"For I haven't any excuse except that I want to stay here and be fucked by Jack, and I can't possibly give that as a reason for not going!" she added with a quizzical smile; "Oh! isn't it unfortunate!" she exclaimed.

"Cheer up, dear!" I cried as I laughed at her really comical despair—"Don't forget that I now have to make week ends to see my sweetheart, who says that you and Helen may borrow me! So it is not as bad as it might be!"

Maud brightened up at once. "Thanks for reminding me, Jack!" she answered smilingly—then turning to Alice she said "And thanks to you darling, for as kind and unselfish a thing as ever one girl did for another!" and going over to Alice she kissed her gratefully and lovingly. "Jack!" she exclaimed, "you must plan a regular orgie for tonight, one that will keep me going for a week!" and she laughed happily.

"All right!" I replied, joining in her gaiety,— "Let us adjourn to the garden out of earshot, and

330

see what brilliant ideas we can raise!" and we all trooped off merrily and settled ourselves under the trees, and set to work to think hard.

I broke the silence after a little time by asking, "Has anyone anything to suggest?" They all nodded negatively with a conscious laugh. "Then let me put my idea before you, such as it is!" I added, smiling at the eagerness with which they all leant forward to listen, their eyes fixed expectantly on me.

I proceeded. "When I was in Budapest I saw a game played by three girls and a man; its name translated into English was "The Victim and her Torturers." One of the girls was chosen by lot to be the Victim, the others then became the Torturers, the man being the Chief Torturer and the others were to obey him implicitly. All four stripped themselves naked—the Victim was then tied down securely on a bed, and for a certain specified time the others did just what they liked to her, their object being to make her spend as often as possible by teasing and provoking and exciting her, no pain-causing play being allowed. Every now and then some two of the Torturers seemed to find the game too exciting—then they would mutually satisfy each others lustful desires while the third looked on and let the Victim have a bit of rest in which to pull herself together a little.

"How would this game suit us for tonight? We are three women and one man. As Maud wants as much as she can get tonight, we might make her Victim and give her a good hour's doing—during which we Torturers can also enjoy ourselves as our natures may demand! Or I shall be Victim. The Victim, I ought to have explained is considered to have the best of the fun. Or each of you can have a twenty minutes turn, drawing cards to settle the order!

Helen, Maud, and Alice looked interrogatively at each other, then broke into hearty laughter. "A most excellent idea, Jack dear!" exclaimed Helen, —"what do you say, girls?" Maud and Alice nodded delightedly. "Carried unanimously!" declared Helen, adding with an affectionate glance at me "With our best thanks to Jack!"

"Now I had better leave you to settle among yourselves which of the three alternatives is to be the order of the evening—I'd rather that you decided this without me. So I'll stroll to the river and back," and I rose.

"One moment, Jack!" cried Alice excitedly, "We want to know if the Victim will be ... fucked!" she asked with pretty blushes. We all laughed merrily. "The girl I saw as Victim was fucked twice, dear, in the hour—once by the Chief Torturer and once by me,—they saw how the game excited me and they kindly made me free of the girl! It was a piquant sensation to fuck a tied-down girl and she seemed to approve of it also!"

"Ah!" Alice exclaimed, her eyes sparkling. Then

I moved off, and they fell to work eagerly to discuss and arrange the evening's programme.

In a remarkably short time, I heard them calling me and I rejoined them. "We've settled everything, Jack!" said Helen—"We'll each have a twenty minutes turn: Maud first, Alice next and I last; you're to be Chief Torturer and boss of the show and we others will do as you may direct."

"Capital!" I exclaimed laughingly, "We'll have a great time!" whereon they all burst into hearty laughter.

"Now Mother, come along and help me to pack!" cried Maud as she hooked her arm into Helen's—"Alice, we leave Jack in your charge!" and off they went to the house, laughing merrily.

"What shall we do dear?" I asked of Alice, "Another row?"

"Oh yes, please, Jack!" she exclaimed delightedly, and soon we were off in the boat, she steering and I rowing. As we neared the backwater, I began to wonder whether she would take us in—and sure enough with a conscious smile she steered the boat in. I made fast as on the previous morning and then seated myself by her on the stern cushions.

"Why have you brought us in here, dear?" I asked softly as I slipped my left arm round her waist and drew her to me.

She yielded herself sweetly to my pressure, then whispered with a blush, "To thank you, darling, for what you did so sweetly to me last night!" And with love in her eyes she kissed me tenderly.

"But it is I who should thank you, Alice dear!" I replied softly, "For you let me take from you forever your most precious possession, your maidenhead!

Alice shook her head and looked tenderly at me. "If you only knew how bad I've often felt dear, and how wonderful I'm feeling now, you would understand my gratitude!"

I kissed her lovingly. "Let it be so, dear!" I replied softly, and let me show you tonight how I appreciate the privilege of fucking you!" She blushed and laughed merrily.

"Did I hurt you much, darling?" I whispered.

"Very little,—you were so gentle with me, Jack!" she said softly—"I am a little sore—but I don't intend to let it rob me of tonight's pleasures!" and she laughed gaily.

"May I judge for myself?" I whispered mischievously. Alice blushed and nodded, and slightly shifted herself so as to facilitate the movements of my eager hand which already had found its way under her clothes and was travelling along between her thighs. Soon it passed through the opening of her drawers and reached her cunt, she flinching deliciously as she felt my finger touch her cunt gently and caressingly.

"It is a bit swollen, dear," I whispered as I tenderly played with her hairs. Alice nodded, smil-

334

ing happily and evidently enjoying having her cunt felt by me. After a little more toying with her hairs and her delicious flesh I gently forced my finger into her down to where her maiden barrier used to be; she winced in spite of herself as my finger touched the sore spot, but to my delight she allowed me to gently soothe the inflamed flesh, whispering "Oh Jack, that's nice!" as my finger entered the sheath-like passage now open for life, and penetrated deeper and deeper into her—the feel of her moist juicy folds of flesh being exquisitely delicious!

"Don't you think that your cunt will be all the better for a little of your own lubricant, dear, your very own manufacture?" I asked with a significant smile. For a moment Alice looked puzzled, then suddenly grasped my idea, blushed prettily, then nodded delightedly with sparkling eyes. Lovingly I set to work to frig her, agitating my finger inside her cunt—at first slowly then more and more rapidly as she wriggled and quivered with pleasure, till I attacked her excited clitoris—when she spent voluptuously, inundating my finger with her sweet essense of love, which I proceeded to distribute all over her inflamed flesh to her evident satisfaction. Then withdrawing my hand I helped her to adjust her disordered clothes, and soon we were again on the river homeward bound, mutually delighted with the little episode.

On the way home Alice told me with a rogueish

smile that they all were so eager to taste the sensation of being fucked while fastened down that they unanimously adopted the twenty minutes turn suggestion. Then she exclaimed archly "Jack, tell me some special way to excite Auntie Helen and Maud when they are tied down!" I laughed, and replied "Get your cook to give you half a dozen long and finely pointed feathers, and tickle their cunts, dear!" She clapped her little hands together in delight at the idea, exclaiming with sparkling eyes "Oh Jack! how lovely! how I'll make them wriggle tonight!" evidently overlooking the fact that any specially brilliant idea of hers would be adopted by the others when her turn to be tied down came; but the anticipation of witnessing the struggles of the three ladies in turn when the feather was applied to their respective cunts was so tempting that I refrained from warning her of the probable consequences of her enterprise.

CHAPTER SEVEN

The day passed away uneventfully, and at half-past ten we all met in Helen's room, the three ladies in visible but suppressed excitement. "We won't waste time," I said briskly, "So everyone naked please!" and in a trice, I again had the pleasure of viewing their naked charms. Then I produced the wristlets and straps, the sight of which produced much laughter; and quickly under my directions Helen and Alice fastened them on Maud's wrists and ankles.

I made her lie down face upwards on her mother's bed and secured her wrists to the opposite bedposts by the straps; then to her surprise and consternation and to Alice's undisguised delight I directed Helen and Alice to pull Maud's legs widely

apart and strap her ankles to the corner posts, so
that she lay spread-eagled, exposing all her most
secret charms to us and utterly unable to prevent
us from doing what we liked to her! In silence we
gloated over the provoking spectacle—then turning
to Helen and Alice I said, "Now dears, Maud is at
your absolute disposal for fifteen minutes—then I
shall want her to myself! Now, go ahead!"

With a cry of joy Alice threw herself on Maud's
prostate and helpless self and excitedly showered
kisses on her lips and cheeks and eyes, then turning
herself slightly she seized hold of Maud's breasts
and after kissing the pretty coral nipples, she took
them between her lips and sucked each breasts in
turn, all the while squeezing and handling them—
Maud lying helpless in shame-faced confusion, the
colour coming and going on her cheeks, and a
nervous smile passing over her face when her eyes
met ours. I glanced at Helen—her eyes were rivetted on her daughter's naked body and glittered
with a peculiar light, and as I stealthily watched
her I noticed how she was shivering! It certainly
was not from cold, and recollecting how she was
fascinated and excited on the first evening when her
daughter stood before her naked for the first time
and how she from that moment seemed never tired
of looking at Maud's naked beauties, I guessed
that unknown to herself a lusting desire after her
daughter had sprung up in her. Seeing that Alice
and Maud were absorbed with each other, Alice in

338

the hitherto untasted pleasure of playing with another girl's naked charms, Maud with the also hitherto untasted sensations of having her most private parts invaded and handled by feminine fingers, I drew Helen out of earshot and whispered to her "You look as if you want to have Maud, eh dear?" She coloured vividly and nodded vehemently with a conscious smile, too embarassed to speak. "Why don't you then?" I continued. Helen stared at me in surprise. "Get on Maud, grip her tightly, and rub your cunt against hers sweetly."

"Oh Jack, really?" Helen stammered in growing excitement, her bosom heaving with her agitation.

I nodded with a reassuring smile, adding, "Try it, dear!—Lots of women solace themselves in this way when they cannot get what they really want!" She looked incredulously at me. I smiled encouragingly; then her eyes wandered to Maud, who was lying motionless save for an occasional quiver—Alice had deserted her sweet breasts and was now busily engaged with her cunt, which she was kissing and stroking and examining, the procedure evidently giving Maud the most exquisite pleasure judging from her half-closed eyes and her beatific expression,—a most voluptuous sight, which apparently swept away Helen's hesitation. She turned to me and murmured almost inaudibly "I long to do it, Jack, but she wouldn't like it!"

I took her trembling hands, that betrayed her lust, and whispered coaxingly "Maud has got to put up with anything that any of us wish to do to her during her twenty minutes turn, dear—when she guesses what you contemplate she probably will protest, but as soon as she feels your cunt on hers she will love you more than ever! Try her, dear!" Helen hesitated, looked hungrily and longingly at Maud, and then at me, then back at Maud. At that juncture Alice exclaimed "I'm only keeping on till you come, Auntie!" Helen shivered again, her eyes now glittering wildly with lust and desire, then with an effort she muttered huskily "Jack! I must ... have her!" and moved towards the bed.

"Come along, Auntie! I've got Maud nicely excited, and you can now finish her off in any way you like!" exclaimed Alice merrily; and after imprinting a farewell kiss on Maud's cunt she rose as if to make way for Helen, while Maud languidly opened her eyes and dreamily smiled a welcome to her Mother; but when she saw Helen scramble on to the bed and place herself between her widely parted legs in an attitude that could only indicate one intention and noted the lust that was glittering in Helen's eyes she became alarmed, and cried "No, no, Mother, no, no!" as she desperately tried to break loose,—while Alice flushed as red as a peony, her colour surging right down to her breasts as she intently watched Helen with eyes widely open and startled surprise. Helen paused a moment as if gloating over the naked beauties of her daughter, then she let herself down gently on Maud who again cried "No, no, Mother, no!" as she felt her Mother's weight come on her and her Mother's arms close firmly round her as Helen arranged herself on Maud—first breast against breast, then cunt on cunt—then having her daughter at her mercy she began to move herself on her lasciviously, just as if she was lying impaled on a man!

Hardly had she commenced to agitate herself on Maud than the latter exclaimed in an indescribable tone of astonished delight, "Oh! ... oh! ... oh! ... Mummy . . dar ... ling!" which sent Alice's blushes surging again all over her bosom as she glanced shame-facedly at me. I crossed over to her and slipped my arms round her, noting as she nestled against me how she was quivering with erotic excitement! Helen had evidently set her daughter's lust on fire, for Maud now was wildly agitating and tossing herself about under her Mother and heaving herself furiously up as if to press her cunt more closely against her Mother's as she passionately kissed Helen. Suddenly she wriggled violently, then spent in delicious thrills and quiverings,—Alice's gentle but subtle toyings had so inflamed her that it needed but little to finish her! Recognizing what had happened Helen suspended her movements and rested lovingly on Maud whom she set to work to kiss ardently, evidently enjoying the thrills and spasms that convulsed her daughter as she spent. Soon Maud began to respond to her Mother's provocations and agitated herself under Helen in the most abandoned and lascivious way, which set Helen off in a fresh frenzy of uncontrollable lust. With wildly heaving buttocks and tempetuous wrigglings of her hips and bottom Helen pressed her cunt more closely than ever against her daughter's, rubbing her clitoris against Maud's till Maud again spent rapturously. Suddenly Helen's body stiffened and grew rigid—then an indescribable convulsion swept violently through her, and with incoherent ejaculations and gasps she spent madly on Maud's cunt— then collapsed and lay inert on her daughter, motionless save for the voluptuous thrills that quivered through her with each spasm of spending! And so Mother and daughter lay in a delirium of ecstasy, their cunts pressed against each other, utterly absorbed in the sensations of the moment and the divine pleasure that for the first time in their lives they had mutually given to each other!

In delighted silence Alice and I watched this voluptous episode and when the delirious climax had passed she turned to me and huskily whispered "Jack! oh Jack!" and looked pleadingly into my eyes. I saw what she wanted; I drew her closer against me and slipped my hand down to her throbbing and excited cunt. She was so madly worked up that it only required one or two quick but gentle movements of my finger to make her spend ecstatically, and her thrills of rapture as she stood upright supported by me nearly sent me off! But with a strong effort I controlled myself, for in a minute or two I had to fuck Maud. So I bade her run away and freshen herself and to bring the feathers with her when she returned; then being curious to see how Helen and Maud would regard each other when they came to themselves, now that their fit of lust had been satiated, I watched them closely.

Very soon, with a long drawn breath of intense satisfaction Maud dreamily opened her eyes—she seemed hardly conscious; but when she found herself unable to move hand or foot and recognized that her Mother was lying on her the happenings of the evening instantly flashed through her brain and sent the hot colour surging over her cheeks and bosom at the consciousness that she had just been ravished by her Mother; and when her eyes caught mine she coloured more furiously than ever, but smiled gratefully as I noiselessly clapped my hands together with a congratulatory smile. Then she turned her face towards her Mother and a look of intense love came over her as she regarded her still unconscious Mother. She brought her lips to bear on Helen's cheek and kissed her lovingly, whispering "Mummy! ... Mummy! ... Mummy darling! ... " Then with a deep sigh Helen came to herself; she quickly realised the position and flushed scarlet as she half-timidly sought Maud's still humid eyes; but when she read in them her daughter's happy satisfaction she kissed Maud passionately and murmured in evident relief "Oh my darling! I couldn't help it! ... you looked so sweet! ... and you were so lucious!" and after another long clinging kiss she slipped off Maud.

Alice had just rejoined me, and as Helen rose to her feet our eyes inquisitively sought her cunt and that of Maud. They were a curious sight; both mother and daughter must have spent profusely as their hairs were sticky and plastered down by their joint spendings.

Noticing the direction of our looks Helen glanced at Maud's cunt and then at hers, and horrified at what she saw she exclaimed in charming confusion, "Oh Alice, do see to Maud!" and rushed off to her bathroom followed by our hearty laughter, in which Maud merrily joined with pretty blushes when we told her the cause.

Helen soon returned and joined me. "Well?" I asked mischievously. She blushed and replied softly, "Jack, it was just lovely, just wonderful!—I couldn't have believed it! Maud was simply lucious!" I laughed. "*Make* Alice do me presently, Jack!—I'd love to feel her on me!" I nodded laughingly—then glancing at the clock I exclaimed, "Only seven minutes more for Maud!—she must now be really tortured for four minutes, and then she is to be brutally outraged in your presence! Now set to work and give her a severe tickling!" and I handed a feather to each.

"No, no, Jack!" cried Maud, flushing painfully and tugging at her fastening—"no, no, don't tickle me! I can't stand it!"—But Helen and Alice joyously arranged themselves one on each side of her and with a smile of anticipated enjoyment they began to touch her lightly with their feathers—first in her armpits, then under her chin then all round and over her lovely breasts, Helen taking one and Alice the other—Maud all the time struggling and squirming in the most provocative way as she begged them to desist. From her breasts they passed to her navel, then on to the lines of her groin, and finally along the soft and sensitive insides of her thighs, Maud now plunging wildly and evidently suffering real torture from the subtle titillation she was being made to undergo. Then after a short pause and a significant glance at each other they applied their feathers to Maud's cunt!

"Ha! ... ha! ... don't!—in mercy's sake stop!" Maud almost shrieked, writhing frantically and straining at her fastenings. Half alarmed at the effect of their action Helen and Alice stopped and looked at me as if for instructions. I glanced at the clock, there was rather more than one minute left —I felt positive that Maud could endure the sweet agony for that time and that it would make the ensuing fuck all the more delicious to her—so I determined that she should go on being tortured, so I signalled to them to re-commence—and to prevent the house from being alarmed I held my

handkerchief firmly over Maud's mouth so as to
stifle her cries. Promptly Helen and Alice complied,
their eyes gleaming with lustful enjoyment at the
sight of Maud's naked body quivering in agony;
applying their feathers again to her cunt they tickled her delicately but cunningly all along its sensitive lips and when these poutingly opened involuntarily under the stress of the titillation and disclosed the coral flesh of her interior, Alice delightedly plunged her feather into the tempting gap
while Helen amused herself by tickling Maud's
clitoris, now distinctly visible in angry excitement!
Maud by now was nearly frantic,—twisting, wriggling, squirming and screwing herself madly in vain
attempts to escape from the torturing feathers—
and in spite of my handerchief the shrieks and cries
were distinctly audible to us. It was evident that
the limit of her powers of endurance was being
reached and that she was on the point of hysterics,
so I signalled to Helen and Alice to stop; just as I
did so she cried frenziedly "Fuck me, Jack! Oh
fuck me!" In a moment I was on her, with two
strokes I buried my prick in her raging volcano of a
cunt and began to fuck her. Hardly had I started
than she spent deliriously! I suspended my movements for a few moments during which I kissed her
ardently—then with renewed lust and unsatisfied
desire I again began to fuck her, the sensation of
holding her naked struggling but helpless body in
my arms and the knowledge that she was tied down

346

and at my mercy imparting a most extraordinary piquancy to the operation! Furiously I rammed into her, deliriously she responded to my fierce downthrusts by jerking herself madly upwards! Then the heavenly climax overtook us simultaneously—and just as she for the second time spent rapturously I shot my boiling tribute frantically into her, she receiving it with the most exquisite quiverings and thrills

As soon as Helen saw that the ecstatic crisis had come and gone, she and Alice unstrapped Maud; and as soon as I slipped off her they carried her off, while I retired to my room for the necessary ablutions. But to my surprise Helen came in before I had commenced. "Alice is looking after Maud, so I have come to attend to you, dear!' she said archly, and sweetly she sponged and freshened my exhausted prick, finally kissing it lovingly.

I asked her if she thought that Alice would be equal to twenty minutes torturing such as we had administered to Maud, also whether Alice's cunt was fit to receive me again. To the latter enquiry she gave a decided affirmative and added that Alice was eagerly looking forward to be fucked, and she agreed with me that we had better reduce the term of Alice's torture to fifteen minutes. I asked with a smile if either she or Maud proposed to fuck Alice, so that I might arrange accordingly—she replied that she would not as she must reserve herself for her approaching turn, but she would not be sur-

347

prised if Maud was tempted, only Maud was very
exhausted by her struggles while being tickled,
and, she added with a conscious smile and blush,
"I am almost sure she intends to have me when my
turn comes!" So we settled that Alice should be
thoroughly well felt by her and Maud, then I was
to suck her, then we should tickle her cunt, and
finally I should fuck her.

When we returned to Helen's room we found
Maud busy attaching the straps to Alice's slender
wrists and ankles, and soon she and Helen had
Alice securely fastened to the four bedposts. I
noted with amusement that they pulled Alice's legs
much wider apart than I would have done, in fact
so widely did they separate them that lips of her
cunt were slightly open. She looked perfectly delicious in her helpless nudity, her pretty cunt being
exhibited to perfection—and as Helen and Maud
gazed silently at her I could see that their erotic
desires were being rekindled. Suddenly they threw
themselves on Alice and showered kisses on her—
then they proceeded to feel her all over, their
hands visiting caressingly her most private parts,
after which they squeezed her dainty breasts and
kissed her cunt, laughing delightedly as she wriggled and flinched under their provocative touch-
ings.

"Come Mummie, let us see the result of Jack's
work last night!" cried Maud merrily—and with
gentle fingers they opened Alice's cunt and eagerly

inspected its interior, noting with amusing animation the changes caused by her violation. Presently Helen gently inserted her finger into the newly opened passage watching Alice carefully as she did so, laughing when in spite of herself Alice winced when the sore spot was touched; but she confirmed her opinion that Alice was fit to be fucked, thereby receiving from Alice a smile of satisfaction. Then they glanced at me as if awaiting instructions.

"Now Alice, you're going to be sucked!" I said with a meaning smile, to which she responded, evidently not objecting to this sweet form of torture. Turning to Helen and Maud I directed them to play with and suck Alice's breasts while I attended to her cunt; and with charming eagerness they addressed themselves to the exquisite morsels of Alice's flesh and blood allotted to them, preluding their operations with ardent and salacious kisses and then proceeding to feel and stroke Alice's dainty bubbies, now holding them up by their little pink nipples, then imprisoning them between both hands and gently squeezing them,—Alice betraying her rising excitement by her quick flushes and nervous laughs.

Presently Maud pressed between her hands the breast she was torturing so sweetly so as to make the delicate nipple stand up—and then she lovingly took it between her lips. "Oh Maud!' ejaculated Alice squirming voluptuously. Helen promptly followed suit, her action eliciting another irrepressible cry from Alice, now rosy red at the sight of her breasts in the mouths of Helen and Maud and the caressingly tickling sensations imparted to her by the play of their warm tongues on her sensitive nipples. I considered it was about time I joined in the play, so lowering my head I placed my lips on Alice's cunt and fondly imprinted lascivious kisses all along her tender slit. "Ah Jack!" she cried, as she instantly commenced to wriggle divinely; and when I ran the tip of my tongue gently along her cunt's lips and delicately licked and tickled them, she began to agitate herself voluptuously, twisting herself as much as her fastenings would permit and wildly thrusting her cunt upwards to meet my tongue. Presently I noticed that its lips began to open involuntarily; as they did so I forced my tongue between them, thrusting, darting and stabbing downwards as deeply as I could into the almost virginal interior and creating in her almost ungovernable erotic fury, under the influence of which she writhed and tossed herself about in the most lascivious fashion. It was clear that she was quickly approaching the blissful crisis—so withdrawing my tongue from her sweet orifice I seized her clitoris between my lips and sucked it fiercely while my tongue cunningly tickled it. This finished Alice off—with an indescribable wriggle she spent in delirious bliss and collapsed in rapturous delight, punctuating the spasms of her ecstasy with the most voluptuous quivers and thrills, then lay inert and exhausted, with turned up and half-closed eyes. But very soon she opened them again, and murmured faintly "Oh, please kiss me!" Instantly Helen and Maud threw themselves on her and showered loving kisses on her helpless cheeks till they restored her to life again; then they tenderly sponged and washed her cunt and gently got her ready for her next torture, while I removed from my lips and moustache the traces and remains of her spend.

When I returned I found Alice was herself again and keenly curious to know what now was going to be done to her. In response to the enquiry in her eyes I leant down and told her we now proposed to tickle her cunt—did she think she could stand it? She trembled nervously then said "I'll try—only stop me from screaming!" "Then we'll gag you, dear!" I said, and carefully I twisted a large handkerchief over her mouth. "Now, darling,"—and I signalled to Helen and Maud to commence to torture Alice.

It was just as well that I gagged her, for at the first touch of the feathers on her sensitive cunt the muscles of her arms and legs violently contracted as she involuntarily tried to escape from or at all events to dodge the tickling tips—then when this natural movement was frustrated by the straps she shrieked in spite of herself as the feathers continued to play on and between the lips of her cunt then struggled and wriggled frantically! A delighted smile now appeared on the faces of Helen and Maud at the sight of the delightful agony that Alice was suffering and joyously they continued their delicious occupation of tickling her cunt! Alice now was an exquisite spectacle—in her desperate efforts she twisted and contorted her lovely naked body into the most enticing attitudes, while the sound of her stifled hysterical screams was like music to us! And although it was only a few minutes since I had fucked Maud, my prick became rampant and stiff, as if eager to renew acquaintance with Alice's cunt. It was evident that the subtle titillation was trying Alice severly, but so delightful was the sight of her struggles and wriggles that I allowed Helen and Maud to continue the sweet torture, till Alice hysterically begged me to stop it—which I then reluctantly did.

As I removed the gag from her mouth she gasped "Oh Jack! It was awful!" "But you liked it dear!" I said with a smile. "Well, yes!" she admitted with a constrained laugh, "but it is too exciting for me! —please don't torture me any more!" she begged prettily. "Very well, dear!" I replied, "But then you must end my torture!" and I pointed to my rampant prick. Alice blushed, smiled, and then nodded lovingly to me—and promptly I slipped between her legs and bringing my prick to bear on her excited cunt I gently forced it in—using every precaution not to hurt her—till it was completely buried in her warm, throbbing and fleshy sheath.

"Ah!" she murmured rapturously as she felt herself possessed again by me but this time without pain! I clasped her closely to me till her breasts were flattened against my chest—and then I set to work to make Alice taste the pleasure of being fucked!

She was terribly excited both by the tickling her cunt had received and by her eagerness to again experience the exquisite raptures she had enjoyed in my arms the previous night in spite of the pain of her violation; and as I commenced to move myself on her slowly but sweetly I could feel how she was straining at her fastenings in order to accommodate herself to the sensations of the moment—then as I proceeded to fuck her she murmured ecstatically "Oh! ... oh! ... my darling! ... how . . heaven ... ly!," as she closed her eyes in rapture and wriggled and quivered under me voluptuously as she felt my prick working up and down in her cunt. Soon the blissful ecstasy began to overwhelm us both—Alice agitated herself under me in a perfectly wonderful way as I rammed furiously into her; then her body suddenly stiffened, an indescribable thrill quivered through her as she rapturously spent—at the same moment I shot into her frantically my boiling tribute of love —and then we both collapsed in delicious transports, oblivious of everything but our voluptuous sensations!—Alice enraptured by the exquisite pleasure that she was now fully able to taste, and I overjoyed at again having fucked her deliciously dainty self.

We soon came to ourselves. Meanwhile Helen and Maud had set Alice at liberty; and so after a long passionate kiss I slipped out of her and retired to my room accompanied by Maud, Helen taking charge of Alice. Sweetly Maud attended to me,— then somewhat eagerly she asked what I proposed to do to her Mother, confessing with a blush that she was longing to enjoy her!

"Certainly do, dear!" I replied, delighted at the prospect of again seeing the Mother and daughter relieving their lust by means of each other, naked. Joyfully Maud kissed me, and we hurried back as Helen an Alice had returned and were awaiting us.

Alice evidently was full of elation at her newly acquired sexual freedom; and eager to enjoy her privileges she caught hold of Helen and drew her to the bed, at the same time calling to Maud to help her to fasten Helen down to the four corner posts. With great glee Maud complied, and very soon Helen lay extended on her back with her limbs strapped to the four posts and a hard pillow under her bottom, absolutely at our mercy.

"Now Maud, you may have your Mother to yourself for the next five minutes," I said; a vivid blush surged over Helen as she heard her fate and glanced half shamefacedly at her daughter, who however smiled lasciviously at her with the assured

354

air of a conqueror. Alice ranged herself alongside of me, slipped her arm round me and with her unoccupied hands gently played with my balls.

Maud bent down and kissed her mother first on her lips and then salaciously on each breast and finally on her cunt; then seating herself alongside Helen she gently ran her delicate forefinger along the lips of her mother's cunt.

"Oh Maud, don't!" cried Helen, shifting herself uneasily and squirming deliciously under the licentiously free touches of her daughter's finger—but Maud continued deliberately to irritate her mother's cunt till she had worked Helen into an almost uncontrollable degree of erotic excitement, making her plunge and wriggle and twist herself in the most voluptuous manner. It was a charming sight to watch the daughter's delicately slender forefinger at work on her mother's sexual organ half hidden in the luxuriant growth of hairs that crowned Helen's cunt, driving her slowly to the very verge of spending but forbidding her the blessed relief, and making her tug wildly at her fastenings in her semi-delirium—till no longer able to endure the maddening desire to spend Helen cried agonisedly, "Oh Maud, to finish me!"

With a gratified smile Maud leisurely mounted on the bed and placed herself between Helen's widely parted legs, and with eyes glistening with lust she arranged herself on her mother so that their breasts and cunts rested on each other—then

355

fiercely seizing Helen's helpless body she set to work to rub her cunt against her mother's. "Ah! darling!" exclaimed Helen in ecstatic delight, as with half-closed eyes she surrendered herself to be fucked by her daughter, jogging herself spasmodically upwards so as to press her cunt more closely against Maud's. Soon their movements became furiously tempestuous, especially Maud's who plunged and rammed and curvetted herself on her mother s fastened down body in her efforts to bring on the madly desired crisis. Suddenly she cried, "I'm coming!"—and with a hurricane of downthrustings she spent deliciously on her mother's cunt just as Helen with an irrepressible ejaculation of "Ah!... Ah!" yielded to nature and collapsed, spending ecstatically in her daughter's arms.

As soon as her paroxysms of pleasure had died away Maud kissed her mother lovingly, rose off her and rushed to the bathroom, shielding with her hands her cunt from our inquisitive eyes; but Helen, being tied down, had to remain as she was with her cunt fully exposed, all glistening and sticky from her daughter's spending. With charming confusion and shamefaced blushes she endured our amused scrutiny—then catching Alice's eyes she murmured, "Please, dear!" whereupon Alice prettily proceeded to remove all traces of the double spend; and by the time Maud returned Helen was ready to be submitted to Alice's caprices.

"What now, Jack?" she asked hesitatingly. I

pointed to Alice. "You've got to satisfy her lust now, dear—go ahead, Alice!—" and installing myself comfortably in an arm-chair I drew Maud on my knees so that together we might watch Helen under Alice's hands.

For a moment Alice stood undecided, her eyes wandering over Helen's helpless and naked self; but she set to work to play with Helen's beautiful breasts, which she stroked and squeezed and caressed, finally sucking each in turn, keeping her eyes fixed on Helen's tell-tale face as if to access the result of her toying. What she concluded evidently encouraged her, for with a wicked smile she armed herself with a finely pointed feather and placed herself by Helen s side in a position from which she could command Helen's cunt.

"No, no, Alice! Don't tickle me!" cried Helen hastily as she nervously tugged at her fastenings, laughing nevertheless at her predicament. Alice however only smiled mockingly at her and proceeded to apply the feather to Helen's cunt, passing the tip lightly but searchingly along its sensitive lips that were still excited from the friction induced by Maud's cunt. "Don't, Alice!" again cried Helen, squirming charmingly—but seeing that she was doomed to undergo the sweetly subtle torture she nerved herself to endure it, clenching her teeth and firmly closing her lips so as not to cry out.

Then followed a lovely spectacle! Having had her

own cunt severly tickled, Alice had learnt where the most sensitive and susceptible spots were and also the most telling way in which to apply the feather to them. Availing herself of this knowledge she so skillfully tickled Helen's cunt that in a very short space of time she had Helen struggling and writhing in the most frantic contortions, straining at her fastenings so frenziedly that the bedposts began to creak—her closed eyes and clenched lips and her heaving breasts and palpitating bosom heightening the provocative effect of her naked tossing and agitated self. But although she heroically refrained from screaming it was evident that she was fast reaching the limits of her powers of endurance; and the gaping of her cunt dumbly indicated the excitement erotically raging there. I succeeded in catching Alice's eye and signalled to her to stop, which she instantly did—and not unwillingly, for her flushed face and glittering eyes betrayed the lustful concupiscence that now possessed her and which she was longing to satisfy by means of Helen's naked helpless body. She dropped the feather and impulsively threw herself on Helen, and was proceeding to work herself on her as she had seen Maud do, when Helen gasped brokenly "Wait ... a moment ... darling! ... " Although she now was absolutely trembling with unsatisfied lust Alice sweetly and sympathisingly suspended her movements; she clasped Helen tightly to her, her breasts resting on Helen's and showered ardent and salacious kisses on Helen's flushed cheeks and quivering lips till Helen had sufficiently collected her disordered faculties—when she opened her eyes and smiling amorously at Alice and murmured "Now, darling!"

Alice needed no encouraging! Gripping Helen tightly she furiously rubbed her cunt against hers, her deliciously youthful figure and her frenzied and uncontrollable but exquisitely graceful movements forming a wonderful contrast to Helen's matured but voluptuous body so rigidly and relentlessly strapped down into practical passivity. So new was Alice to the art of fucking that in place of prolonging the exquisite pleasure and slowly bringing on the sweet climax she concentrated all her energies to procuring the satisfaction of her erotic lust. Wildly she rubbed her cunt against Helen's till the ecstatic crisis overwhelmed them both—then simultaneously they spent, Alice with a rapturous cry of "Auntie! ... oh! Auntie! ..." accompanied by the most voluptuous thrills of carnal delight while Helen ejaculated deliriously "Oh! ... oh! ... Alice! ... dar ... ling!! ..." as she lasciviously quivered in her amorous transports!

In silence and spell-bound, Maud and I had watched Helen and Alice, but the sight was too much for Maud; and when Alice set to work to fuck Helen, Maud whispered hoarsely to me "Jack! ... Jack! . . ." and agitated herself on my knees in such a way that her desire was unmistakeable

359

Instantly my hand sought her cunt—there was no time for any sweet preliminaries, my finger went straight to her throbbing clitoris and so adroitly did I frig her that just as Helen and Alice were surrendering themselves to their lust and began to spend, Maud also distilled her sweet love-juice with an ecstatic discharge all over my hand!

I let the three women rest undisturbed till the throes of their spending had ceased; then when Alice slipped off Helen after passionately kissing her, Maud seized her and dragged her to me, exclaiming "Show us your cunt, dear!" Bashfully, Alice stood still as we delightedly inspected her sexual organ, all smeared with the love-juice that had proceeded from herself as well as from Helen. I showed her my hand—"This is Maud's!" I said with a wicked smile, wiping it gently on her hairs I added "Now your cunt carries the sweet essence of all three of you, darling!"—to her blushing confusion, which Maud terminated by dragging her off to the bathroom. Helen was still in her semi-swoon looking most fetching in her exhausted nudity; quietly I armed myself with sponge and towel and gently set to work to clean her cunt. This roused her from her torpor—she slowly opened her eyes, but when she recognized me and what I was doing to her she started into full life and hotly blushing exclaimed, "Jack! ... oh darling, that is not for you to do!" Suspending my work for the moment I replied smiling significantly "My darling Helen, as

I am about to be the next occupant of this sweet abode of love, may I not put it in order for my self?"

She smiled tenderly at me and raised her face as if inviting a kiss; and as I bent downwards she whispered softly "Darling, may I suggest my next torturing?" I nodded with an encouraging smile. Helen blushed deeply, then murmured bashfully "Do you mind ... sucking me? I have never had it done to me yet, and I would like to try it!' "Certainly, dar!" I replied, delighted at her request, then added, "and after that?" She blushed again then replied softly "Fuck me, darling!" Enraptured, I kissed her passionately in token of compliance; then I set to work again, and thoroughly sponged and purified her sweet cunt inside as well as outside—and by the time Maud and Alice reappeared Helen was herself again and eagerly anticipating the new experience she was about to taste.

When the two girls returned I placed them on the other side of Helen—they guessed from my position what I was going to do to her and with expectant smiles they quickly took their places. Then lowering my head I brought my lips to bear on Helen's eager cunt and kissed it sweetly, first in the very centre of her clitoris—each kiss making her shiver with pleasure. Next I began to pass my tongue backwards and forwards along her slit, licking it delicately but provokingly. "Oh Jack! ... oh! ... oh!" Helen exclaimed agitating her bottom and hips voluptuously while a smile of beatitude crept over her face! Seeing that she was now revelling in the erotic sensations aroused by my tongue I continued to lick and tongue-tickle her till her cunt became to gape and pout amorously, when I darted my tongue into her orifice as deeply as I could and tickled the deliciously warm soft interior. This set Helen raging with erotic lust "Oh! ... oh! ... Jack! . . . my . . . dar . ling! . . ." she gasped brokenly as she violently wriggled in lascivious transports as I first tickled this sensitive part of herself with my tongue and then took it gently but firmly between my lips while I passionately sucked it! This finished Helen! Her struggling body suddenly stiffened, a violent convulsion swept through her, and with an incoherent half-strangled cry she spent rapturously with the most lascivious quivers and thrills!

As I reluctantly raised my head from Helen's cunt the two girls noiselessly clapped their hands gleefully, evidently delighted by what they had witnessed; and as Helen was still absorbed in her ecstatic oblivion they accompanied me to my room watching with more amusement the removal from my lips and moustache of the traces of Helen's spend "What next, Jack?" they eagerly asked. "The usual finale, dears" I replied smiling—"only I am going to pull the straps so tight that Helen won't be able to move at all, and also will lie like a log while she is being fucked! When I give you the signal just tighten the straps as much as ever you can, even if she cries out!

Helen had come to herself when we rejoined her, and welcomed us with her usual kind smile; the girls at once kissed her warmly, and eagerly enquired how she liked being sucked. Helen blushingly confessed that she had found it just heavenly! "As good as ... what you are about to receive, Mother dear?" asked Maud teasingly. Helen laughed. "Do not forget, dear, that I have tried it only once, while the other—well, I know and love!" she replied evasively. "Well Helen," I intervened, "I was going to fuck you—would you prefer to be sucked again?" She blushed, hesitated, then said gently "The old way, Jack, please; I like to be in your arms, dear, and to feel myself possessed by you, and to ... spend in response to you!" "Then fucked you shall be, darling!" I replied as I kissed her tenderly—"Shall I do it now?" "Give me a minute or two, please Jack!" she pleaded, then turning to the girls she said softly "Dears, will you try to work me up." "I know a better way for both of us," I said—and straddling across Helen I seated myself on her chest, placed my prick between her breasts, and with my hands I pressed the latter together round and over it, at the same time lasciviously squeezing them as I gently logged my prick backwards and forwards between them, revelling in the delicious contact of Helen's full and soft breasts against my now excited organ—its stiffness together with the provoking friction seeming to communicate to Helen some of its ardour, for in spite of her shame-faced confusion at the sight of her breasts being put to such a use her bosom soon began to heave and palpitate and her colour to come and go. I nodded to the excited girls, and they immediately set to work to pull the straps as tight as ever they could, laughing merrily at Helen's dismay and protests when she found herself practically unable to move at all! "Now, darling!" I said—and working myself backwards over her stomach I slipped into position between her legs, threw myself on her helpless and rigidly extended body, and with one powerful stroke I drove my prick up to its roots in Helen's longing cunt! As I took her in my arms and began slowly to fuck her.

"Ah! . . .Jack!" she breathed blissfully. My sensations were extraordinarily piquant! Although Helen lay motionless under me I could feel that she was involuntarily struggling desperately against her fastenings by her muscular contractions and broken breathing and the agitated movements of her only free part, her head, which she rolled and tossed so restlessly and unceasingly that I had the greatest difficulty in catching her lips to kiss them —while her up-turned eyes, clenched teeth, and half-closed lips indicated that her inability to indulge herself in the relief afforded by even slight wriggles was concentrating the whole of her erotic lust and lascivious cravings in the battle field itself, her terribly excited cunt! The tension was evidently getting too much for Helen, so I set to work to fuck her hard, plunging and ramming myself into her quicker and quicker and more and more wildly till the blissful climax arrived—then madly I deluged the recesses of her thirsting cunt with a torrent of boiling lobe-juice which Helen received with incoherent ejaculations of rapture as she herself spent ecstatically in transports of lascivious delight!

Leaving Helen to lie in happy oblivion I slipped off her, and with the aid of the girls I freed her from her fastenings. Just as this was achieved she came to, and dreamily rolled off her bed; Maud at once took charge of her while Alice accompanied me into my room and again sweetly bathed and dried my exhausted prick—then suddenly stooped down and kissed it lovingly, blushing hotly as she did so. It was the first time she had let herself go, and I augured so favorably of her action that I ventured to whisper as I kissed her "Before long, dear, you must let me teach you how to suck it as well as kiss it!"—in response to which she looked lovingly at me and nodded her head with a tender smile of promise!

We re-entered Helen's room simutaneously with herself and Maud. Helen threw herself into my arms and kissed me lovingly, seemingly overjoyed by her experiences. We chatted together for a little, and then after affectionate goodnights we all sought our respective rooms well pleased with ourselves and each other.

CHAPTER EIGHT

After breakfast next morning Maud started on
her visit, Alice and I accompanying her to the
station to see her off,—and as it was a fine morning
we decided to walk back. While en route a Tele-
graph lad on his bicycle overtook us, and recognizing Alice he pulled up and handed her a telegram
addressed to me; it was from my Solicitors, and it
asked me if I could attend at their office at noon on
the next day but one to meet the vendors of a
property I was desirous of buying. I showed it to
Alice and explained that I practically had no option but to attend, and I wired back agreeing to do
so; she was very downcast at so unexpectedly sudden a termination to my visit, but when I told her
that I could return within three or four days if
Helen could again receive me, she cheered up.

But on reaching home we were startled to find Helen in her boudoir wrapped up in a shawl and sitting by a low wood fire. She told us that when she was dressing that morning she was afraid she had caught a cold,—"I certainly have been exposing myself to the air a good deal since you came down Jack!" she said laughingly—and since morning it had become worse, and she was trying to stop it.

I told her that I had been recalled to Town and must go up on the following morning, but that I could be back within three or four days if I might then resume my visit. "Of course, Jack dear!" she replied warmly, "surely you know that we will be only too delighted to put you up again and as often as you like!"

"May I take it that I shall be put up both in the house and in my hostesses?" I asked audaciously. "You may, Jack!" Helen replied with emphasis, as she and Alice broke into merry laughter at my casuistry,—then more quietly she added, "I mustn't put you up myself to-night, darling, for with this cold on me it would be very inadvisable, but I do not know why Alice should not be your hostess tonight, for she has now qualified herself!" and she smiled affectionately and meaningly at Alice, who with sparkling eyes threw herself on Helen and kissed her gratefully exclaiming "Oh Auntie, it is sweet of you!—You don't know how I've been longing to have Jack all to myself for a

368

whole night!' And so it was settled that I should pass the night alone with Alice in her room.

In spite of her protests, Alice and I kept Helen company all the afternoon and evening, during which I managed to find an opportunity of asking Alice to put on her daintiest underwear when she dressed for dinner and also to let me undress her when bed time came,—to both of which requests she gave a blushing promise.

In due course bed time came,—Helen kissed us both lovingly and then said somewhat pointedly to Alice, "A sweet time to you, my darling, please be very careful and run no risks!" With a conscious blush Alice faithfully promised; then we retired to our respective rooms, and when half past ten chimed I slipped noiselessly into Alice's bedroom attired only in my dressing gown, and was rapturously welcomed by her. True to her promise she had not begun to undress; and when I took her in my arms in all her pretty finery, the thought that I was about to take off her dainty garments one by one till she stood naked before me made me thrill with lascivious emotion.

As may be well supposed I had never been in Alice's bedroom, nor had I ever caught a glimpse of its interior. It was a veritable little nest, furnished simply but in exquisite taste, and curiously in keeping with its sweet occupant. On the walls hung some beautiful water colour paintings, and scattered all over the mantel, dressing table, the top of the chest of drawers etc., were her girlish treasures, nick-nacks, framed photos and the hundred and one trifles girls love to accumulate. But in my present frame of mind two articles attracted me—first, Alice's bed, a pretty single bedstead of white enamelled wood covered with a dark bed-spread,—then next, an unusually large cheval-glass that stood across a corner; on the first Alice would lie quivering in my arms as I fucked her, while the second would reflect our naked figures as our hands wandered audaciously over each other.

She seated me in a low easy chair, placed herself on my knees, then threw her arms round my neck and kissed me passionately, murmuring "Oh my darling! it is nice to have you here all to myself, and to feel we can do just whatever we like!" "And what are you going to like, dear?" I asked as I returned her kiss. "Something naughty, darling?" she replied, blushing prettily, "I feel ... wicked tonight!" she added laughing gaily. Clearly my presence in her room and the prospect of having her clothes taken off her by me had inflamed Alice's imagination; and promptly I resolved that I would take the opportunity to initiate her into some of the finer mysteries of the art of fucking!

"We won't waste any time, darling!" I said softly, "I'm not going to leave you until you have drawn out of me every drop of my love-juice, —so you'll have every opportunity of being ... naughty!" Alice hugged me to her in huge delight at this announcement, and kissed me passionately; then obedient to my unspoken suggestion she rose, and with an indescribably subtle gesture she intimated that she stood at my disposal!

I also rose, and throwing off my dressing gown I exhibited myself to her stark naked save for my shoes and stockings. She blushed prettily at the sight, her eyes dwelling fondly on my prick which was beginning to show signs of interesting itself in the proceedings. I slipped my arm round her waist and drew her to the cheval-glass saying, "Let us see how we look!" "Oh Jack!," Alice exclaimed, half shocked at the contrast of my naked self with her fully dressed self so faithfully reflected in the glass—then laughed merrily as she watched my hand wander amorously over her bosom and also her hand as it gently took hold of my prick and caressed it!

"Now, darling, let me undress you!" I said tenderly to her,—" you'll have to show me how to get your dress off you, but the rest I can manage myself!" Alice laughed somewhat constrainedly, then under her whispered directions I removed all her jewellery and ornaments, unfastened and took off her dress, unbuttoned and slipped off her petticoat,—she yielding herself to me but blushing furiously as her attire became scantier and scantier, till she stood in her corset, under which the fringe of her chemise hung provokingly nearly down to her knees and revealed her pretty and slender calves cased in black silk stockings and dainty shoes! I feasted my eyes on her charming dishabille, making her turn herself so that I could view her sideways as well as before and behind, she colouring delightfully at witnessing my admiration —then I resumed my delightful occupation by unlacing and removing her corset after first inspecting her sweet little breasts as they nestled in its pouches. Then I made her draw her arms through the shoulder staps of her chemise and let it fall to her feet; I dealt with her practically transparent vest in the same way,—and then Alice stood before me naked to her waist and wearing only the daintiest of deliciously frilly drawers, black silk stockings and shoes!

"Now see how you look, dear!" I said, and led her again to the glass. "Oh Jack!" she cried, laughing shame-facedly, "I'm positively indecent!" and her blushes redoubled. "I'm going to make you look more indecent still, darling!" I said with a meaning smile, "Please get out that large black hat with the dark feather and put it on." "Oh Jack! what an idea!" she exclaimed in fits of laughter, but nevertheless sweetly complying she put on the hat! "Now darling, stand again in front of the glass and watch yourself as I take down your drawers, and step out of them!" Now red as a rose and trembling with erotic excitement, Alice placed herself in front of the mirror—I knelt behind her, undid the tape fastening of her drawers but kept them in position with my hand—then watching her intently in the mirror I suddenly pulled them down to her feet. "Oh Jack!" she cried as her eyes caught sight of herself naked to the knees, and involuntarily she shielded her cunt with both hands! "Raise your feet one at a time, darling!" I whispered; obediently she did so. I threw her drawers on to a chair, rose, and standing behind her and looking over her shoulder I grasped her slender wrists and drew her hands apart and backwards, revealing the sweet triangular patch of hairs that my soul so loved. "There darling," I whispered, "now you do look both indecent and naughty!"

Alice blushed beautifully as she surveyed her naked self in the glass, smiling at her bizarre nudity with something suspiciously akin to admiration of herself, "Isn't a pity that you can't fuck yourself, darling!" I asked with a teasing smile. Alice turned to me with eyes bubbling over with merriment at my suggestion, and nodded vigorously her assent, then broke into hearty laughter at the idea.

"Well darling, that's impossible—but come to bed and I'll teach you how to fuck yourself on me!" and I led her gently away and stripped her absolutely naked by removing her hat, stockings and shoes. Then I placed myself on my back on her bed, with her pillows beneath my bottom.

Alice looked at me with undisguised astonishment. "Come darling, straddle across me and put me into yourself!" I said invitingly. At once she comprehended the arrangement, and with pretty blushes she followed my whispered directions; and while I supported her with my arms she with her dainty hands lovingly seized my prick and inserted it into her cunt—and when she had sank down on it until it was buried inside her I lowered her gently till she lay on me and cardled in my encircling arms, when I whispered directions; and while I supported her with my arms she with her dainty hands lovingly seized my prick and inserted it into her cunt—and when she had sank down on it until I was buried inside her I lowered her gently till she lay on me and cradled in my encircling arms, when I whispered amorously "Now my darling, the game is in your own hands! I shall simply lie still and leave you to fuck yourself slow or fast as your fancy may dictate!" and kissed her lovingly.

Alice's eyes sparkled with delightful anticipation as I explained her duties to her. She passed her arms round my neck as if to anchor herself on me, kissed my lips ardently as she murmured "Oh darling, it is just heavenly!"—then looking me straight in the eyes and smiling lasciviously she commenced very gently to agitate herself on my prick, pressing her Mount of Venus so strongly down against my groin that our hairs intermingled! She continued this delicious agitation for a little, then her eyes began to flicker and her breathing to be broken—while her bosom heaved and palpitated

374

excitedly against my chest. Soon her movements became more tempestuous—her bottom began to waggle and jog itself up and down more and more fiercely as her sexual concupiscence grew hotter and hotter. She now was in the throes of lust. She pressed her cheek against mine, clutched me more closely round my neck and worked herself furiously up and down on my prick—then spent deliciously with voluptuous thrills and quivers!

True to my undertaking I lay like a log under Alice, holding her plunging body firmly and closely against mine and encouraging her with salacious kisses—but when she collapsed after spending and lay limp and inert of me, I slipped my hands on to her glorious bottom and set to work to stimulate her to fresh exertions by caressing and fondling her rich and plump flesh. Presently with a sigh of deep content Alice raised her head from off my shoulder, and with humid eyes she looked tenderly at me as she imprinted a long sweet kiss on my lips. "Go on again, dear!" I whispered stimulatingly. Instantly Alice's eyes brightened and her limpness disappeared. "Oh Jack, may I?" she exclaimed excitedly. I nodded encouragingly. "Oh darling!" she ejaculated rapturously as she kissed me passionately —then tightening her grip round my neck she re-commenced to work herself voluptuously up and down on my prick!

This time I left Alice to maintain her balance and position on me without the help of my encir-

375

cling arms; and while she fucked herself blissfully I gently encouraged her by stroking and tickling her breasts as they rested sweetly on my chest, squeezing them amorously when I noticed that the estastic climax was overtaking Alice. Soon she again spent rapturously, kissing me passionately as the spasms of pleasure thrilled through her—then with hardly a pause she set to work to fuck herself more furiously than ever, plunging and raging riotously on me with wild frenzied down thrustings of her tossing and agitated bottom. My powers of self control succumbed under her fierce assault; deserting her breasts I threw my arms round her, gripped her tightly to me, jerked myself madly upwards—then shot my hot discharge into Alice just as she for the third time spent in delicious transports, flooding my happy prick with her sweet essence of love!

As soon as the spasms of pleasure ceased to thrill through her Alice slipped off my prick, and whispering, "Lie still, darling, till I return!" she disappeared, remindful of Helen's parting admonitions. Meanwhile I lay peacefully on Alice's dainty bed, thrilling at the recollection of the exquisite pleasure I had just been privileged to taste with her in my arms, and endeavouring to decide what next I should do to her: but before I could come to any decision Alice returned armed with basin, sponge and towel, and deliciously bathed and refreshed my now flaccid prick—then lay herself down by my side, encircled by my arm.

"Well, dear?" I said interrogatively as I smiled lovingly at her. Alice blushed prettily. "Darling, it was just heavenly!" she replied softly, then whispered, "Jack, I went off three times!" I laughed, then replied, "I know you were very ... naughty by the way you were wriggling on me, dear—any naughtiness left?" Alice nodded roguishly, then broke into merry laughter. "And what particular naughtiness are you now yearning after, dear?" Alice hesitated for a moment, then whispered bashfully, "Darling, may I watch your ... thing grow from what it now is the the big stiff thing it is when you ... put it into me?" "Certainly you may, dear!" I replied smiling approvingly, "and if you like to use your hands and lips you can greatly expedite the resurrection!" Alice raised herself on her elbow and looking radiantly at me exclaimed, "Darling, I'd love to do so!—and at the same time have a real good look at your ... thing for we've been too ... busy up to now!"—and she laughed wickedly. "You're evidently going to be very naughty again, dear, but I suppose I must put up with it! Now let me arrange ourselves for your special benefit!" And shifting my position I placed myself so as to lie on my back across Alice's bed, then carefully guiding her I made her straddle across me and lie face downwards on my stomach, reversed in "soixante-neuf" style, so that her cunt hung just above my face while she had right before her eyes my penis and balls, and free hands with which to manipulate them!

"There, darling! I think that is about right," I said, for while you are satisfying your natural curiosity and ... amusing yourself, you are giving me something to look at and perhaps to kiss if you sufficiently excite me."

"Oh Jack! you are clever—this is just lovely," Alice exclaimed delightedly as she voluptuously wriggled herself on my stomach till she had settled herself comfortably on me—then I felt her soft but intensely exciting fingers gently seize my penis and balls!

As I thrilled with pleasure at the contact of Alice's hands with my genital organs, I accidentally turned my head in the direction of her tiolet table, and to my great delight I saw ourselves reflected in the glass, visible to me but not to her. Meanwhile Alice, thinking herself unobserved, threw off all constraint and set to work openly to indulge her curiosity. I could see the sparkle in her eyes as with rapt excitement she examined my penis and balls, handling them with wonderful gentleness as she pulled my hairs and drew back the loose skin off the rubicond head and caressed my balls, and generally investigated thoroughly every feature of my sexual equipment.

Presently I felt a premonitory shiver run through her, and I could see by the reflection of her tell-tale face in the glass that some fancy or caprice was tempting her, but that she had not yet surrendered herself to it! Alice was evidently hotly debating something in her mind—whether to do it or not —for her colour came and went and her bosom rose and fell in pretty agitation as she played with my private parts!

Intuitively I guessed that the idea of sucking me had suddenly suggested itself to her—and with the object of seeing whether it was so as well as to encourage her into doing it I softly kissed her cunt, then watched her intently in the glass. She shivered violently, blushed hotly, raised my penis towards her lips—then as she lowered her face to meet it she checked herself as if in doubt. Again I kissed her cunt—again another quiver followed by a strangely yearning look at my penis, which now began to swell and assert itself as it rested between her gentle fingers. I tried the effect of a third kiss, and to my huge delight I saw Alice lower her lips to my penis, and felt her lovingly kiss its sensitive head—then after regarding it fondly she kissed it over and over again! With each kiss my penis grew stiffer and thicker and angrier-looking, till it stood erect and rampant; Alice had not only witnessed its resurrection but had brought about the miracle, and a smile of gratified triumph played on her face as she regarded her handiwork!

Now she had to be induced to suck me! Following the same tactics of suggestion I began to lick and tickle her cunt with my tongue. Alice quivered voluptuously and half-closed her eyes for a moment in bliss—then to my surprise she kissed my balls ardently as they lay in the palm of her hand; and after a little hesitation she commenced to apply her tongue to them, the exquisite sensation together with the provocative sight sending me wild with delight! She now was fairly wriggling on me with lust—I thrust my tongue into her cunt as deeply as I could with a darting stabbing action. Alice now raised her mouth from my balls, her face aflame, her eyes simply blazing with lust; then slowly she guided my prick into her mouth and began to suck it ardently while her tongue played lasciviously on and round its now excited head!

My sensations were just heavenly, and the sweet knowledge that I was engaged in taking the maidenhead of Alice's mouth only heightened my ecstasy. My hands had been playing alternately with her delicious bottom and her breasts—but now I flung them round her dainty waist; and clasping her firmly so as to control her plunging wriggles I set to work to suck her into spending. Every now and again I caught a glimpse of her face as reflected in the glass. Alice seemed as if she was in a delirium—her eyes were almost closed, her right hand held my balls and her left hand clasped my penis—she had nearly half of my prick in her mouth, and instinctively she was working her lips up and down on it as if to pump up my love-juice, driving me mad with pleasure. Just then she must be on the verge of spending, so I fiercely attacked her clitoris, and seizing it with my lips I tickled it with my tongue. A violent convulsion swept through her, then Alice spent rapturously, suspending her suction of my prick while the spasms of pleasure thrilled through her, but retaining it in her mouth. I felt myself going! "Stop darling! ... I'm coming!" ... I cried as I struggled to drag my prick out of her mouth—but Alice kept it imprisoned and tightly held between her lips and teeth, then resumed her suction in so delicious a manner as to break down all my powers of control; and no longer able to restrain myself I jerked myself upwards violently and spent frantically in Alice's mouth, shooting my hot essence down her throat, jet after jet in my ecstatic bliss; but as I did so, in spite of my delirious rapture I turned to see how Alice bore the sudden flooding of her mouth with my love juice. To my surprise and intense relief she absorbed my deluge without flinching, swallowing each jet as it shot into her mouth and keeping her lips tightly closed round my prick till the last drop had oozed out and it had begun to shrink—when she drew it out of her mouth, and with an amused expression she watched it shrivel up and dwindle away to a third of its size. Then without a word she rose off me and disappeared, leaving me in a state of confusion and apprehension that can easily be imagined. But whether I had offended her or not, I had to purify myself; and having done so I awaited events.

In a few minutes Alice returned rosy red but smiling happily. I took her in my arms murmuring "Oh darling!" She kisses me warmly and whispered, "Did I do it all right, Jack?" Relieved beyond measure I kissed her passionately, then whispered back "Darling, you sucked me like an angel!" which set her off into silent but merry laughter; and then we lay down together again, Alice this time placing herself on me with her cunt resting on my prick and her arms round my neck.

"Why did you call out to me to stop, Jack?" she asked presently, with a half-smile on her lips, "didn't you want to . . . finish?"

"I didn't know whether you would be willing to let me . . . finish in your mouth, darling," I replied, "and so I tried to make you stop before it was too late, but you wouldn't, and I had to let myself go. Were you expecting it?"

"Yes," she whispered with a blush and a smile— then continued, "you may remember that just before you . . . violated me" (here she tenderly kissed me) "Maud sucked you till you got stiff! Well, when I was helping her to pack yesterday I asked her about it and she told me how to do it and that you would . . . finish in my mouth and that I was to swallow what came from you! So I was looking out for it—but I didn't expect such a lot," she adding roguishly, "it was hard work to get it all down."

I kissed her lovingly. "And you didn't mind, dear?"

"Not after the first swallow," Alice replied laughing and blushing prettily.

"And you'll do it again?" I asked with a tentative smile.

"Whenever you like as as often as you like, darling," Alice replied tenderly as she sweetly kissed me. I gratefully hugged her, and we lay silent for a moment, our lips pressed against each other.

"And what else did you learn from Maud, dear?" I asked with some interest.

"Oh, lots of things, Jack," Alice replied, laughing merrily. "We talked a lot and she told me a lot! Jack, when she comes back, we are going to have a night together in her room, and she is going to teach me some ... tricks," and again she laughed merrily.

"I wish I could be there to see you!" I murmured regretfully, "you two will make a perfectly lovely pair—and to watch you experimenting on each other stark naked would be a treat for a King! You and Maud haven't yet fucked each other, have you?"

"No, not yet," replied Alice, colouring slightly, "no one has fucked me except you, darling, but I fucked Auntie last night!" she added with evident satisfaction.

"And you no doubt will be doing so again before long!" I added with a meaning smile, whereupon Alice kissed, "but don't practice too much with her, dear, for Maud will have been chaste for a fortnight and will take a lot of satisfying, and to have your charming self at her disposal will excite her more than ever. Mind you write and tell me all that you do with her and also with your Aunt," I added, and with pretty blushes Alice nodded a promise.

Meanwhile her sweet hand had not been idle but had business itself by playing with my prick and endeavouring to restore it to life, and it now was beginning to show signs of returning animation. "Jack, you're coming again," Alice whispered delightedly as she redoubled her delicate attentions, "And how will you take it this time, dear?" I whispered. She hesitated for a moment, then whispered back. "Under you darling, just like the very first time!" and slipping out of my arms she bent herself forward, lowered her head, and took my prick into her sweet mouth, and began to tongue it divinely while she stroked and caressed my balls with her gentle little fingers. Promptly my prick responded to her invitation and became stiff and rampant—but so delicious was the sensation communicated by her soft lips, warm tongue that I let her continue to suck me till fear of a catastrophe impelled me to stop her.

Almost regretfully Alice released my prick from its sweet imprisonment in her mouth, and after a final kiss of its now excited and throbbing head she resumed her original attitude at my side and whispered, "Darling, was that all right?" "Simply heavenly, dear!" I replied as I kissed her gratefully, "now turn over on your back and receive the reward of your sweet kindness!"

With sparkling eyes Alice quickly complied, then separated her legs widely, exhibiting her exquisite cunt in the most inviting way. Without delay I slipped on to her, and taking her luscious body in my arms I slowly and voluptuously pushed my prick into her longing cunt, till it was completely buried in her and our hairs intermingled, Alice quivering with rapture as she felt her cunt being thus deliciously invaded. "Twist your legs round me, dear," I whispered. Instantly comprehending Alice threw her legs across my loins and gripped me tightly to her as if trying to force my prick still deeper into her, at the same time hugging me closer against her breasts with her arms.

Our mouths sought each other, and as our lips met in passionate kisses I began slowly to fuck Alice. The moment she felt my prick moving in her cunt she gripped me more tightly than ever with her legs and then commenced to wriggle under me in the divinest fashion, arousing in me the most voluptuous sensations of lust sweetly being satisfied. Never in all my life had I been in such close contact with a girl as I then was with Alice. I was absolutely locked up between her arms and legs and rightly pressed against her soft warm luscious flesh, while with fierce desire I clutched her to me till her delicious breasts were flattened against me and I could feel every pulsation of her quivering self as Love's sweet frenzy by degrees overwhelmed us both, till no longer able to restrain myself I spent deliriously into Alice just as she for the second time flooded my excited prick with her warm love-juice. But our lust was not yet satisfied, we were made to enjoy each other again, and my prick remained stiff and rampant in Alice's cunt. So, after a brief pause during which our lips were sweetly engaged with each other, we re-commenced our now lascivious pastime. This time our pleasure was deliciously prolonged as our carnal rage had been gratified, and we could devote ourselves to voluptuous copulation as connoisseurs and revel in the exquiste raptures attending the satisfaction of our lust as little by little we approached the heavenly climax. How many times Alice spent I cannot even guess—she seemed to pass from one blissful ecstacy to another, her half closed eyes and slightly parted lips, her incoherent ejaculations and voluptuously involuntary movements as she wriggled beneath me testifying to the rapturous transports she was tasting as I slowly fucked her. But before

386

long it became evident that Alice was getting exhuasted, and by now I also was furious to "dissolve myself in ecstacies" in her delicious interior. So I whispered to her, "Now, darling, let us finish together." She opened her eyes langourously with a smile of ineffable pleasure, kissed me lovingly, then set to work to second my now vigorous rammings and thrustings. Soon we were fucking each other madly with the most unbridled lascivious fury. Suddenly Alice gasped, "Now, darling . . . now!" at the same time wriggling hysterically under me. Promptly I let myself go, and just as I felt her warm essence bedew the head of my prick again, I spent convulsively into her with a rapture I have seldom tasted, shooting into her every drop of love-juice that I could discharge.

Under the excess of our rapturous pleasure we both lost consciousness. I, at all events, was in a state of oblivion till the chiming of a clock aroused me. It was 2 a.m. I still lay on Alice locked up between her arms and legs, my prick was still lodged up her cunt, and she was still clasped closely to me and apparently sleeping happily. I was loath to disturb but it was imperative that we should separate and retire quietly for the rest of the night. So reluctantly I roused Alice with loving kisses; she opened her eyes in bewilderment, and when the position of affairs dawned on her she flushed rosy red, then whispered shame-facedly and hurriedly, "Oh do let me get up, darling," at the same time hastily releasing me from my sweet imprisonment between her arms and legs. Gently I slipped out of her embrace and set her free in turn —then hurriedly we assumed our night gear; and after a tender "Good night" accompanied by many kisses I noiselessly slipped out of Alice's room and regained my chamber.

Next morning I was delighted to see Helen appear at breakfast, and apparently all right again, though a little pulled down. She had been into Alice's room, and in the absence of the latter she gently chided me for allowing Alice to indulge her newly acquired sexual privileges to a possibly injurious txtent. Just then however Alice appeared, radiant, a vision of happy satisfied girlishness which effectively dispelled Helen's anxieties; and she then proceeded to chaff us both in her usual kindly way—till Alice seized her and with eager insistence made Helen promise with pretty blushes that on the first night of my return she would place herself at my disposal for the whole night.

In due course the hour of my departure arrived, and after a tender farewell and many kisses I tore myself away from the hospitable mansion where I had passed as delicious a week end as ever had been vouchsafed to mortal man!

THE END

BOOK II

Herewith a novelette which has been handed down by private collectors for a number of years. We feel it covers most comprehensively, the subject of discipline and corporal punishment as it is generally practiced in the home.

OLD FASHIONED DISCIPLINE

It has been said that truth is stranger than fiction. Perhaps that depends on what one considers strange.

In our town, just big enough to have a high school, are two families with a good deal in common. My family and the Turners, both comfortably well off, are both headed by a widow, 35 and 40 years of age respectively. They have between them five children of school age. Mrs. Martin, my aunt, adopted me five years ago. I am now 17 and her daughter Cora is 19.

The Turner family consists of Mrs. Turner, tall, beautiful, and stern, and George, 16, Vera, 17, and Doris, 18. We are all students at high school and Cora will graduate this year.

About four years ago Auntie and Mrs. Turner, firm friends for many years, apparently came to the conclusion that their families were slipping out of control, and they decided to do something about it. Well, they settled on a course of action that for them has been a complete success; for us kids, however, their scheme has been painful and humiliating. They must have thought out everything with great care. They made rules of conduct and set out penalties for their breach to include us all. As a safeguard against possible resistance, the two of them tackled us separately and privately, and within a few days they brought us all safely under the rule of the rod.

There were great outcries of indignation, but I don't think any culprit has ever made any real resistance. I cannot say we are unhappy under the new order, painful as it is, and our stern parents boast that they have the best behaved family in town. Over this somewhat remarkable background, I draw a veil of anguished tears and go on to tell of an episode that profoundly affected our lives.

Auntie arranged for Janet, the daughter of an

old friend, to stay with us while taking a secretarial course in town. Janet turned out to be a really lovely, well-stacked brunette with a friendly manner. She was most cordial to Auntie, but, being rather self-important, she was sweetly patronizing to the rest of us and none of us liked that a bit. Cora particularly resented it. She frequently made snippy remarks about our "wonderful behavior." Once Auntie drily observed, "They are not always so well behaved, but rigid discipline quickly improves them."

"Yes, of course, that would account for their nice manners. Indeed, you are to be congratulated, Estelle dear," rejoined Janet airily.

"Thank you, my dear," said Auntie gravely. And then, significantly, "You and I must have some private little talks on the subject of discipline." Janet replied that she would be delighted.

We were sure they did have such talks but had no idea how much, if any, of the Turner-Martin code was disclosed to Janet. However, at the end of Janet's third week with us, Auntie, all smiles, told us.

"There's to be a picnic for all of you tomorrow. Unfortunately Janet and I can't be with you for the fun. We are having Mrs. Turner to lunch, but I think Janet won't miss the picnic too much. She will be entertained here."

Cora and I dutifully thanked Auntie. As soon as we were alone, Cora burst out happily, "This is it,

Gerald! I'd love to be at the intimate little lunch tomorrow. I know exactly what Mamma meant when she said that arrogant cat would be well entertained. She meant well chastised!"

"What makes you say that? And even if you're right, do you think that she'd submit? She's even bigger than Doris Turner."

"Silly boy, haven't you noticed how meek she is with Mamma lately? And how quick she agrees with just everything Mamma says? Oh, she'll submit all right when those gracious ladies start on her. You'll see!"

After the picnic, we all drove back to our house. Cora had guessed right about the reason for the lunch.

Our house is quite secluded, in the midst of a two-acre plot. The most secluded place in the house is the recreation room. It is a very large room and it is here that most of the family punishments are given. In one of its many cupboards are hung in neat array straps, paddles, and Auntie's favorite instrument, the famous—or perhaps I should say infamous—Scottish tawse. It is a wicked little affair of thick leather about three inches wide and fifteen long, and has five slits at the business end, forming sort of fingers; fingers that sting abominably.

There is not much furniture in the room, but one item is outstanding—the massive old chaise lounge that sits before the fireplace. Auntie bought it two years ago and had it remodelled. The high, broad head has a curved depression with a restraining strap on either side, admirably suited and very effective in securing in position the waist or neck of anyone leaning over the head or kneeling on the seat. Along the sides hang other straps for a like purpose. Auntie calls it "the chair of Applied Discipline."

We all trooped own to the rec room. The scene that met our gaze brought gasps of astonishment and then some covert tittering from the Turner kids.

Mrs. Turner and Auntie, wearing severe, plain black sleeveless dresses, were seated on the "chair" nonchalantly chatting and enjoying a cup of tea. Standing in the corner, sobbing spasmodically, dejected, her disheveled hair framing a tear-streaked face, was Janet, her head bowed, her hands clasped before her. She was the very picture of a penitent.

"Did you have a nice time, children?" beamed Mrs. Turner. Then, continuing in tones of quiet authority, she pointed to the sobbing girl. "This girl was an honored guest, but I'm afraid she has been badly spoiled and her conduct here was disruptive to family discipline. So much so, that we decided that she must go home. However, she begged to remain and her wish has been granted. Her status is now very different; now she is one of you. She will share the pleasures and responsibilities of our families and, like you, will be subject to our necessary discipline. She is inclined to be haughty, impudent, lazy, untidy and disrespectful to her superiors. Those faults we shall cure. She has had an exemplary whipping on her bare bottom which, I am sure, she will remember for a long time."

There was a buzz of excited chatter at this cool matter-of-fact announcement, and in a few minutes Auntie brusquely ordered Janet to her room. And, believe me, she lost no time in obeying. The Turners left soon after, and the subjugation of Janet passed into history.

For a few days Janet sulked and avoided Cora and me. I expect the poor girl was ashamed, though she need not have been. We are all in the same boat. However, gradually she settled into her new role. She now said "Auntie" instead of the familiar "Estelle," and was very, very carefully polite and submissive to Auntie, as well as most friendly to Cora and me. I accepted her friendliness at once, but Cora remained cool and distant.

"Why can't you be nice to her?" I asked Cora.

"Listen, Gerald," she answered tensely, "you just don't understand girls. That big simpering Janet treated me like dirt under her feet for three long weeks, and I intend to make her pay dearly for it. Oh boy! Will I ever sting her big fat behind for her when the time comes!"

Her vehemence shocked me. "You actually mean to whip her?"

"I do and I shall. You will see, my sweet passive little cousin!" she purred.

No more than ten days after Janet's initiation, Cora and I brought home unsatisfactory reports from school. Auntie was very angry about the reports. "You should know what to expect for these!" she snapped, waving the offending reports at us. "Gerald's hardly surprises me, but you Cora! I am very disappointed in you. Go to my room, the pair of you, and take the tawse with you. I'll attend to you shortly. And you, Janet, your room is a disgrace. Tidy it at once!"

On what small things our fate sometimes hangs. Had Janet meekly answered, "Yes, Auntie," and obeyed at once, I suppose that would have ended the matter. Maybe she was tired and irritable. At any rate, I was amazed to hear her say petulantly, "Oh all right Auntie, I'll do it, but not right now, I'm too tired."

For a moment there was dead silence; then, white with anger, Auntie exclaimed, "Mistakes I can overlook, but deliberate disobedience, coupled with insolence, I punish with pleasure! You go with the others, Miss!"

"Oh Auntie! Please! I didn't mean what I said. I'll tidy my room this very instant!" cried Janet, realizing the wrath she had provoked.

"You will go to my room this very instant instead, for a sound whipping on your bare bottom!" Auntie promised.

397

A strange thrill went through me at her words, and I flashed a picture of lovely, curvaceous Janet, half naked, her bottom dancing and bouncing under the tawse. I'd never had such thoughts about seeing Cora or the Turner girls in that position, perhaps because they were all so much like sisters to me, and I was usually too busy anticipating the feel of the whipping on my own rump to be aroused by what I saw. But Janet, a near stranger whose body I had bared in my mind often, produced a gush of excited blood through my veins as I followed her still clothed swaying buttocks down the hall.

Cora had fetched the tawse, and while we were waiting in Auntie's room Janet bemoaned her careless words. "Oh, what ever possessed me to answer like that? Oh Cora, I'm terrified!" She trembled a bit as she looked for comfort to my gloating cousin.

"I've no sympathy for you. If you are silly enough to practically ask for a tanning, I hope you get it good. Or perhaps you were rude on purpose and really want a spanking—is that how it is?" inquired Cora searchingly.

Janet blushed to the roots of her hair. "Well, not with that awful tawse," she said.

"So our proud, haughty darling welcomes a smacking from those in authority over her, so long as it doesn't sting too much. Is that right?" queried Cora softly.

398

"Why, I—er I—well, I adore your mother," stammered the blushing, embarrassed girl.

Cora laughed sarcastically. "Oh, don't bother confessing, I can see through you like glass. You really want it, but gently. Well, I'm sure you will get what you want, and much more besides—and that part will be most interesting. Instructive to you and enjoyable to me!"

At that moment, Auntie appeared. To our surprise, she was dressed to go out.

"I find I must go out at once. I may be very late, so your correction will have to wait until tomorrow evening. Reflect about it and your naughtiness until then. That will put you in a proper frame of mind for your punishments."

"Please, Mamma, may I say something?" cooed Cora demurely.

"Well, yes, what is it?" said Auntie impatiently, "I'm in a hurry."

"I was just thinking, Mamma dear, that it might put us in an even better state of mind if you order each of us to give the other two a preparatory spanking now."

Auntie pondered for a moment, then she smiled broadly. "It's a novel idea, Cora, and may be a good one. Very well, you arrange it, and we will see how it turns out. Now I must go. Let them be good spankings, mind. Good night children, and remember tomorrow evening!"

My pulse had quickened frantically as I realized

what had just passed between Cora and my aunt. The only thought in my head was that soon I would have Janet across my lap and actually feel her bottom bounce under my hand. I knew I was growing an erection, but was not the least concerned at the moment. I did manage, though, to conceal the excitement from showing in my voice and face. Cora's vow of vengeance never crossed my mind.

Cora assumed command as soon as Auntie had gone.

"All right, let's go. Gerald, you spank us first."

"Okay Cora, over you go across my knee," I grinned. She promptly put her slender body in the time-honored position. I flipped up her clothes and gingerly spanked the seat of her panties with my open hand. I neither dared nor wanted to spank her hard. I smacked for about a minute, and when I released her she smoothed her dress down and said primly, "You silly boy. Mamma intended you to give a real spanking and you know it."

I paid no attention to her words, but nodded cheerfully to Janet to assume the position Cora had taken. I was trembling inside as she draped herself over my lap and I felt her warm curves on my thighs. I was tempted to pull down her panties and remove her girdle. I burned with desire to uncover her bottom but lacked the nerve, and so the opportunity passed. I gave a few tentative pats to both cheeks and thrilled to their soft firmness.

Then I began spanking a bit harder and the resilient flesh shook and wobbled under the impact of the blows. The spanking was probably a bit harder than what I had given Cora, but I knew I couldn't have produced more than a pink glow on the white mounds. As I let her off my lap, Janet smiled and kissed me, saying, "I love you for that cruel whipping, Gerald darling."

Cora was less than pleased, though, and said again, "All right for you, but it's not obeying Mamma. Now, you take over, Janet, and you'd better do as you were told."

"Oh, don't be so stuffy, Cora. What Auntie doesn't know won't hurt her." Janet laughed as she seated herself in Auntie's upright chair and drew me down across her knees. Lowering my pants, she smacked noisily with her hand until it stung her too much, then pushed me off to make room for Cora.

"Now to spank Miss Sobersides," she exclaimed with evident amusement, indicating that Cora should get face down across her lap. She gave the merest make-believe spanking and let Cora go.

Perhaps I should have known better, but I fully expected Cora would carry on the farce we had begun. I had forgotten her vow to make Janet suffer for her earlier treatment, but there was an eager light in her eyes as she took her place on the chair.

"Come, Miss Naughtiness, get properly face

down across my knees," cried Cora as she turned back her skirt and spread her knees to receive her victim. Janet looked a bit alarmed at the sharp command, hesitated for a moment, then lowered herself until her lovely form was sprawled across the lap of correction. Cora held Janet firmly by the waistband of her skirt. Her eyes flashing, her voice slightly trembling with emotion, she spoke imperiously.

"Now, you arrogant minx, you are just where I've wanted you since we first met. In utter ignominy, dangling helpless across my lap, anxiously awaiting to have your big bottom bared for a good sound whipping. I'm going to whip you with the tawse. You will remember how beautifully it stung you when Mamma used it on you."

Janet couldn't help but realize she was in for a real good spanking, and she began to squirm and plunge desperately in an effort to get free, protesting with indignation as she struggled.

"No! No! Cora! You can't mean that! Don't you dare! If you use that awful tawse on me I'll tell Auntie! I will! I'll tell!"

"Yes, do tell her, by all means. But you will get the tawse on your bare bottom just the same," trilled Cora, as Janet continued to struggle even more furiously. Her feet slipped on the broadloom, her hands could reach nothing to grab for leverage; she was, as Cora informed her in honeyed tones, helpless. But she struggled on and on for fully five minutes before she dropped exhausted, still where she had started, with her rear in one of the very best positions for spanking. I could see that all through her frantic squirming and jerking Cora held her in place with the greatest ease.

The rebellion thus ended with Cora triumphantly saying, "Have you quite finished your silly wriggling? Because I can wait, you know."

"Yes," whispered Janet choking with emotion.

"Splendid! and now, with your ladyship's kind permission, or without it if necessary, we will arrange your skirt and slip suitably," Cora said, with a great deal of sarcasm.

I watched fascinated as Cora deftly dropped her right knee and pulled the front of Janet's skirt forward and again raised the knee under the more than ample posterior. Then she flipped up the back of the dress, revealing the spank spot clad in frilly flared leg panties over her taut girdle. Cora unfastened the garters, then pulled the cute little panties down to Janet's knees. The girl squirmed under this indignity. I gasped at the sight before me—long, well molded legs, topped by her big round behind, tightly encased in its girdle, out of which popped most alluringly three or four inches of plump, pale pink cheeks. I held my breath as Cora made the final act of preparation for a whipping. Amid pathetic little protests, Cora rolled and tugged the girdle well up on the culprit's waist. I sood transfixed for a moment until Cora snapped:

"What are you staring at? Hand me the tawse this instant!" Then taking the tawse—that most dreaded of instruments—from me, she gripped the rolled up girdle firmly and began to whip Janet.

Her technique for imposing the utmost in anguish and humiliation was superb in its simplicity. She waited after each stroke for her victim to regain her composure enough to truly appreciate the next stroke to the fullest measure. Meanwhile, she lectured Janet to shame her still further.

The tawse cracked down with explosive force to the tune of Janet's yelps of pain as her beautiful behind bounced and quivered.

"This is the reward of naughtiness!" Smack! Smack!! "And to respect your superiors!" Smack! Smack!

By now Janet was sobbing wildly, writhing and gasping out little broken pleas to be let off. Her frantic movements were exposing far more than her scarlet bum, and I was torn between sympathy for her plight and the arousal her nakedness caused. Cora gave a mocking laugh at her unahppy pleas and went on with the work she seemed to enjoy with great relish.

"Let you off indeed!" Smack! Smack! "Of course I will, when I have whipped you to my entire staisfaction!" Smack! Smack! "And I'm not easily satisfied!" Smack! Smack! "Your bottom shall be well whipped!" Smack! Smack! "Like this!" Smack! "And this!" Smack! Smack! Smack!!!

Smack!!! "Now, will you promise you will obey?" Smack! Smack!

"Ow!!! Yes! Yes!! Y-e-s-!!" Janet panted frantically between her sobs and squeals.

"Then this will remind you of your promise!" Smack! Smack! Smack smack smack!!!

At this stage, Janet was practically hysterical, so Cora lectured her no more, but continued to whale the red, unprotected seat on the lap of correction with, if anything, increased vigor during the last flurry of smacks.

At long last, she pushed disdainfully the well whipped girl off her lap and ordered her to bed.

In a daze, I watched the subjugated girl leave the room. I say subjugated because no doubt was left that Cora had done just that to her. I was so completely engrossed in the masterful demonstration I had witnessed, as well as the animated display of Janet's intimate parts, that I had forgotten my turn was yet to come. My memory was quickly refreshed.

Cora, dominant and supremely confident, turned to me: "Well, Gerald, are you prepared to receive your spanking?"

I had no illusions now that she intended to let me off with a token spanking as we had done with her. Truly I was in a dilemma. A thousand crazy thoughts chased each other around in my brain. Cora, tawse in hand, seated herself, ready for my chastisement. Could I appeal to her sense of fair play to treat me as I had her? One look at my determined, imperious cousin told me I could not. She wouldn't even listen. Could I make a break for it and stay out till Auntie returned? No, for my thoughtful cousin had sweetly locked the door and also removed the key. Suppose I simply defied her? Well, she had Auntie's orders and far more important, she had that formidable tawse in her hand. And, if I did manage to resist, I'd only get a double dose later from Auntie. She seemed to read my thoughts.

"If you have any foolish idea that you can evade your just punishment, forget it! For you know perfectly well in your heart that you are going to be well spanked, don't you?"

I sat on the bed twisting my hands in dispair. It seemed an eternity when I heard myself answer in a low choking voice, "Yes, I know, bbbut—"

"There's no 'but' about it boy. Stand up! Hand me your belt!"

My mouth was dry as I shamefacedly pulled off my belt and handed it to her.

"Hold out your hands!" she ordered.

"You don't neet to tie me."

"Hold out your hands!!" I obeyed and she strapped my wrists tightly together.

With that act, I passed the rubicon. Resistance was out of the question, and she could now punish me at leisure.

She drew me close to her right side and gripped

either side of my beltless pants, pulling them down slowly and surely until they collapsed in a heap at my ankles. Faintly I hoped that she would leave me my brief shorts, but alas, they followed my pants, thus depriving me of my last shred of dignity. That is if a fellow about to be spanked can be said to have any dignity.

Having cleared the decks for action, she folded back her skirt to avoid crushing it into wrinkles, and incidentally giving me a generous glimpse of gorgeous silk clad legs and creamy thighs, that on another girl at another time would have been most interesting. Just now I was much too preoccupied with other thoughts. And how!

She drew me down and balanced me across her lap, tucking my shirt well up on my shoulders. I quivered as I felt her cool hands slowly gliding, appraising the area she meant to whip. Strangely, it seemed proper and right for my upstart cousin to punish me. All I really thought about at the time was the pain to come.

Without more ado, she picked up the tawse and started to lash my rear in the same methodical way she had tanned Janet's. The stinging was simply awful and it didn't take me long to commence roaring and squealing. Between strokes I found myself almost incoherently promising—to be good, to be obedient, and above all, pleading to be let go. For indeed I'd had enough.

Cora paused, draping the tawse across my hot

stinging seat. "Why Gerald! You are making more fuss than Janet did. Actually, I've barely begun to warm your bottom yet. And I promise you most sincerely I am going to whip you every bit as soundly as I whipped her."

With that, the awful sonorous smacks resumed. How many I got, I've no idea—but it was far worse than any whomping I'd had from Auntie or Mrs. Turner. The next thing I remember, I was on my tummy in bed, sobbing bitterly and stinging like fury.

It must have been hours later that I heard a soft sound at my door. I twisted my head to look just as the door quickly opened and closed. The room was quite dark, but I could dimly make out a form leaning against the closed door. A moment later Janet, wearing a cotton nightgown, was standing over my bed. I made a grab for the covers but she stopped me, saying, "It's all right. I've brought some salve for your bottom. Did she whip you badly too? I could hear you sobbing."

"No worse than you," I said, stunned by the fact that she was standing by my bed and I was naked. The burning in my seat was for the moment forgotten.

"This will be nice and cool on your hot skin. Let me rub it in and take some of the sting out of it." Not waiting for me to answer, she sat on the edge of the bed and opened the jar in her hand. I jumped as I felt her gentle hand touch my soreness, but then the soothing salve was being rubbed tenderly all over my buttocks, and the fire behind was gradually replaced by new fires within. "What awful welts," she murmered sympathetically, as she traced light fingers over the raised skin.

I gave a great sign as she stopped massaging, both for the easing of the sting and the pleasure of her touch. She hesitated for a second, and then said haltingly, "Would you please do the same for me, Gerald dear? I just know it would feel wonderful."

I somehow managed, in my excitement and confusion, to take the jar from her hand. Then I boldly brushed my lips across hers and said, "That was awfully sweet of you, Janet. It feels much better now. Lie down here and let me soothe your poor bottom now."

I made room for her on the bed and knelt beside her as she lay face down. I felt more eager than shy as I liftd her nightgown well above her scarlet rump, and put a gob of salve on my hand. I rubbed as gently as I could until I could feel that some of the heat was leaving her sore flesh. It was as if my hands were moving without any directions from me as they continued to glide over her bottom long after the salve had done its work, and I heard a little contented coo from Janet that told me that for her too, the salve was not the only consolation she received. Without any conscious thought on my part, my hand lingered at the top of her thighs and

I had an almost unbearable compulsion to stroke the softness between them. Janet must have sensed my desire—more likely, shared it—because just then she rolled onto her side, turned her head toward me, and whispered:

"Gerald, we'd be punished terribly for this if Auntie or Cora should find out. But we could make each other feel so good, and after a whipping like that ..." Her voice trailed off for a moment. "Let's just kiss and touch though, dear, and be very quiet."

My blood was pounding furiously and my body felt like one great throb as I lay back on the bed and took the beautiful, once haughty Janet into my arms.

Next morning I was siff and sore. My seat was a mass of ugly dark red welts and, though the sting had gone, it still hurt abominably. I had to force myself to concentrate on the ache in my bum as Janet came down for breakfast in order to hide the flush of pleasure I felt at the thought of what had happened the night before. Janet had left my room only a few hours before. She sat down very, very gently, and I gave a wince of sympathy as her pained bottom made contact with the chair. Cora and Auntie were all smiles.

"Cora has given me a full report of all that happened last night and I'm sure you both richly deserved what you got. Now, off to school with you.

410

I shall speak to you again after dinner," Auntie declared sternly.

Janet went off to her school and I to mine. I could hardly bear to sit on the hard seats. It was torture; and, in addition, I couldn't work for thinking about what might still be in store for us at home when Auntie meted out her share of our punishment. What conflicting feelings surged through me, between dread of Auntie and eagerness for the meeting Janet and I planned for the next day, which was Saturday.

We ate dinner that evening in silence. My eyes kept wandering, but always ended up on the tawes which ominously lay on the buffet. We were so uncomfortable that I was really relieved when Auntie spoke sharply, saying:

"I was shocked that you two would dare to disobey my orders to spank each other soundly. And did you both disobey? Did you Janet?"

"Oh, I wish I had obeyed. She couldn't have whipped me any harder in any case," said Janet with a wan smile.

"It's too late to think of what you might have done. And you, Gerald, did you disobey too?"

"Yes, Auntie," I sighed.

"Very well, you must both know that I'm very annoyed and most disappointed in you. And I am more then pleased with Cora, who not only obeyed, but proved herself most capable by giving you a thoroughly sound whipping. Indeed her conduct so impressed me that I have talked with Mrs. Turner and we enthusiastically agree that Cora shall be allowed and encouraged to help enforce discipline in our homes. So my children, I hope you will be delighted to know that Cora now has our full approval to punish any of you if you break any of the rules. You should know them quite well, so there should be no difficulty there. I have decided you shall take over between you Cora's share of the household duties, since she is to take over this disagreeable task. Now, as a symbol of her authority, I am presenting her with this good tawse, which she has used so well, and also with this key to the instrument cupboard."

Cora looked most demure but underneath I'll bet my charming cousin was just reveling in her triumphs.

She thanked her mother meekly and said she would try to be worthy of the confidence placed in her. Janet and I looked at each other goggle-eyed. We were utterly bewildered at this new turn of events. Sort of stunned, I asked Auntie, "And will Cora still get punished?"

Auntie smiled sweetly and said, "Yes, Gerald, of course, if she is naughty in the future. But I rather expect a great change for the better in her deportment since by the same agreement, you two shall punish her if she misbehaves. I think she'll want to avoid that. Now for the good news. The chastisement I promised you for this evening is cancelled. I think you have already paid the penalty, and if Cora hasn't paid fully, it is the fault of the two of you."

"Don't you think they should be punished for deliberate disobedience last night?" asked Cora silkily.

"If you think so my dear, but postpone it and consult Mrs. Turner. She may wish to see you demonstrate your prowess."

Janet and I commiserated with each other later about the new situation. Cora had fallen into her position so quickly and we knew she would show no sympathy for us or have any qualms about using her power at every opportunity. We were quite sure there was no way we could avoid frequent punishments in the future.

It was late the next evening when we met in the woods a quarter mile or so behind the house. I was much bolder now, and took her in my arms at once for a long, exciting kiss. As we lay down on the soft grass Janet told me of the summer she had spent at camp the year before. She had learned quite a lot from the boys in the neighboring counselor's camp when she and a girlfriend would sneak down to the lake shore after hours. I was trembling with eagerness as she described in whispers what had taken place. We spent a long hour in the darkness then, as she patiently and thoroughly shared her experiences with me. By the time we made our way back

413

to the house, Cora and the terrible tawse seemed a distant threat.

It was no easy matter, though, to keep and renew our glow of pleasure in the days that followed. Cora gave us imperious orders to do this and do that whenever we were within earshot. I was really kept jumping, what with housework and school work as well as my regular duties.

Cora certainly blossomed. She no longer looked nor acted like a school girl. She wore high heeled shoes and did her hair in a more mature fashion. She was unmistakably the mistress and we the underlings. She gave her orders with supreme confidence, usually ending with a "And do it quickly and properly or I'll smack your bottom."

Happily, we must have pleased her, for she didn't carry out her threats—possibly because she was afraid that if she proved to be too great a tyrant Auntie would remove the favored status from her. At any rate, when most of her threats failed to materialize, our anxiety began to abate. Unquestionably she was enthralled with her new status. She also meant to graduate and so worked hard at her school work. She hoped to graduate with honors and thus cast shame on Janet and me. Meanwhile, we did her chores and met, whenever we could, behind the house for respite from the slavedriver.

Unfortunately, the quiet was the lull before the

storm. One Friday just as dinner was over, she gave commands.

"There is a small matter to be attended to children," (she copied Auntie's form of address in the most humiliating way), "you will recall your disobedience when I last punished you. I shall reward you for that little mistake tonight. Report to me at the rec room at seven thirty sharp. You, Miss, put on your tightest panties, skirt, blouse and slippers—that's all you'll need. And I warn you both—be prompt now. Go and change for you have only ten minutes."

We hurried down, Janet trembling and clutching my hand. "Oh, Gerald, she's really got a rod in pickle for us. She's been saving it up for us, I just know it, and I'm all goose pimples!"

"Me too," I whispered. As we entered the rec room, every light was on. Cora, seated on the chair, was grim and businesslike. The ping pong table was pushed to the wall and Auntie sat primly on one of the chairs in front of it.

"You may sit down, culprits," said Cora sternly.

Hardly had we done so when Mrs. Turner swept in majestically with her tall and willowy daughter Doris in tow. She is a stunning blonde of 18, nicely rounded and curved in all the right places. Instinctively I knew the reason for her presence. Indeed, Cora's authority seemed to be increasing as rapidly as her appetite for domination. Mrs. Turner significantly locked the door and sat beside Auntie, motioning her daughter to sit beside us. Doris seemed a bit bewildered at seeing Cora sitting where only our parents had sat before.

"Cora, as I told you, my daughter has been impudent, lazy, and disobedient during the last week, thus earning for herself a good whipping. And this punishment I wish you to administer here and now."

Full of confidence, Cora stood up and kicked off her high heeled pumps as she replied, "I shall be charmed to oblige and obey you, dear Mrs. Turner." Doris jumped up, her eyes blazing with outraged indignation as she croaked, "Mom! what nonsense is this? That cat Cora won't touch me! You can't really be serious Mom. I will take it from you, but not from a school kid! Let her just try— I'll show her!!" Then, turning to Cora, she stormed, her face red with anger and humiliation, "You go to hell! Don't you dare lay a finger on me or you'll be sorry!"

Undaunted by this outburst, Cora stepped up to her. Without her pumps, Cora is about four inches shorter than the formidable looking opponent Doris. Cora's hand flashed out slapping Doris' face hard, right and left. The fight was on. They grabbed each other's hair and yanked furiously, swaying and circling around the ample space between us and "the chair." They both squealed with pain and rage and soon it began to look as though Cora had met her match. When, suddenly, Cora

416

drew back her right hand, balled her fist and drove it with terrific force into the pit of Doris' tummy. The girl gasped for breath and relaxed her hold on Cora's hair. Following up her advantage like lightning, Cora let her have two more punches, right and left to the stomach. That ended the fight, Doris collapsed to the floor, all doubled up, gasping and moaning. Instantly Cora pounced like a tigress. She flipped Doris on her face, then straddling her bounced with all her might, knocking out any bit of breath left in her body and leaving her like a limp rag.

Cora by now had the situation well in hand; calm and serene she asked Auntie for a restraining strap from the chair. Receiving it, she wrenched the limp girl's arms behind her back and strapped the soft forearms to the elbow at each side so that they were folded above her waist.

By this time Doris had got her wind back and began to struggle, but it was too late. Cora had won and no matter what the culprit did now, she had no chance of escaping her punishment. She should have realized that, but foolishly when Cora got off her, she got up and started to kick out wildly. Several good ones landed on Cora's shins before she got behind the refractory Doris and pushed her by the ears to the high end of the "chair."

In one swift fluid motion, she pushed Doris down into the depression in the "chair" head and

cinched the restraining strap in place about Doris'
waist. This had the effect of forcing Doris down
until she was bent over at an ideal angle and she
was, of course, completely immobilized. Auntie and
Mrs. Turner were delightd.

"Congratulations, my dear," beamed Auntie.

"And mine too. You managed her splendidly.
And don't spare the guilty girl's bottom after the
trouble she's been," smiled Mrs. Turner.

"For her silly rebellion, I thought of giving her a
dozen strokes with Mamma's nice thin, bendy cane
and a good spanking with the tawse as the chastisement she came for," said Cora in a most re-
spectful tone.

"Certainly, my dear. I quite agree with you and
I hear you have found the tawse most satisfac-
tory."

"Oh yes, I really have, Mrs. Turner," answered
Cora silkily, as she went over to her helpless victim,
swishing the cane as she went. Doris' skirt and
petticoat went up over her shoulders. Her little
panties soon glided to the floor. Her garter belt
Cora removed with a flourish. She was devastat-
ingly beautiful to behold. The pale ivory of her
glorious hemispheres and long smooth legs all un-
draped reminded me of a huge peony, her white
petticoat the petals, her luscious legs the stem. Her
symmetry was almost perfect. It seemed, no matter
how naughty she had been, a pity such beauty
must be marred by the rod even temporarily. And

418

that soon Cora's competent hands would have her behind a fiery red.

Doris took her caning like a trooper; she gasped with pain as the awful cane came singing down, but she didn't really yelp before the sixth stroke. Then as the next six hissed down relentlessly, she had to kick, dance and squeal, her lovely form bouncing to the time of the rod. Twelve very red, well spaced welts marked her from waist to thighs when Cora laid down the cane. Then she picked up the tawse and, cracking it in the air a couple of times, she stood and began to spank.

"Now, Miss Impudence, you are going to learn it does not pay to disobey your mother. I'm going to apply three dozen good sound smacks to your very spankable bottom and I hope you will enjoy it as much as I shall," said Cora sarcastically to the weeping Doris.

Doris shrieked and sobbed from the very first stroke, writhing, twisting and squirming her bottom under the smarting caresses of the tawse. Now the tempo of her dance was fast and furious, her shrieks filled the room.

At the thirty-sixth stroke, Cora with smug satisfaction written all over her face, laid aside the strap and left the well punished girl palpitating in her humiliating pose, sobbing her heart out, her whole rear a deep crimson crossed with the deeper marks of the cane, and turned her attention to her next victim.

"Janet, you are to be punished for disobedience, are you not?" she inquired sharply.

"I suppose so," answered Janet.

"You suppose so!" snapped Cora. "I told you to prepare and I hope you did so! You suppose!! Take off your skirt!"

With nervous fingers dear Janet fumbled with her zipper and in a moment stood revealed in nothing but a white frilly blouse and a pair of skin tight nylon panties.

"Hand your panties to me, you naughty girl, as an abject token of your submission," Cora ordered.

Quivering noticeably, poor Janet stepped out of her panties and meekly surrendered the little garment symbolic of her ignominy.

"Now lie over the lounge Doris has just vacated. You shall have two dozen excellent stingers with the tawse. Doris will stand close and watch closely to realize the spectacle she was—if she can see through her tears," said Cora scathingly.

While the ladies discussed Cora's performance, Doris sobbed and moaned in anguish as Cora applied the tawse with vigor to Janet. Quickly Janet's shrieks and sobs joined Doris in a duet of misery as Janet's rear squirmed.

I sat watching the humiliating and painful spectacle of Janet's punishment, all my desperately protective urges squashed by Cora's oppressive presence, and waited fearfully and anxiously for the moment I too would be yelling and squirming under that hellish tawse. I grew more apprehensive as each stroke brought my turn nearer.

Having finished with Janet and allowing her to don her panties behind the head of the chair, Cora led me by the ear to an ordinary chair, then hauled me across her knee as though I was a small boy. A shudder of humiliation and a thrill of fear went through me as she yanked down my pajamas. She held me firmly and slipped a new device on her hand—a glove with a palm and fingers of stout leather stitched to it.

"Your disobedience was not as flagrant as Janet's, so I'm going to let you off lightly and just smack your bottom with my nice new leather spanking hand. I hope it will remind you to obey in the future."

My tanning probably only lasted five minutes, but it felt like an eternity. Like the others, I yelled and wriggled. The "hand" stung like fury and of course it was humiliating, but it was just nothing to what she'd given me before with the tawse.

"There now, stand with your back to the ladies and don't dare move!" she snapped.

Loud were the praises heaped on the triumphant Cora. "You are really wonderful, my dear—a disciplinarian par excellence if ever there was one. You will certainly command respect and obedience," gushed Mrs. Turner.

They must have gone on chatting for more than half an hour. Presently Cora, excusing herself, announced, "They are sufficiently composed now. I will have them serve coffee."

"Splendid! and you will join us, of course," exclaimed Auntie, still beaming with approval. I was sent to don a pair of bloomers with an opaque front but a transparent rear. When I returned, the girls were bare from the waist down with a little apron concealing the front of their bodies and leaving them some little modesty. The white aprons accented the red of their bottoms greatly.

In the kitchen the girls, sobbing and burning, prepared the coffee. I didn't know what I was supposed to do, I only knew that I was only too glad to be out of that awful room.

"I'll get Cora for this if it's the last thing I ever do," swore Doris as she gently touched her red behind.

"Oh come, Doris, be sensible. How can we 'get her,' as you put it? She simply conquered us. We had to submit and we will continue to submit. After all, you have to admit that she is really and truly a super whipper," replied Janet.

"I don't care. I hate her and she'll never whip me again," choked Doris.

"Like to bet?" asked Janet archly. "Well let's get in with the coffee—and don't forget, honey, Mistress Cora has that tawse and she may find your bottom irresistible, so for Pete's sake let's not drop anything."

Doris made no misstep and, coffee over safely, Mrs. Turner rose to go home.

"Before you go, Doris, I want to speak to you. You have been punished for disobedience and daring to resist, but I recall you dared to say I could go to hell. That was an unladylike expression and I will not tolerate it, do you understand?" said Cora sternly, the tawse swinging in her hand.

Poor Doris didn't feel defiant now. She took one look at the tawse and mumbled, "Yes."

"Say 'yes, Miss,'" demanded Cora.

"Yes, Miss," Doris repeated sullenly.

"Good. Now for that unladylike language, come here right after school next Wednesday. Be here at 4:30 sharp for a little lesson in manners, my dear child."

By that time, Cora had subdued and whipped both Verna and George. Cora was well entrenched and in full, undisputed authority over us. Auntie and Mrs. Turner seemed happily satisfied to leave most discipline to Cora. She applied it strictly and all work and duties were carried out promptly. What more could they desire? As time passed, Cora revealed more and more her capability for ruling. Every punishment she gave was calculated to impose the utmost in pain and humiliation to the offender of the moment. She made a ceremony of the act of submission and usually insisted that the culprit go through a long and elaborate preparation for chastisement. She added to the stock of punishment accessories. She had invented the spanking glove and now she made a pony pole—a broomstick with three short straps about nine inches apart at one end. This ingenious device fastens on the folded forearms behind the back. Thus secured, the operator grasps the protruding end of the stick and the culprit can be made to control his movement to a small circle around which he or she is urged with the tawse.

"Why do you stay, Janet?" I asked one evening as we lay exhausted on the grass.

"Oh Gerald, I just don't know. It's too complicated for me to give a straight answer. You see I truly do adore Auntie. At first I was shocked and then enthralled when she told me of the spanking arrangements you'd undergone for years. And how the home now ran like clock work and how your behavior had improved. Well, I had never, nver been so much as slapped and living with you I used to wonder and imagine what a spanking was like. There is some subtle magic about it, you know, Gerald," she smiled. "Frankly, I was dying of curiosity, and Auntie sensed it, I'm sure. Well, one day she said, 'You know, Janet, you really are a spoiled girl and glib as you are I really ought to treat you as I do my own children. I think perhaps I'll phone your mother.' Well, that decided me. Blushing, I answered, 'Oh no, Estelle, don't phone mother! If you think perhaps—'

"She said, 'I certainly do, my dear, but I warn you, my hand is heavy and when I spank it hurts.'

"And so I got my first spanking there and then. And I have to confess that although I smarted I loved her for it—and felt strangely excited. She gave me many more spankings right up until that fateful picnic day. True, they were a little harder each time, but still they were mere child's play to what we all endure now. I guess Auntie was just conditioning me for that first real severe whipping she and Mrs. Turner gave me. Oh boy, was I ever surprised!"

"So now the big spanked girl is as resigned to the code as the rest of us?" I grinned.

"I think I am," said Janet pensively. "You know, at secretarial school I've heard it said my manners are charming. And anyway, I'm attracted to the whole business, painful as it is. So there!"

We talked a bit then about Cora. Certainly she is a different proposition from the adults. They simply and only punish to maintain discipline and improve us. But with Cora, her personal triumphs have brought out a natural, arrogant pride. There seems nothing she won't do to increase and exalt her wide authority. One would think she was a despotic queen and we her servants to be whipped at her merest whim.

"You may be attracted, honey. I don't think I am. But we are powerless anyhow," I mused, a little chilled by my thoughts.

"You know, Gerald, I have an idea. At present she has five targets to hit. If she had more, we wouldn't get it so often," said Janet.

"It's an idea, but where do we get more targets?" I asked.

"You may be surprised, but there are others. I've been thinking a lot—" she replied. "There is a wonderful subject in class and I know she's ripe for subjugation. She's a woman, 25. To conquer her would flatter Cora's ego enormously. I know it'll work because Sandra and I exchange some confidences and she has confessed that she would like a taste of the strap."

"A taste," I snorted. "Why, our Cora would flay her alive."

"So what?" shrugged Janet. "I'm really only obliging her anyway. If she gets more than she bargained for that's her lookout. Anyway, I've spoken to Cora and she's really elated at the prospect. I'm to have Sandra here at 7:30 tomorrow. There, now, I've told all. Clever, hm?"

At 7:15 on the eventful eve, I stole down to the rec room and waited in comfort, sitting on a folding chair in a cupboard of mammoth proportions. Soon Cora entered and switched on two spot lights centered on a space around the "chair." Then she sat down to wait.

Cora was dressed in a clinging black satin sheath, low cut and without sleeves, long black gloves and high heeled black shoes, her raven hair confined at the nape of her neck. She was authority personified. Even I was a little awed.

The "chair" was covered with an afghan, thus hiding its awful purpose. Cora was positively majestic to behold. Her whole being exuded relentless dominance. I thrilled and shuddered at the thought of what I was about to watch. At 7:30 on the dot, Janet came in leading Sandra by the hand to the circle of light. She hadn't exaggerated a bit. Sandra was ravishing. A tall blonde—big and exquisitely proportioned. She wore a long, smart coat and a little red hat. Looking rather ill at ease, she stood there gracefully in the spotlights. I am sure she was on the verge of tears—her hands were twisting nervously.

"Stand there darling," said Janet, taking her coat and hat, under which Sandra was clad in a short tight skirt, barely knee length, and a ruffled white blouse—no doubt dressed according to instructions. Janet stood beside the uncomfortable girl and made a low bow.

"This, Miss Cora, is Sandra Watt, the willful young lady I was telling you about."

"I am aware of that," said Cora imperiously. Then with a contemptuous glance she addressed Sandra:

"Well, I'm told you are 25 and so far have never been whipped?"

"Yes, Cora, that is so," she admitted, blushing under Cora's searching gaze.

427

"You will address me as Miss!" snapped her inquisitor. "Stop fidgeting and stand rigid and at attention when I speak!"

Immediately the girl straightened and put her hands stiffly at her sides.

"Janet tells me you would not find a taste of the strap unwelcome?"

Sandra, blushing furiously now, stammered, "Well—I—er—that is—I didn't exactly say that. I meant—well, something like that might be interesting—but—."

Cora cut her off sharply. "I agree it will be interesting—very! Now understand your position: if you surrender to my authority, and I think you will—won't you?"

Faintly Sandra whispered her reply, "Yes—er—yes Miss."

"You are a sensible girl, but I warn you I shall tolerate no nonsense. I expect and will have instant obedience or you will suffer the penalty. This evening you shall have your taste of punishment and unless I miss my guess, you will need whipping quite frequently in the future. You'll find I have a stong arm and a good variety of instruments to chastise you warmly with."

"Oh—but—please, er, Miss, I think—I hope—I'm sure one experience will be enough," Sandra cried in distressed tones.

"I will be the judge of that. Consider yourself lucky I allowed you to come here. You will do well to forget you were an independent young woman and to remember you are just another naughty girl under my authority about to have your posterior whipped."

Sandra, almost on the point of tears, wailed, "Oh Cora—I mean, Miss Cora—you look so severe. I didn't think—I didn't expect it to be like this—I can't—I don't want to go through with it. Please!"

At this, Cora smiled disarmingly, "Of course I look severe. You should expect that, my dear."

Sandra seemed to have reached an emotional crisis. She smiled back at Cora. "Forgive my foolish protest, I forgot myself for a moment." And so saying, she sank to her knees and kissed Cora's shoes. "I'll submit most humbly," she said fervently.

How very different she was from the fighting Doris. She was even more passively willing than any of us to lick the hand that chastises.

Cora, obviously well pleased, raised Sandra's face between her hands and looked deep into her eyes. "Come, get up—I wish you face down across my lap."

Sandra's big moment had arrived. Meekly she rose and bent over. Her skirt was flipped up, her panties lowered, and her rear was well clapped by Cora's gloved hand. It was humiliating and stinging, but it didn't seem to shame the girl. Frankly, she looked as though she was enjoying it.

Set once again on her feet, she murmured in a dreamy voice, "Thank you, Miss Cora. I thank you from the bottom of my heart for spanking me."

Cora gave a silvery laugh. "You are quite welcome, my girl, but a little premature with your thanks. The ceremony is not over yet. Janet, turn the spots on the chair and turn on the rest of the lights, then strip Miss Impudence to her bra. Let her kneel on the chair and fasten her at the chest and knees—now be smart about it, or I'll warm your bottom for you too!" concluded Cora with a stamp of her foot.

Janet lost no time. In less than two minutes Sandra was in position, her rounded rear sticking out bewitchingly. She looked fearful of what was coming but was docile and allowed Janet to handle her without a protest.

"Oh, my dear Miss Watt, let me congratulate you on having so ample a posterior to offer for correction! It will be amusing to make it bounce!" exclaimed Cora with glee. "Now Janet, lay on the floor before her the cane, the tawse and the martinet. And get me out of this dress—I want freedom of movement," said Cora, extending her hands for Janet to remove her gloves. Then with much solicitation Janet helped her out of her dress. There she stood, completely lovely, in only black satin bra and matching lace trimmed panties, ready to whip.

"Your bottom is perfectly posed. Now I will introduce you to your dancing partners. First you shall have six marks of esteem from this nice swishy cane." The cane hissed down smartly, leaving well spaced welts on the already pinkish buttocks. Sandra gave an agonized yelp as each stroke stung her, but she took it stoically and neither bawled nor pleaded to be let off.

"Hand me the tawse, Janet," snapped Cora. "This delightful instrument has the loveliest caress and will kiss your bottom just twenty-four times," remarked Cora as she applied the tawse with devastating effect. Sandra's bottom was now writhing wildly, her sobs and squeals almost continuous, and her behind and thighs really crimson. Then Sandra was released from her bonds and ordered to stand in the corner. Meanwhile, Cora refreshed herself with a cup of coffee served by Janet. Presently Sandra had composure enough for Cora's purpose and was called over.

"Strap the pony pole on her, Janet." I'm sure she didn't know what the pole was for, but Sandra meekly folder her arms behind her and allowed Janet to buckle the pole in place.

Cora grasped the end of the pole firmly and could now control her victim, who was able to move freely but only around the pivot of her castigation. Arming herself with a long, fine martinet, Cora began to thrash the plump, outraged target. The awful martinet whistled down again and again relentlessly. Sandra shrieked and danced. She leaned forward, she arched her back, but she was unable

431

to escape a single stroke. Cora's aim was deadly accurate. Sandra seemed to get an idea—she bounded round and round at the end of the stick, urged faster and faster by the stinging blows to her rear. Cora laid on stroke after stroke. I was spellbound gazing at the girl's frantic contortions. Abruptly, Cora threw down the martinet and ordered the culprit released and to kneel at her feet. Somehow Sandra managed to obey, choking on her sobs, tears streaming down her face.

"Your first lesson is over. Remember it well. Now you know what to expect in the future?"

"Yesss, Missss," sobbed Sandra brokenly.

"Very well. Janet will take you home now and I will continue your lessons in obedience very soon."

I was cramped, but I dared not move in my secret place while Janet comforted and petted her well whipped friend. Finally they were ready to leave and Janet, full of sympathy, said, "Oh, darling, I'm sorry. I should never have brought you here."

"Don't have any regrets, Jan dear. I have none. Truly I was scared and I didn't dream she could whip like she does. It was awful, but I guess I'll get used to it like you. All I can say right now is that Cora is the most!"

Janet was quite right. Now that Cora has so ardent an admirer of her technique, she is much easier to get alone with and doesn't spend nearly as much time checking us up and punishing us for the merest trifling error. Cora has taken to spending more and more time devising new instruments. Oh, we still get our fair share, but not nearly so much as before Sandra came along to distract Cora.

Janet and I still meet frequently in discreet places, and I am proud to say that our pleasure skills are improving as well as Cora's punishment techniques. All in all, I can't say I regret the change in household operations that Janet's presence produced, strange though some of them may seem.

VICTORIAN EROTIC CLASSICS
AVAILABLE FROM CARROLL & GRAF

☐ Anonymous / Altar of Venus	4.50
☐ Anonymous / Autobiography of a Flea & Other Tart Tales	5.95
☐ Anonymous / Black Magic	6.95
☐ Anonymous / Careless Passion	5.95
☐ Anonymous / Confessions of an English Maid & Other Delights	5.95
☐ Anonymous / The Consummate Eveline	4.95
☐ Anonymous / Court of Venus	3.95
☐ Anonymous/ Best of Erotic Reader	6.95
☐ Anonymous / Eroticon	4.95
☐ Anonymous / Eroticon II	4.95
☐ Anonymous / Eroticon III	4.50
☐ Anonymous / Fallen Woman	4.50
☐ Anonymous / Harem Nights	4.95
☐ Anonymous / The Intimate Memoirs of an Edwardian Dandy	4.95
☐ Anonymous / The Intimate Memoirs of an Edwardian Dandy, Vol. II	4.95
☐ Anonymous / The Intimate Memoirs of an Edwardian Dandy, Vol. III	4.95
☐ Anonymous / Lay of the Land	4.50
☐ Anonymous / The Libertines	4.50
☐ Anonymous / Maid and Mistress	4.50
☐ Anonymous / A Man with a Maid	5.95
☐ Anonymous / Memoirs of Josephine	4.50
☐ Anonymous / The Merry Menage	4.50
☐ Anonymous / The Oyster	4.50
☐ Anonymous / The Oyster II	3.95
☐ Anonymous / The Oyster III	4.50
☐ Anonymous / The Oyster V	4.50
☐ Anonymous / Pagan Delights	5.95
☐ Anonymous / The Pearl	6.95
☐ Anonymous / Pleasures and Follies	3.95
☐ Anonymous / Romance of Lust	5.95

☐ Anonymous / Rosa Fielding: Victim of Lust	3.95
☐ Anonymous/ Sharing Sisters	4.95
☐ Anonymous / Secret Lives	3.95
☐ Anonymous / Sensual Secrets	4.50
☐ Anonymous / Sweet Confessions	4.50
☐ Anonymous / Sweet Tales	4.50
☐ Anonymous / Tropic of Lust	4.50
☐ Anonymous / Venus Butterfly	3.95
☐ Anonymous / Venus Delights	3.95
☐ Anonymous / Venus Disposes	3.95
☐ Anonymous / Venus in India	3.95
☐ Anonymous / Victorian Fancies	4.50
☐ Anonymous / The Wantons	4.50
☐ Anonymous / White Thighs	4.50
☐ Anonymous / Youthful Indiscretions	4.50
☐ Cleland, John / Fanny Hill	4.95
☐ van Heller, Marcus / Adam and Eve	3.95
☐ van Heller, Marcus / Lusts of the Borgias	4.95
☐ van Heller, Marcus / Seduced	5.95
☐ van Heller, Marcus / Unbound	5.95
☐ van Heller, Marcus / Venus in Lace	3.95
☐ Villefranche, Anne-Marie / Passion d'Amour	5.95
☐ Villefranche, Anne-Marie / Scandale d'Amour	5.95
☐ Villefranche, Anne-Marie / Secrets d'Amour	4.50
☐ Villefranche, Anne-Marie / Souvenir d'Amour	4.50
☐ von Falkensee, Margarete / Blue Angel Confessions	6.95
☐ "Walter"/ My Secret Life	7.95